THE TICKING TERROR
MURDERS

THE FEATHER CLOAK
MURDERS

Darwin L. Teilhet

THE TICKING TERROR MURDERS

Darwin L. Teilhet

THE FEATHER CLOAK MURDERS

Darwin and Hildegarde Teilhet

The Adventures of the
Brave Baron Von Kaz
in the Northern States of America

Vol. 1

COACHWHIP PUBLICATIONS
Greenville, Ohio

DARWIN AND HILDEGARDE TEILHET, COLLABORATORS

The Ticking Terror Murders by Darwin L. Teilhet
  / *The Feather Cloak Murders*, by Darwin and
  Hildegarde Teilhet
© 2022 Coachwhip Publications edition
Introduction © 2022 Curtis Evans
Cover image: © Channarongsds

The Ticking Terror Murders first published 1935
The Feather Cloak Murders first published 1936
Darwin L. Teilhet, 1904-1964
Hildegarde Teilhet, 1905-1999
CoachwhipBooks.com

ISBN 1-61646-518-2
ISBN-13 978-1-61646-518-6

GOOD COMPANIONS
The Story of Darwin Teilhet and the Baron

Curtis Evans

Detective novelist Freeman Wills Crofts once recalled that back during the 1920s, when he was in the process of developing his famous policeman detective, Inspector (later Superintendent) Joseph French, he had firstly to decide whether his sleuth would be a "character" (by which Crofts meant a remarkable outsized individual drawn along the lines of Sherlock Holmes) or, conversely, an "ordinary humdrum personality." With disarming frankness the mild-mannered railroad engineer turned mystery writer admitted that since "striking characteristics, consistently depicted, are very hard to do," he had opted for going with the humdrum sort of detective. With Inspector French, the author thereby fashioned—directly in his own image, as it were—"a perfectly ordinary man, without peculiarities or mannerisms."

How different from Joseph French in all particulars, aside from his keen knack for cracking crimes, is American author Darwin Teilhet's Baron Franz Maximilian Karagôz und von Kaz, detective and protagonist of four highly praised mystery novels published over a five-year period shortly before American entry into World War Two: *The Ticking Terror Murders* (1935), *The Feather Cloak Murders* (1936), *The Crimson Hair Murders* (1936) and *The Broken Face Murders* (1940). In creating Baron voz Kaz, Teilhet opted (like such noted mystery authors as, for example, Agatha Christie, Dorothy L. Sayers, Margery Allingham, S. S. Van Dine, Ellery Queen and John Dickson Carr before him) to create a colorful "character" detective, one whom mystery scholar Douglas G. Greene has highly lauded as "one of the great humorous detectives."

Unusually for fictional sleuths of the Thirties, the comical Baron von Kaz owed his inception to deadly serious contemporary real world affairs, specifically the violent political upheaval which was then occurring in the central European country of Austria. The year 1934 had seen Austrian Chancellor Engelbert Dollfuss' overthrow of the First Austrian Republic, which fifteen years earlier, in the aftermath of the First World War, had been messily carved out of the carcass of the defunct Austro-Hungarian Empire. Now a newly empowered authoritarian ruler, Dollfuss established in the Republic's stead an Austrofascist dictatorship under the title of the Federal State of Austria. All political entities besides Dollfuss' own Fatherland Front were outlawed, including the Social Democrats, whom Dollfuss and his forces had vanquished in the bloody five-day Austrian Civil War in February. Dollfuss himself was assassinated in July at the instigation of Adolf Hitler, on account of his opposition to the German dictator's schemes to absorb Austria into Germany, but the Nazi coup attempt which followed Dollfuss' murder was thwarted by the strongman's successor, Kurt Schuschnigg.

As befits his title, the Baron von Kaz is neither Austrofascist nor Social Democrat, but rather a fervent monarchist desirous of bringing back to power the exiled House of Hapsburg, which had been formally dethroned in Austria in 1919. The Baron's injudicious support for the restoration of the monarchy while serving as no less than the Chief of the Viennese Police Section concerned with political crimes and foreigners led to him ingloriously fleeing Austria for his very life—whereupon he ended up, with little to succor him barring "his agile wits" and a certain remarkably lethal green umbrella, in the United States, a strange land which he haughtily terms the "barbaric states of North America."

The proud baron tends to look on Americans as peasants and parvenus and generally treats them accordingly. Frequently in the series he quotes (rather imperfect) Latin to presumably ignorant Americans and he is invariably nonplussed when he finds that some of them understand the dead European language rather better than he. With aristocratic hauteur he never hesitates to sponge off other, lesser beings or to put off paying—or even run out on—his debts. Yet withal he shows a wiliness and gritty determination to survive against odds that should impress the most avidly bootstrapping American. A braggart and a mountebank who at times resembles Baron Munchausen, (von Kaz's war stories tend toward the highly imaginative), the Baron nevertheless is a lovable rascal whose detective feats and other adventurous exploits charmed and intrigued readers of the day. One widely syndicated rave review in American newspapers of the first Baron von Kaz case—that of *The Ticking Terror Murders*—indicates the baron's appeal in the "barbaric states of North America":

> The modern method of writing a detective story seems to be to invent as outlandish and eccentric a detective as your imagination can contrive and then turn him loose, trusting that he will carry by sheer force of human interest whatever deficiencies the plot may develop.
>
> Ordinarily this leads to some excruciatingly bad mystery stories; but I am here to testify

that it has provided at least one good one—to wit, "The Ticking Terror Murders," by Darwin L. Teilhet.

Mr. Teilhet has invented the Baron von Kaz, a penniless but jaunty Austrian who drifts out to California on his uppers, connives his way into the employ of a movie star and unexpectedly finds himself with a string of murders to solve.

There are times when everybody (including the reader) suspects the baron of being a pompous and windy faker—a sort of Austrian Major Hoople [a reference to a braggadocious character in the popular American comic strip *Our Boarding House*]—but in the end he triumphs, and his antics are so engaging, and the mystery he tackles so cleverly constructed, that the book is a delight from start to finish.

A half-century later crime writer and critic Bill Pronzini amply praised the Baron von Kaz's recorded cases as "great fun" and pronounced the baron himself "an engaging character." Aside from their memorable sleuth and intricate plots, Darwin Teilhet's Baron von Kaz detective novels (the last three of which are co-credited to his author wife, Hildegarde) are distinguished by their well-conveyed settings, drawn from places the Teilhets had actually lived (Carmel, California, San Francisco, the Hawaiian islands, the western Mexican coast). In the climactic sequence in the exotic *Feather Clock Murders*, for example, readers surely can almost feel themselves stumbling through those sinister lava tubes along with the Baron and—well, I will leave them to see for themselves!

Unusually for detective novels at that time, the Baron von Kaz mysteries were deliberately conceived as a short series about a character that evolves over time. Events in previous cases are recollected and they indeed matter, as the baron struggles against capricious fate to achieve what he deems his fitting destiny in life. Just what this is, readers will find in the last novel in this entertaining series, *The Broken Face Murders*. The book was published in 1940, two years after the March 1938 Anschluss, or Nazi German annexation of Austria, which extinguished, for the next seven strife-torn years, what feebly trickling fonts of freedom had remained in that troubled country and finally put paid to the Baron's fond hope of returning to his fatherland.

* * *

Like his brave baron, Darwin LeOra Teilhet (pronounced, American fashion, "Teel-et") was a wanderer with an ample stock of colorful tales to tell about his life, some of which may even have been true. As Darwin LeOra *Tillia* he was born on May 20, 1904 at Wyanet, an agricultural town of under 1000 souls in northwestern Illinois, one of three children of Henry John Tillia, a farmer, and Cora Johnson Tillia, a farmer's daughter. (Some records give Darwin's birthplace as Buda, an even smaller town in the area.)

Darwin's father was the son of French immigrant John Tillia, who married native Louisianan Emma Miller in Wyanet, probably in the late 1860s. According to a newspaper interview which Darwin gave in 1934 to freelance journalist Henry F. Pringle, author of a recent Pulitzer Prize winning biography of Theodore Roosevelt, John Tillia migrated to the United States around 1880, after "his vineyards in France were ruined by [the insect pest] phylloxera." He started growing grapes in Ohio along with several other Frenchmen, (some of whom worked for the family of Nicholas Longworth of Cincinnati, the Father of American Grape Culture), then he moved to Wyanet, where his efforts met with indifferent success, prompting his son to sell off the family farm.

It is unclear how much of this story of an immigrant Frenchman romantically tilling grapes in the American Midwest is accurate. For one thing, John Tillia was born in 1834 and he was living in Wyanet in the years immediately following the Civil War, so obviously he had migrated to the U. S. more than a decade prior to 1880. However, it is established that Henry Tillia was residing in Wyanet and working as a farmer in 1900, when he married Cora Johnson, and that sometime between Darwin's birth in 1904 and 1910, the family had moved west to Des Moines, Iowa, where Henry established a lucrative practice as a realtor and housing contractor.

Described as a big, "handsome, breezy" boy who "cut quite a swath," Darwin distinguished himself at West High School with his outgoing flair for journalism, advertising, art and the stage. (In 1920 he played, for example, the title role in a performance of the recent hit stage crime farce *Officer 666*.) After graduating from West in 1921, Darwin matriculated at Drake University, where he was a cheerleader (or "yell leader"), a member of the varsity debate team and co-founder and co-editor of a satirical college magazine, *Caprice*, wherein were "tucked rich, roistering, merrily absurd, and comical jests in buffoonery worship of the pagan gods." Unfortunately *Caprice* went a mite too far in its comical roistering in the eyes of Drake's newly installed president, Daniel Walter Morehouse, pagan gods notwithstanding, and the magazine was ignominiously suppressed, obliging Darwin to take a delivery job on an ice wagon in order to help pay off its debts.

Clearly at Drake Darwin was an extrovert with a store of seemingly boundless energy. At the university's 1921 football clash with Iowa State, the *Des Moines Tribune* reported, Darwin, then just a freshman, devised a highly original "stunt to thrill spectators." Suspended by his knees from a rope ladder, Darwin swooped down over the stadium in a small plane, unfurling a huge Drake banner and leading the home crowd in lusty Bulldog yells. This stupendous cheering feat, which happily resulted in no fatalities, evidently impressed college administrators rather more than had Darwin's editing of *Caprice*.

After completing his junior year at Drake in 1924, Darwin departed Des Moines for the rather less censorious city of Paris, France, where for a year he attended classes in art and foreign languages at the Sorbonne, sending back to the *Des Moines Register* colorful dispatches about his experiences. (Whether he crossed paths at this time with Richard Wilson Webb of "Patrick Quentin" mystery fame is unknown.) Darwin seems to have spent less time in class than in touring France, Italy and Spain on a motorcycle, taking especial interest in "circuses and clowns, and extemporaneous Italian comedy." Returning to the United States, he registered as a senior at California's Stanford University in 1926, though only after taking another foreign trip, this one to the Far East. While in China, he claimed to Henry Pringle, he made an adventurous trip several hundred miles to the interior with "a half-caste Chinese who sold kerosene."

Wanderlust briefly satiated, Darwin graduated from Sanford in 1927 and in October, at the age of twenty-three, wed pretty twenty-year-old Blanche Hildegarde Tolman, the daughter of distinguished Stanford geology professor Cyrus Fisher Tolman. After stopping off in Birmingham, Alabama, where Darwin's parents had relocated with his two younger siblings, the newlyweds set out to Europe to spend a year of study and travel in France and Germany, in the event settling mostly at the city of

Heidelberg, soon to become a major stronghold of the Nazi party.

Upon returning to the United States, Darwin, having legally changed his surname to Teilhet (he claimed that "Teilhet" was the original version of the surname in France), took a position in Philadelphia, home of nascent mystery writer Richard Wilson Webb, as a copy writer with the advertising firm N. W. Ayer & Son (which in the Forties would employ Oklahoma mystery writer Todd Downing). The couple remained in Philadelphia for two years, departing for California in 1932, when Darwin transferred to the company's San Francisco office. With their three daughters (their only son tragically died in infancy) the Teilhets would mostly remain in California for the rest of their lives, although for a time in the Thirties they resided in the Hawaiian islands, when Darwin worked as a copy writer with the Hawaii Pineapple Company (aka Dole). In this capacity he devised some of the early ads for Dole pineapple juice.

A couple of years after the Teilhets settled at San Francisco, Darwin—now a portly and prematurely balding, pipe-smoking, tweeds-wearing thirty-year-old with a short-cropped mustache who looked like he had lived life to the fullest—regaled Henry Pringle with picaresque accounts of his many adventures abroad. "Mystery novels are only one phase of his variegated career," Pringle breathlessly divulged, "which reminds his friends a little of Lightnin' Bill Jones [the comical fantasist title character of the Broadway smash hit play *Lightnin'*], except that all of it has actually happened. It is astonishing to think that anyone, in a mere 30 years, can have covered so much ground." The mysteries which Darwin's real life interests and activities inspired were important indeed, however, for they firmly established him in his "moonlighting" career of over three decades as a novelist.

* * *

Darwin Teilhet's first detective novels, both of them avi-
ation mysteries, were published in 1931, when he lived
with Hildegarde in Philadelphia. This was the same year in
which Richard Wilson Webb along with Martha Mott Kel-
ley, both of whom were then residing as well in the City of
Brotherly Love, published the first "Q. Patrick" detective
novel, *Cottage Sinister*, which rather tempts one to wonder
whether Webb knew the Teilhets and had a sort of creative
synergy with Darwin at this time, whereby the two men
were simultaneously inspired to take the plunge into mystery writing. Suggesting a certain intimacy between Webb
and the Teilhets, Webb in May 1936 inscribed for Darwin
and Hildegarde a copy of the Q. Patrick novel *S. S. Murder*
"with best wishes Q. Patrick." Beneath this inscription are
the signatures "R. Wilson Webb and H. C. Wheeler," the
latter of which belonged to Webb's later writing partner
and companion of two decades, Hugh Callingham Wheeler
(who in fact had not co-authored *S. S. Murder*).

Whatever propinquity Webb and the Teilhets may
have had in Philadelphia, however, both of Darwin's early
detective novels actually more resemble those of another
recently launched young American mystery writer who was
well-travelled in Europe: John Dickson Carr. As Douglas
Greene has noted, both *Murder in the Air* and *Death Flies
High* "are fine examples of the ingenuity of Golden Age
detection" that "are part of what Carr called 'the grandest
game in the world' in which the reader is challenged to unravel a fiendish puzzle along with the detective." In particular, Greene notes, *Murder in the Air*, which I have found
Darwin partly based on the bizarre real-life Alfred Lowen-
stein case of 1928, "features a clever dying message and
an impossible disappearance on a single-engine plane over
the English Channel." It was claimed to have sold thirty

thousand copies in the United States, an impressive number indeed for any fledgling mystery writer. Both of Darwin's novels featured as sleuth a French detective from the Sureté, like Carr's early series French policeman sleuth Henri Bencolin, and both of them recall the daring plane stunt that Darwin had staged when he was a flamboyant yell leader at Drake University.

Three years later, in the summer of 1934, about a year after Chancellor Adolf Hitler staged his murderously lethal Night of the Long Knives, there followed Darwin's next detective novel, *The Talking Sparrow Murders*. The author set the novel in Heidelberg, topically filling its pages, as Associate Press New York music and arts editor John Selby in one of the book's many rave reviews noted, with "striding Nazis, Jew-baiting and other features of modern Germany to good effect." As Douglas Greene noted in an introduction to a 1985 reprint of the novel, not until the late Thirties did the vast majority of popular writers start "to feature Hitler and the Nazis in their novels." Darwin daringly had beaten most of his mystery-writing brethren to the bloody punch by several years.

Although not as overtly political as *Sparrow*, Darwin's Baron von Kaz mysteries, which followed *Sparrow* into print between 1935 and 1940, regularly reference the deteriorating political situation in the baron's homeland of Austria (which as mentioned above was finally annexed by Nazi Germany in 1938); and the last novel in the series, *The Broken Face Murders*, which the Teilhets published after war had broken out across Europe, brings the fascist menace to home to America. Most reviewers heartily welcomed the brave baron's return and the highly relevant real world subject matter, although in the *Honolulu Star-Bulletin* columnist and Unitarian minister Arthur Wakefield Slaten sourly complained of "the anti-Hitler allusions dragged in by the ears." About this he testily complained: "The Teilhets would have us forget that Hitler was an Austrian and that Austrians greeted the Anschluss with joy. Of course, there is intermittent rasping on the anti-antisemitic string—which makes for sales appeal."

While Reverend Slaten's criticism was very much a minority view, Darwin was increasingly turning his eyes and his bountiful imagination toward other fields of fiction. Indeed, the last three Baron von Kaz detective novels had been co-credited to Hildegarde, although even as far back as 1934, Darwin had allowed to Henry Pringle that his spouse "types all his drafts and works with him with very closely." Of Hildegarde Darwin earnestly avowed to Pringle: "She does . . . at least a third of my work. I wouldn't be able to do any of it without her." In his own name alone Darwin in between mysteries during the Thirties published two mainstream novels, *Bright Destination* (1935) and *Journey to the West* (1938), the latter a well-received, sprawling picaresque tale set in California with a von Kazzish sort of protagonist (though an American by birth). After the Thirties he turned almost exclusively to writing historical fiction and children's adventure tales, one of the latter of which, *The Avion My Uncle Flew* (1946), was short listed for a Newbery Medal.

Exceptions to this new emphasis were the wartime espionage tales *Odd Man Pays* (1944) and *The Fear Makers* (1945), and three Fifties paperback crime fiction originals written under the pseudonym William H. Fielding. Once again Darwin had first lived what he later wrote, having retired from advertising with U. S. entry into World War Two and served in Washington, D. C. and London as a major in the Office of Strategic Services, which coordinated espionage activities behind enemy lines for all branches of the United States Armed Forces. The best known of Darwin's later crime novels, *The Fear Makers*, was a lauded effort in which Darwin additionally drew cleverly (and scarily) on his extensive experience as an adman. In 1958 this perceptive and indeed prophetic crime novel was adapted under the same title as an underrated spy film drama, directed by esteemed genre director Jacques Tourneur (*Cat People, I Walked with a Zombie, The Leopard Man, Out of the Past, Night of the Demon*) and starring highly regarded American leading man Dana Andrews, best known today as the gruff and tough police detective who falls in love with Gene Tierney in *Laura*.

Shortly before his untimely death at the age of fifty-nine on April 18, 1964, Darwin returned once more to the crime genre with his final novel, *The Big Runaround* (aka *Dangerous Encounter*), a far-seeing tale of California high tech industrial espionage, of which prominent crime fiction reviewer Anthony Boucher, a fervent admirer of Darwin, in his notice uncharacteristically implored the author: "[Darwin Teilhet still] knows how to plot an intricately surprising thriller. . . . The hell with readers of historicals, Teilhet; we need you here." Sadly, the dreadful bell tolled suddenly for Darwin and he instead passed away within three months of Boucher's review.

The earthly remains of Darwin LeOra Teilhet were interred south of San Francisco in the Golden Gate National Cemetery, followed thirty-five years later by those of his wife Hildegarde, who herself had independently enjoyed a successful crime writing career during the 1940s and 1950s. With the exception of International Polygonics' 1985 reprint of *The Talking Sparrow Murders*, the Teilhets' work remained entirely out-of-print in English for more than five decades, despite the praise afforded the authors by such eminent crime fiction authorities as Bill Pronzini and Douglas Greene. This makes these new volumes of the Baron von Kaz's extraordinary investigative adventures published by Coachwhip in 2021, ninety years after the appearance of Darwin's first detective novel, all the more satisfying to introduce.

THE TICKING TERROR MURDERS

*The First Adventure of the
Brave Baron Von Kaz
in the Northern States of America*

To Jehan Van Steen Tolman

In the Hope That It Will Embarrass Him Greatly

1

The Brave Baron Von Kaz

"Baron, I'm terribly confused," she said.

"So?"

"Henry thinks Charlie's causing the ticking noises—"

"If you please, the—"

"Ticking noises. Tick-tick—like that. At night."

"Ah." He nodded politely. "So."

"But, Baron. I'm certain Charlie's not causing the ticking noises at all. Charlie's really harmless. Besides, Charlie doesn't suspect—" She regarded the Baron Franz Maximilian Karagôz von Kaz across the Chinese-red breakfast table. "You do understand this is very confidential?"

"Assuredly, my dear lady."

"Henry and I are going to be married," she virtuously continued, pouring herself a second cup of coffee. "You won't have a cup, Baron?"

"One thousand thanks, dear lady. I finished a large breakfast before I came to your hotel. And these—" He rubbed his nose. "These ticking noises?"

The telephone bell rang shrilly. Lucille Tarn excused herself, rustled elegantly and gracefully to the whirring mechanism across the living room of the hotel suite she had taken in San Francisco to await the Baron's arrival. She was a tall, handsome creature with glittering platinum-gold hair, moody gray eyes, and a figure which had

been reckoned by Solar Pictures, Inc., as one of the loveliest contrivances of its kind ever to operate on the screen
for a profit.

As soon as the Baron saw the golden flowered back of
Lucille Tarn's lounging pajamas, he snatched one of the
triangular morsels of toast from the plate and swallowed
it in one gulp.

She lifted the receiver. "Oh, it's you, Henry."

On the other end of the wire Henry Kerby apologized,
explaining that he had gone out for a shave and hadn't
been informed until he returned, about two minutes ago,
for breakfast, that she had called him.

"He's here. The Baron's here. He arrived twenty minutes ago. I'll send him over to see you at once."

Although Lucille had told him Sunday that she had
wired for a detective, and had persuaded him into finding
an excuse to leave Carmel Monday to come to San Francisco
in order to meet the man, Henry Kerby was still dubious as
to the wisdom of a detective and said so. Meanwhile, the
Baron crossed his legs, gazed innocently out of one of the
curtained windows as though he were unaware of the fact
that his left hand was occupied in reaching for a second
slice of toast. At times it was surprising how innocent
and guileless the Baron could appear.

While Henry spoke, Lucille Tarn patiently listened.
She knew something was wrong. Although repeatedly she
had assured herself that Charlie couldn't be responsible
for those sly ticking noises, she hadn't been able to escape
an uneasy feeling. It frightened her. If Charlie did know,
he might divorce her first. She wouldn't get a property
settlement. She was pretty tired of Charlie. But she didn't
want him to do the divorcing.

For a year and a half now she had been married to Charlie Tarn, and it was over six months ago that he had introduced his wife to Henry Kerby. God knows since she had

given up Hollywood for marriage, and all the excitement and adulation which went with Hollywood, all the premiers, all the glory of being Lucille Delay, Solar Pictures' star—well, perhaps the good Lord, reputedly an Admirer of the simpler pleasures of existence, didn't fully appreciate just how dead it was for her in Carmel. With the days sliding away under that bright empty sunshine and Charlie everlastingly weighing his chances for running as governor at the next election, nothing ever happened. Nothing ever happened! Not until she had encountered Henry Kerby and they had fallen in love, totally disregarding the hard and cold fact that they both were married . . .

"I told you," she insisted over the telephone when Kerby had stopped protesting, and while the Baron consumed the last piece of toast and wondered if it would be too obvious if he emptied her cup of coffee. "I told you that the Baron von Kaz is perfectly reliable. He helped me in Vienna."

"If he's so thunderingly reliable," Kerby wanted to know in a voice loud enough to go through the telephone receiver to the Baron's ear, "why didn't he show up yesterday as he wired you he would? I tell you, Lucille, Dave's asking what the hell I'm doing in San Francisco. He called me last night about the script."

"You're working too hard on that terrible script," she informed him soothingly.

"Maybe I am. Do you know, now that I've had some sleep, I think I probably imagined those idiotic noises."

"If you want to know what I think, as I've said before, they're made by someone right in your own home. It's Caryl, trying to worry you by—"

That resulted in an explosion: Caryl wouldn't do such a thing. Caryl wasn't revengeful. In addition, Caryl knew nothing for her to revenge. While Lucille waited for the explosion to diminish in volume, the Baron uncrossed his

legs, speculatively eyed the flowered silk back of Lucille
Tarn's expensive pajamas, glanced around the ornate room,
reached for the cup of coffee and drained its contents and
sighed happily.

Abruptly the explosion ended. "I'll send the Baron
over," Lucille said, and terminated the conversation.

The Baron drew out her chair for her. She thanked
him. She raised her coffee cup, set it down. "Henry's at the
Bohemian Club. I think you had better see him at once.
He's expecting you."

She frowned at the empty cup. She hadn't seen the Baron
for two years; no, three years. And that is a long time when
you are a motion picture star and then are married to a
man who is supposed to be the next governor of California.
She wondered how much she should tell the Baron . . .

Even in Vienna, she had only seen the Baron twice.
She had forgotten all about him, almost that is; she could
never entirely forget him and how he had helped her. And
six months ago she had read in the papers that, among
others, a Baron von Kaz had been arrested by the Austrian
government for participating in a plot to restore the monarchy. She had half-considered if this were the same man
who had aided her and then had dismissed the story, not
to think of it or the Baron until she had received his dignified note, forwarded to her at Carmel from the studio,
saying that he was now in Hollywood and would be pleased
to call upon her at her convenience.

That was all. She hadn't immediately replied. She had
been too concerned about Henry. He was complaining of
ticking noises which seeped into his bedroom at night.

The whole thing was so damnably senseless and impossible that half the time when Henry talked to Lucille,
he wasn't willing to admit that he even heard them. He
had started to worry regarding himself, speculating if the

noises were only in his imagination and were an indication of mental trouble. Lucille was too well acquainted
with him to think that the noises were hallucinations. He
was a great, red-bearded man at the peak of his fame as a
humorist, entirely too sane and earthy ever to be troubled
by mental phantoms. And appreciating that, Lucille had
grown more concerned than he, if it were possible.

It was difficult to believe that Charlie had discovered
her affair with Henry Kerby. But if Charlie *did* know, and
in his smooth way was already waiting for her to bring
divorce charges, he would have the upper hand.

Both she and Henry were terrorized by the possibility
of a scandal. They had conducted their affair expertly and
secretly. She was confident that no one was aware of it until the ticking noises intruded upon her sense of security
with a shattering unreality which was much more frightening than something normal, something tangible. Henry
had become obsessed with the idea that it was her husband
who, somehow, had hit upon a means of revenge. Either
that, he had decided, in talking it over with Lucille, or he
was going batty. It was then that Lucille had recalled that
the Baron was now in Hollywood.

She had wired the Baron, requesting him to meet her
Monday afternoon at the St. Francisco in San Francisco.
She had managed to see Kerby alone Sunday afternoon
on the golf course. Here she informed him what she had
done. Kerby disapproved. However, Monday morning he
had found an excuse to go to his club in San Francisco.
Lucille had told her husband that Ransahoffs were having
a sale and as she needed new clothes she was driving in to
the city.

But the Baron had failed them. He had failed them pri-
marily because the pawn shops were closed on Sundays and
he was unable to raise money for the trip until Monday.

Lucille had persuaded Kerby to stay over until Tuesday
morning. The Baron had taken the Monday night bus from
Los Angeles, arriving at the hotel as Lucille was finishing
her breakfast . . .

So now she considered him; trying to decide how much
to tell him. He remained standing, his head inclined slightly. Noticing that his frayed cuffs too shamelessly revealed
their age, he dropped his hands into his pockets. His suit
was worn, dusty. He had managed to shave, but that was
about all.

"Didn't I read," she asked, entirely too carelessly, "that
you had been arrested or something?"

He bowed.

"A mistake, I suppose?"

"A very serious mistake, my dear Miss Delay—" He
corrected himself, "Mrs. Tarn. I committed the grievous
error of choosing the wrong political party."

"But you are here now."

"Ach so, I am here." He ended the matter, "To assist you."

"You have heard of Henry Kerby?" A faint frown shadowed her forehead. Perhaps if they hired an American detective it would be wiser. "The famous author?"

"Assuredly," he said, smiling. His underlip was full and
heavy. Usually he remembered to hold in this Hapsburgian
heritage from a distinguished if prolific grandfather, but
now his underlip thrust out normally. He had observed
that frown passing over Lucille Tarn's forehead where it
appeared as incongruous as a wrinkle on the surface of a
white alabaster vase. She was his only, his last resort in
these barbaric Northern States. "The famous author? Ach,
so. I have often read him, hundreds of his books—"

"Hundreds? He's only written about twenty."

"Hundreds of times, dear lady. Thousands of times.
Yes, I know him. He is a great man."

"I'm not certain whether you can help or not."

"If you require a brave detective, dear lady, then I am certain that the Baron von Kaz can help."

"Mr. Tarn isn't responsible. You understand that, of course?"

"Entirely. If you please, who is living in the same house with Mr. Kerby?"

"His wife, Caryl Kerby. I want you to watch her."

"That is all?" he asked politely;

"There's David Blane; he's nice. He wouldn't—he wouldn't have a reason to start those ticking noises. He's on leave of absence from Solar Pictures to work on the motion picture script. I'm going to play the lead in it. And—there's Alice Rittenhouse. She's the daughter or niece of Henry's publisher; she's been staying with the Kerbys for the past month."

"Perhaps I shall meet her?"

Incontinently, Lucille glanced at her watch. "Heavens! It's nearly ten. Our Garden Club's giving a charity show at the Carmel Theater and I have to be there this afternoon. Charlie and I are on the committee. Are you certain you understand everything, Baron? I've tried to make it clear but with a foreigner it's difficult—"

He bowed, his lips touching her hand. "Charming lady, when you explain even to a foreigner your words are delightful."

This pleased her. He picked up the green umbrella he had so carefully placed across the arms of one of the chairs, and she went with him to the door and dubiously watched him walk down the long hall to the elevators.

Although he was in a hurry he stopped in the rental library off the lobby of the hotel to inquire if the young lady had any books written by Henry Kerby.

Yes, she had. Four of them: *The Green Hedge, Hawaiian Summer, The Day Before Yesterday,* and *Two Men on an Island.*

Soberly he examined them. *Two Men on an Island,* according to the title page, was the most recent and that was published three years ago. "Have you nothing newer, if you please?"

"That's his latest."

"Thank you." He walked away. At the next intersection he asked a newsboy how to reach the Bohemian Club . . .

"If you permit, my dear sir, I present myself. The Baron von Kaz." Heels together, back stiff, he inclined forward in his curious bow which was strictly according to the military rules of another era with one exception: Instead of inclining respectfully, his head was always held up, wary and saturnine, as though even when bowing he was too distrustful to take any risks during those seconds of extreme courtesy.

Of such stuff was his nature compounded. In a country where bowing is a lost art he would continue to bow as though he had never departed from his beloved Vienna; and, in Vienna, where not yet has this form of manners been extinguished, he would invariably ruin the effect by the lifting of his head.

Henry Kerby, a big, broad-shouldered man, with intelligent, amused eyes above a blunt nose, looked at the individual who was bowing. Kerby's short whiskers were flame colored and now, as he lowered his head to inspect this detective recommended to him by Lucille, the whiskers spread out like fire on the wide chest. He offered his hand. "Sit down." He wondered why the fellow carried a green umbrella when the sun was shining, hot and warm even for San Francisco.

"Glad to meet you, Baron," Kerby began. "Mrs. Tarn said you had been of great service to her in Vienna."

"It was nothing, my dear sir," was the modest reply.

"Well, she thought it was. But blast it! Baron, I don't see that I need—"

"For a man of my ability," continued the Baron blandly. "When she was in Vienna acting in a cinema picture, I learned that two men were threatening to throw acid upon her face unless she gave them twenty thousand kronen. I assure you, I could not permit such an occurrence. Where another might have bungled the matter, in—ach!" He snapped his fingers. "In two days I had arrested the men, forced a confession. She was so grateful that she kindly suggested that should I ever come to Hollywood, that I inform her of my presence. And so I did. Ad litteram." He glanced up to make certain his erudition was appreciated. "That means—"

"Look here," said Kerby impatiently. "That's fine. That's all right in Vienna where you know your way around. But triple thunder! I don't need a detective. And if I change my mind, I'll get an American detective. Lucille—Mrs. Tarn shouldn't have told you about those idiotic noises."

"That means 'to the letter'."

"What?"

"Ad litteram. It is Latin." In Austria and also in England the Baron had been warned that the Americans were barbaric, devoid of all education, and easily impressed by superior minds.

"Oh." Kerby swallowed. "But what I was saying, that is if you're interested, Baron, is now that I've had some sleep I'm not so sure but that the ticking noises were purely imaginary."

The Baron said, "The entire world would be appalled should any grievance befall to so great an author."

Kerby lit his pipe. "You've read my books?"

"My dear sir, *The Green Hedge* was splendid."

"Well." Kerby unbent a little. "I'm glad you liked it."

"And *Hawaiian Summer* and *The Day Before Yesterday* were superb!"

"Thank you." Kerby sat on the bed, trying to get his pipe going, gaining a more favorable impression of this dark-faced person across from him. The man seemed to have sense after all. "Look here, Baron," he said more kindly, "I'm sorry Mrs. Tarn and I had you come here from Los Angeles. I don't think I need a detective—"

"However, my favorite book," continued the Baron, "is the magnificent *Three Men on a Boat*." He smiled, watching Kerby suck ineffectually on the cold pipe, automatically bringing forth a heavy, old-fashioned cigarette case. He wished to be as gracious and courteous to the author as he had been to other clients who had entered the forbidding office of the Baron von Kaz in Vienna.

"Eh?"

"Yes, *Three Men on a Boat* was the best."

"I've always thought so myself." Grimly Kerby stood up. "So good I wish I had written it. As a matter of fact, I tried something like it. *Two Men on an Island.*" He strode to the door, "Well, Baron, as I said; I don't need a detective."

Rapidly the Baron asked, "Will you have a cigarette, my dear Mr. Kerby? My special brand?" The silver case clicked open. Kerby stared at the case. The case contained no cigarettes. Too late did the Baron recollect his disturbing phenomenon. "In my suitcase at the bus—at the train station, I have one thousand cigarettes," he declared loudly, standing. "Two thousand. All of a special make. I forgot them. In the excitement of considering these lethal and deadly ticking noises, I forgot them." Wishing he had said "three thousand," he sat down.

"Deadly?" bellowed Kerby, taken unawares. "Lethal?"

"Exactly. And before I can say whether or not even the great von Kaz can protect you, I must be told more concerning these ticking noises."

"Protect me?"

"We must consider whether they are imaginary or real. Whether you are insane—" Noticing a package of cigarettes on the table, the Baron helped himself after considerately proffering the package to Kerby who weakly waved his pipe in refusal. With a flourish the Baron lit the cigarette, for a moment closed his eyes. It was his first cigarette since last night when he had borrowed two from the bus driver. "Ach, excuse me. Where were we?"

With feeling Kerby replied that as nearly as he could remember one of them was supposed to be insane. Also, he wanted to know why the Baron had called the noises "lethal and deadly"? The Baron asked when had they started? What were they like? Kerby wished he knew just what Lucille had told this confounded foreigner. He sat on the table. He sucked at his pipe. At first, he explained, when they had begun he had thought that they were caused by a clock, or a watch; or, perhaps by some blasted bug or cricket which had become trapped in between the walls.

He lit his pipe again. Or maybe they were made by a leaky faucet dripping. They bothered him. He couldn't go to sleep. He complained to his wife. She and the servants searched the entire house. Well, they hadn't discovered a thing. The plumber arrived. There was nothing the matter with the pipes or faucets. The architect had stated most emphatically that the walls were of solid concrete. No bugs could be trapped to produce noises in a house that he had designed. The clocks near and in Kerby's bedroom were stopped completely. But night after night, when Kerby was in bed and the lights were out and the house was quiet, the damned noises would come.

As Kerby described them, almost could the Baron hear them: sly, furtive, ticking noises. So soft that you could not decide from what part of the bedroom they originated. "Blast it!" Kerby tapped his pipe on the heel of his shoe.

"I had to stop complaining to Mrs. Kerby, Baron. She began to look at me every time I mentioned them as if she thought something were the matter with my head. And I didn't want the servants to talk. I may be goofy, Baron, but if so I'm not ready for all Carmel to hear it." He grinned, one-sidedly, embarrassed by his own harassed frankness. "As a matter of fact, that's why I haven't changed to another bedroom. I'm planning to sell a script to Solar Pictures and I can't risk having some columnist find out I'm afraid—I'm troubled by silly noises and write a story on it."

"Thank you," said the Baron, thoughtfully.

"There you are." Kerby again went to the door. "You can see that I don't need a detective. To tell the truth, now that I've had my sleep, unless the noises return I'm not going to a doctor. I'm damned sorry we wired for you—"

"Excuse me. If, as I said, you are insane, I cannot assist you. But once I spend two, perhaps three nights in your home, I will decide whether or not are the ticking noises there."

"In my home? You in my home? I wouldn't have you in my home for five thousand dollars. What would my wife say if—"

"My dear sir." The Baron's blue eyes held a glacial glitter. "That is essential. Otherwise, despite my high regard for the gracious Mrs. Tarn, I must refuse to assist you and her."

"Good." Kerby put his hand on the knob of the door. "I don't need a detective. And if I should ever decide that I do need one, I'd want one who was an American." He dropped his hand. "Before you go I want to know what you meant by saying those noises might be deadly? I mean; if there *are* actually noises?"

The Baron had no intention of going. "They offer terrible possibilities, my dear sir," he stated in precise, metallic tones. "First you grow worried and nervous as you are

now. You cannot sleep. The situation becomes a patholog-
ical process. It is a most highly refined torture for a man
of your temperament. Ach, sir, an ingenious and diabolical beginning—" He tucked his green umbrella under his
arm, bowed. "However, if you do not wish the services of
a great and brave detective, I have, if you believe you are
in no danger, nothing more to say. Please carry my kindest
regards to dear Mrs. Tarn. Good day, my dear sir."

"Wait a minute," demanded Kerby awkwardly. "Don't
be in a thundering rush. Sit down, will you? Ticking noises
can't *hurt* anyone."

"No?" questioned the Baron politely.

"Of course they can't. That is, they can be confoundedly
irritating and if they're really there why they're probably Charlie's or someone else's idea of a—well, damn it! a
practical joke." Kerby looked at him. And then, with less
assurance, "Don't you think so?"

The Baron shrugged. "Ach, perhaps practical. Not a
joke. No."

"What in blazes would anyone want to—"

"They may be most serious, my dear sir. So very serious
that you should engage the services of a great detective."

Kerby shook his head, half to himself, as if such conceit weren't possible. "Well, how much would these services cost?"

"Five thousand dollars. When I determine the source
of the ticking noises, stop them from tormenting you, tell
you who is responsible for their presence I receive my fee.
If I fail," he snapped his lingers, "nothing."

"Great almighty Lord! I'm not sure whether I want your
services, Baron. I wouldn't give an American detective over
two or three hundred dollars."

"If you please. I am not an American detective."

"And besides, the noises are probably imaginary."

Coldly the Baron regarded Henry Kerby, pacing back and forth in front of the door like a large, lumbering Newfoundland dog worried by some smaller object, and puzzled by it, and not knowing whether to recognize the source of the worry or ignore it.

It was now, decided the Baron, that he would either lose or obtain the case. He couldn't afford to lose it. In Vienna, admittedly, this would be an ordinary triangle: The wife. The husband. And the other man. Not entirely ordinary, he thought, because there *was* something strange and sinister about the ticking noises, a queer compound of viciousness which might possibly be removed from the ordinary.

Kerby didn't appear to be a man who would suffer from hallucinations. He was too vital, not at all the nervous, irritable type which so often is an easy prey to morbid mental ailments or disturbances. And a man suffering from mental delusions rarely has the forthright courage to question his own condition, and to consider means of curing it. No, concluded the Baron, this man *was* being tormented by something.

Mr. Kerby must be forced to doubt that this was the simple triangle he seemed to think it was. Mr. Kerby must be convinced that only could a brave and accomplished detective unravel the solution. And so, the Baron asked quietly, "My dear sir, if these noises are not in your head, you assume that they are instigated by a jealous husband as a manner of revenge, no?"

"By Charlie?" Kerby's pacing halted. "Certainly. He's the only one who might have anything against me." He grinned lopsidedly. "As a matter of fact, Baron, I wouldn't blame Charlie but—blast it! You know how a man and a woman—well, you can't help it sometimes if you happen to like a woman?"

"Unfortunately no," admitted the Baron.

"There you are. And any American detective, for a hundred dollars, could find out if those noises are being caused by one of my servants bribed by Charlie Tarn to—"

"Mr. Tarn? Impossible, my dear sir. Did I not understand from Mrs. Tarn that he wishes to be the next governor?"

"Yes. But what has that—"

"Then doubly impossible."

"Doubly impossible, hell! See here, Baron—"

"No politician, my dear Mr. Kerby, would possess this remarkable imagination. Nor the patience required to drive you to kill yourself!"

2

The Dacrokoff Disappearance

Three hours later, the brave Baron von Kaz emerged from the bus station with his battered pigskin suitcase, deposited it on the pavement, and with the aid of his green umbrella enjoyed the supreme luxury of beckoning for a taxicab.

Complacently he stepped into the cab, read the address his first American client had given him:

HENRY I. KERBY
12 LA HONDA DRIVE
CARMEL-BY-THE-SEA

"Carmel," he ordered.

The taxi driver pushed a disbelieving nose through the window. He inspected his fare. He saw the worn suit, the disreputable hat, the bulky green umbrella. "Trying to be funny? Where do you want to go?"

Carmel was one hundred and thirty miles from San Francisco. The Baron had no money; never had he a sense of distance nor an understanding of financial matters. Now that he at last had a client, these matters were trivialities. He raised his head. "Carmel," he repeated a little less mildly. "Carmel-by-the-Sea."

The gentleman conducting the cab, a large Irishman by the name of Tivvits, looked at the dark, clean-shaven face, and the more he considered the icy blue eyes the more difficult it was to develop an adequate reply. There was a clear, unfeeling steadiness in the blue eyes; it was as if they passed through the driver, as if this individual had been taken care of and no longer mattered any more than any other instrument in the car. Tivvits felt all this. He said, "Okay, boss!" uneasily, lamely deciding that there wasn't need to antagonize a fare who evidently was going to pay for a hundred and thirty mile drive.

The Baron leaned into the cushions, contemplating the future pleasantly. Mr. Kerby had agreed to the fee of five thousand dollars providing the Baron could determine who was responsible for the ticking noises. The Baron frowned. He perceived a small dark cloud in this roseate future. He had been forced to frighten Mr. Kerby into accepting a great and brave detective instead of an ordinary American one.

That was very fine. Mr. Kerby now had a great and brave detective. The Baron had the case. But he had begun to wonder where the devil he would find a suspect. To frighten, to convince Mr. Kerby that he was threatened by a complex danger, the Baron had cheerfully eliminated the husband of Mrs. Tarn. The Baron had proved that Mr. Tarn couldn't possibly be responsible for placing the ticking noises in Mr. Kerby's bedroom.

Ach, thought the Baron. He stuck his head through the window to the driver's ear. "My dear sir, are you married?"

Tivvits was married, and recently, and said so at great length. It was a long drive to Carmel and if his fare wanted to talk, Tivvits had no objections.

"And if your wife should fall in love with another man, what would you do?"

"What?" Tivvits took his foot off the throttle pedal. "If she *what?* Why, say! I'd kill the guy! I'd crack his head between my two hands. I'd—"

"Thank you," said the Baron, reclining upon the cushions. It was obvious what Tivvits would do. With Mr. Tarn eliminated the Baron was forced to discard the jealous husband motive. The Baron began to appreciate that perhaps he had been somewhat premature. But he reassured himself: Mr. Tarn *was* a politician; no politician would be capable of conceiving such an insidious revenge, subtly designed to drive a man to suicide. But even as he reassured himself, he became less optimistic. He had no intention of permitting his client to kill himself; at least not until the five thousand dollar fee had been paid. But unless that fee were earned, and quickly, the Baron wondered if he might not find himself with a dead client and no future whatsoever in the barbaric states of Northern America.

After the taxicab left the Santa Clara valley, the highway wound through green mountains. The rains had been heavy this spring and the mountains were all smooth and soft, dotted with solitary oaks and then crowned with cypress and pine. The air was fragrant, filled with mingling odors of sweet grass and the scent of pine; Indian paint brushes, lupins and poppies sprinkled the bright green with brilliant patches of purple and blue and shades of orange-yellow and reds. Golden mustard flowers hid entire embankments.

This was a new country, a strange new country for the Baron. The sky was blue, a clear sterile blue as if from morning until night the color was never disturbed by passing storms nor by the acrid shattering of lightning. Between the blue sky and the sun a faint, barely perceptible haze filtered out all of the harsher rays. Only a benevolent golden light passed down upon these endless mountains, an illusory light which contained little warmth. The Baron shivered, closing the windows. He did not approve of this unnatural radiance and this untamed landscape. Resolutely, he ignored both. His eyes closed and he recalled that country he loved so well . . .

The taxi stopped suddenly and the Baron awoke immediately in full possession of his faculties as though he had not slept for the past fifty miles. Tivvits opened the door and through the door the Baron was conscious of a long, two-storied house shaped like an "L." The sunshine splashed against the white plaster. The house was flat-roofed, with green vines climbing the walls. The driveway led past the house to a garage, with a large flower garden at the right of the garage, the greater part of it concealed by the house.

The Baron stepped from the taxicab and looked around. The house was on a point, separated from the white sands of the beach and the shining blue water by the winding road. He could see a small town on the other end of the bay and assumed that it was Carmel. Confronted by this magnificent estate, Tivvits visibly grew more respectful. He touched his hat as the Baron pointed to the battered pigskin suitcase and the green umbrella, and plunged into the rear part of the cab to remove this luggage. On the other side of the driveway there was a tennis court and the Baron saw a girl in shorts practicing against the stone wall at the back. Her yellow hair was cut in a long bob and the soft breeze swirled it about her shoulders as she drove the ball with swift hard strokes at the wall. Down near the garage a man was cutting the lawn and the Baron could hear the sound of bees coming from the rose bushes and above him, in that clear empty blue sky, seagulls circled.

Tivvits read the meter. "That'll be exactly fifty-four dollars and thirty cents," he said, now very, much pleased with himself for having the instinct to spot a fine fare when he saw one.

The Baron didn't answer. The girl had jumped over the net and as she turned toward him, courteously he lifted his hat and bowed as he would to any woman, whether he had been introduced to her or not, whom he should meet upon one of the estates of his friends. The girl flashed him a smile, waved her bare arm cheerfully and not until she had closed the gate of the tennis court and approached the house did she realize that she did not know the man.

He walked up to her. "Permit me, I introduce myself, von Kaz. Baron Franz Maximilian Karagôz von Kaz."

She was small. She had a pert little nose placed where it should be between slightly perplexed gray eyes and a mouth which, thought the Baron without the slightest premeditation, he should enjoy kissing and thereupon decided that this was an idea which he should not neglect in the future.

The perplexed eyes suddenly brightened. "Oh, you're the Baron!" She gave him her hand. "Henry said he'd learned that you were in San Francisco and invited you down here. Henry knows so many interesting people."

Tivvits, standing respectfully beside his cab, heard all of this. A Baron? Wait until he got back to San Francisco and told them how he saw this nobleman wandering bewilderedly through the streets of San Francisco and wasn't fooled just because the nobleman was dressed like a foreigner but walked right up to him, smartly, saying, "Wouldn't you like to ride in one of our fine new cabs, sir?" and the nobleman says, "Yes, I would," and ends by going to Carmel and paying fifty-four dollars and thirty cents and a tip of eight dollars. Tivvits knew that this was his lucky day.

"I'm Alice Rittenhouse," the girl told the Baron. "Henry's working with Dave on that damned script of theirs and I suppose he's forgotten that you were coming." She nodded toward the house. "Caryl's gone to the theater. The Garden Club's sponsoring a show tonight. You'll probably have to attend. And as long as Caryl isn't here, I'll be the hostess. Come along, Baron."

The Baron followed her up the flagstone walk, motioning for the driver to bring his things. Alice opened the door. "Sit down and I'll see if I can get you a drink. Put your bag there in the hall and I'll ask Maggy if Caryl told her what room you're to have."

Alice's shapely bare legs carried her through the cool hall into a long living room from where she disappeared through a door. The house was quiet. Standing there in the hall, the Baron could hear from somewhere the faint clattering of a typewriter and now and then the murmur of men's voices. The driver was standing on the terrace, hat in hand. He appeared to be in a trance; his lips were moving. This was his luckiest day. He was repeating what he was going to say to the office in San Francisco. Maybe they'd appreciate how important it was to have a smart man at the wheel of one of their cabs now. If he handled it rightly it might even mean that they'd take him off the day shift and give him a regular job like checking the stands.

Waiting for Alice Rittenhouse to return, the Baron looked into the tall mirror and was acutely aware of his appearance. Now that he had a client and had at last started to carve a successful new career for himself in these raw states of America, it was eminently befitting that he clothe himself in a new suit. His meditations were interrupted by Tivvits, who respectfully advanced a step.

'That'll be all, your Lordship?"

"What?" The Baron turned and gazed upon this eccentric.

"You don't require me no longer, your Lordship?"

The Baron shook his head, marveling at this strange form of address.

"It'll be—" Laboriously Tivvits wet his lips. "It'll be fifty-four dollars and thirty cents."

Alice returned with a tall glass, followed by a dumpy woman in a clean black dress. "Maggy this is the Baron—" She laughed, "I'm afraid you'll have to repeat the name for me."

"Von Kaz." He lifted the drink.

Maggy curtsied. "He's to have the room upstairs next to the study, Miss Rittenhouse."

Tivvits commenced again but the Baron silenced him by pointing to the pigskin suitcase, then put down the glass and accompanied Alice. Alice stopped at a door near the white stairs. "Maggy, show the man where to leave the Baron's bag." She spoke to the Baron, "I think you'd better give him your umbrella. I'm sure it won't rain. Not while we're in the house anyway. We'll risk disturbing Henry and Dave."

She knocked and then opened the door.

Kerby was sitting at a huge Italian desk, his pipe clenched between firm white teeth, his beard blazing red from the reflected sunlight which streamed through the wide windows. Near him at a smaller table, bent over a portable typewriter, was a tall, fair-haired man in a silk shirt and flannel slacks. Kerby turned his head at the interruption and the tall man jumped up.

"What in thunder do you want?"

The Baron stepped in beside Alice and bowed formally.

Kerby took off his plain, silver-rimmed glasses, dropping them carelessly on the desk, adding to the confusion of papers, open books, pipes, and pipe cleaners. "I was wondering when you'd arrive. Get your baggage all right?" He grasped the Baron's hand, pumped it vigorously, and turned abruptly. "Dave, I want you to meet a friend of mine." He paused, glanced at the impassive face of the foreigner, adding, "Knew him in Vienna. As a matter of fact, I knew him very well in Vienna. Found that he was staying in San Francisco and invited him here for a visit.

Mr. Blane, the Baron von—" He ran his hand through his
red beard and grinned. "Forget those blasted titles. Dave,
meet the Baron."

"How do you do," said Blane distantly.

The Baron inclined. "Delighted, my dear Mr. Blane."

"You've already met Alice?"

Alice laughed. "I'm playing hostess. Caryl's gone to the
theater so I took charge of him."

The Baron murmured, "Os magna sonaturum," looked
around modestly. "That is Latin. It means a mouth from
which comes beautiful—"

Kerby good-naturedly clapped the Baron on the back.
"No doubt. But as a matter of fact, I think you'd better
unpack."

Blane eyed the Baron, lit a cigarette. "Good game of
tennis, Alice?"

Alice shook her head. "Couldn't find anyone to play
with. Caryl had to go to the damned theater early."

The Baron looked at the mass of manuscript piled on
Kerby's desk.

Kerby rumbled, "I'm trying to rush through ten pages
as I promised my wife I'd pick her up at the theater." He
sat down and shuffled a sheaf of papers, already his mind
returning to his work. "I'll see you at dinner then. You'd
better plan to go to the show with us tonight." Then he
once more glanced at his new guest, at the shabby suit,
and added awkwardly, "That is, if you're not too tired."

The Baron said stiffly, "Not at all," nodded to the other
man who was lounging by the window seat, and withdrew
with Alice.

His room on the second floor looked comfortable
and cheerful. The walls were of rough plaster, the bed
was large and soft, the furniture was heavy, serviceable,
well-polished and in a style which he assumed was a mixture of Spanish and Californian. Alice Rittenhouse poked

her head through the door. "I'm going to change while you have a chance to wash and unpack."

According to the clock on the dresser it was three-thirty. He handled the clock and found that it was electric and silent. He sat down, trying to form his plans when there was a knock on the door.

Maggy said hesitantly, "The taxi driver is waiting; He says you owe him for the fare, sir."

Downstairs, the Baron closed the front door and faced Tivvits.

"Fifty-four dollars and thirty cents," said this gentleman.

"Very reasonable," amiably replied the Baron. He inserted his hand in his pocket, drew it out with an air of annoyance. "Ach, my dear sir. You could not possibly cash a letter of credit for five thousand dollars, could you? I but recently landed and I find I have spent all my small change."

The illumination slowly faded from Tivvits' wide face. He shook his head.

"I am so sorry." The Baron shrugged. "I am afraid you will have to return tomorrow."

"Return? I got to drive back to San Francisco tonight. I can't make another trip tomorrow of one hundred and thirty miles each way." Then the radiance returned to Tivvits' face. "It's only three-thirty. I could take you to one of the banks in Carmel."

It would not do to start a vulgar discussion concerning a miserable bill of some fifty dollars in front of the house owned by his client. Ach, if he were only in Vienna where taxi-drivers sent their bills to the office of the great Baron von Kaz and had the breeding and courtesy to wait until he was pleased to pay. He sighed and made up his mind.

"Excellent. I shall go with you. Excuse me one minute."

He returned with his green umbrella.

In Carmel, the Baron with his green umbrella tapped Tivvits on the shoulder, ordering him to stop in front of an exclusive men's clothing store. "If you do not mind, my dear man, I shall take advantage of this opportunity and step in to purchase a suit. My trunks have not yet arrived. It is annoying to have to wear this—ach!—this old traveling suit."

Tivvits was content to wait. The meter clicked happily. Now the bill was past fifty-seven dollars. With any luck at all it would amount to sixty.

Inside the store the Baron selected a well-tailored, dark brown suit. He regretted that he had not the time to have one made to order, but this suit, except that it was slightly tight in the shoulders, fitted him admirably. One thing, he admitted, these North Americans were efficient, and they could manufacture clothes with the same facility they produced automobiles. He then decided on a supply of linen, ordered this to be sent to the home of Mr. Henry Kerby and credited to the account of the Baron Franz Maximilian Karagôz von Kaz.

Given these two imposing names, the clerk had no thought of questioning the Baron's credit. The clerk complimented the Baron on his selection, suggesting that a new hat and shoes were all that were required to complete the outfit. The Baron glanced up at the clock. It was ten minutes to four. "If you please, could you tell me what time the banks close in Carmel?"

"Four o'clock."

He shrugged. "Show me your shoes. I can attend to the bank later."

Thus it was that he emerged from the store at four twenty-eight. And strangely enough, when Tivvits made the round of the banks, all were closed. "Do not mind," declared the Baron carelessly, as he returned to the cab after trying the door of the third bank. "To be frank with you, my dear man, I find you a most competent driver. I shall probably require your services for the next few days and you shall prepare a statement to cover the entire time when I no longer need you."

"Say—" commenced Tivvits.

"And we shall add, shall we say, five dollars a day in addition to the regular charges to recompense you for your admirable services?" The Baron sank into the cushions.

This was a fortune. A gold mine. Tivvits was unable to speak. He could merely nod. In order to prove what a tremendously effective driver he was he took every turn on two wheels. When the Baron stepped out of the cab, Tivvits touched his cap. "I got it up to sixty-four on that last straight away," he said modestly. "I bet not another man in California could do the same."

"No doubt. You had better stay at one of the hotels. Let me know which one. What is your name?"

"Tivvits, your Lordship."

"Tivvits? An excellent name. I am the Baron von Kaz."

"I know that already, your—"

"Baron is all that is necessary, Tivvits." He nodded at the cab. "I suggest that you telephone your company and request them to send a more suitable automobile than this affair. Can you do that?"

For a tip of five dollars a day, Tivvits was ready to do anything. "Certainly, your Lordship." He climbed into his taxi. "I'll have a car for you tomorrow morning . . ."

That evening in the theater, Alice Rittenhouse smoothed a print silk skirt over the most ravishing pair of knees the Baron had seen since departing in such haste from Vienna.

"How do you like Carmel's theater, Baron?"

He was gazing intently seven rows ahead. Here a woman with glittering yellow hair was seated. He recognized Lucille Tarn. He was speculating on how he could get in touch with her.

"I beg your pardon." When he faced her, Alice Rittenhouse forgot the domineering Hapsburg profile. She was
only aware that the man could be strangely charming. She
was about to repeat her question when Caryl Kerby spoke.

"We had quite a time persuading Dacrokoff to perform
for our little charity show, Baron. I hope you will enjoy
him. He's Austrian, I believe. Terribly famous. Played all
through Europe. I hope you haven't seen him?"

The Baron was seated between Alice Rittenhouse and
Caryl Kerby. Caryl was twenty-seven or eight, about five
years older than Alice, and as dark as Alice was fair.

"Uhm," replied the Baron. "I do not recall the name."

Then David Blane walked down the aisle. Kerby was
sitting to the left of his wife. He grinned and pointed to
the one empty seat on his right, three seats removed from
Alice. "I told you not to wait and finish that scene, Dave."

After eyeing the bloody idiot who had the impudence
to sit next to Alice and receiving a bland smile in return,
Blane took the empty seat. Ever since that confounded
Baron chap had arrived in a taxi from San Francisco the
scenario editor had suffered from one of his frequent
attacks of indigestion.

The attack had commenced from the moment Alice
Rittenhouse had brought the fellow into the study, rising
to critical proportions at the dinner table, when she had
changed her chair to sit by him.

The little theater quickly filled. In the auditorium
lights were dimmed as the footlights flashed on. The curtain jerked upwards. Dacrokoff the magician stalked to
the center of the stage and bowed and waited for the applause to end.

"He's supposed to be the greatest magician in the
world," Caryl Kerby whispered.

"You have seen him?" Somehow the Baron had received
the opposite impression.

"Twice." In the darkness her small, olive face turned. "Last Wednesday in San Francisco and a couple of weeks ago at a party Dave gave for Mr. Goldenstein of Solar Pictures."

"I'm sure you'll think he's marvelous," Alice chimed in. "I saw him, too, at the blowout Dave had for his boss."

Under the spotlight the magician's face was gray, like crinkled rubber. He posed before a purple cabinet six feet and a half high, three feet wide, and approximately one and a half feet from front to back.

The side facing the audience was covered with thick velvet. He called a huge negro from the wing; together they lifted the base to prove that neither in the base nor in the stage floor were there openings.

"Why that's 'Dude'!" exclaimed Alice. "He's helping?"

"Dude" was the negro, whispered Caryl. A general handy man for Carmel who worked in Caryl's garden. Kerby was rumbling about the scenario to Blane, who moved restlessly, wondering if it would be too obvious if he swiped the Baron-person's seat during intermission. Caryl said, "Sh-h-h!"

"Ladies and gentlemen," Dacrokoff was announcing, "you have seen that this cabinet is empty. I have demonstrated to you that it contains no means of entrance other than the opening in front. The three sides and base of the cabinet are walnut, three inches thick. . . ."

The windows of the theater had been closed. Through them the Baron could see the soft, gray fog. Ach, he thought, I do not like this, and he felt for the handle of his green umbrella.

When Dacrokoff asked a member of the audience to come onto the stage you could feel the hush settling upon the audience. A woman tried to titter. A fat man in the first row coughed nervously. In the following stillness as the magician waited, you could hear the faint beating of waves as they broke and rolled on the near-by California shore.

No one answered. Everyone would like to see Dacrokoff make someone disappear. But someone else. The spotlight followed the negro as he descended from the stage and walked up the center aisle.

He stopped by the woman with the glittering platinum-gold hair. "Maybe you'd like to be made disappear, Mrs. Tarn?"

"Oh, no, Dude. Get someone else." A man sitting next to her said in a jovial, public-speaker voice, "Why not, Lucille? Don't spoil the fun for these good folks."

And several of her friends began to laugh and clap: "That's right, Charlie!" "You tell her to, Charlie!" "I'll do it after you do, Lucille!" And so on.

Seemingly reluctant, she followed the tall negro to the stage. "You think you can cause me to disappear, Herr Dacrokoff?" she questioned, and provocatively swayed her body as though she were before a camera because Henry Kerby was down there somewhere in the blackness and she wished him to see her and realize what she meant to him.

Dacrokoff's hands fluttered as he circled her, intoning a sing-song chant, "O great invisibles, aid me tonight I implore you: O great invisibles, assist me with your presence tonight, thus do I implore of you . . ."

And, eyes intent upon that tall man in the spotlight, the Baron knew that he *had* remembered correctly. The years might have changed Dacrokoff's face but never that habit of his, the nervous fluttering of those terrible hands which could so quickly strangle a man. How many years ago had it been, thought the Baron, as he concentrated on the stage with the dull throb of the guttural voice droning into his ears. "O invisible ones thus have I implored you; thus do I request of you," and the audience now quiet and still and slow weaving tendrils of fog curled at the windows of the theater.

How many years? Ten, perhaps. It was after the war. It was before the Baron had been promoted to head his section and that bungler, that bloated Hjiek was in charge. Three women, wives of government officials, had been strangled near the theater where Dacrokoff was playing, although his name had been different then. What was his name? Never mind, it would come; all his faculties were strained toward the stage. When he was ready the name and all the incidents relating to it would come trooping into his acute perception, marshaled but not necessarily in order.

"O invisible ones, assist me to send this woman into eternity, into a movement of time," came the guttural voice. The Baron had heard that voice in the theater on Göffstadt in Vienna. He had gone there one evening after the third woman was found strangled, her body crumpled at the base of a lamp post, but old Hjiek had thought it was the sailor with the scarred fade and refused to permit the Baron to interfere with the case. And so Dacrokoff—what was his name then? Lichtbrunne, Lichtbrenne—had departed. To Canada, they learned later after the sailor had furnished a water-proof alibi.

The chant ended. With her back to the audience the magician assisted Lucille Tarn into the cabinet. Except for the glaring blue spotlight, the lights on the stage had been dimmed. At a command from Dacrokoff the negro performed sweeping motions with his hands behind the cabinet, starting from the floor and extending to the top of the box-like structure, proving that no trickery existed to permit the woman to vanish at the rear via the back-drop curtains.

Then with swift, chopping motions of his own hands, Dacrokoff drew shut the purple curtains and stamped his

foot. "Go!" he cried. "Go into eternity." Perhaps there was
a faint scream. Of that the Baron was never certain. Later,
he wondered if Lucille Tarn might not have realized, realized with all the terror of which she was capable, just what
eternity meant after the curtains closed and . . . screamed.

With dramatic suddenness Dacrokoff ordered the negro
to pull aside the curtains. The interior of the cabinet was
empty. Lucille Tarn had disappeared.

Well, that was what the audience had expected; it was
for this that they had paid their money. Dacrokoff was a
famous magician. It was an unusual trick, a startling trick,
but that's what famous magicians are hired to produce.
So while people in the audience gaped and uttered, "Oh,
she has gone, hasn't she?" and other intelligent remarks
worthy of the cultured community of Carmel, the tension
relaxed. Everyone was pleased. Observers wiggled in their
seats. They opened their mouths and breathed normally
and while Dacrokoff grimaced triumphantly, fog pressed
ever thicker at the windows.

Next Dacrokoff raised his arms, crying, "Bring back to
me this form you have taken," stamped his foot, remained
motionless perhaps a minute, and with a great flourish
whipped apart the curtains without troubling to glance
inside.

Astonished at the swift draught of silence which flooded through the theater, Dacrokoff twisted his head toward
the cabinet. By now most of the spectators were on their
feet. The silence was shattered by gurgling notes of surprise and the shoutings of men from various sections of
the room.

The negro peered into the cabinet, rolled his eyes,
and blubbered in amazement to Dacrokoff that the lady'd
fainted.

Charles Tarn, the man who was to be the next Republi-
can governor of California, ran down the aisle.

Lucille Tarn was in the cabinet. She was there. Everyone could see her. But she wasn't standing, proud and defiant. She was crumpled in a pitifully awkward heap. She should have known better than to faint in that position. Any motion picture director would have been astonished to have Lucille do a trick like that.

"Lucille! What's the matter?" Charles Tarn leaped onto the stage. "Get up. People are staring at you!"

Yes, everybody was staring at her. Get up, Lucille. Get up now and smile and be adored again.

There were calls for a doctor in the house.

But Lucille didn't get up. Dacrokoff and her husband pulled her out of the somber, box-like cabinet with three sides of wood. The glittering hair spread over her shoulders and when her husband lifted her in his arms, her head dropped back unnaturally and on her dress was a splotch of the brightest red the Baron had ever seen.

Ruthlessly he elbowed through the hushed circle gathered around the cabinet.

He saw the husband place his finger on that crimson spot blossoming over her heart on the white dress. The husband cried out hoarsely. He pulled something from the crimson spot, something long and thin and sharp; something which had penetrated into the breast and to the heart.

Tarn dropped his wife, crying, "Murder! Murder!"

"Oh, it's a joke," a woman declared unbelievingly. "Get up, Lucille! Get up!"

But never again would Lucille get up.

The Baron turned quickly as Kerby urgently whispered, "For God's sake come and help me. Blane's fainted."

3

The Five-Pointed Triangle

The crowd was jamming around the cabinet. Tarn was on his feet now, with the dripping hatpin in his hand, and two or three men were lifting the limp body of the murdered woman. More men had corralled the magician, Dacrokoff, and the negro near the back-drop. Someone had smashed the magician on the face and his lips were bleeding. The negro was blubbering, "Ah don' know nothin'. Ah don' know nothin'!" Dacrokoff refused to speak, folding his arms, gazing above the heads of the surging crowd.

A short man called to Tarn, "Say, see this? There aren't any holes in the wood." Excitedly he thumped the wooden cabinet. "How'd the hatpin get—" Another man ordered savagely, "Shut up you fathead," as Tarn swayed and was supported.

"Watch out for the hatpin," Tarn muttered. "Maybe there are fingerprints. Have you called a doctor?"

"He's on his way. We got the police on the phone."

The Baron edged his way through the thickening ring of people, using his green umbrella when necessary, working toward Blane and Kerby. Kerby took Blane by the arm. "I'm all right," the Baron heard Blane saying. "Sorry to trouble you. Terribly sorry. Too close in here."

Blane hadn't fainted but he looked as though he were on the verge of doing so. He was leaning against a plaster

angel ornamenting one of the columns by the side wall.
A tall rugged man with ample jaw, he wasn't the type of
man, thought the Baron, to be so affected by the sight of
a dead woman.

The spotlight stabbed a blue glaring light through the
yellowing haze. The aisles were swollen with two conflicting, shouting, struggling streams of people; one eddying
rush driving for the stage, the other trying to get away
from that horror on the stage.

"Baron, you take Dave, will you?" Kerby asked. "Caryl
and Alice went to the car. I'm going to Lucille."

The Baron unfeelingly left the scenario editor and
plowed into the mass and jerked at his client's arm. "You
will come with us, please."

It was hard to hear in the confusion. Men were shouting. A woman in the far corner was squatting on the floor
screaming while a frenzied husband attempted to lift her.
Sirens were blasting their shrill, tearing shrieks in front of
the theater as the ambulance and police arrived.

"I'm not leaving," Kerby cried. "You take Dave."

An elbow caught him sharply in the pit of the stomach, directly in the solar plexus. He staggered. If the Baron hadn't grasped him, drawn him out of the wriggling,
thrusting flow of humanity, Kerby would have fallen. He
shoved the Baron away, breathing hard. "By God! You did
that. I saw you."

"Suppose one knifes you in this crowd?"

"You're not in Austria. Take Dave. No one is going to
knife—"

"At present," declared the Baron coldly, "you are worth
five thousand dollars to me. I will not permit you to jeopardize my fee."

In amazement, Kerby looked at this suddenly ruthless
and resolute guest of his, anger receding before the indu-
bitable fact that the Baron was in deadly earnest.

"If you please," the Baron pointed to Blane, "he requires our assistance."

They worked their way through the crowd. Caryl Kerby was waiting at the gate. "Alice is hysterical. What took you men so long?" She noticed Blane's greenish face. "What's the matter with you?"

Blane sagged, apologizing faintly. "Too stuffy in there or something. Dreadfully sorry."

They crossed the street. Alice was sobbing softly in the rear of the big town car. David Blane climbed in, taking the folding seat, followed by Caryl and Kerby, who for a moment stood with one foot on the running board, his face haggard and drawn by the dripping light of the street lamp.

The Baron murmured gently, "We can be of no help in there," and waited for Kerby to slowly enter the car.

The Baron shut the door and was opening the front door to get in next to the chauffeur when a large figure appeared by the fender and dutifully lifted a hand to a hat slightly askew above a round, broad-beamed face. "Evening, your Lordship," said a voice hopefully. "I saw you come out. The taxi's at the corner."

"Not tonight, Tivvits," said the Baron patiently.

"Not tonight?" asked Tivvits mournfully, touching his hand to his hat again and sadly watching the Baron enter the town car and drive away . . .

Lucille Tarn was mysteriously murdered in the Carmel Theater at seven fifty-six, Tuesday evening April the ninth.

At nine forty-eight the same night, Kerby and Blane stopped their forced conversation regarding tomorrow's work. Kerby crossed his study and turned on the radio, while Blane finished his third glass of whisky and soda. He had refused to go to bed when they arrived at the house, saying that the ride had cleared his head. Kerby entered

the low-ceilinged living room, removing his glasses and
dropping them in his pocket. Caryl Kerby was playing sol-
itaire, expertly and carefully as she always did everything.
Her face reminded the Baron of a beautifully carved cameo
as he watched her playing from the depths of a great, easy
chair near the fire.

There was something quiet and still in the smooth olive
face, accentuated by the lustrous black hair parted in the
middle and drawn smoothly from her forehead, that puzzled him. It was as though all her hopes and her thoughts
and her wishes were forever hidden behind that cool forehead and only when her brilliant black eyes opened, revealing a sudden flash such as might cross a sky on a sultry night, and then half closed again with the long lashes
brushing the warm olive cheeks, did the Baron realize that
here was one who could be a dangerous enemy and still
smile at you with those wide, scarlet lips. And he remembered what Lucille Tarn had said.

Kerby spoke gruffly to his wife, "Ten o'clock news report." He glanced around the room.

"Alice is all right," Caryl said in her low voice. "I left
her a sedative to take if she needs it." She glanced at the
Baron from under level eyebrows. Death, itself, meant little to the Baron; he was callous to death and he held no
false sentiment about it. Although he would not even admit to himself how Lucille Tarn's death, so brutally unexpected, had shocked him both from an emotional and professional standpoint, now that she *was* dead he could not
understand why anyone should not want to talk about her.

After reaching the Kerby house, he had speculated
upon how her death had been accomplished, asking the
others to describe in minute detail what they had seen in
order to view the events upon the stage not alone with his
eyes but from theirs too. In this he had been extremely
unsuccessful. Kerby had indicated several times that this

was not precisely the time to discuss her death. Blane had immersed himself in a glass of whisky and soda, his eyes on Alice, feeling very sorry for her and for himself because, as the Baron's conversation centered on the scream he insisted he had heard after Lucille Tarn had entered the cabinet, Alice's color changed from chalk white to a sickly yellow white. She had produced a stricken little whimper, suddenly put her hands over her eyes, announced that she had a splitting headache, and rushed upstairs. Caryl had followed her, to return after Blane and Kerby had retired to the study to plan tomorrow's work.

And so, when Kerby entered with the announcement about the radio, Caryl had glanced at the Baron, and then accompanied her husband into the study. The Baron shrugged. These people were sentimental barbarians. He walked into the study in time to hear the radio wish happily; "A good, good evening, folks. The Consolidated Oil Company brings to you the latest reports of the day. Flash! Mrs. Charles Tarn, wife of the prominent Carmel lawyer and important political figure of California, mysteriously murdered a few hours ago in the Carmel Theater . . ."

And for the next twelve minutes the fine, rich, throbbing, insensate voice of the radio told sixteen million civilized listeners all that was known concerning the murder of Lucille Tarn, concluding:

"Although the magician Dacrokoff is strongly suspected, at this hour no one has yet been able to solve how the hatpin could have penetrated into her heart without leaving a mark of its passage through the wooden cabinet! I have in my hand the latest information from Chief of Police Zack Watson of Carmel. Here is what he reports to Radio-Press:

"'Dacrokoff's cabinet is built of wood. It is six feet and a half high. The front is open, covered by heavy velvet curtains. The two sides and the rear of the cabinet are composed of solid wood two and one quarter inches thick. The cabinet is approximately as wide as a large man's shoulders, an inch under three feet. From front to rear the length is exactly nineteen inches. The top of the cabinet is also of wood, joined securely to the three sides by screws. The base is thick, three inches and a quarter, with a hidden trap concealed by false beveled wood strips running around the interior of the cabinet. Just above these wood strips are several small slits for ventilation purposes when the heavy curtains are drawn.

"'This cabinet was examined with minute care by trained men from the Monterey County Sheriff's office. Because the cabinet is so narrow, it was definitely established that Mrs. Tarn could not have committed suicide by secreting the hatpin upon her when she entered the cabinet and then piercing her own breast. Her arms would be pressed too tightly to her sides to permit her to raise the hatpin to her breast. Mrs. Tarn was five feet, four inches in height, in her shoes. From her shoes to the point where the hatpin entered her breast, we have measured fifty-one and one third inches. That implies that the hatpin must have been inserted somewhere into the rear end of the cabinet approximately fifty-two or three inches, allowing a little over an inch for the angle of penetration, from the base; and, approximately seventeen inches from the right hand side of the cabinet.

"'Examining this spot on the wooden rear section of the cabinet by high-power microscopes we were unable to detect any indication that the wood had been entered by a hatpin or any other instrument. It has been suggested that the hole supposedly left by the hatpin could have been immediately puttied up with plastic wood after the murder. It is necessary, therefore, to repeat: *No hole exists in the wood, neither in the rear section nor the two sides, either filled or unfilled.* Until the method of the murder is more clearly established it will be impossible to advance a more definite statement to the newspapers or to the Radio-Press.'"

The radio took a breath. Quickly the Baron glanced at the two men. Kerby was sitting at his desk, pipe clenched between his teeth, shaking his head as if he were refusing to believe the amazing statement given by the Chief of Police over the radio's press service. Blane's jaw was thrust forward, and there was an angry, bewildered expression on his bronzed face. He had recovered from his sickness and he no longer appeared to be the same man who had dazedly apologized in the theater. He looked lean and hard, and his two hands were gripped so tightly around the glass that it was in imminent peril of being shattered.

The radio continued:

"In addition to the report issued by Police Chief Watson, the Radio-Press offers us the following last minute flashes. Both Dacrokoff and his negro helper, a local Carmel man by the name of 'Dude' McKay, who has worked as a gardener and general handy man, are being held. Meanwhile, Benjamin Lennock, manager of the Carmel Theater, has explained the trick of the so-called 'Dacrokoff Disappearing Act'. The secret trapdoor found in the cabinet by Police Chief Watson, communicates with a hidden opening sawed through the stage floor. In the basement, Dacrokoff had a rough elevator hidden from view by a wooden framework. Lennock operated the hand-winch to lower and raise Mrs. Tarn. Although he was unable to see her he states positively that he was the only person in the basement at the time. Police Chief Watson examined the wooden framework in the presence of a number of reporters and proved beyond a doubt that it contained no holes which would permit the hatpin to attain Mrs. Tarn's heart while she was in the elevator.

"Thus, folks, again California is shocked and astounded by a murder of terrific intensity just as Consolidated

Gasoline will astound the wise motorist by the terrific intensity of power for uphill and down." The radio took another breath. "And folks, you too, can have . . ."

Caryl twisted a knob on the radio. "I think that's sufficient for one night."

"I can't figure it out." Blane scratched a match for his cigarette with such force that he tore the box. He dropped the box in the waste basket. "The negro did it. He was standing behind the damned cabinet all the time. They'll find that he plugged the hole if they look for it."

"Uhm," came from one of the chairs.

"Well?" asked Blane sharply.

"If you will excuse me," said the Baron, "we all agreed a short time ago that we could see the blackman's—ach!— the negro's hands as he extended them beyond the cabinet, waving them that the audience might know nothing existed between the cabinet and the back drop."

"It wasn't the negro," rumbled Kerby. He pointed his pipe at the Baron.

"I'm sure," countered Blane, "it wasn't the magician. He wasn't even near the cabinet."

"What puzzles me," murmured the Baron, "is how the hatpin was able to penetrate exactly into her heart. If you wish my opinion—"

"Your opinion!" said Blane scornfully.

"My opinion is that the Police Chief should consider the hatpin more carefully. The puzzle is not that it passed through apparently solid wood but that it was able to strike a vital spot."

"Perhaps Ben Lennock knows more than he indicated." The men were so intent upon their argument that they had forgotten Caryl until she spoke from the doorway. "Lucille did her best to have him discharged as theater manager two weeks ago."

"She did?" But Caryl had vanished up the stairs, not replying to her husband's question.

Inside the Baron's bedroom, Kerby glanced at the book the former had taken from one of the library shelves before ascending for the evening. It was Kerby's last one, *Two Men on an Island.*

"Don't waste your time on it," he advised moodily. "It isn't much good. From now on the movies are going to be my bread and butter. I'm through with books." He fumbled in his pockets for his pipe, sat on the bed, staring at the floor. When he lifted his head, "Well, you heard Charlie Tarn urge Lucille to go onto the stage. What do you make of that?"

"Ach, so. Mr. Tarn."

"Why did he have Lucille go up there? It's clear enough to me. Charlie's been after us both. Now he's got Lucille and he's trying to get me. What are you going to do about it?"

The Baron swallowed. "It could have been merely a coincidence that Mr. Tarn urged his wife—"

"It's damned suspicious, isn't it?"

"Suspicious?" The Baron shrugged uncomfortably. "However, how could Mr. Tarn have murdered her? He did not go on the stage. No, Mr. Tarn could not be so clever as to murder his wife while sitting in the audience."

Wearily Kerby shook his head. "Blast it, *I* don't know. That's your business. I guess you ought to know." He sucked at his pipe. "Who did it then? What's your idea? I can tell you, I know what an American detective would say. He'd be just simple enough to pay a little more attention to Charlie. However—" He squinted sourly at the Baron. "Lucille believed in you, Baron. You've got your chance. If you think Charlie didn't do it, I'm not going to argue with you. Find out who did it. That's all I want to know." His big hands clenched together.

The Baron extemporized, trying to convince himself as much as his client that this annoying Mr. Tarn was blameless. The Baron suspected that he had got himself into a hole. If he should now admit that he was wrong in eliminating Mr. Tarn, he might forfeit all confidence from his client. Ach, and that five thousand dollar fee? The Baron became stubborn. It wasn't Mr. Tarn. "Is there anyone in *this* house, my dear Mr. Kerby, who might wish to frighten you against marrying Mrs. Tarn; and, failing, would wish her death?"

"What?" Kerby got up. "You've met everyone here. Look here, Baron. Are those ticking noises going on in my head or in my room? If they're in my head, I'll go to a doctor. If they're in my room, I'm paying you five thousand dollars to tell me who's behind them. You're to tell me," he declared grimly, as he took a match from the table and held it in his fingers. "And no one else." He scratched the match and then discovered he'd forgotten to put tobacco in his pipe.

The Baron bowed. "Assuredly, my dear sir."

Kerby opened the door, closed it. "Call me 'Henry'. I'm not your 'dear sir'. Nor, as a matter of fact, your 'dear Mr. Kerby'. Suppose you come into my room tonight? The noises are probably nothing but my imagination, but I'm tired of worrying. I'll leave my door unlocked."

"Please do not trouble tonight, my dear sir." The Baron yawned, excusing himself politely, "I am tired. Much already has taken place tonight." He smiled, "Tomorrow night."

"You won't come?"

"Yes, if you are frightened."

"Frightened? Hell no. No noises can frighten me." He opened the door again, said in a lower voice, "I just don't like to stay in that room because—because, as a matter of fact, I can't sleep. Goodnight."

The Baron was closing his door when from down the hall he heard another door open and a soft voice say, "Henry. Is that you?"

Kerby halted in front of Alice's bedroom. "What's the matter?"

"I'm afraid, and I don't want to take that stuff Caryl left."

"Go on to bed and forget what's happened," he told her with a curious rough kindness. "If we don't be careful we'll all get so afraid of our shadows none of us will sleep."

Quietly the Baron shut his door.

He sat in front of the table, reimpressing in his mind the second floor plan of the Kerby house.

Built in the shape of an L, the longer section of the L faced the road and the ocean. At the tip of this longer section was the game room; followed by four bedrooms, occupied respectively by the brave Baron von Kaz, one that was empty, Alice Rittenhouse, and David Blane, Solar Pictures' scenario editor.

The stairway was at the angle of the L, opposite Caryl Kerby's large, cool Colonial bedroom with the great four-poster bed her father had brought with him from France when he settled in Monterey. Henry Kerby's room occupied what would correspond to the base of the L. A long unobstructed hall hung with aberrations of Kerby's artistic friends ran from the winding stairway down to the game room, Where the hall turned to the left, leading toward Kerby's bedroom, a large linen closet narrowed the passageway. The servants lived over the garage, so the guests were particularly free and before Kerby's marriage to Caryl, the rumor was in Carmel that many of the parties had been exceedingly riotous.

The upstairs plan established in his head, the Baron smoked one more of the excellent cigarettes dear Mr. Kerby

provided for his guests, emptied what remained in the silver box into his right hand coat pocket, and turned off the
light. Next he opened his window as silently as possible.
He remained motionless at the window, peering into the
darkness, listening to the muttering thunder of the surf.
Tonight the fog had swept in and the shredded veils of
mist obscured the stars. He reached and felt a cold object
and withdrew his arm and closed the window.

And he nodded his head thoughtfully.

To his left he had discerned a copper waterspout running down to the ground. It was within reach of the window. Without taking off his clothes he threw himself on
the bed and in a quarter of an hour was sound asleep.

He awoke a little after three in the morning, making
certain of the time by counting the slow, tolling strokes of
the mission bells which came faint and doleful from across
the bay.

"Excellent, my dear Franz. Excellent." In the darkness
of his bedroom he complimented himself. He had wished
to wake at three in the morning. And although you would
have thought by now he could accept this minor faculty
for waking at whatever hour he wished, he was inordinately pleased with the accomplishment each time. Without
turning on the lights he felt for his suitcase in the closet
and removed one of the few instruments he had carried
with him when he had escaped from Austria. This was
a German instrument made by an ex-locksmith. His talents, unfortunately, were not appreciated by the Viennese
police because they shot him before he could explain why
he was found in the middle of an Ambassador's dressing
room clutching most tightly a box of state secrets.

Noiselessly, the Baron closed his door from the hallway,
inserted the long tweezer-like affair through the keyhole,
and turned the key in the latch from the outside.

This done, he stealthily walked down the silent hall. At the staircase he turned left, passed the door of the linen closet, entered the narrower and shorter hall which led by Caryl's bedroom to that of Kerby's. Here he paused, breathing very lightly.

The Baron waited for perhaps half a minute. Then he inserted his illegal instrument into the lock of Kerby's door. Very slowly he turned it, waiting for that fragile click of the tumblers as the tweezer-shaped nose encountered the key. Gently he touched the door after withdrawing the thief's tool. The door squeaked and he waited, one, two minutes, before pushing it again.

The door swung sufficiently wide for his body to slip through and into Kerby's bedroom. Here he remained for several more long seconds, motionless by the wall, a shadow mingling with the other shadows, until his eyes were ready to dissociate the details of the room. On three sides, windows permitted the misty, dark light from the few stars now out to crush into the room and dilute the total blackness.

Turning his head, he distinguished a writing table, a large bulky object which he assumed was a bureau, four or five chairs, and in one corner a great bed. Kerby's clothes were scattered on the floor and when the Baron felt it was safe he approached the bed. The sheets and covers were disturbed. For a time, at least, the bed had been occupied.

Reflectively, he laid his finger by the side of his nose, thinking. Kerby was not in his room. Caryl's bedroom adjoined her husband's. He crossed the room, placed his ear to the intervening door without the slightest feeling of embarrassment. Listening, he could hear a faint stirring in the next room.

He smiled in the darkness. Ach, this Kerby, he was not so brave as he would have you believe. But if the ticking noises had driven him from his bedroom into his wife's, where then were these sinister noises? Could they cease as soon as the man fled?

For all of ten minutes the Baron remained, his back to the wall, merely as a precaution. However, no noises produced themselves. With a feeling of irritation mounting, directed at these strange sounds which seemed almost human in their ability to appear and disappear, the Baron closed Kerby's door. He locked it by the same process which he had employed for his own door. Quietly he gained the stairway. He had much to do before he could return to his bed.

He was half-way down the stairs when he stopped. Lieber Augustin! he thought; no, it could not be possible. . . .

Nevertheless, he went back up the stairs, going right down the long hall which led to his room and the game room. But he stopped, two doors from his own bedroom.

And in front of Alice's door he also applied his ear and when he raised his head, if your eyes were as sharp in the dark as the Baron's, you could have perceived a ridiculously puzzled expression on his face. For Alice, too, was restless that night.

In his thoughts, he had considered this case as resembling a triangle. With Tarn eliminated, Lucille Tarn and Caryl Kerby formed the two points at the base of the triangle. Henry Kerby was sitting on the sharp third point as all gentlemen who stray into other men's pastures must risk doing. This was the traditional triangle abhorred by cuckolds, producer of romance and death, love and virulent hatreds.

However, after listening, he wondered if it might not be necessary to revise the triangle and construct one hitherto entirely unknown to the mathematical profession; a triangle with five points instead of three, including Alice as well as David Blane.

He shrugged, hurried down the stairs and out into the night.

The Kerby residence was situated on the farthest tip of Pescadero Point, some five miles from Carmel. Not until the Baron reckoned that he was near the outskirts of Carmel did he stop his easy lope and light a cigarette before continuing toward his destination. Toward the solution of the murder of Lucille Tarn.

4

One Act in Several Drops

A block from the Carmel Theater the Baron saw an official and portly gentleman sitting on the top step beneath the single light. This gentleman yawned, broke his cigar in two, lit one half, wiggled on the cold cement step, and yawned again. This sleepy gentleman, decided the brave Baron von Kaz, was the policeman delegated to guard the theater.

Accordingly he slowed his approach, pressing close to the buildings. A milk wagon clattered up the empty street. The horse stopped and the milkman jumped to the pavement. "I got what you wanted, Bill."

The policeman walked to meet the milkman, taking a bottle which was neither the size nor the shape of a milk bottle. "It's tarnation lonely sitting here," complained the policeman. "Come back behind the pillar and have a drop to warm your body and soul."

"Can't, Bill," replied the other regretfully. "That there mare's liable to light out with the wagon."

"Look at her. Why she won't leave you. I know mares, Jim, and no mare like her, is going to leave you. It's lonely here. Zack ought to try a spell of it. What sense's there watching the theater anyhow. . . ."

Having heard all that was necessary to indicate that the policeman had little of the bloodhound in his veins, the

69

Baron cautiously retraced his steps, returning to the next intersection. From here he circled two blocks through the thickening fog to reach the rear of the theater.

He found a gate opening into the rose hedge running all the way around the theater, planted a year previously when Caryl Kerby was president of the Carmel Garden Club. He waited, expecting that the policeman would make his rounds. But the policeman apparently believed that all that was required of him was to guard the front door. Either that, or he was too engrossed in persuading the milkman to forget the mare and have one more little drop.

Stealthily the Baron ran across the space between the rose hedge and the steps to the rear door of the theater. While the fog and coldness penetrated into him, he wasted ten valuable minutes with his thief's tool, trying to open the door. His fingers were numb. His instrument merely turned around in his hands. Evidently this lock was a new American contrivance, not susceptible to German instruments. He swore softly.

He was wasting too much time. He knew that. He gave the lock up, placed the tool in his pocket. Exasperated, he grasped the knob and shook the door. In shaking it he accidentally turned the knob. The door opened. It had not been locked. Incredulously he ascertained that these singular residents of Carmel had left the rear door entirely unprotected, either by guard or lock. He entered, feeling disappointed at such a simple procedure of entrance.

High above, a spectral glimmer seeped into the vaulted theater, hardly a glimmer, a shading from the night's oppressing blackness into the deep, pitch-like quality which filled the theater as thickly as if it were liquid and tangible to the touch.

The Baron whirled, his arms lifted, as a squeaking rat scuttered across the boards. He did not wish to risk a light, hoping to find his way through this back-stage clutter and jumble of canvases and props to the cleared area behind the asbestos curtain. He advanced warily, hands before his face, moving one step at a time. Something coarse and rough rasped his cheeks. "Gott!" He leaped back, landing on his toes and froze immobile. Could someone still be in this theater? Hiding here, perhaps, after the murder until it should be safe to escape? His groping hands again touched that coarse swinging thing and he grasped it, jerking it. It was a rope hanging from the beams. He let it go, accusing himself of childish nervousness. Nevertheless, he pulled out his cigarette lighter and let it flicker momentarily to sight his bearings.

At one side, shadowy sets loomed. An owl, stirred from its haunts in the rafters, flopped through the musty air and the Baron ducked, shielding his head. Then there was silence. A heavy, dusty kind of silence. It was the silence of an empty theater. It was the silence where every fragmentary creaking is magnified. As the curling phantoms of the fog pressed in at the windows and doors, the applause of forgotten audiences and the voices of forgotten actors seemed to lift once more, faintly and secretly. And the cracked canvas sets rustled eagerly, welcoming stray breezes creeping into the building.

It was the silence of an old theater, where gray rats leave their holes, sniffing and calling their families, perhaps prancing around in their own rat-produced tragedies; a silence where even the building itself stirs. Beams and rafters bend a little as the dryrot creeps in and fibers give. Within the theater the night takes form. Impalpable shadows come; and go . . .

That was the devil of it. True, the Baron was a brave man. He admitted it. However, he had the imagination of twenty brave men. And he tiptoed toward the curtains of the front stage, cracking his shins twice, once on a chair, again on a ladder; nearly hanging himself on a second rope conveniently looped; and, after tumbling over a roll of canvas and going flat on his face, he at last attained the wing and from there the center of the stage.

Standing there, tenderly massaging his bruised elbow, he debated with himself whether or not he dared risk employing his cigarette lighter for the second time. His imagination was stimulated by the darkness and the clammy fog. He imagined a hundred intruders besides himself, lurking, waiting for him. His hands perceptibly trembled. His forehead was dampened with moisture other than the fog.

Unquestionably, he declared to himself, he required a light. He was hesitating there with the empty auditorium in front of him and no more of it to be seen than had a sodden black cloth been crushed against his eyes. Logically, he decided, if he required a light, then it was a reflection upon the bravery of the great von Kaz should he be afraid to use it. Thus, having sensibly reasoned this matter, he flicked the lighter, cupping the feeble flame in his hands.

With the aid of this light, he proceeded to examine meticulously the cabinet of Dacrokoff, wherein so mysteriously had been murdered Lucille Tarn. Either the woman had been killed from the inside of the cabinet or the outside, and by means or device which had escaped the examination of the Chief of Police. Indeed, Chief Watson had feared this; and, so fearing that he had missed something relevant to the solution, had ordered the cabinet and the apparatus concerned with Dacrokoff's act to be left as it was until the state investigators could examine it the following day.

At the rear of the cabinet the Baron stooped, poking his fingers through the ventilation slits, judging how thick was the wood and, if possible, whether or not it was composed all of one single thickness or two or three laminations pressed together. There were three ventilation slits, each about four inches long by a half an inch or so wide, in all the three wooden sides of the cabinet. His sensitive finger tips ran around the slits, and from the evidence he was satisfied for the moment that each side of the cabinet was formed from one solid piece of wood. These slits were less than a half inch above the thick base of the cabinet. From the slits, he went over every inch of the three wooden sides, now trusting entirely to his finger tips.

In this move, the blackness aided him rather than hindered. His strong, muscular fingers had been trained for too many years of searching for hidden openings and drawers, seeking out minute impressions too faint to be seen by the eye, to miss any indication of a hole no matter how smoothly filled it might be. But there were no holes, as far as he could determine, either filled or unfilled, which would allow a hatpin to enter through the wood to Lucille Tarn's heart.

He was not discouraged. He had not expected to find a hole. Whoever was the murderer had planned the death more cunningly and ingeniously than by means of any hole. When he had thoroughly covered the exterior of the cabinet, he paused, withdrawing from it and glancing around, again trying to pierce the pressing blackness. The faint noises of the theater and the night came to him with renewed intensity. He pulled the collar of his coat up. The theater seemed to be growing colder as the minutes went by.

He approached the front of the cabinet, flicking his lighter more frequently, cocking his head from one side to the other with each brief flare of light, putting himself in the place of the murderer, wondering what he would do if he were confronted with the problem of killing Lucille Tarn after she had stepped into the cabinet.

The thick velvet curtains closed the entrance of the cabinet. The cigarette lighter shed a feeble radiance as he lifted it over his head, next down to his feet. The rings supporting the velvet curtains jangled noisily when he drew the curtains apart. He blew out the lighter and waited. The rats had returned to their holes. The wind from the mountains had died away. The beams stopped their sagging and for the moment the theater had returned to a silence as if black unseen wings had folded upon it and shut out all scurrying sounds and hushed the night into silence.

Nervously the Baron flicked the lighter. The wick sputtered, flared, died. He shook the lighter. This time the wick caught the spark but the little point of yellow was weak. He shoved his head into the cabinet and the motion of his body extinguished the light. In here, had Lucille Tarn stepped unto her death. It had come to her, unknown and terrible, stinging into her breast, through to her heart. The Baron withdrew his head. He started, straining his ears. But if he had heard a clicking that noise did not repeat itself.

He swore silently for displaying such nervousness. Bravely he flicked on the light, not without, however, glancing over his shoulder, and then stepped face forward into that cabinet, just as a few hours previously a woman had entered to have her breast and heart opened by a sliver of steel. His shoulders were wider than Lucille Tarn's had been. Squared directly toward the rear, he found that the two sides pressed tightly against his shoulders and arms. From the front and sides he was protected, but as he stood in the cabinet, trying to search but the secret held by death, increasingly he had an uncomfortable sensation that his back was unprotected; behind him was the vast emptiness of the auditorium. More and more often he would halt his exploration by his finger tips and strain his head over his shoulder. But all that he saw was the blackness; he could have closed his eyes and seen as much.

By turning sideways, he was able to lift his right arm. Angrily he held the tiny flame of the lighter close to the dark grain of the wood, scowling at the inanimate surface. By so turning, it was also possible for him to cover his heart with his left hand. If a hatpin could thrust itself through solid timber to attain a woman's heart without leaving a trace of its passage through the wood, the brave Baron von Kaz did not desire such an experiment repeated upon himself.

At the far end of the theater a door softly closed. However, the Baron was too engrossed to hear the faint creaking of a door. He was interested in the base of the cabinet. He dropped to his knees. He could imagine that there still was a trace of wood violets, a lingering scent of that woman who had preceded him; who had counted upon him, the great Baron Franz Maximilian Karagôz von Kaz to protect her from all danger. "So!" he murmured. Neatly countersunk in the wooden base, concealed by false edges, was the hidden trapdoor mentioned in the radio broadcast. His fingers felt the slight ridge. His head bent over what his fingers had discovered and he grew absorbed in estimating the dimensions of the trapdoor.

Feet moved stealthily down the center aisle of the theater. Feet softly pressed the thick carpet. And the Baron? He who would assure you that his ears were attuned to the most minute sound? To the drop of a pin. Was he already planning a way to safety? Or was he bravely standing his ground, ready for this unknown who so silently crept along the long east aisle?

Not at all. The Baron was gently tapping the trapdoor. The Baron had an idea.

A figure, wide and squat, as of any marauder of the night, slowly moved up the steps of the stage.

Massive shoulders edged along the drop curtain toward that cabinet from where fluttered the uneven, ebbing glow of the cigarette lighter. And inside the cabinet, the brave Baron von Kaz irritably dug his long tweezer-like pliers into the grooves of the trapdoor, then pocketed the pliers, and lifted his light in order to examine in more detail the base.

Someone crossed the space between the drop curtain and the cabinet, a shadow stretching upon the stage.

Lined with triumph, a face looked down upon the unsuspecting outline of the Baron as he teetered on his toes. Underneath the cabinet and the stage flooring an insecurely wedged spring trembled. The Baron was experimenting with an idea. He wished to learn whether any one could open a gap sufficiently wide between the trapdoor and the base to thrust upwards with an instrument, fine as a hatpin, but sufficiently long to touch Lucille Tarn's breast.

Ach, Gott! No, it was impossible. The trapdoor seemed to give. But not enough. A man would have to be in the basement who was acquainted with the Dacrokoff trick. Then perhaps he could release the spring to the trapdoor and shove an instrument of his own devising upwards and so high as to penetrate into Lucille Tarn's heart. And even then, thought the Baron as he rested discouraged on his knees, unaware of that menace behind him, the trapdoor would drop first before one could kill Lucille Tarn.

Behind him a gun showed dully.

He glared at the wooden base. Du lieber Augustin! He had been stupid. These North American police officials were very stupid, also. Never would they think of such a simple solution—

He rocked on his knees as behind him a voice ordered, "Don't move. You're covered."

The Baron did not move.

"Jim!" cried the voice. "Come on. I've got him. I told you there was someone in here when we saw the light."

The Baron started to lower his cigarette lighter, drawing in his breath to blow out the flame.

"No tricks or I'll plug you. If the light goes out, I shoot. Stay on your knees and back slowly."

Many ideas flashed through the Baron's fertile brain. In Budapest, for example, he had outwitted the ferocious Mornoff with a handful of pepper; and, it was in Prague, that five had thrown themselves upon him and he'd fought like a demon and escaped. . . .

"Hurry or I'll let you have it. Jim, come on with that rope!"

A hollow voice floated from the other end of the theater. "I'm coming, Bill."

A hand grasped the Baron by the shoulder.

No matter how brilliant is the brain, sometimes there is nothing to do. In the obscure cavity of the Dacrokoff cabinet he shifted his knees to comply when the strained spring-latch below suddenly gave way.

A void opened under the Baron.

He clutched at his cigarette lighter. The upward rush of air engulfed the flame. He landed with a jarring thud. A gun roared and echoed, roared again. Two bullets smacked dully into the cabinet overhead. Above him the astounded policeman shot a third time. This was magic. "Jim!" he shouted to the milkman, hovering fearfully somewhere in the blackness near the left wing. "Jim, come here."

"That mare of mine, maybe she'll run away," said Jim. "I'd better go and see."

"You come here!" This was sheer, tarnation magic, the like of which he'd never seen. The policeman couldn't believe it. Having a man disappear before his very eyes. Fortified to the gills with fine old Monterey brandy, the policeman feared neither man nor devil nor ghost. Gun held in front of him, he bellowed into the darkness for Jim to strike a match, and not waiting any longer, stepped into the cabinet, shrieked in outraged surprise as his feet struck air instead of solid wood, and dropped like a plummet.

The milkman was paralyzed. He tried to speak. He was alone in the theater. When he finally tried to light a match, the match fell from his fingers. His knees sagged. "Help," he said. The word was as a drop of water touching a great ocean. He thought of his family. He thought of his mare alone and deserted in the empty street and of all his poor customers asleep, expecting their milk in the morning, and they would have no milk because he had got drunk with Bill instead of going along with his mare. He was drunk. That was it. He was drunk and terribly drunk and good old Bill hadn't disappeared but was out there on the steps guzzling brandy instead of behaving as a decent upright man should and those rushing, roaring things were shadows and phantoms. He would get back to his mare. Jim rushed from the theater, climbed into his wagon on the third attempt, clucked at his horse, and the horse galloped down the street.

Now the Baron was a wiry man, with extremely supple muscles, but the policeman had long ago given up all exercise more strenuous than hefting a bottle that was filled and lowering one that was empty. Needless to say, between these two exercises, the one up and the other down, there is a considerable space of elapsed time for even one so accomplished as the policeman. As a result, it may be stated that the sum total of his exercises did him little good. Consequently, a fall of eight feet was practically as disastrous for him as falling off Point Lobos.

The Baron, on the other hand, had landed like a rubber ball, instinctively doubling his feet, dropping his head between his arms, rolling forward and cushioning the fall on the thick pad of shoulder muscles.

The policeman descended through the traphole without any foreign airs, falling upon his pate such as any simple, God-fearing American might do. And, thereafter, he had no further discernible interest in murders of any variety for a number of days.

Almost as soon as he had recovered his breath from the fall, the Baron barely escaped being crushed in the plummet-like drop of the policeman. Only because the Baron was standing, his back against the boards of the makeshift elevator shaft, did he escape. As it was, the policeman struck him a glancing blow, was deflected by the Baron's shoulders, and hit the floor in the aforementioned manner.

Despite the pains in his shoulders, the Baron remained perfectly quiet in this well of absolute blackness until the milkman had overcome his paralytic fright and rushed out of the theater.

When the theater had again returned to its approximate stillness, the Baron judged that it was time to leave. In some respects the Baron had a single track mind, so he did not deserve all the credit he later took upon himself for ignoring the danger of his situation long enough to examine his surroundings.

With the aid of his lighter he discovered that he was in a kind of elevator shaft, boarded on all four sides, about eight feet high. He ascertained that he was standing on the platform proper of the elevator. Four wires, attached to each corner of this platform, led to four pulleys near the top of the elevator shaft. These wires, he assumed, and correctly, were attached to the winch outside the shaft and by means of the winch, raised and lowered the platform to or from the trapdoor.

In the rough boards enclosing this shaft there were no cracks or holes which would permit a hatpin to be inserted when Lucille Tarn was lowered. That he saw. He glanced at the policeman, slumped in an awkward position at his feet. The man's head touched the side of the shaft. Whether or not the man was alive was a factor which held no consideration for the Baron. The policeman had stupidly interfered; he would cause no more trouble for the next few minutes, and that was all that interested the Baron.

He stepped upon the body of the unfortunate gentleman of the law, grasped two of the wires supporting the platform, and pulled himself up until his head approached the hole in the ceiling. Then, by extending his knees until they pressed firmly against either side of the shaft, hanging onto one of the wires with his left hand, he was able to remain in this insecure position and to employ his lighter with his right hand.

The two trapdoors, closing the floor of the stage, had lowered when the spring had broken, permitting the bottom of the Dacrokoff cabinet to give way and fall to the elevator platform resting upon the basement floor. The Baron shoved his cigarette lighter through the opening. Here he saw something which interested him greatly: Concealed in the thick base of the Dacrokoff cabinet were two sections of what evidently was a false bottom.

The mechanics of the Dacrokoff Disappearance Act at once became apparent to the Baron. When the real or movable bottom was lowered, these sections were slid over the opening, and as far as the audience could determine the cabinet would appear to be without structural change. He had seen all that he desired. Later he would draw a diagram of this cabinet and the elevator to reconstruct the disappearance more clearly, but now his head held all the essential details.

This examination had taken between twelve and thirteen minutes. It was a foolhardy thing to do under the circumstances, and any intelligent American would have probably immediately clambered out of such a prison. But the Baron was not an intelligent American. He had made this trip to the Carmel Theater to investigate not only the

Dacrokoff cabinet, but also this elevator which had been mentioned by the effulgent radio voice.

His objectives were accomplished. Furthermore, his left hand ached mightily with the strain of holding to the wire, and his knees had grown numb. He extinguished the lighter, groped for another one of the wires with his right hand, and without undue trouble hauled himself through the traphole, into the narrow confines of the cabinet, and from there crawled onto the stage. . . .

Not until he was outside the theater, padding effortlessly along the Seventeen Mile Drive toward La Honda road did he recall that he possessed a chauffeur, Tivvits, who supposedly was on tap at all hours. Somehow this tickled immensely the fancy of the brave Baron von Kaz. Without slowing his long, steady lope, he laughed. It was a small, quiet laugh. It died away as quickly as it had commenced.

Then, as he ran through the night, he complimented himself upon outwitting his assailant; transcendentally ignoring fate, an insecurely fastened spring, and a milkman who was passionately fond of his mare. . . .

The Baron had reason to compliment himself. He now knew how Lucille Tarn had been killed.

And he knew who actually killed her.

5

The Black Man

With the aid of the copper waterspout he climbed into his bedroom via the window, and immediately was sound asleep. He awoke late, shivered through a quick, cold shower, cursed the English race for ever inventing so barbarous a custom, and shaved leisurely.

It was after nine when he descended for breakfast, ravenously hungry. Only Alice was at the table, her ripe, corn-colored hair glossy from a recent brushing. Ceremoniously he inquired if she had slept well and his dark face was expressionless when he was informed that she had, except for nightmares concerning poor Lucille Tarn. Alice supposed that terrible magician had done it. But why?

He shrugged sadly.

From her he learned that Kerby and Blane had already started on their morning's work, while Caryl had departed without breakfast to be present at a hastily called meeting of the Garden Club to decide what should be done about the tickets sold at the theater last night: Some were for returning the money; others wished to arrange for a performance later; more practical minds were for doing nothing at all.

Alice forgot her manners, yawned prettily. She got up. Her headache was returning. She guessed she'd lie down for an hour or so unless the Baron would like to play

tennis with her? With a deliberate boldness he scrutinized
her as she came around to his side of the table. She was
in shorts again. And she had ravishing legs, he thought,
and her white sweater was so snugly fitted that his eyes
required no assistance from his imagination.

"They are nice, don't you think?" She looked at her
legs, and then at him sideways.

Whatever the Baron would have said was stopped by
Blane's appearance from the study. "Henry's going to work
with him—" He nodded at the Baron, "for half an hour on
his Austrian notes, so we've time for a set, Alice."

"But I promised to play with the Baron, Dave."

Kerby shouted through the door of the dining room,
"Blast it, Baron! Aren't you through breakfast yet? Come in
here. I can't wait all morning to start you on your memoirs."

Resignedly the Baron folded his napkin. Blane said,
"So sorry you won't be able to play, Baron," and he didn't
sound sorry at all. "Hurry, Alice. Perhaps we can wrangle
two sets."

Kerby locked the study door. "I've told them you are
working on your memoirs. That'll hold anyone who asks
questions about you. Now—" He thrust the morning
paper at the Baron. "See what's happened while you were
sleeping."

Displayed across the front page was the news that the
policeman guarding the theater had been found unconscious, evidently having been attacked and thrown into
the basement of the Carmel Theater. The Baron read this,
lit a cigarette from his now full case. Plainly he evidenced
his lack of interest. The ocean was unusually blue this
morning, the cold fog of the night was swept away, and
he stared out of the window. The curve of the shore was
something like that beach he remembered near Trieste
where his grandfather had gone for the summers.

Kerby exploded. "Haven't you any interest in the fact that Lucille's murderer returned to the theater and assaulted Bill Leeds? Almighty thunder, Baron, you're supposed to be a detective. Why don't you *do* something?" He stamped over to his desk, growling, "As a matter of fact, you weren't interested in finding the ticking noises last night. You had to sleep. Sleep!"

Brought back from this reverie of another shore in another country, the Baron asked with coldness, "If you please, my dear Mr. Kerby. Did you hear the ticking?"

"Did I hear it?" Kerby reminded the Baron of a small boy who has stolen cookies and was trying to decide whether to lie or not. "Well, no. As a matter of fact, I didn't. But that hasn't a damn—"

"Mrs. Kerby? Does she sleep with you? In your bedroom, I mean?" The Baron sat down in the big green leather chair by the window.

Kerby's shaggy, reddish eyebrows met over his eyes. He asked with considerable temper what the hell business it was of the Baron's. "See here, Franz," he began less explosively. "You're accustomed to Austria and to Austrian manners. No doubt you were a great detective in your own country, but don't you honestly think that this—" He gestured. "Isn't this a little above you? Suppose we call it off and I bring in an American detective who doesn't have to sleep all morning and who can get out and find what in thunder's going on."

"You wish to terminate my services?"

Kerby waved his hand for the Baron to keep his seat. "Good thundering Lord! Don't get sore. I like you. So does Caryl—all of us. I'm not saying it is your fault. But an American understands this kind of work."

"You do not desire the services of the great von Kaz?" came incredulously.

"Don't you see? You're accustomed to Austria and intrigue and all that sort of thing. We act differently over here, Franz. Take Charlie, for example. He may or may not be mixed in all of this, but an American detective would soon determine that. And you, you want to make it complicated and before you know it something else happens."

The Baron was becoming heartily sick of references to Charles Tarn. In his mind, by proving so frequently that Tarn had no connection with the case, he had at least convinced himself. And now, perhaps because there was still a faint unquenched doubt deep within himself, his pride and his temper inflamed at the suggestion that the great von Kaz could be wrong. In addition, to suggest that a doltish American could be superior to a man trained in Austria was too much. After all the insults he had had to swallow before persuading Kerby to employ him, and now—on an empty stomach—and after a night of hard work, for this to come! His pride was struck as though by a saber blow. The old scar on his cheek showed as the color receded from his dark face.

That was the trouble with the Baron. He was so busy quarreling over rents in his pride and conniving with himself on how to shock and astonish people by his brilliance that the world always seemed against him. Consequently his limited but highly developed talents for boring through to a solution of a problem in crime were often hard put to wriggle out of difficulties blasted up by the man's enormous conceit. If you told him that he was merely an acutely gifted specialist in what is ordinarily a prosaic and sordid profession he would have remained awake the greater part of the night devising sufficiently refined revenge for such an insult.

"My dear Mr. Kerby—"

"For God's sake, don't keep on saying 'my dear Mr. Kerby.' I've told them here that you're an old friend of mine." Kerby pushed the papers off his desk. "I didn't mean to shout at you like that, but blast it! I'm getting jumpy myself."

The Baron stood up. "When you engage your next detective, my dear sir, have him get in touch with me and I will inform him who killed Mrs. Tarn. I will give you my address when I send you my bill for five thousand dollars."

Kerby did not hear the Baron's acid remark concerning the five thousand dollars. *"You* know who killed Lucille? You're not saying it just to—"

"I beg your pardon."

"Now you've lost your temper again. Will you sit down? *Who* killed Lucille?"

"The blackman." The Baron unlocked the door. "Please present my sincere regrets to Mrs. Kerby that I was unable to wish her good-by before departing. I have my own chauffeur. He will—"

"Wait a minute!" Kerby yelled. "What black man?"

The Baron stood in the doorway. "I am certain that your American detective will satisfactorily handle all details."

"What American detective?" Kerby took the Baron's arm, pulled him into the study and locked the door. "Why didn't you tell me you knew? Forget what I said. There sit down." He pulled forward a chair. "Shall I call Zack? What black man? What do you—" His excitement slowly vanished as he squinted sourly at the Baron. "You mean— 'Dude'? The negro?"

"Exactly, my dear Mr. Kerby." Highly pleased with himself, all insults now forgotten, the Baron reseated himself in the green leather chair. Gott! These Americans. They were as children. They required firm handling.

"You think 'Dude' did it? Look here, Franz, I like you, but I won't stand for your pulling in sharp stuff on me. Only last night you were proving that he couldn't do it."

He tugged angrily at his beard. "I thought for a second you were serious and really had discovered who had done it. . . ."

"So? Do you know this—'Dude'?"

"Sure, I know him. He's as harmless as—thunder! As you are. Worked for Caryl in her garden. Lord almighty! For a lot of people around here."

"Mrs. Tarn?"

"Yes. Look here." Frowning, he pointed his pipe at the Baron. "I still think that Charlie's somehow mixed in it, but just because 'Dude' worked for him doesn't mean a confounded thing."

"I did not imply, my dear sir, that Mr. Tarn is suspected. I only say: The black—the negro killed Mrs. Tarn. There can be no doubt that he killed her."

"'Dude'?" Incredulously Kerby stared at the Baron. "You think you can prove it, do you?"

"If you have time this morning to listen."

"Time? God almighty! I've got all day."

"It will require half an hour. I suggest that you make certain that Mr. Blane—"

Kerby opened the door. "I'll tell Maggy no one's to disturb me for forty-five minutes."

"I shall require a pencil, paper, and—" He rubbed his nose, "Uhm, two sheets of carbon paper."

"Carbon paper?" Kerby looked at him as if he had gone mad. "All right," he assented after a moment. "You'll find the paper and pencil on my desk. The carbon paper is in the typewriting desk."

The Baron found the necessary material, arranged the two sheets of carbon paper between the three sheets of white paper so that he would have one original and two copies of what he evidently planned to draw.

Kerby returned, locked the door, and saw that the Baron was engrossed in outlining a sketch. Kerby reloaded his pipe. Curiosity finally overcoming him, he stepped behind the Baron's chair.

"To illustrate most completely exactly what occurred the night Mrs. Tarn was so ingeniously murdered," he said, "I am going to prepare a cross-section of Dacrokoff's cabinet, showing part of the stage, and the elevator shaft connecting with the cabinet from the basement."

"But blast it!" Kerby leaned over the Baron's shoulder. "Why the carbon paper?"

"We are to have three identical cross-sections," replied the Baron, rapidly ruling in the lines. Completed, he withdrew the three papers, glanced at the three sketches complacently, finished by labeling them "Cross-section A", "Cross-section B", and "Cross-section C". "Now," he said, "we shall produce an animated drawing, as it were, the first showing Mrs. Tarn as she appeared *in* the cabinet, the second as she was being lowered into the basement, and the third as the elevator has finally brought her down into the basement."

He wet his pencil, said casually, "At one time, in my youth, I considered the profession of an artist. It is extremely fortunate that I possess this artistic talent, otherwise it would be necessary for us to go to the theater where I would have to show you the Dacrokoff cabinet." With his pencil he labeled the ventilation slit in the rear of the cabinet "1"; the false bottoms sliding into the base of the cabinet "3"; the trapdoor in the stage floor "4"; the elevator which was raised and lowered in the rough wooden shaft "5"; and the winch "6", which tightened the four wires attached to each corner of the elevator platform, thus lowering or raising it.

"What are all those numbers, for?" impatiently demanded Kerby. "And where's number '2'? You've forgotten to put that in."

"We march slowly," replied the Baron. "The murder of Mrs. Tarn was simple. However, to understand it, first you must comprehend the method of the 'Dacrokoff Disappearance Act'." He indicated "Cross-section A", sketched in a figure, presumably of Mrs. Tarn, as she would stand in the cabinet after the curtains were closed.

"Good," he murmured to himself. "Excellent . . . Now, my dear sir, we shall march. First the 'Cross-section A'. You understand it?"

"I guess so," grunted Kerby. "You've forgotten your number '2'—"

"We shall make certain, if you please. And I have not neglected number '2'. That is important. It comes a little later. Unless you are familiar with the arrangement of the Dacrokoff cabinet, a murder which was in reality simple and highly uncomplicated, appears bizarre and impossible. Without doubt, the murderer thus wished to confuse us."

"Can't we omit the lecture, Franz? As a matter of fact, just what does all this have to—"

"'Cross-section A' represents the Dacrokoff cabinet as it would look if the right wooden side were removed. Mrs. Tarn has passed into it, facing the rear wooden wall. You will note that I have indicated the ventilation slit near the base by the arrow attached to the figure '1'. Now this ventilation slit is directly above a wide and thick wooden base. There is a reason for the unusual extension of that base which, in a moment, I shall exemplify. Now . . ."

He drew the figure of a man standing behind the cabinet. "Here, my dear sir, is the black man, 'Dude'.

"You will recall that he went behind the cabinet. You will recall, also, that he crouched, and then immediately afterwards extended his hands so that they projected from the cabinet and stood up, waving his hands, thus proving that there was no means of exit for Mrs. Tarn existing between the rear of the cabinet and the back-drop curtain."

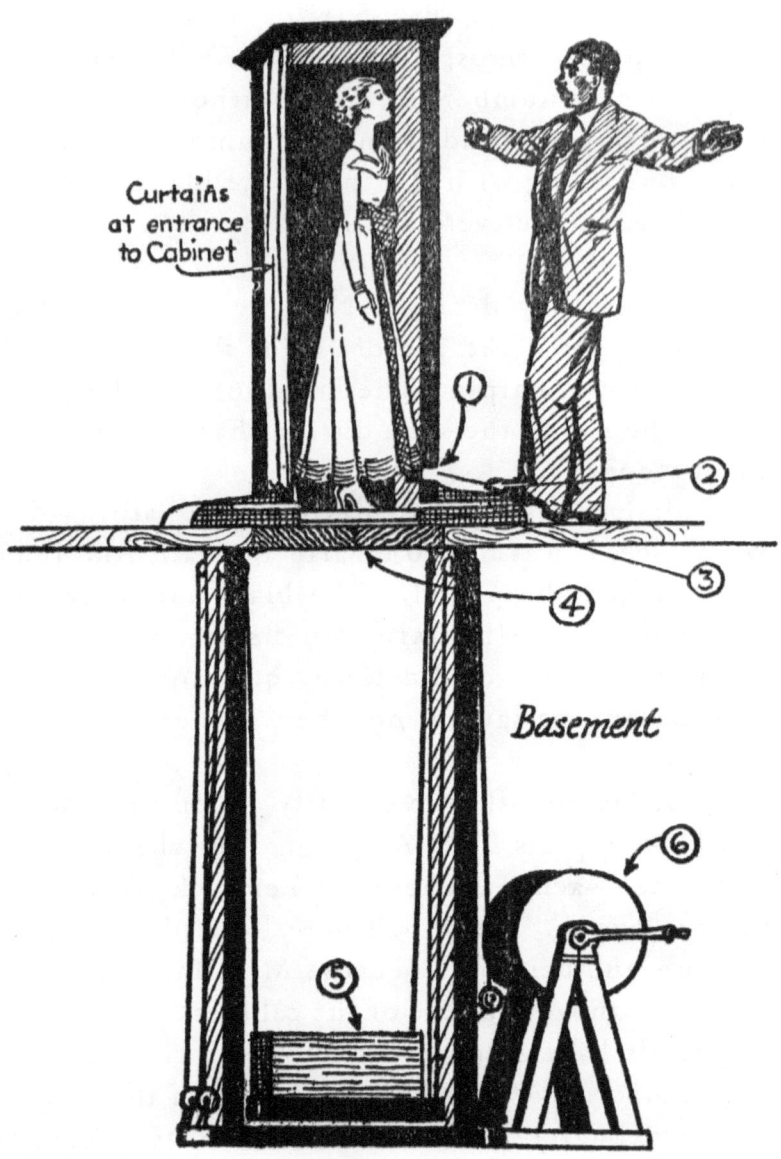

Curtains
at entrance
to Cabinet

Basement

CROSS SECTION A

(1) Ventilation hole in cabinet. (2) This is HATPIN in "Dude's" left shoe, watch "2!" (3) False bottom hidden in base. (4) Trapdoors in stage floor. (5) Elevator. (6) Winch outside elevator "shaft."

Kerby agreed.

"Now," declared the Baron with a solemnity which he enjoyed to the utmost, "we will draw the number '2'. Thus. It is a nice number '2', no?" Without waiting for a reply, he continued, "And from this number we will place an arrow connecting with the toe of the black man's shoe. So. Ach, that marches very well."

"But what—"

"One minute, my dear sir. Now we draw a fine little line extending from the toe of 'Dude's' shoe. This little line represents a hatpin. The head of the hatpin was wedged in the toe of the shoe during that instant that the blackman stooped."

"Lord almighty!" breathed Kerby. "The hatpin—"

"As you see, it was not so bizarre after all. And remember—" He lifted the pencil, "The blackman knew at the *exact* moment when Mrs. Tarn would start to descend."

"He did?" No longer did Kerby question the truth of what the Baron was saying; now he was merely asking for information.

"Did not Dacrokoff conveniently stamp his foot? And why did he stamp his foot? As a signal for the man—what was his name?—ach so. The good Lennock. For Lennock to wind the winch. The winch here." He placed the pencil point on number "6." "Because Mrs. Tarn's breast was some five feet above the base of the cabinet, the sheriff and other officials have assumed that to penetrate her breast, the hatpin must have been inserted through the wood at a height approximately the height of her breast. Fortunately," he asserted dramatically, "that was not compulsory."

"Fortunately, for God's sake?"

"For the criminal who conceived this plan, if you please." He handed Kerby the sheet of paper containing "Cross-section B". "After hearing the signal, Lennock turned the winch. The winch lifted the elevator platform.

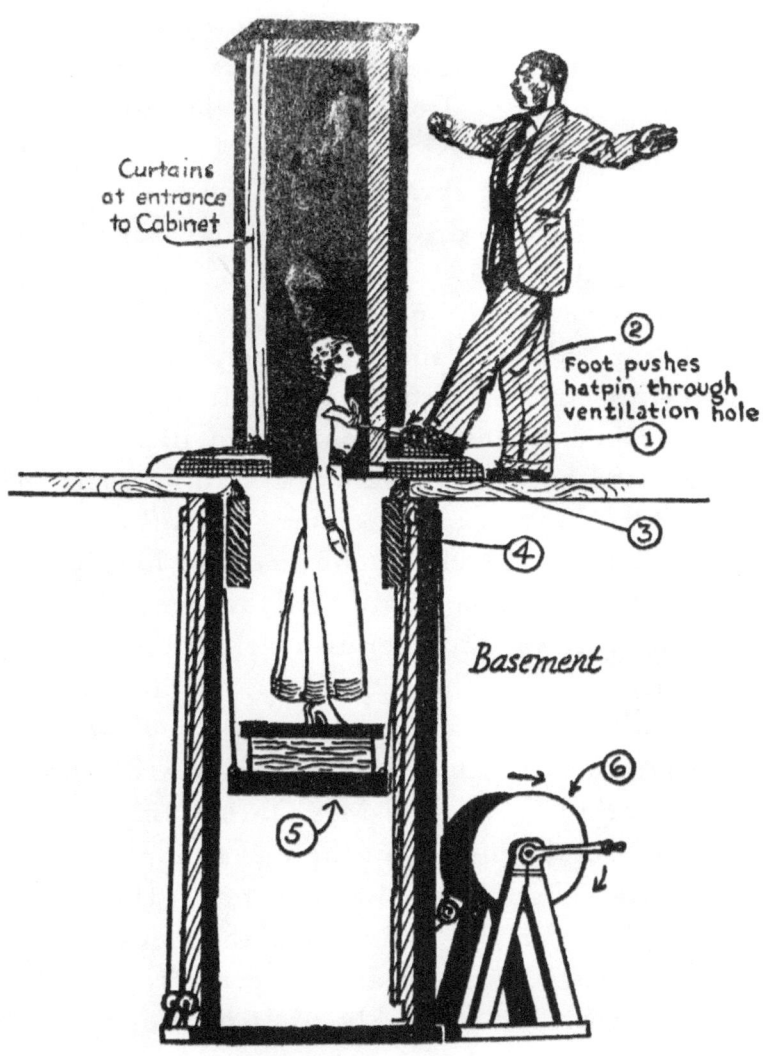

Curtains
at entrance
to Cabinet

② Foot pushes
hatpin through
ventilation hole
①
③

④

Basement

⑤

⑥

CROSS SECTION B

As elevator (5) lowers Lucille Tarn, trapdoors (4) have dropped open. "Dude's" left shoe has pushed hatpin (2) through ventilation hole (1), piercing Lucille's heart and . . .

At a certain point, the wires drawing up the platform must have disengaged a catch holding the trapdoor in the floor. This is a minor point," he explained modestly. "Last night I had not the time to determine exactly how the trapdoor was dropped, but I believe the wires caused it. Nevertheless, the trapdoor *did* drop, and the elevator platform— Number '5'—came to rest beneath the base of the cabinet. In so doing, a second spring must have been disengaged, permitting the base to drop upon the elevator platform. Is that clear, my dear sir?"

Kerby frowned. "Go on."

The Baron took the sheet of paper, again sketched in the negro this time with the negro's left foot in a position of being pushed against the ventilation slit. "Waiting for a second after he heard Dacrokoff stamp, until the elevator platform was lowering, taking Mrs. Tarn down the elevator shaft, the blackman pushed the hatpin through the ventilation slit. That is all." He shrugged. "The hatpin pierces Mrs. Tarn's breast; her own weight does the rest. As her head drops below the stage floor, the hatpin has been forced into her heart and is completely drawn through the ventilation slit. The blackman moves his foot. And in 'Cross-section C' we find Mrs. Tarn slumped upon the cabinet section supported by the elevator platform. Mrs. Tarn is—dead. That is what I discovered at the theater last night when I was in the cabinet and the elevator shaft—"

"When you—" Kerby became speechless.

"That is why I was unable to listen to your ticking noises."

"You attacked Bill?"

"My dear sir," protested the Baron. "The man interfered."

"Oh, my Lord!" Weakly Kerby dropped to the arm of the chair. "Oh, my God! He didn't see you?"

Blandly the Baron shook his head.

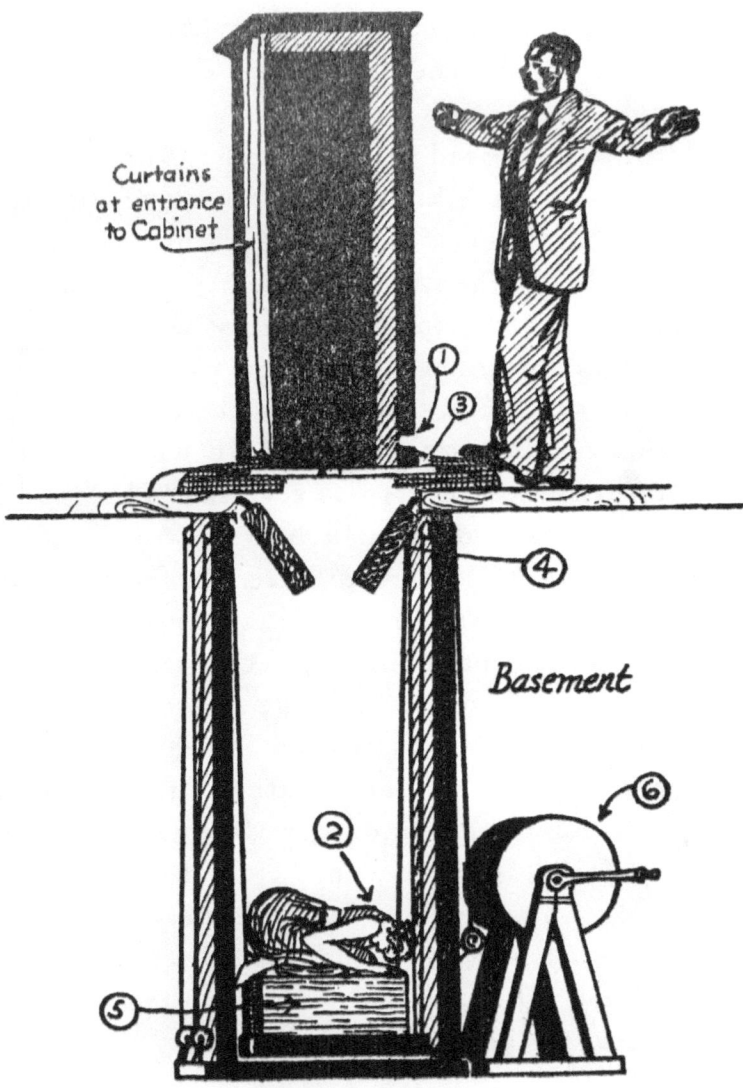

Curtains
at entrance
to Cabinet

Basement

CROSS SECTION C

As elevator (5) drops to bottom of shaft, the hatpin now
embedded in Lucille Tarn is drawn completely through ventilation hole away from "Dude's" shoe. False bottom (3)
slides shut, closing base of cabinet.

"The ticking noises were bad enough, but if you keep on . . ." He bent over the desk and took the three sheets of paper, studied them, asking at last, "After Lucille was killed, Franz, just how the devil did she get back up into the cabinet?"

The Baron was pleased. Already he had thought of that point. "Ah so? I do not know how Dacrokoff did it, perhaps when he drew back the curtains, but somehow he managed to slide out the false bottom after Mrs. Tarn 'vanished'. Thus the cabinet appeared empty, with no opening. And—" He again pointed, "After she was at the bottom of the elevator shaft, the trapdoor in the stage swung upwards once more, closing the hole. Next, when it was time for her to return, the process was reversed. The good Lennock applies himself to the winch. The wooden sides of the elevator retain Mrs. Tarn despite the fact that she is dead. Her body is pushed into the cabinet; under her, the false bottom has slid back into its recess in the base, and the trapdoor closes for a second time. Dacrokoff pulls the curtains, thinks that she has fainted."

Kerby walked across the room, turned again to the desk, picked up the telephone, and then dropped it. "But see here." He squinted at the Baron. "How did 'Dude' know that the hatpin would go into her—her heart?"

"How?" The Baron ceased admiring his sketches. "Oh, he did not know. That was purely an accident. Undoubtedly the hatpin was poisoned."

"Poisoned?"

"That is what I should do. Then, no matter where the hatpin penetrated, Mrs. Tarn would die. One of the cyanide poisons would be satisfactory. However, apparently there was no indication of poisoning when the good Mr. Watson examined the body. If the hatpin were coated with a crystalized solution of—ach—strychnine sulphate, that would work very nicely. Unless they analyzed the heart or the veins the strychnine would not be particularly notice- able. And a few minute crystals dried on the hatpin would be ample. Perhaps after Mr. Watson has time to think he will consider the hatpin—" The Baron sprang up. "If you please, dear sir?"

Kerby had lifted the telephone receiver for the second time. "I'm going to get Zack at once."

"Do you believe that wise?" The Baron cocked his head. "A day or so wait would not hurt, no? The blackman? Would you say he is intelligent?"

"Intelligent? Damned if I know. Probably not. I see what you're driving at—"

"Good! Then I must have that day or so to find this bizarre intelligence behind the blackman, the intelligence which devised this plan, which hired the black man, which hates you and hated Mrs. Tarn."

"You think those ticking noises are made by whoever planned Lucille's death?"

"Exactly. That is why we must not warn the police because, who can say? Ut fata trahunt. That is Latin. It means 'as destiny guides'."

"As *what?* Listen, what's that got to do with not calling Zack?"

"My dear sir." The Baron concluded that this was not a practical opportunity to display his classical erudition. "In other words," he said rapidly, "who knows whether this one for whom we seek might not learn through the Police Chief that the perfect murder no longer is perfect? And then, this one will act before we can lay our own plans."

"Don't be so damned melodramatic!" protested Kerby. "What are you trying to do? Frighten me? And how do you know those ticking noises are connected with Lucille's death?"

"Tonight I shall find out for certain," declared the Baron, pushing back his chair. "Tonight *I* shall listen for them after you have retired."

"Well if you don't," came decisively, "I can tell you I won't stay in that room."

When the Baron smiled, tiny wrinkles appeared at the corner of his eyes. "Now, can you do this? I wish to talk with Dacrokoff alone. His tongue and mine are the same. Let me speak to him in his own language. He may know something the very significance of which he does not realize."

"Carmel one six nine," Kerby said into the mouthpiece; and, to the Baron, "I'll get Zack. I'll tell him I have a guest who's Austrian and suggest that Dacrokoff might confess to him. I can fix that all right, with Zack."

The jail at Carmel had only been built recently.

It was on Jasmin Road, two blocks off Ocean Boulevard, a handsome yellow stucco structure designed by two of Carmel's most prominent artists. As an artists' and writers' colony, Carmel had fought against a jail. And when the shopkeepers and real estate men had protested that a growing town the size of Carmel had to have a jail, the two divergent elements in the community finally had compromised with the understanding that a jail would be designed and built which was in keeping with the other buildings of Carmel.

Only in Carmel, where even the roads were deliberately kept unpaved (except for the main thoroughfares) to preserve the noble country atmosphere, would such a jail be constructed. The offices and gymnasium faced the road; the cells were placed in the rear, divided by a corridor, one row overlooking a narrow alley. The Carmel Garden Club planted flowers and shrubs around the jail and along the alley. With the barred windows of the cells hidden from the

tourists passing on Jasmin Road, the jail had the appearance of a country club. The two artists were enormously
proud of their work. Until the murder of Lucille Tarn,
arrests had been infrequent and then of a minor character;
a few drunks, a few speeders, and a Mexican now and then
who insisted on beating his wife in public. And if his wife
should come in the evening, with a black eye, and hand
food up to her husband from the alley, the jail-keeper had
no objections. It lowered the cost of supplying prisoners
with food. The inhabitants of Carmel considered it quaint
and primitive and altogether amusing. "Such a darling
jail!" that was what a prominent woman author had said
when she inspected it; and her opinion had been accepted
with overwhelming delight by the taxpayers of Carmel . . .

Tarn was with the Chief of Police.

The Baron noticed that Tarn's clothes were rumpled.
They looked as though he had slept in them. His face was
drawn, his eyes were red. "So you think if you talk to the
magician alone you can get something out of him?" demanded the Police Chief Zack Watson. He was not greatly
impressed by this foreigner. "You think he'll tell you how
he killed Mrs. Tarn?"

The Baron politely shook his head.

Tarn's narrow, bronzed face contorted. "What Dacrokoff needs, Zack, is a rubber hose. No foreigner's going to
make him talk."

"Take it easy, Charlie," advised Watson. "I thought
Kerby said you could make him talk, Baron?"

"I did not say, my dear sir, that I could persuade him
to tell me that he killed Mrs. Tarn."

"You're not afraid to be alone in the cell with him? He's
disarmed."

"The Baron von Kaz is a brave man."

Tarn eyed the Chief of Police. This latter spat. "Oh . . ."
he said, helplessly. "You're a brave man, eh?"

The Baron bowed.

"Karl," the Chief of Police called the jailer lounging by the door. "Take him to cell twenty-one. It won't hurt to try, anyway," he said, half apologetically to Tarn.

"Pardon." The Baron paused at the door. "Have you analyzed the dried blood on the hatpin which killed Mrs. Tarn?"

"Have we—" Watson hadn't thought it was necessary to give the hatpin to a chemist. The hatpin had killed Mrs. Tarn by piercing her heart.

"Does it not seem peculiar, my dear sir, that the hatpin so fortunately struck her in such a vital spot?" The Baron bowed, departed with the jailer. He had had no intention of bringing up the matter of poison when he had entered the jail, but the attitude of the two men had irritated him; he would teach them to appreciate the Baron Franz Maximilian Karagôz von Kaz.

The Baron leaned on the door of the cell, listening to the heavy clumpings of the jailer's feet as they hit the cement floor and died away. Dacrokoff was sitting on the bunk, his head level with the barred window. His face was gray and his long arms were folded. The Baron saw the red flowers growing outside the window. A cart passed in the alley and a man's head was visible through the bars. The man was whistling. The sun was strong and bright. Bees were humming, busy with the flowers. The Baron frowned.

The silence between the two men hung heavily. Dacrokoff spoke first. He couldn't stand the silence. "So it's you?" He spoke in German.

The Baron leaned on the green umbrella, nodding absently.

"I thought they shot you?"

The Baron shrugged, his gaze going past Dacrokoff toward the barred window.

"How did you come here?"

The Baron looked at him. It was the same man. He had remembered the name, "Liebermann." "We nearly caught you in Vienna," he said pleasantly.

Liebermann, or "Dacrokoff," to use the name he had taken, stirred, stood up menacingly. "I was innocent. Officer Hjiek said I was innocent. They let me go."

"So? Hjiek was always an imbecile."

"You won't try your gypsy tricks on me here, von Kaz!" Dacrokoff's terrible hands fluttered. "Not here, do you understand?"

For reply the Baron placed the point of his green umbrella on the man's chest, shoved gently. "If you please. Not so close."

"I could strangle you, von Kaz. You drove me out of—"

"Did you hear? *Not so close!*"

Dacrokoff reached for the Baron.

The Baron leaped backwards, grasping the umbrella by the handle, and asked, "So? Hümgarten did not tell you of my green umbrella?"

Hümgarten had been one of Dacrokoff's associates who had foolishly remained in Austria after the Baron was appointed as head of the Special Division.

"Hümgarten?" Dacrokoff's little pig-eyes glanced at the green umbrella. "Christ God! Baron, that is not *the* umbrella?"

"If you please, sit down."

As though fascinated, the magician stared at the silver-tipped umbrella. "Did you hear?" the Baron asked crisply. Dacrokoff humbly sat down as far away as possible from the Baron. The little pig-eyes glinted ominously.

"One day I shall catch you without that—" he jerked his head. "Then what will you do?"

"Run probably."

Dacrokoff slapped the seam of his trouser leg. "You would? Ah, no one can compare with you, Baron von Kaz."

"What do you know of the murder of this unfortunate American woman?"

This question instantly sobered the magician. "No." His hands fluttered. "I will not talk. I know nothing. You waste your time, Baron."

"As you wish." The Baron swung around and pointed through the window. "Do you see that tree? They are talking of lynching you. That is not pleasant. When they place the cord about your neck, remember that the Baron von Kaz offered to help you. Good day."

"Baron!"

"I do not believe you did it," came coldly. "I do not think you even implicated. However, if you do not wish to talk, that is your own affair."

Dacrokoff looked out at the dark tree in the bright sunlight. He had heard of these terrible American lynchings. His fingers touched his throat. He offered,

"I will talk, Baron, but Christ can have my soul if I know anything."

"How did you happen to be at the theater?"

"An Englishman, a man of the cinema, your Excellency, knew of my work in Los Angeles."

"Blane?"

"That was his name. He wrote for me to come to Monterey, to entertain at a party he was giving."

"And then?"

"I went to San Francisco." Dacrokoff's mouth twisted. "Now I am a famous magician. I am billed at the Orpheum. After an afternoon performance a woman attended me. She had been at the party in Monterey—"

"What was her name?"

"She was tall, slim. Not like these American women—"

"Her name?"

"I do not recall, Christ take my soul if I do. Her Garden Club was planning a benefit show. She would have me."

"Rittenhouse?"

"Rittenhouse? That was not the name, your Excellency. When I arrived I did not see her except once. I worked with the theater manager, Lennock. I needed an assistant. I told Lennock. This woman—"

"Mrs. Kerby?"

Yes, that was the name. He and Lennock had been making their arrangements and Caryl Kerby had appeared, asking if everything was satisfactory. She had suggested "Dude", that is how "Dude" chanced to assist Dacrokoff. At one time in his life "Dude" had been a carpenter. It was he who had worked with Dacrokoff in sawing the trapdoor through the stage floor, setting up the winch and the elevator shaft.

"The blackman knows!" Dacrokoff waved his hands. "You ask him, your Excellency. What?" He lifted one foot and then the other. "These are the shoes I wore."

The Baron ordered the magician to remove them.

Apparently he was satisfied with his inspection because he handed them back to the magician, then thumped on the door of the cell to signify to the jailer that the interview was ended.

Upstairs, Tarn, sitting on the desk of the Chief of Police, listened sceptically. "So you didn't learn anything, Baron?"

"Nothing," replied the Baron regretfully. "That man has no knowledge, no idea of how the regrettable murder was planned or executed."

Watson spat, briefly thanking the Baron.

Tarn was saying to Watson, "We'll cut a length of rubber hose and if you can't get anything out of him, I'll attend to it myself. You're too lenient with—" and he noticed that the Baron was still in the room. "Thank you for your services," he said sharply.

At the door the Baron paused, "Excuse me, if you please, but have you seen the blackman?"

"The black man?"

"He means 'Dude'," explained the Chief of Police. "Don't worry about *him*, Baron. He's a local man. We're softening him with thirty hours' silent treatment. When we get around to him, he'll talk. Tell Henry we appreciate his sending you over." Elaborately, when the Baron had departed, Watson winked at Tarn.

The Baron returned. "If you please, I forgot." He hesitated. "If you wish to speak to the blackman this afternoon, I suggest that you remove him from a cell directly overlooking the alley. Good day, my dear Mr. Tarn." And to the head of the police department, "Good day, sir."

Tivvits was waiting for the Baron in the shiny new Lincoln town car rushed to Carmel late last night when it was learned that a millionaire nobleman who was spending his money like wild fire wanted first-class transportation.

Tivvits opened the rear door, touching his hat. "All ready, your Lordship—"

"Tivvits," reproved the Baron.

Tivvits blushed. "Your Baronship. Want me to take you back to Mr. Kerby's house?" He added hopefully, "It's a wonderful day, your Baronship. Maybe a little drive? This car can do ninety without even panting."

"I do not think so," said the Baron slowly. "In fact, Tivvits, I have a presentiment that I will be needed here." Over his shoulder he saw the Chief of Police dash out of the door, glancing around wildly. "Tivvits," he ordered quickly. "Go to Mr. Kerby at once. Tell him I require him at the jail immediately."

"Hey, you!" shouted Watson. He ran down the steps as the Lincoln purred away. "Come back here! Me and Charlie want to see you."

A cluster of men were gathered in front of the door of the next to the last cell in the outside row, overlooking the alley. "Right in here," commanded the Chief of Police harshly. "We thought you might like to try talking to 'Dude' yourself."

Something was lying on the bed. The feet, the arms, and the body were distinguishable. They weren't harmed. But where the head should have been was a pulpy, grayish and red ooze as if an egg filled with blood had been smashed . . .

"Ugh." The doctor wiped his hands. "You don't need me on this, Zack. 'Dude's' deader than a doornail." In the middle of the mass above the shoulders the Baron saw the handle of a small hammer. The iron head of the hammer was buried in the negro's skull.

"What we'd like to be told," came from Zack Watson, "is just how you guessed, that 'Dude' was killed when you said—"

"Good God!" The doctor suddenly leaned over the negro, gingerly placed his handkerchief upon something near the bloody head, and then showed a long hatpin to the amazed Police Chief.

6

The Black Day

Wednesday, April tenth, the day after the sensational murder of Lucille Tarn became the blackest of all days for the brave Baron Franz Maximilian Karagôz von Kaz.

During the course of the day he was humiliated, twice was his pride irreparably damaged, and he committed one serious mistake. More than once during the day he concluded that his time would have been far better employed sitting beneath one of the shade trees of the Kiràlyi discussing the merits of Palugyay Szmorodner with a pretty and admiring young singer waiting to rehearse at the opera.

In sad truth, the Baron required admiration as a tree does water. Because of this thirst for admiration he made his mistake and thus suffered grievous humiliation. Unable to contain his desire to astonish Police Chief Zack Watson and Charles Tarn by his superior talents, after giving them to understand that the hatpin which had killed Mrs. Tarn should be examined, he made the mistake of not permitting them to discover for themselves that "Dude" had been murdered. He couldn't wait for them to enter the cell and attempt to wake the dead negro. No, as soon as he saw how accessible one row of the cells was from the alley, already suspecting how important it was to whosoever had planned the murder of Lucille Tarn that the one weakness in the plan—the negro—be forever hushed, he had asked the jailer which cell "Dude" occupied and then he had to explode his suspicions under the very nose of the Chief of Police.

The doctor was a busy, efficient man. He handed the hatpin wrapped in the handkerchief to Watson. "It was stuck right here in the pillow, Zack."

"I'll be damned," said Watson. He turned to one of the men. "Garaghty, see if there's any fingerprints. Probably won't show on a bit of steel but might as well try."

The doctor closed his bag. "You don't need me?"

"How long's he been dead, Doc?"

"Can't tell." The doctor lifted one of the negro's arms, let it drop. "Rigor mortis hasn't started to set in. 'Sides, it was warm this morning. Want an autopsy?"

Watson again reluctantly examined the negro. "Looks like someone stuck his hand through the window and bashed 'Dude's' skull with the hammer."

"It would take a lot of force wouldn't it, Zack, to do that to a man's skull?" asked Tarn.

The doctor closed his bag. "Not so much, Charlie. Even a woman swinging a heavy hammer like that one could bust open the skull. A negro's head's no thicker'n anybody else's. Sometimes not so thick. I got to get along. You don't need an autopsy, do you Zack?"

Watson decided that he didn't. He turned to the Baron, to repeat the question the doctor had interrupted by his discovery of the hatpin: How had the Baron guessed that "Dude" was murdered or going to be? The Baron shrugged. Anyone who had designed such a jail as this, he stated with unnecessary acidity, should have been arrested for criminal negligence.

By this time, inasmuch as the news had got out that "Dude" was murdered, the corridor was filled with report-ers representing the San Francisco papers who were cov-ering the Lucille Tarn case. Watson hastily shut up the

Baron, ordered the corridor cleared. He sent for the police photographer. He grabbed the jailer by the coat lapel. "Get that magician into a cell across the corridor away from these windows. Put a guard outside the door and do it right now. We don't want three murders."

A stoop-shouldered young man entered and proceeded to photograph the body from all angles while Tarn and the Chief of Police stood in one corner, discussing the latest sensation.

While this was going on, the Baron stepped to the barred window. It was, he figured, some seven feet from the window to the alley.

A small man with glasses ran down through the corridor, entered the cell and whispered to the Chief of Police. "I'll be damned!" exclaimed Watson. "Strychnine sulphate?"

The police chemist nodded.

Tarn grabbed the chemist by the arm. "You're sure?"

"Just finished now. Started on it as soon as Zack gave me the idea. The hatpin was coated with a solution of crystallized strychnine sulphate. That stuff's easy to get. Want me to examine Mrs. Tarn's body? We'll find traces in her heart and veins. There's no doubt of it."

"Come here, you!" ordered the Chief of Police to the Baron. "Now just why did you think the hatpin was poisoned?"

"Ach. I would do it that way myself."

Watson had to get between Tarn and the Baron. When Tarn was quieted, the Chief of Police told the chemist to give him a written report as soon as possible. The photographer had finished. Watson commanded the Baron to stay where he was, and then extracted the clotted hammer from the negro's head, and gave orders for temporarily holding the body at a local undertaker's.

"What about the hatpin?" asked the photographer as he put away his camera. "Garaghty said you gave him a hatpin."

"Garaghty'd better hold his goddamned mouth," Watson stated angrily. "Tell him to give it to Jacobs after he's checked it for fingerprints and see if there's strychnine crystals on it."

"What do you intend to tell the reporters?" Tarn stepped forward, his eyes redder than before, his hands thrust into his coat pockets.

"As soon as we've checked on the hatpin, I'll give them the story. I'll take Jacobs' word for the strychnine. We won't cut—won't have an autopsy on Mrs. Tarn."

"Thanks, Zack." Tarn dropped his hand heavily on the Police Chiefs shoulder, nodded significantly at the Baron who was standing, frowning and thoughtful, near the window. In the Baron's mind there was no doubt of what had occurred: Sometime during the night, the murderer had silently come into the alley, either climbed on top of an automobile or had brought a ladder to stand on, called to "Dude," and when the negro had stood on his knees on the bunk beneath the window, had bashed in the man's head. "Excuse me?" The Baron looked at Watson when the latter spoke.

"I'll give you one more chance to answer. How did you suspect that 'Dude' would be murdered?"

"My dear sir, was that not obvious?"

"Lock him up!" savagely suggested Tarn. "These goddamned foreigners have to be taught that they can't flout American institutions. Lock him up until he decides to talk civilly, Zack. Maybe he'll understand we're serious."

And so, because he had made the mistake of stating the obvious, the great von Kaz suffered the humiliation of being thrown into a cell until he was willing to explain civilly to the police. They thrust him into the room formerly occupied by Dacrokoff. "These goddamned foreigners!" Tarn complained to Watson. Thenceforth, throughout the entire case, the unforgiving Austrian extended no effort to be of assistance to constituted law and authority.

Kerby arrived fifteen minutes later, shortly after eleven o'clock. He asked for the Baron, was informed that he had been thrown into jail for suspected complicity in the death of "Dude" McKay. "'Dude's' murdered?" shouted Kerby. The reporters, now gathered in the Police Chiefs office, knew Kerby and liked him and so they quickly related how "Dude" had been discovered, giving Watson no time to explain.

Tarn defended the Chief of Police's actions.

Kerby's temper, never too securely fastened, blew up completely.

"Charlie, you had the Baron arrested?"

"Take it easy, Henry," protested Watson. "He wouldn't tell why he thought 'Dude' had been murdered before we saw—"

"Blast you to hell and gone, Zack! Just because the man's five times as smart as you are, you throw him in prison!"

Tarn interfered again. "I take full responsibility for having him put in jail, Kerby. You writers seem to think that you have a God-given right to dictate what's to be done in this town. Well, you listen to me: this isn't any funny story. My wife's been killed—"

"See here, Tarn." Kerby squinted malevolently at the man, his red beard cocked at a fighting angle. "Let me tell *you* something. Some of us writers and artists are beginning to wonder if you haven't controlled this town too long. Remember, we pay the taxes. We have a few votes of our own. And I'll tell you this, Charlie Tarn, if your political machine has filled this town with such incompetent fat-heads that they can't even discover who murdered Lucille, then by Lord! some of us are going to raise so much hell that you won't be able to be elected dog-catcher, to say nothing of governor of California!"

Tarn sputtered and walked out of the office. Kerby pointed his pipe at Watson. "Baron von Kaz is my guest. He had the courtesy to come here to assist you at my suggestion. Now you get the hell down there and release him and apologize to him or I'll telephone Jack MacNamra and see if he can't get the governor to find out what's going on in Carmel."

James MacNamra was legal counsel for a great chain of California newspapers, a close friend of Kerby's. Hoping to retain full glory for himself in a case that threatened to be one of the most celebrated in California criminal annals, Watson had no intention of doing anything that would bring in outside assistance. With Tarn gone, Watson cleared the room of the reporters and then declared that perhaps he had acted too hastily with the Baron, admitting reluctantly that he had no other evidence than that offered by the Baron himself to connect him with the second crime.

The telephone rang. Watson picked the receiver up, listened, said, "All right, Jake," and turned to the Baron who had entered. "Jake says there's nothing on the second hatpin except blood spattered off of 'Dude'. They can't find any fingerprints on it or on the hammer. Both must have been handled with gloves. Well?"

The Baron said nothing.

Watson told Kerby that the first hatpin had been coated with crystallized strychnine sulphate. "It isn't reasonable," he complained, "that the Baron should be such a damned good guesser, is it?"

Kerby looked bewildered, recalling the Baron's insistence that the police not be told of the probability of poison, and said the Baron was a brilliant man and the Baron smiled and bowed and the Police Chief sourly watched the two go out of the door.

When the Baron appeared on the jail steps the reporters crowded around him. He was more afraid of the reporters than of being thrown into any jail except one—and that one was in Vienna. He had visions of an inquisitive immigration officer reading that a Baron von Kaz was in Carmel.

"Ach," he said plaintively, "it is nothing, gentlemen. A misunderstanding." They followed him to Kerby's car. Kerby came to the Baron's assistance. "You're on the wrong track, boys. The Baron is a guest of mine. As a matter of fact, I heard that the magician refused to talk, and knowing that the magician was an Austrian, I thought he might talk in his own language and the Baron kindly offered to serve as interpreter. That's all." He waved them away, grinning at them happily, his anger altogether forgotten.

Behind Kerby's Mercedes, the Baron saw the imperishable Tivvits hopefully waiting at the wheel of the town car. Kerby asked, "When in thunder did you get a chauffeur and a car? Your man came steaming up to the house with the information that you had to see me at once. Lucky for you he did."

"Ach, in Vienna always did I have a chauffeur, dear Mr. Kerby. Now, if you will pardon me, I have affairs to attend to."

"What about 'Dude's' murder? And the ticking noises you were going to—"

"This afternoon and tonight, if you please. We will discuss the murder, let us say, after lunch."

Perplexed, Kerby watched the Baron climb into Tivvits' car and give the driver instructions to proceed down Ocean Boulevard.

Kerby drove home.

David Blane was waiting in the study. "I believe we
were in the middle of the balcony scene at the last interruption," he said dryly. "You suggested that the heroine
blindfold the comedian—"

Kerby placed his hand on the scenario editor's shoulder.
"See here, Dave, I'm worried. Give me a minute, will you?"

The minute extended into half an hour.

Blane finished his twelfth cigarette. "I can't believe it,"
he insisted.

"There you are." Kerby lit his pipe.

"I remember Caryl had the servants hunting for a
cricket or something that was in your bedroom, but I'd
imagined you'd found the—whatever it was that caused
the noises. You didn't mention them after the first week or
so. And that's why you've been so worried lately?"

"The Baron proved to me it wasn't Charlie, Dave. And
now I think he thinks it is Charlie. I can't make out what
he thinks, to tell the truth."

"The Baron?" Blane was angry. "You mean you told him
and didn't tell me? That mountebank? And yet you didn't
trust me as a friend—"

"Don't go off half-cocked, Dave. I trust you more than
anyone else in this world. That's why I'm telling you this—
the Baron is a detective. As a matter of fact, Lucille knew
him in Vienna."

"A detective? Oh, for God's sake!" Blane laughed sarcastically. "Henry, I've never seen anyone do as many crazy things
as you can do. And what for God's sake makes you think
he's a detective? I knew Lucille at the studio before you did.
She hadn't much more practical judgment than you have."

"You knew her?"

"Slightly." Blane searched his pockets for a match. "Before she was a star. Well, if you want to know," he added
steadily, "when she first came to the studio I knew her
very well."

"You never told me."

Blane smiled crookedly. "You never asked. Besides what good would it have done? Anyway, I knew her and I realize that she'd be just the type to select a mountebank like that so-called Baron of yours and think he was the finest detective in all the world. He probably kissed her hand a couple of times in Vienna and she fell for him."

"Dave," Kerby stopped him quietly. "I don't give a hoot what you thought of Lucille, but—"

"Oh, I'm not going to quarrel with you," Blane assured Kerby. "She might have changed after she was a star. . . ." He inserted a sheet of yellow paper in the typewriter. "If you want my advice, you'll hire a real detective."

"But good Lord, Dave. The Baron's already learned how she was killed."

"Think so? The way he talks, both you and Lucille— well, you are gullible enough to believe anything. I know a first-class detective in Hollywood whom I could get for you. He's reliable. You can trust him."

Kerby tapped his pipe on the palm of his hand. "Damn it! How the hell can I get rid of the Baron without hurting his feelings?"

"Hurting his feelings? Is he a baby?"

"I kind of like him, Dave. He's so damned touchy and conceited—"

"Oh, for God's sake," exclaimed Blane, exasperated. "We're in the middle of the balcony scene. The comedian falls into the wine barrel. What next?"

And Kerby closed his eyes, leaned back in his comfortable chair, stuck his pipe in his mouth, and returned to that world of dreams all of his own where people fall into wine barrels and impossible and extravagant things happen, and where even Death, if it comes, is something ludicrous and not at all tragic.

"Tivvits," asked the Baron, as they arrived at the end of Ocean Boulevard, "how far is it to Hollywood?"

"Three hundred miles, your Lordship?"

"I told you not under any circumstances to call me 'your Lordship'," sternly reprimanded the Baron. Penitently Tivvits nodded. "How long would it take you to drive to Hollywood?"

Three hundred miles to Hollywood; three hundred miles back. Why the bill would be nearly two hundred and fifty dollars for the drive alone. "Seven hours, your honor."

The Baron got out. "I wish you to go there at once."

"Yes, your honor."

"I have a friend of mine here. A very good friend." The Baron winked. "He claims that he is not married. I think he is. I wish to fool him. In the North American states, do you have a government official who records marriages?"

Tivvits had been married for three months. There was such a place. He was positive of that.

"Very good, Tivvits. You will locate this office in Hollywood or in Los Angeles, and ascertain if a man by the name of David Blane is, or was, married. You will find to whom he is or was married. If you can learn nothing at the city offices, telephone his studio—the Solar Pictures—and say that you are a newspaper reporter. Say anything." The Baron thought for an instant. "Wire me at the Kerby house the result of your inquiry. You should be back here in Carmel by tomorrow. Good day, Tivvits. Whatever is the cost of the trip, I am certain that it will be eminently satisfactory. Good day."

Tivvits started for Hollywood. He had reached the state where, if his client had said "London," Tivvits would have attempted the journey without hesitation.

The Baron returned to the neighborhood of the jail. He sauntered into the alley. Ahead of him he saw a cluster of men standing. He heard one of the policemen saying to the reporters, "These here must be the identical boxes the criminal used. They was kicked into the ditch."

There were two boxes, one piled upon the other, against the yellow stucco wall of the jail. Two photographers were taking pictures. One of the reporters climbed upon the boxes, reached through the bars, "I can nearly touch the bed with my hand. What a jail this one is!"

The Baron turned and left.

In his own mind the Baron believed that he had already narrowed the murderer down to two suspects. Steadfastly he refused to consider Tarn as a potentiality, although he was not so obstinate as to refuse to admit to himself that Tarn had equal opportunities with the two suspects to plan the murder, in fact greater opportunities.

Tarn had a reason to hate Kerby, if it were true that he had learned of the affair with his wife, and thus might have reason to originate the ticking noises. He had the same motive for hating Lucille Tarn and could have engineered her death. Rightly or wrongly, the Baron had told Kerby that no politician could have the astuteness and ingenuity to devise the ticking noises and so, rightly or wrongly, he was not going to start suspecting Tarn as yet. And the more the Baron considered Tarn, the more he felt that the man was incapable of murder.

The Baron thought that Caryl Kerby had the best motive. He was far from being convinced that Caryl was unacquainted with her husband's affair with Lucille. Caryl, he thought, might first have tried to frighten her husband; then, she might have struck relentlessly at the man's mistress.

He had the following facts to build this belief:

1. Lucille had been afraid of Caryl.
2. Caryl, as the wife, had an excellent opportunity to contrive the ticking noises,

to conceal the source when her husband
searched for it.

3. "Dude" had worked for Caryl.

4. It was she who had arranged for "Dude" to
assist the magician after she had watched
the latter's trick twice.

Not yet was the Baron ready to decide whether or not
Alice was involved. When he thought of her, as he did
with increasing frequency, his mind would accept nothing
more than that she was pretty and charming. . . .

More or less stalemated, then, the Baron was obliged to
consider David Blane.

He knew little about him.

However, Blane had fainted, or as good as fainted, when
Lucille Tarn was murdered. That was a strong indication
of an overpowering, emotional upheaval. And Blane was
scenario editor for Solar Pictures, Inc., where Lucille Tarn
had been starred as Lucille Delay.

The Baron had attributed more complex motives for
Blane's possible guilt. These motives troubled the Baron.
If Blane, in the past, had been married to Lucille Tarn,
or greatly in love with her, was it not conceivable that he
would feel a great resentment against Tarn for, thanks to
his wealth and influence, taking the woman he loved? So
much was predicated on what the Baron hoped the invaluable Tivvits would either find or not find in Hollywood or
Los Angeles records.

If Blane hated Tarn, then how much more would he
hate Kerby? It would be the corrosive hate of injured ego-
tism. And if Blane could kill Lucille Tarn and drive Kerby
to suicide in such a manner that Tarn would be incrimi-
nated, he would have established his revenge on the three
who, knowingly or unknowingly, had injured him. Blane,
the Baron already had ascertained, had taken his residence

in the Kerby house about a week and a half before the ticking noises commenced.

Devoutly, the Baron hoped that Caryl Kerby was a murderess.

If she were the one he did not believe that she would attempt to kill her husband. The death of "Dude" would end her killings unless she were pressed, the ticking noises would stop after a week or so, long enough after the two deaths so that there would appear to be no connection with them.

But if it were Blane, then, plausibly, there would be one more death before he was finished. . . .

7

Love in Bloom

The Baron arrived at the Kerby residence at five minutes to one in a taxicab, saw Blane standing thoughtfully in the yard, and requested him to pay the taxicab fare with the explanation that he had absent-mindedly forgotten to take his money with him. Blane paid it unwillingly.

As the Baron hurried upstairs, into the hall toward his room, Alice's door opened and Henry Kerby backed out, laughing. Forgetting all manners, the Baron promptly crouched behind the banister, hoping that no one would enter the downstairs hall and see him in such a position.

He heard Alice Rittenhouse's voice, "Well, I'll have the Baron for lunch anyway," and then the door closed.

The Baron resumed his normal position, walked down the hall where he encountered Kerby, who was wiping his lips with his handkerchief. "Oh, it's you?" he said, half-sheepishly, half-startled. "What did you discover?"

The luncheon bell rang.

Blane called from below, "Henry! Are you ready? It's one o'clock."

"Damn," said Kerby unhappily. "Look, Franz. I promised Dave I'd have lunch with a friend of his in Monterey today, at Pop Ernst's. I've got to go. Caryl's going, too. I'll see you here around three because I want to talk to you."

"Henry! Come on. Caryl's waiting."

Henry Kerby went downstairs. Almost the Baron shouted for him to stop, but even as he ran to the head of the
stairs he halted, realizing that he could say nothing to
warn the humorist. Anything that he could say now stood
too great a chance of being disbelieved. And, if the humorist should lose his head, unwittingly warn either Caryl
or Blane, then the danger would be greater.

The Baron, a few minutes later, joined Alice at lunch.
He was somber throughout most of the meal. This intrigued
Alice. Inasmuch as she was a little angry that the two men
had left, taking Caryl and not her, she laid herself out to
be especially nice to the dark, gloomily romantic foreigner. First they talked about the murders; rather she did, and
the Baron responded with intelligent "Uhms", "Ahs", and
even a "Yes". Alice said Lucille was to be buried Friday.
Poor Lucille. Wasn't it a shame?

Then she changed the subject, inquiring how soon he
was going to start on his memoirs. He didn't know. Although he didn't say so, he had almost forgotten that he
was supposed to be writing memoirs. "What you should
do," she said, "is to dictate."

That would be too difficult.

"But to me?" she pouted. "I could take it down for
you."

After she had graduated from college she had taken
a business course and often her uncle in the publishing
business dictated to her. She was taken with the idea. As
soon as they finished lunch he must start his memoirs.
She would change first to something cooler, indicating her
natural linen two-piece dress, because she wanted to play
tennis later. She jumped up, blew him a pretty little kiss.
"I'll be terribly cross if you're not ready in ten minutes. In
the game room."

Alice kept him waiting fifteen minutes. She entered
in a navy blue silk shirt, a new pair of shorts, carrying

pencils and a shorthand book she confessed she had swiped from Henry's study.

She drew a chair close to the ping-pong table. "All set, Baron," she announced and waited.

Apparently she had no idea of the havoc her smooth and well-furnished underpinnings were causing upon a gentleman who enjoyed nice legs and particularly that delectable brand which had a peach-bloom skin and lines which swoon more or less from a soft curve to an ankle sufficiently small to be encompassed by the thumb and forefinger.

She had a small mouth, a sulky little mouth which easily opened in laughter; and her nose, decided the Baron, was especially American, altogether at home in a face which was round, which owned eyes whose brightness was frequently hidden by the silky lashes. "Dear Alice," he said amiably, "several days ago I saw a lovely brooch in San Francisco. Perhaps when we both have the time you would experience pleasure in accompanying me to San Francisco to look at it?"

There was a silence while she looked at him and he at her.

She marked the book with her pencil. "You'd better begin on those memoirs of yours, Baron. If you're stuck, just start anywhere. In Vienna, for example. I'd like to go there some day."

"So? Possibly some day I could—"

"You never can tell." She lifted her eyes. "But now you start on the memoirs."

"Ah, yes." He frowned. He did not wish to waste too much time before kissing her. "We will start during that year preceding the war."

"You were in the war?"

He showed his surprise.

"Not all through it?"

"I was captured by the English in nineteen-fifteen. That is why now my English is so perfect. . . . In that year before the war, my dear Alice, the flowers bloomed more beautifully than ever before and I recall those flowers as if it were today. I recall one day in June when I went down the Schlossallée." As he spoke, he placed his hands on the back of her chair. "Down the Schlossallée and to the Kursaal where it was that Ganthur von Meyer was to play . . ."

When he stopped she glanced at him, smiling.

"You are very charming, Alice."

"You want me to write that?"

Ah! she *was* charming. So he bent his cheek, brushing her hair, and kissed her, expertly and full on the pouting lips. When she tried to draw away, his hand was at her neck holding her head.

"Very, very charming," he assured her and released her. And, as if nothing had taken place, carefully wiped his lips with his handkerchief, replaced the handkerchief in his pocket, and gazed out through the window at the ocean. "Where were we, dear Alice?"

"You really should be slapped—"

"So? For only one little kiss?" His blue eyes held an amused glint. The two lines deepened on each side of his dark face, and the heavy underlip thrust forward normally as he impudently stared at her. "But perhaps for two kisses, yes?"

"You're terrible!" She laughed at him and probably would have permitted him to kiss her again, but he had other things upon his mind and so lost an excellent opportunity to have his face slapped. A little later they both agreed it would be wiser to defer the memoirs to another day when it was cooler. Alice left to practice tennis shots. The Baron entered Kerby's study, discovered a bottle of good brandy and had consumed approximately a fourth of it when Kerby returned with his wife and Blane.

Kerby asked the Baron to come with him into his bedroom. "Dave can get to work downstairs," Kerby explained. "I want to change into some easy clothes. Caryl's going to dig in her garden so we can talk safely enough. I had a chance to read the San Francisco *Examiner* in Monterey. It had the story of 'Dude's' death blasted across the whole front page."

Kerby threw his coat and pants on one of the chairs, stripped, grunting from time to time as he heard the Baron's theory of how "Dude's" death was accomplished with the help of the two wooden boxes, the hammer, and the night. The hatpin was added, according to the Baron, undoubtedly as a ferocious act of bravado. It hadn't been poisoned. "What was the big idea you had? You weren't going to tell Zack the first hatpin was poisoned and then you went and told him?"

"Hein?" The Baron had conveniently forgotten that he had planned to withhold this information from dear Mr. Watson. "Ach, the poor fellow. He aroused my sympathy."

"Sympathy?" grunted Kerby as he ducked into the shower. "Zack evidently got you talking."

The Baron protested this undeserved calumny but the noise of the water drowned out his explanations; it was just as well, because as explanations go they weren't very convincing.

During the next few minutes the Baron had ample time to extract the handkerchief from Kerby's coat and insert it into his own pocket.

While Kerby was drying himself, the Baron asked, "Mrs. Tarn, did she ever play costume roles on the screen?"

"Huh?" Kerby opened his drawers, selecting fresh linen. "Guess so. Thunder and hell!" He threw a shirt on the floor. "Do the laundries butcher every shirt in Vienna, too?"

"Has she retained those old costumes since her marriage, my dear Mr. Kerby? Particularly old hats?"

"Franz," complained Kerby, "don't keep saying 'my dear Mr. Kerby'. You're supposed to be a friend of mine." He took a second shirt from his drawer and pulled it over his head and looked into the closet for his old flannel suit. "I don't know whether she had on to her hats or not. Damned if I can say. I see what you're driving at, Franz, but as a matter of fact this is all getting too complicated for me. If Lucille *had* old-fashioned hatpins, you can lay all the money you have that Charlie Tarn'd be too smart to use them."

He brushed his hair, ran his fingers through the red beard, and grinned when he saw that the Baron was watching him. "I'll have to shave these bushes off one of these days." He looked for his pipe, finally finding it in the coat he'd tossed on the chair. "Now don't get sore, Franz. You think you've reconstructed how 'Dude' killed Lucille, and I give you credit for it. However, just what the deviled hell does it all signify? Where do the tickings come in? *You* haven't been able to answer that, have you?"

"Tonight, my dear sir—excuse me. Tonight, Henry, I investigate the noises."

"That's fine. See here, Franz." He puffed his pipe, thinking of his conversation with Blane concerning this Austrian detective. "Going back to what we were talking about this morning, what would you say to this? Suppose I hire another detective to assist you? You'd be in charge. We'd get an American detec— All right," finished Kerby hastily, "forget it. And tonight then, you'll try to decide if I'm nuts or if there are ticking noises? I tell you, Franz, I'm damned if I'm going to sleep in my bedroom if you don't find out. There aren't any noises in the other bedrooms."

"If you please, and how do you know?"

"How do I—" If anything, Kerby's beard turned redder than usual. "Because—well, as a matter of fact, no one's complained of them, have they? Isn't that proof?" He swung open the door. "I've got to work with Dave until dinner. See you then."

In his own bedroom the Baron withdrew two handkerchiefs from his pocket, holding them to the sunlight. On each handkerchief was a stain of lipstick red. Obviously, the red stains were from the identical lipstick. The Baron was quite pleased because the stain on his handkerchief was considerably larger than on his client's.

Then the Baron became serious.

He sat down by the window. To the right he could see the tennis court; he could see Alice, with her honey-colored hair and her flashing legs as she drove the ball hard against the brick wall. The drives were powerful, even vicious. There was strength and power behind those drives. He rubbed his nose in that odd gesture of his when thinking or perturbed. The girl in the tennis court could give him the clue he required so desperately. He had two objectives; Caryl Kerby and David Blane. And with luck, Alice Rittenhouse might be induced to give him that clue leading to what he wished to learn.

He smiled grimly as he got up. In a way it was like taking a blood test. If it turned positive then he would know that Caryl was innocent. But if it turned negative, then there was still a chance that Caryl might not be the murderess because Blane was involved. . . .

It was nearly four-thirty in the afternoon when Alice and the brave Baron von Kaz arrived at the end of their walk. She was gazing out across Sunset Point, the wind whipping the yellow skirt she had buttoned on over her abbreviated shorts. He felt the warm, white sand, resting on the embankment which shielded them from the road. The sun was bright. The sea was covered with small whitecaps. Far in the distance a tramp ship was laboriously churning its way toward San Francisco. "Pretty, isn't it?" she asked, dropping beside him. "Cigarette?"

He handed her one, lit it.

She puffed at it contemplatively, then suddenly and maliciously inquired concerning his experience in the Carmel jail.

This so unhinged the Baron's indignation that he temporarily forgot what he had brought her out here to obtain. He spent ten minutes proving to her how incredibly imbecilic everyone had been except himself.

She was pert and flip. Gradually their talk died away. They looked at the ocean and her shoulder brushed his and he was conscious of the faint, exciting perfume from her hair.

Finally she thought it necessary to remind him, "You're not in Austria now," and smoothed her hair, completely at ease.

"Ach, even in America the Baron is always a brave man." With courteous insolence which, although she frowned, did not displease her, he grasped her hand.

Again his underlip was thrust forth in a wicked grin, surprisingly youthful. The dark polished face was handsome, she decided. In growing panic she wished to God she'd never left the tennis court to take this walk. She sighed softly. She tremulously lifted her mouth, closing her eyes.

That damnable one-track mind of his began to function, reminding him most sternly that while he was not exactly wasting time, he had taken this walk for a definite purpose; that purpose, while not conflicting with his present occupation, would be lost should he wait until she was in a less confiding mood.

"Dear Alice," he began.

"Darling why talk? I'm sick of men who talk. Somehow you seemed different."

"Alice." He had a little trouble disengaging her arms. "But what would Mr. Kerby say—"

"Henry?" She gave him a shove and jumped up. "What do you mean—what would he say? What has he got to do with us?"

The Baron attempted to be diplomatic. "There is no need for us to act as children, my dear Alice. After all, I, too, was attracted to you. You have known Mr. Kerby for some time, no? I respect, I admire dear Mr. Kerby. He is— ach!—a good friend. If you are not free you should speak frankly with me before we go on."

"Well," she said, her lips curving a little although her eyes were wary. "I'll say this for you; you're cold-blooded. I presume that's the way the men are in Vienna?"

He took her by the elbows, feeling the smooth skin, feeling her as she came close to him, half-reluctantly.

"That saves much hurt . . . later."

She frowned suddenly, as if she'd thought of something, and twisted free. "Just a second, Franz. What made you mention Henry?"

"Ach!" He lit a cigarette. "After all, was he not with you last night?"

"Why you—" Her eyes narrowed.

"Alice, is it not so, no?"

"Caryl Kerby told you?" she blazed at him. "Caryl's paying you to spy on me." This time she came close to him, declared bitingly, "You contemptible fraud. Dave said you weren't a Baron and I didn't believe him. Why you—get away from here."

"Dear Alice," he protested.

She slapped him twice on the cheek and his cheek turned red and under the red the scar stood out livid. "Do you hear?" she cried.

"As you wish." He bowed formally and walked off without once looking back, having learned what he wanted to know, but considerably more disturbed than he ever had expected to be.

8

The Flying Cow

David Blane had not spent much time working on the
scenario that afternoon. Both he and Kerby were restless.
They had dropped the comedian into the barrel of wine
and neither of them could think of an excuse to extract
the comedian. The way Blane felt, the comedian could
drown. That attitude of mind was not conducive to progress. Kerby gave it up first. "Blast it! Let it go for today,
Dave." He went out. Caryl, he learned, had changed her
mind and driven in to Carmel to market before gardening.
The house was quiet. He returned to the study but Blane
already had wandered from the house toward the tennis
court. Kerby filled his glass with brandy and soda, put
under his arm the latest biography published, and went
upstairs gloomily. . . .

Blane decided that Alice and the Baron fellow had gone
for a walk. This annoyed him immensely. The afternoon
was warm and, perplexed with a problem of his own, he
sauntered around the house into Caryl's rose garden at the
rear.

He leaned on the lattice work, smoked two cigarettes,
when all at once he threw the third cigarette which he had
just lit away. After ten somber minutes he reached a decision. He went to the garage and told the chauffeur he was

131

going to Carmel to get more manuscript paper. He backed out his own roadster, drove to Carmel, then changed his mind and went to Monterey. Here he parked his car and entered a drugstore where he was not known.

He asked long distance the cost to telephone to Hollywood. The price learned, he changed four dollars into quarters, returned to the telephone booth, closed the doors tightly, and telephoned Hollywood, fortunately getting the person to whom he wished to speak.

Then he went three blocks to another drugstore where he purchased five capsules, recommended to cure a dog of worms. "You want to be careful," warned the clerk. "That's powerful stuff and if you give your dog more'n one every twenty-four hours it'll tighten him up instead of loosen the worms and drive him nearly crazy. Too much is like a poison. Why, I had a customer—"

"I know," Blane advised grimly. "I've used this before."

Arriving at the Kerby house and meeting Caryl who had just come in from shopping, he explained his absence by saying that he'd driven on from Carmel to Sur Chiquita to say hello to two acquaintances of his whom he had assisted at one time in Hollywood and who were now attempting life on a small ranch. Alice was still with the Baron, at least she wasn't in the house. Blane went for a walk, passing through the garden, taking the trail which led by the old stable to the slope behind the house. Here he turned, heading for La Honda Drive.

The Baron, returning from his walk with Alice, was in a vile mood. Blane had the misfortune to encounter this gentleman about a mile from the Kerby residence. Noticing that the Baron was alone, Blane was pleased. Alice then had not gone for a walk with the beggar after all. And feeling pleased, regrettably he became jocose:

"Ah, our brave Baron? I see the salt air has brought color into your cheeks. You should walk more, Baron. It's good for you."

The Baron halted, rigid. His hand went to his cheek where he had been slapped, dropped immediately. Mistaking the cause for Blane's joviality, at that moment he could have killed the man, run him through from groin to kidney without a qualm. Believing that Blane had intentionally insulted him, he stepped forward. Disregarding all his carefully planned maneuvers with which he was going to lead to this delicate question, he put into cold, edged words that which was derived from a conjecture based on Blane's obvious shock at the sight of Lucille Tarn's dead body:

"Is it true, my dear Mr. Blane?" He cocked his head slightly. "Is it true that you and the late Mrs. Tarn once were in love when you both were working for Solar Pictures?"

Blane's smile faded. His face turned the color of old stone.

"One thousand pardons," murmured the Baron, already ruing his stupidity, for now Blane would be warned that his past was of interest. The Baron ineffectually tried to slide out of his blunder. "I did not appreciate that it was so painful a subject. If you please, forgive me." Never would the Baron learn to control his pride, keep his inflammable temper sufficiently dampened. Otherwise, despite his volatile imagination, he would have made an admirable detective.

He left the scenario editor rooted there in the middle of the road with the shadows of the stunted cypress trees on the fine sand turning orange; with a gull soaring lazily in the purple sky of early evening, coasting along, thinking what a fine day it had been. . . .

As long as the day had turned out so abominably, the
Baron decided that he might as well finish it with perhaps
the most unpleasant task of all, that of approaching Caryl
Kerby.

She was not in the house.

He located her in the garden. He bowed and she was
there in front of him; a little amused by his stiff bow,
with her wide scarlet mouth twisted in a smile which gave
the Baron to realize that here was one who was not in her
place. Coming from Alice to this woman, not so much
older in years but infinitely more so in wisdom, with a
lithe poise that was the heritage of her French blood, he
wondered why it was that suddenly her cool dark beauty
contrasted so greatly with Alice's bright shallowness. This
was not a woman who could be won in a day; and, once
won, her hate could be as penetrating and constant as ever
had been her love.

At least so he thought as he kissed her hand. As has
no doubt already been perceived, at times the Baron was
of a deplorably romantic nature. Place him in a garden at
sunset with a woman of grace and charm and he would ask
nothing better than to stay all night conversing with her,
about himself to be sure.

"Gracious madame, what a beautiful garden!" He raised
his head, inhaled the perfume of a thousand roses. "I am
enchanted. It is a symphony of color." He thought that a
pretty phrase and when she agreed, he took a deep breath.
It was delightful to talk to a woman of understanding, even
if in a few moments that understanding would be shattered.

He swept his hand, indicating the harmonious array of
bushes, cleaved by the radiating gravel paths. "It *is* a symphony as only a magician could create. You have a piano.
Is it that you are a musician?"

She shook her head. "Hardly."

"Such a pity, dear madame."

"I have no feeling of rhythm, Baron."

"You should have trained with a metronome, my dear lady."

"Oh, I tried one. But I threw it away. . . . Have you noticed these roses? The clippings came from your country."

In the gathering twilight, she showed him the prize roses and where her new flower house was to be built between the garage and the old stable which at present was occupied solely by a cow. The old glass greenhouse, between the stable and the house, was too small. At times, as Caryl Kerby grew eager and excited in discussing her garden, the Baron would secretly consider the fine nose, the small determined chin and sigh half-audibly and wonder if he were about to commit a gross mistake.

When some of her slow, graceful reserve had vanished, and the time for dinner was drawing near, he stated with ruthless directness, "Your garden is most beautiful and fragrant, dear Mrs. Kerby. In fact, when Mr. Kerby so aptly compared its beauty and fragrance with that of Miss Rittenhouse, I felt I must see it."

A rose fell to the ground as the scissors clicked. Caryl stooped and picked up the flower. "Alice is very lovely," tranquilly she replied.

The Baron was enthusiastic. "You knew her in the East?"

"This rose is—Alice? Her uncle formerly published Mr. Kerby's books. Mr. Kerby met her in the East and when she decided to come to the coast for a vacation, naturally he—we wished to have her stay with us. This rose, Baron, comes from France."

He glanced at the rose held between her fingers. "I presume that you have been married long to Mr. Kerby—"

"If you wish to learn of Mr. Kerby's first wife, and divorce, I suggest that you apply directly to him or to any of the villagers." Still holding the rose, her smooth, graceful stride carried her into the greenhouse.

And thus dismissed, with that sly, infantile gesture of his, he touched the side of his nose and cocked his head and nodded most astutely to himself. Ach so? he thought. . . . And how soon would she notice the tiny drops of blood on her forefinger where the rose thorns had pricked into the flesh? Kerby was not the man for a woman like her. He required someone light and gay, someone who would not demand everlasting faithfulness, one who could laugh at his failings, not mind them, not consider them as tragic mishaps.

And so thinking, as he walked to the house to bathe and shave before dinner, he thought of Alice.

And thinking of her ruined his bath. Usually he liked to lie in warm water, dreaming idly, forgetting that on the morrow he would have to suffer the shock of a deluge of cold water, as did the English with inhuman delight. Secretly he admired the English race and sought to achieve their great vigor by emulating their practice of cold showers. He had learned the English language with facile ease when he was a war-prisoner in England, but the thought of cold water was still as abhorrent to him as it had been in the prison camp. And that was why, at evening, his warm bath was so enjoyable.

However, this evening he derived no relaxation from his bath. His rancor at the slap was now forgotten. He pitied Alice. For if it were Caryl Kerby who had struck at Lucille Tarn in demoniacal jealousy, what would Caryl do to Alice? Alice, who was a smaller, fresher edition of the late movie star?

The Baron considered these people living in this house with him: Alice in danger if Caryl were a murderess; Kerby in danger if Blane were a murderer. And when he thought of these four people he now wished that he had not so quickly and firmly declared that Tarn could not be the intelligence behind the ticking noises. It would be so simple if Tarn were only responsible for the noises, for the deaths. But as the Baron made this admission to himself, his mind closed firmly on it like one of those steel traps his grandfather's gardener had employed against moles years before. No, said the Baron to himself; ach no! Tarn is not implicated. This matter, my dear Franz, you have decided once. You waste time and energy going over that empty trail. He opened the drain, and his revived speculations concerning Tarn vanished as did the swirling warm water down the pipe. . . .

When the dinner gong sounded, the Baron bethought himself of his preparations for the night.

Therefore, as if to smoke a cigarette before eating, he wandered casually into the garden, thence into the garage. On the work-bench he saw a package of tacks. These would be satisfactory. Helping himself to a handful, he thrust them into his pocket where he hoped the bulge would not be conspicuous.

That night at dinner, Mr. and Mrs. Henry I. Kerby and two of their three guests were singularly silent. Inasmuch as the Baron had succeeded in insulting all present except Mr. Kerby, you might have expected him to remain silent; at least to conduct his conversation with tact. But not the Baron. Only he was talkative. In fact, he enjoyed telling of the one hundred and twelve Englishmen he had killed that time in the fall of 1914 and had almost reached the climax when Blane pushed back his chair, apologized to his hostess, and left the room.

The Baron was disappointed. He felt as an actor would who watches one fifth of his audience walk out on him. "David," said Caryl, in the following quiet, "is an Englishman. Henry, give the Baron more wine."

From then on no one talked very much. After dinner, the Baron managed to see Kerby alone. He told Kerby to go to bed, to leave his door unlocked, and not to worry. If the ticking noises were there, the Baron would investigate. Kerby appeared relieved and worked on the script until ten.

Caryl retired to her room early.

When the Baron entered the living room, Alice quite haughtily departed, probably for *her* bedroom.

The Baron finished reading *Two Men on an Island* by eleven o'clock. He took the handful of tacks from his pocket and spread them on the floor of his bedroom, points up, in the space between his bed and the door. This completed, he switched off the light and went to bed to sleep until two in the morning.

He had placed his clothes on the chair between the bed and the window where no tacks had been strewn. He dressed quickly. There was nothing at all dangerous or particularly exciting in the process of climbing from the second story window to the flat roof. By standing on the window ledge, one hand grasping the thick vines for support, he could touch the roof. He pulled himself up as easily as an acrobat going over a bar.

Inasmuch as he had no one present to gasp and shudder at his daring, he flowed upwards like a fleet shadow and reached the tar and sand covered roof without any panting or other discernible demonstrations.

The moon was out, but still obscured at times by fleecy clouds, dense and blue on the fading drapes of night. He crawled to the brick chimney where he gazed across Carmel Bay, past that dark hump of Pescadero Point, until he could discern the scattered lights of Carmel. An automobile's headlights briefly swept the trees from Cabrillo Road and vanished. Clouds marched past the curved horn of the moon. In the stable behind the garden, the milk cow enquiringly mooed. It was one of those early mornings when even a cow should be stirred and long for other things.

Very carefully the Baron moved until he was above that portion of the L-shaped house occupied by Henry Kerby. Near the edge of the roof a tall plantain tree rustled brittlely and the Baron held his breath as if death itself were clambering onto the ledge.

Then he heard it.

And as soon as he heard it he knew it wasn't caused by a clock secreted in anyone's bedroom. It had a different, a harsher ticking. As the Baron crawled closer to the ledge of the roof he was aware of a more insistent, sinister beat to the ticking.

He peered over the ledge. Dimly he saw a round metal grill set into the attic, three or four feet below the flat roof. In order to examine the grill more closely, he swung out, then lowered himself by grasping the slippery branches of the plantain tree. When he descended a little below the metal grill, the ticking actually increased in volume; and, as he stepped on a branch only a foot or so from one of the wide open windows of Kerby's bedroom, he could hear very plainly the ratchet-like clicks, monotonous and deadly.

He leaned out toward the window. Inside Kerby was sleeping soundly. His enthusiastic snores left no doubt in the Baron's mind as to why Caryl had her own bedroom. Planning to explore the probable source of the ticking noises, he gripped the tree trunk to climb to the roof, but as his weight shifted the slim branch bent. For the next few instants neither the coldly metallic tickings nor Kerby's inspired trumpeting interested the brave Baron von Kaz.

To have matters more enjoyable, somewhere beyond and below was a splintering as if a gate had been broken, followed by a series of crashes. Then the Baron's hands slipped. The branch broke. The Baron hung head downward, left foot caught in a crotch of the tree. By a superhuman effort he restrained his indignation. He closed his mouth on a torrent of blasphemous adjectives directed at a fate which had crowned his misfortunes with this crushing disaster. Just as he managed to lock his hands around the tree trunk, from below ascended an interested, highly sympathetic moo-o-o.

It was Gertrude, the Kerby's Guernsey milk cow.

Gertrude contentedly swished her tail. She opened her mouth. She absorbed several flowers which had cost Caryl the price of a whole wagonload of milk, chewed with extravagant delight, lifted her head, mooed passionately and rubbed her sides on the tree. The tree jerked violently. The Baron lost his grip. As he fell down toward her, he had the illusion of the cow and the earth flying up to him. As the hard kicking object landed directly in front of her in the middle of the bushes, Gertrude let forth an unladylike bellow, decided that this region was no longer safe, and started for her stable.

"What the thundering hell is going on?" Kerby shoved his head through the window. Two hundred dollars worth of flowers separated Gertrude from her stable. But she was not a cow that respected the finer things in life. "Bill! Bill! Caryl!" Kerby withdrew shouting, "Caryl! Wake up. That blasted cow's ripping your garden to pieces."

Lights blazed in the second story of the garage. Lights flashed downstairs in the Kerby house. Kerby ran out, dressing gown floating behind him. The yawning chauffeur opened the garage door.

Coyly, Gertrude stopped at the end of the garden, thought perhaps she wouldn't go to bed after all, and lunged through a select stretch of hibiscus as Caryl emerged from the sun porch with a flashlight in her hand.

The porch light fell full upon her face. Hidden in the wet bushes, resting on hands and knees, the Baron waited until she fled into the garden, promising vengeance on a race of cows.

Undoubtedly it was Gertrude who saved the Baron. When she turned playful and Kerby started to swear in earnest, a whole army of Georgian princes fully equipped with shoes could have marched to the front of the house without attracting attention to say nothing of one highly circumspect Austrian Baron.

He climbed the copper spout to his room and with a huge sigh of relief started to undress. Naked, he stepped to his bed to get his pajamas. His bare foot came down upon a tack. He froze, stock still. No longer did the ticking noises disturb him. He believed he knew their cause.

But a tack between his bed and the window, when he had placed no tack there, could mean only one thing! Someone had entered his room after he had left. Someone who might still be in the room, waiting. . . .

9

The Deplorable Manners of the Brave Baron Von Kaz

Alice Rittenhouse heard the soft, insistent tapping at her door. She switched on the bed light as the tapping continued. "Who's there?" she whispered, and she heard a muffled reply; she thought it said "Henry," but she wasn't positive. Nevertheless, she took time before the dressing table to fluff her yellow hair, hastily dab powder on a pert little nose, and pat perfume behind both ears.

She unlocked the door, pushed it part way and when she saw the dark, sardonic face grinning at her she exclaimed haughtily, "What in Heaven's name do *you* want at this hour?" and she was going to say more, threaten to scream if necessary, but the Baron slipped inside before she realized it.

She tried to bite his hand when he clamped it over her mouth. She scratched at him. With his free arm he picked her up and while she offered a remarkable display of fancy barelegged kicking, unceremoniously dumped her on the bed. Here he said wickedly, "Ach, dear me!" and still holding his hand tightly pressed against her mouth, employed his other hand to arrange the peach crêpe de Chine night dress somewhat lower on her thighs. This courteous gesture produced another series of convulsive wiggles and kicks.

A portion of his thumb was between her teeth and she gnawed voraciously upon it. These American girls, he thought, were sheer hell-cats. Finally he managed to place his knee upon one arm, and slapped her lightly on the left cheek.

Her mouth opened in horrified amazement. That the man might be so enamored of her that he would wish to enter her room at night was something that Alice could understand; but that a gentleman could ever cruelly slap her, and in such an impersonal fashion, was so abnormal to her way of thinking that she stopped struggling. "If you will not scream, my dear Alice, I will henceforth keep my thumb far from those sharp teeth of yours."

She lay on the bed, her snug little breasts rising and falling from her exertions. He pointed to her legs, sprawled cater-cornered, "If you will permit me." And his lower lip thrust out, grinning at her all the time in the most malevolently good-natured fashion.

"My manners are deplorable." He sat on the bed and lifted her left foot as though he were a shoe clerk preparing to fit a young lady with shoes. When she attempted to wrench free her leg, "Quiet!" he ordered softly. She lifted up on her arms. Without releasing her foot he pushed her back on the pillow. She watched him examine the sole of her left foot. He repeated this procedure with her right.

Both soles were covered with tiny, bloody punctures. "So?" he asked genially.

She was utterly outraged. She thought she would try shrieking. But she looked at his face. She decided she'd better not, not right away at least.

He got up, crossing to the dressing table. Hastily, she pulled the covers over approximately three-quarters of her body. She raised, apprehensively watching him take the square bottle of perfume. He poured a drop into the palm of his hand. He sniffed it, nodding approvingly to himself before replacing the bottle.

Then he turned, waggled his finger at her. "Next time permit me to suggest less perfume when paying early morning calls. You had a von Kaz frightened until he sniffed that delectable fragrance in his room remaining after you departed."

"I don't know what you're talking about. If you don't get—"

"And also," he advised with implacable cheerfulness, "you should have worn shoes."

"I'll—I'll scream."

"As you wish."

"After all, Franz," she attempted a different tack, pouting a little, "if you take French leave by your window, you can't object if I try to find what it's all about, can you?"

He was startled. "You heard *me?*"

"I couldn't get to sleep and was looking out of the window at that insane ocean. How anyone can sleep in this house with the ocean always sloshing is beyond me. And I saw someone climbing out of your window."

No longer disturbed now that he had heard her explanation, he regarded her, tilting his head to one side. No one *ever* heard the Baron when the Baron decided to move quietly. In Austria they could have told you that. However, this wasn't Austria. Gott! he thought; if he were only there again where people did what an intelligent man could plan upon their doing. "And how did you come in my room?"

"With my door key. If you're so smart, you'd know that all the guest bedrooms have the same door key."

"So?"

Her fear had vanished. Accordingly, her anger mounted. She shook the hair from her eyes, twisted the bed lamp shade so that the light would rest upon her visitor. "I suppose," she asked tartly, "that Caryl expects you to come in my room every night now to make certain that—"

"Do not be an idiot, my dear Alice. Pardon—" He moved her feet to the other side of the bed so he could have room to sit down. "We must understand each other. . . ." He adjusted the lamp shade. He did not want to say too much. You could not tell with this little scatterbrain. If he frightened her she might let everything out and, as yet, he had no actual proof against anyone. And he did not wish to be awakened some morning in the near future with the information that Alice Rittenhouse was found dead with a hatpin thrust into her heart. So those blue eyes of his became candid and frank; his dark face grew solemn, it looked the face of an honest, friendly, and sincere man. "You must believe me, my dear Alice, when I swear to you that Mrs. Kerby has said nothing to me concerning—"

"Do I seem that dumb?" asked Alice, her head on the pillow, her yellow hair curling and framing her pretty and pert face. "Are you going to get out or not? Caryl's jealous. That's all. There isn't a damn thing she can be jealous about. If she wants to hire you or anybody else to keep an eye on me or Henry or the cook, that's fine, *I* don't care. My conscience is clear. Now you get out or I'll yell. And hand me a cigarette before you go because I'll never get to sleep now."

He offered her one from her own package on the night stand and then helped himself. "Try to listen to me," he said amiably, lighting the cigarettes. "You revealed your own secret this afternoon."

"*I* did?" Her eyes grew round. "That's not true!"

"Please do not be ridiculous. Was that not why you slapped me? And tonight? Did you not drop a tack where I would step on it?"

She pretended to laugh. "It was a joke—"

"A joke? So? I will tell you why you did it. *You wished the Baron von Kaz to discover that one living in this house knew he had departed from his room, no?*"

"Don't be silly. I simply did it for a—"

"Not so loud if you please. You placed the tack there for a good reason. You thought the brave Baron would be frightened by the knowledge that someone had learned that he had left the house; and so, perhaps you could frighten him and he would leave for good in the morning. That marches, hein?"

She lifted her head from the pillow. "If I tell the police, then what?"

"As you wish, my dear Alice."

"You were arrested once," she reminded him sharply. "If Mr. Watson was told you were ducking out at midnight, he might be interested."

She would tell the Police Chief, he realized, and that would be considerably more than annoying. He demanded bluntly, "You, who have an affair with Mr. Kerby? *You* will call the good Mr. Watson? You, who wish the Baron von Kaz away from this house because you are afraid that the Baron will tell—not Mrs. Kerby—but dear Mr. Blane, who appears to be rapidly falling in love with you. Is Mr. Blane wealthy? That is it?"

Her pretty mouth lost its bow-like shape as her upper teeth clenched into her lower lip.

He continued, "*You* will call the police? You, my lovely Alice, who had an excellent reason for wishing Mrs. Tarn dead? Ach no."

She jumped off the bed, forgetting that the lace top of her nightgown was not equipped with shutters.

"Your ticking noises were admirable to frighten a man of Mr. Kerby's temperament. No wonder the unfortunate man was ready to sever his friendship with poor Mrs. Tarn—"

"It's not true! I didn't cause the tickings. Caryl's doing it, and he won't believe me."

So the charming Alice Rittenhouse was thoroughly aware of the ticking noises, evidently knowing that they still were present. . . .

She caught sight of the amount of bare space revealed in the mirror, blushed nicely, and did something to the upper part of her gown which didn't help much. She snatched the blue quilt and draped it demurely over her shoulders. The Baron delighted in the changing expressions shading one into the other as they passed over the girl's face; anger, consternation, fright, and then sweetly forgiving. She extended her small firm hand. "After all, Franz, I wonder if we're not being just terribly silly?"

"Now that is better," he approved.

"Let's forget it?"

He bent, gravely touching the hand with his lips. "What if you did sneak out?" Wisely she shook the corn-yellow hair. "Heavens! A man like you *would* find a girl friend in Carmel. Who is she?"

And now she will be the shrewd little cat, wondered the Baron, and have me for the mouse? He dropped her hand as both turned when they heard a gentle knocking on the door.

"Hide!" she whispered. She whirled, pointing to the closet door.

A minute later the door was open.

Caryl Kerby was flushed and indignant. "I saw your light, Alice. I guess you heard that damned cow? Ruined my entire garden. Sorry the noise woke you. I thought you might be frightened—"

"Oh, was that it?" Alice yawned beautifully. "The cow."

"I can't think what's got into the beast. Henry sent me up here to see if I could rouse Dave or the Baron. The cow seems to have gone quite mad. We can't drive her back into the stable."

"Perhaps I could help?"

"No, you go back to bed, Alice," Caryl said firmly, "Sorry for the racket. Those men! The Baron won't answer and Dave's door's open. He isn't in his—"

Caryl's voice halted. For a moment she forgot her troubles with the cow and her garden. Looking past Alice, she saw the corner of a man's dressing gown jerking agonizedly from where it was caught in the crack of the closet door.

"Why, Alice," uttered Caryl. And then she did a surprising thing. She laughed softly. "I *have* been stupid, haven't I?"

"Caryl, you don't under—"

The wide scarlet mouth smiled. "Better than you think. I believe it will require at least fifteen minutes more before we manage to corral that infuriating cow," she said in a matter-of-fact voice.

Caryl hastened down the hall. For a young woman returning to protect a ruined garden, her thoughts were considerably detached from devastated flowers.

Alice kicked shut the door. Angrily, the Baron stepped from the closet, lifting his dressing gown. "Did she notice it?"

Alice slowly lit a cigarette. "What are you raving about?"

He took her by the shoulders. "You know what I am talking about. She did, no? Why did she say 'I have been stupid?' She thought it was the Englishman? Blane? Gott! You little imbecile."

He threw her on the bed. "Remain there. I return in ten minutes. If you—" He pointed to her from the doorway, "If you are not here, I shall strangle you." He repeated it, "S-strangle you!" hoping that this would be a sufficiently ferocious threat to hold her.

Then he darted off.

No, Blane wasn't in his room. The bed hadn't been slept in. Noiselessly, the Baron ran downstairs, found his way through the dark rooms into the kitchen. He opened the door, slipped quietly onto the back porch. He could see the cow lunging madly at the far end of the garden, now and then picked out in the light of sweeping flashlights.

Kerby was there. Kerby was shouting. He held a pitchfork in his hands. The gardener was near Kerby. As the chauffeur ran by the porch, the Baron shrank into the shadows. "Here, bossie. Here, bossie . . ."

"Don't call that blasted, triple-distilled hellion 'bossie'," cried Kerby. "Call her—" And then he expounded his idea of what she should be called. Caryl cried from close by the stable for the men to stop their chattering and to try to save what remained of the garden, thus terminating her husband's extemporaneous description.

The Baron counted the running figures; there were four of them. That accounted for Kerby, Caryl, the chauffeur, and the gardener. Blane wasn't there. The cook and one of the maids arrived at the door. The Baron vaulted over the porch railing, doubled around the house, found the front door locked, swore, and wasted a valuable minute swarming up the copper water spout into his own room.

He opened his door stealthily.

The hall was empty. He passed Alice's door and entered Blane's bedroom, closed the door, and turned on the lights. The man's baggage was unpacked. In the upper bureau drawer, under an ostrich-skin collar bag, he found a leather wallet. Inside he saw Blane's English passport. Feeling a stiff piece of cardboard behind it, he removed the passport.

It was a picture of Lucille Tarn, as she was three years ago. She was dressed in a Gainsborough costume with a wide picture hat jauntily posed on her head. She was looking at him, smiling. The picture, he decided, must have been taken a few months after she returned from her Austrian trip. He turned the picture over. On the back was:

"To Dave—
With all the love in the world,
from his Lucille."

He was about to reinsert the picture when he discovered two worn newspaper clippings folded away in one compartment of the wallet. He opened the first. It was a paragraph, an ordinary paragraph, one of those which fill many of the back pages of the Los Angeles newspapers. It stated that on October 3, 1933, Lucille Delay had appeared before Judge Wallace to receive her final decree from D. K. Blane, Solar Pictures' script writer. That was all. The Baron whistled soundlessly. He unfolded the other clipping. This was longer.

It was the account of the marriage between Lucille Delay, Solar Pictures' star, and Charles M. Tarn, prominent California lawyer, on November 18, 1933. There was a three-column picture of Lucille surrounded by well-known actresses, her bridesmaids.

Thinking that he had heard a noise, the Baron turned, his back to the bureau. It was nothing. The wind clattering the Venetian blinds. Rapidly he replaced the clippings, the picture, and the passport in the leather wallet, placed it underneath the ostrich-skin collar holder and shut the bureau drawer.

He had sent the invaluable Tivvits to Hollywood on a useless errand. The evidence for which the Baron had been searching was here, in this house. He glided across the room, glancing once more at the undisturbed bed, and switched off the lights. He would have liked to have entered Caryl's room but he did not wish to leave Alice too long without securing her mouth for the next day and the next.

Outside of Alice's bedroom he hesitated.

He shrugged, irritably snapped his fingers, entered. Then he stepped back against the door when he saw her emerge from the corner. There was a small gun in her hand.

"Get away from the door."

He obeyed, warily.

She was wearing her dressing gown, a golden mandarin coat, now. With her left hand she deliberately caught it at the collar and ripped it open down to her waist. "You think you know so much," she said. "Breaking into my room, attempting to attack me . . ."

"My dear Alice—" He smiled.

"Put your hands up."

He lifted them.

"It won't help to look around, either." She advanced, the gun in her right hand, close to her side, the muzzle aimed at him, dangerous and threatening.

"I'll tell them I shot in self-defense." Her lower lip trembled. He saw that she was dangerously close to crying.

"My dear child." He lowered his arms. "That would be the most foolish thing in the world. And I will tell you why."

"Keep them up." The gun wobbled and he could see the tendons tighten along her right arm as her finger gripped the trigger. "I will shoot, I really will." He watched her nervously. She was so near to hysterics that she might be just imbecilic enough to pull that trigger.

"As you wish." He sat down in the chair observing her in the mirror, his back to her. He could see her mouth move into a shapeless blur. She raised the gun so the muzzle was aimed at his head, closed her eyes tightly.

In that moment the Baron placed both feet against the dressing table and shoved hard. The gun gave a sound like a small paper bag being popped. When the chair went over, he fell upon his shoulders and completed a somersault. The mirror smashed into a thousand pieces.

He gained his feet, snatched at the quilt on the floor and, before she could recover, threw the quilt over her and leaped upon her and the quilt. As he sat on the struggling mass squirming underneath him, he wondered if the sound of the little gun popping had been heard in the garden. He lifted the quilt from the girl's face.

"Will you try to be sensible, my dear Alice?" he asked amiably and proceeded to enroll her in the quilt and took the gun, which had fallen from her hand to the floor and emptied it.

She made a weak sound and shut her eyes.

10
Red-Haired Wife

"Uhm," he muttered, feeling that somehow he had become entangled in a nightmare. When he callously tickled her foot, she did not move. He opened her left eye, reaching above him, twisting the bed lamp so that the light would shine directly into it. Alice showed no indications of returning to consciousness.

He went out, shutting the door and stepped to one of the hall windows overlooking the garden. The moon was now concealed by the fog blowing in from the Pacific. Faintly, through the thickening shreds of grayness, he could see several flashlights twisting weirdly toward the berserked cow.

"Here you triple-distilled monster!" came Kerby's furious voice. Then the Baron heard a crashing and Caryl called, "She's breaking into the greenhouse, Henry. Head off the crazy thing. Oh, damn!"

Caryl had tripped. Truculently, Gertrude the cow again mooed. She was in a fine fighting mood tonight. What with the fog, concluded the Baron, they would be fortunate indeed to coerce that cow into her stable within the next ten or twenty minutes.

Abruptly the Baron reached a decision.

That mad, crazy cow would occupy the attention of the Kerbys, he decided, long enough for him to examine

the Kerbys' bedrooms. Blane's disappearance increasingly worried him. If even now, Blane should be lurking in
the house, or about the house, waiting to take advantage
of the antics of this mad cow . . . Mad, crazy cow? Donnergott! He wheeled at once, running toward the Kerbys'
rooms. But the cow *was* crazy! There could be no other
explanation. It was the climate. This climate with its
superabundance of sunshine and alternating fog which
must be muddling his head; and, with a grunt of exasper-
ation, he slowed as he neared the corner of the hall where
it turned left.

He turned the knob of Kerby's door with extraordinary
caution. Inside, once the door was open wide, the blue
light from the hall touched the polished wood of the huge,
four-poster Italian bed, streaking it with a murky shine
as though a phosphorescent match had been struck upon
the surface. Through the windows came the intermittent
shouts from the garden and more cries and invectives when
another hothouse pane of glass was shattered.

There were two closets in the room. He stood flat
against the wall, unlatched the door at his right, kicked it
open with his foot. He repeated this procedure with the
second closet. Blane was not in there, waiting, hiding . . .

Not until he was close by the bed could he hear the
ticking. Even here the ticks came softly, almost imperceptibly. They were tiny, regular clickings, very like those of
a metronome, but infinitely more faint. He could imagine
them coming through the night with the cutting force of a
rusty razor blade being drawn along a man's skin, pressing
deeper each time.

Outside Kerby's bedroom when he had been cramped so
lovingly around the fickle plantain tree, these tickings had
been more distinct. He placed his ear to the plaster walls,
going around the room in this uncomfortable manner. The
noises receded as he drew away from the bed and they did

not come from within the walls. He opened drawers in the bureau and the table, hoping to find a hidden watch or clock, some device, *something,* which could cause the noises but was unsuccessful. On his knees he crawled under the huge bed. Nothing. He realized that he was losing time.

He sat on the edge of the bed with the noises seeping into his ears. He jumped upon the bed, tried to reach the ceiling. He bounced across the bed to one of the sturdy mahogany posts, shook it, and then pulled himself upwards on it in the manner of a man climbing a greased pole for the five dollar prize. If Gertrude the cow should fail him now, he thought grimly, and permit herself to be captured and someone other than Mr. Kerby should return to see a guest in this position . . . The Baron did not continue the disagreeable thought.

Perched precariously on the quivering bedpost, he lifted his head and managed to touch the ceiling with his right ear. The ticking noises were louder. Then a peculiar expression appeared upon his face. He sighed, very puzzled; and, listening intently, wondered if it could be his imagination. But no. He heard a second sound!

At longer spaced intervals there came a creaking over his head as if there were someone who slowly and cautiously creeped from rafter to rafter, not wishing to be discovered. This did not make sense. But again it came, the heavy, pressing creak.

The Baron bounced back onto the bed, then struck the floor. He closed Kerby's bedroom door and again reached the head of the stairs. During his stay at odd, discreet moments he had explored the house. For one thing, he had learned that this house, in common with many other Spanish-California homes, had a space four or five feet in height between the second story and the flat roof. Secondly, he had already ascertained from Maggy, who thought this guest dafter than most of Mr. Kerby's foreign friends, that the only entrance to this space was through a small trapdoor in the hall linen closet opposite the stairway, just across from the bedroom occupied by Blane.

The Baron sidled through the linen closet door. As a matter of prudence, he closed it, finding himself in a place absolutely without light. In front of him he knew were shelves piled high with linen and spare bedding. He remained where he was for only a second, regretting that he did not have his green umbrella with him and not and not daring to waste more time by going into his bedroom for it. Standing on tiptoe, he could not touch the high-ceiling. He felt for the shelves. Where you might have expected sheets and blankets to be piled neatly and in order, by rapidly passing his fingers over this assortment, he found that they were rumpled, in disorder. More than ever he wished that he had his green umbrella with him as he stepped upon the first shelf, the second, and then the third.

Above him he felt the crevices of the trapdoor leading into the attic. Slowly he pushed upwards, lifting the trapdoor inch by inch, and as he peered through the widening crack he saw a flickering light at the far end of the attic as though a match had been struck and quickly extinguished.

The Baron was trained in silence. Night and darkness were his allies. But as he gently eased himself up through the opening, so slowly that the sweat dampened his forehead from the strain on his shoulder and arm muscles, he devoutly wished for that extravagant California sunlight. If he could have had his way, he would have brought the sun itself into that attic.

The Baron was a brave man. Yet his imagination even surpassed his bravery.

Constantly this imagination impinged upon his bravery. The two incongruous elements pulled and tugged at one another and sometimes when his bravery was overwhelmed by the specters brought forth by that imagination, then he had nothing to rely upon except pride. And when pride alone carries you forward into a dark attic, it has all that it can do when oppressed by an unhaltered imagination stimulated by a soft, deadly tick-tick-tick which seems ever to gain in volume.

The Baron swung his head from side to side. Up here under the roof the smells were sourish and musty, of plaster never thoroughly dried, of wood, of decayed bits of refuse. . . . Once, his hand pressed onto a nail protruding from one of the joists and he had to clamp his mouth shut as he withdrew his hand.

Doggedly he continued forward toward that source of the ticking noises which he thought to lie ahead of him.

Irrationally, because he was afraid, his anger grew steadily. Ave Maria! If whosoever were there waiting for him in that black silence, punctuated only by the soft tickings, would only once be careless and make a little movement, only a fraction of a movement!

But the silence extended and stretched, only broken by that monotonous tick-tick-tick which appeared now to be all around the Baron, intangible, uttering its cloaked and subtle threat of danger. . . .

Halfway across the beamed attic the Baron again stopped. What if this ticking jeopardy should have tricked him, should have circled toward the trapdoor? That thought filled him with such rage that he gripped one of the long beams running the width of the floor and felt the pain come stronger into his pierced hand. He would shout for help. He actually turned, planning to go back. But that infernal pride of his interfered. *He* shout for help? The brave Baron ask for assistance? Permit Mr. Kerby, or Mrs. Kerby, or maybe Alice Rittenhouse, to believe that he had been frightened? Ah no! That would never do. The Baron was a brave man, a very brave man.

In his ears the tickings grew sharper, more definite. Now they were harsh, imperative in their deadly warning. Tick . . . tick . . . tick . . . so it came to him . . . stay . . . away . . . do . . . not . . . come . . . closer . . . He lifted his head, trying to pierce the blackness and emptiness of space surrounding him. Nothing tangible. Now the ticking noises seemed to have swerved; their source was plainly at his right. There was no sense to this, he reasoned. A noise should be stationary. But the noises ostensibly retreated as if there were a singular intelligence directing them and leading him always away from the safety of the trapdoor.

He twisted his head sideways. True, the noises move, argued the Baron to himself. However, such a fact is logically impossible.

My dear Baron, he concluded: If a noise is provided with a means of locomotion then it can move. That also is logic. You are becoming stupid. Engrossed in this majestic piece of deduction, he forgot to advance with due diligence, was thus surprised when his head bumped a sloping rafter at the end of the house.

He had traversed the length of the attic corresponding to the lower angle of the hitherto-before-mentioned L, which was so useful in describing the plan of the house.

And, as he rubbed his head, squatting dolefully, he became aware of a frightful fact: The ticking noises slowly were receding! They were, as he faced the trapdoor now in front of him. They were going toward the trapdoor. The one way of entrance and exit.

He laid himself flat on the plastered floor. He extracted his cigarette lighter. He lifted his arm high in the air, clicked the cigarette lighter, and as the wick caught the spark he waited for the shot to be fired at him as his position was revealed. He hoped that the gun would be aimed instinctively at the glow of light and not a few feet lower as he would do should the situation be reversed. No shot followed.

Like spreading ripples from a pebble dropped into a dank mill pond, the feeble glare spun outwards, striking the heavy rafters, advancing into the gloom.

And near the trapdoor, the Baron perceived a crouching figure lurch as the glimmer filled the attic. The Baron's arm drew back, swung forward. The cigarette lighter left his fingers. An arc of light streaked half the length of the attic. It struck the lurching figure desperately tugging at the trapdoor, sputtered, went out. Dense blackness once more rushed about the Baron with a kind of fury as if the spurt of light had angered the very elements. There was no time for caution after throwing the lighter.

The Baron sprang forward.

The person had raised the trapdoor when the Baron stumbled across a beam, falling heavily.

The person had started to climb down into the linen closet and then stopped. Slowly the person again ascended, approached the Baron, who was lying across the beam, with his head upon another.

The blackness pressed into the Baron's head as if it had grown thicker and when he dazedly shook his head, not believing that such a monstrous thing could have befallen to him, the blackness glowed with prickling lights which blinded. It pierced his head as though by sharp irons. The person considered the Baron, finally risked lighting a match. The Baron's forehead was covered with blood. The Baron half-raised as the match was struck, and a shadow leaned over him, and then he was hit on the temple. His head sagged and dropped to the wooden beam.

The tickings remained close to the Baron, and loud now, as those eyes contemptuously looked down upon him. The noises receded. Feet felt their way through the trapdoor until only a head remained projecting into the attic.

The Baron moved.

Astounded, the other was aware that the Baron again was trying to lift himself. When you hit a man on the temple who is already half unconscious, you don't expect him to attempt to get up. You expect him to lie there, decently, and not move.

The Baron's jaw hung forward. He lifted his head and his shoulders, pushing hard on the floor with his hands as a man weighted with lead. But all the lead in the world, all the blows in Austria and in Carmel, could not extinguish the pride of the Baron Franz Maximilian Karagôz von Kaz, owner of the Order of the Iron Cross, owner of the Order of Leopold, and he reached his knees. He reached his knees and penetrating the blur of darkness and pain, stretched out his two hands. He was groping feebly. He was groping for that enemy. The ticking noises thundered now. He could hear them battering and swirling through that enveloping haze which buffeted him.

And when he was struck for the second time, and when his bloody face was on the plaster, still his arms moved, ineffectually pushing upwards, obeying a will that remained long after all reason and consciousness had been lost.

Eyes looked down upon him, a hand holding a second match. . . .

On that morning the sun broke through the fog after eight. By half past eight it was warm. The heat came in through a window screened by heavy wire. The bright rays fell on a man's face and the man turned irritably from side to side, and, as he turned, something bulky seemed to encumber his head.

With an effort, he disengaged his right hand, drawing it slowly to his forehead where his fingers encountered what appeared to be bandages. He opened his eyes. They were open for a long time before he fully realized that the splotched grayness at which he was staring was the ceiling. He was lying on his back. When he brought his head forward to his chest, an intolerable ache swelled into his temples. Stubbornly, he maintained his head against his chest. The ache gradually lessened. He sighted across an undulating expanse of deep purple and the intolerable ache returned with renewed vigor.

The wave of pain passed. Again he opened his eyes. At the end of this horrendous purple sea were two dark poles. One pole had a round ball upon it. The other held a denuded spike. He centered his attention upon the spike. Hanging from the spike was a curiously familiar object, bulky and green. He focused upon this green.

Gradually he recognized that the green object was an umbrella. That was comforting. Beyond the umbrella, cracked walls of a room formed and upon a small table was a dilapidated pigskin suitcase and he stared at his umbrella and at his suitcase as though they were things definite and concrete upon which his mind could function.

This took time. Minutes added into half an hour.

Still, without moving his head, his eyes retraced their path across the undulating purple sea. He tried moving his feet. At the far end of the sea he perceived a wave creating a response to the movement of his toes. Thus did he determine that he was in a bed.

Because the ache in his head was recurring he shut his eyes. He tried to think. He had been in Mr. Kerby's attic. A figure was at the trapdoor. That much he could remember. This effort of recalling the near past was not quite so painful as was the involved process of moving his head. There was no purple quilt on his bed in the Kerby house. Of that he was certain. He advanced further in his conjectures. The walls of his bedroom, he believed, were covered with paper of an unobtrusive floral design.

Cautiously he risked opening one eye. Ach du lieber Augustin! this cannot be, he thought, appalled. These walls, apparently, had never been covered by anything more permanent than whitewash. At the left of the table was a door. He arduously turned his head toward the right. Through the window he could see nothing but the sheer rise of a mountain, and above the mountain the eternally blue California sky, and that was all.

Near him something stirred.

The Baron wasn't interested. Where was he? he thought dully. Why was he here? What had happened to his client? When for the second time, he felt the stirring of some other object on the bed, he rolled his head to the left. At once he wished he had never looked. On the pillow next to his was a quantity of curling red hair. Only was the hair exposed. Whatever the hair was attached to was covered by the poisonous purple quilt. The Baron took a quick, startled breath,

He did exactly what anyone else would have done under similar circumstances. His sole idea was to get away as far as was humanly possible from this curling red hair with no visible appendage. This silky red hair massed upon the pillow was unnatural. It was bad enough to awake to a room in which never before had he been, to lie in a bed which obviously was not his own. A mighty wave of nausea drenched upon him as he sighted the red hair upon the pillow.

As soon as he attempted to move his body, his own head sadly betrayed him. The walls of the room curved inwards as though they were constructed of flexible material. The bright sunshine dimmed. Unwillingly he sank back. He touched an object close to him which was warm and yielding. He groaned. Disregarding his dizziness, he tugged at the purple quilt, trying to throw it off his legs.

A not unpleasant voice halted this worthy endeavor. "For Heaven's sake, darling, can't you be a little more quiet?" The voice was muffled by the quilt but perfectly understandable.

"Hein?" shouted the Baron, dropping the quilt.

From somewhere a bare arm materialized. It was a nice arm, long, freckled. Sturdy fingers lowered the quilt. A head was uncovered. It was a head that, in other environs, in other conditions, the Baron might have willingly glanced at more than once. The face was wide, the nose was a little too broad, but the lips were practically perfect. They appeared, however, at a disadvantage. There was too much rouge on them. Much can be said for the Baron's training and perception that in his condition he noticed this single fact which would eventually give meaning to his inchoate surroundings.

Sleepily the girl rubbed her eyes. "You might at least kiss me, darling. It's morning, isn't it?"

"Kiss you?" Not in years had the Baron stammered over such a question.

"Naturally, darling. Don't you want to?" She raised her head.

A man came into the room without knocking. He was lank, unshaven. He stopped for a moment when he saw that the Baron was sitting up. Then he shouted cheerfully, "Feelin' better, Baron? 'Mornin', Sally."

"For Heaven's sake, uncle," Sally complained, "you might let us get our sleep."

"What both of you two love-birds need is ham and eggs." The man laughed harshly. "What did you say, Baron?"

The Baron stared at the man, then at the red-haired girl by his side in the same bed.

He didn't say anything.

11

The Green Umbrella

The brave Baron von Kaz was a vain man. Seven or eight hours after he had awakened to find himself theoretically bedded with a red-haired girl, the infernal gyrations inside his head slowed down. And thus, as he began to contemplate matters with something approaching normal lucidity he bethought himself of his probable appearance. Exploring his cheeks with the palm of his right hand—he found the left well bandaged and had no difficulty in recalling the incident of the nail—he was desolated to discover that he was in dire need of a shave.

This fact furnished him with an idea. He recollected when last he had shaved. It was Wednesday, the day following Lucille Tarn's death. More carefully did he the second time feel the thick stubble on his chin and cheeks. A good two days' growth. Today, then, triumphantly he surmised, must be Friday. It was on this day he remembered Alice had said that Lucille Tarn was to be buried.

Fearful that he might overstrain the great von Kaz brain before its brilliant faculties were fully restored by healing rest, he went to sleep, awakening, strangely, just in time to eat supper served to him by the red-haired girl, now presentably dressed. He ate, finding that he was famished, and actually enjoyed a meal concocted from canned ingredients. When he was nearly through the lank man

entered suspiciously, saw that red-haired Sally was deco-
rously perched upon the table waiting for their guest to
complete the meal. She had been most helpful in view of
the Baron's injured hand. The lank man lit an odoriferous
pipe, ran his fingers down Sally's arm with a sly gesture,
spoke at great length and cheerfully of the marriage between his niece and the Baron. When his pipe had burned
low, he said he guessed he'd drop in to town, hustled Sally
out of the room and the Baron heard him lock the door.

The yellow moon steered its course across the sky, covering the mountain side with a somnolent sheen. After
some hours the Baron heard a car grinding up a road, dogs
barked furiously, and a man shouted, "Git down there,
Runt. D'you hear Runt?" and a door squeaked and Sally
said, "'Bout time you were getting home." After desultory
conversation, the man looked in the bedroom, holding a
lamp above his eyes. The Baron pretended to be sleeping.
"Leave him be, Herb," said the girl. "That crack on his
head's still bothering him." The door closed softly.

After thirty minutes or so the Baron reopened his eyes.
Through the window the deceptive radiance from the yellow moon filled the room. He heard a hoot-owl and one of
the dogs barked crossly and then was still. The wood floor
was cold under his bare feet and as he walked to the table,
the floor seemed to undulate and when he had attained the
table he had to grasp the edges to hold on. Shadows danced
in the room. The cold yellow shine through the window
sharpened the shadows providing an unreal quality to the
interior. He fumbled with the bronze clasps of the pigskin
bag. The hoot-owl swept back through the night and rushing wings rustled at the window and beat upwards again.

Every minute was an age. He found the pants to his old
suit crumpled into the top of the suitcase. He got them
on, grasping the table for support. The shadows in the

corners of the room were small and black and when he moved they followed him, creeping from their corners, sprawling across the yellow moonlight. All that he could remember now was that he had to escape; that somewhere, some place, a man was in danger of death and that only he could save that man. Slowly and cunningly he raised the window, his face working with the exertion. The wind rolled down the mountain and struck him cool on the chest and before him, on the slope of the mountain, the tall pine trees waved and he could feel the surge and ebb of the house as it strained and would go to the trees.

His hand conflicted with the screen tacked over the window. With infinite care he thrust at the wire netting, but it would not give and the moon peered at him, yellow and bright and so far away, and he shook his hand at it, clenching his bloody fingers into his palm. Somewhere was a man sleeping and somewhere was death approaching this man. And where was the Baron von Kaz? The brave Baron von Kaz who was so great and so sure of himself, and who would cheat death from its third victim?

He returned to the window. In his hand he held the thief's tool, the one he had replaced in the side pocket of his bag in his room at the Kerby house. Whoever had removed him from the Kerby house had been in a hurry, dumping his clothes into the bag without wasting time by examining the previous contents. Skillfully he pried the nails from the wire, using the fingers of his left hand as little as he could. The sweat stuck to his forehead. He slipped out of the wire netting, unmindful of the scratches on his shoulders and, for a moment, supported himself by the clapboard side of the small house. Near him a great shape growled menacingly. The dog lunged, was brought up sharply by the chain. A second growl followed, with more intimidation.

The second dog was smaller. It did not lunge. Quietly it rose, paddled the full length of the chain to sniff inquiringly. The Baron pushed himself away from the house, ran feebly toward the beckoning pine trees, but he ran as if he were partaking in a hideous dream. All his energy went into the process of running but his feet moved with dreadful slowness. The yellow moon was over him, indifferent, shining down upon him, and the grade grew steeper. Even the wind pushed at his naked chest and he panted, his head low, his arms close to his ribs. Once before he had run like this, but then it was toward a flag that he wanted and tall demons had leaped from the shell hole and pulled him in. Now he was alone. And instead of one flag there were a hundred dark flags ahead waving from the pine trees. . . .

He fell and got up, and fell again. Behind him the dogs were straining at their chains and their high, nervous yelps filled him with panic. He tottered drunkenly, the yellow moon drenching him, and a girl stood before him. Her hair was red under the light of the moon and a coat was around her shoulders. "You poor fool," she said, half compassionately.

"Let me go."

She had his arm was guiding him away from the pine trees. "Herb—uncle'd kill you if he wasn't so drunk he could sleep through an earthquake."

He leaned beside the house and watched her quiet the dogs. She stooped and picked up the shiny thief's tool. "Pliers? Why Baron. Where'd you get it?"

"Let me go, if you please. I am not married to you."

"Married? Why of course you are, darling. Don't be silly. Have you forgotten?"

He shook his head, wearily closing his eyes against the cold yellow light of the moon.

"Can you climb in the window?"

Desperately he tried to break away and he did, but had only advanced a few yards out into that golden circle of moonlight before the earth and the ground and the mountain spread apart to trick his feet and he would have fallen if a strong arm had not caught him. "You'll catch your death of cold. Come on." She was urging him as if he were a child. "You'll have to go through the window. Can't risk having you wake up uncle. Hush, Runt!" The huge dog put its head between its paws and growled.

Somehow he got through the window and she followed him and then he was in bed doing as she told him to do. "Take them off." And he did, kicking his feet weakly, rolling over, and pushing the pants from under the covers. She dropped them into the suitcase. "How do you feel?" She was worried. "Better go to sleep. And don't try any stunts through the window again," she warned seriously. "You'll get shot."

"I assure you . . . I did not . . . marry . . ."

"There. Go to sleep now. You married me all right," she whispered in such a soothing, convincing tone that even as he closed his eyes and slipped into a deep, dark chasm he could hear those words over and over again impressing themselves upon his memory:

"You married me, Baron. Married me. Me. Sally. You married me . . ."

The next morning, Saturday, he was dimly aware that very early he was aroused by the girl pounding outside his window and then he went back to that fitful sleep, feverish and terrifying, and did not awaken until in the afternoon.

Sally brought him food and was relieved when she saw that he looked better; his eyes were clearer. He sat up in bed to eat the heated canned meat and to drink an entire quart of milk. The fuzzy burning in his head had departed.

Only the dull ache remained. He was married to this girl? *Married to her?* "You've got bigger shoulders than I realized for a man of your size," she informed him admiringly, scrutinizing him as he was propped up with the pillows. He had the purple quilt under his armpits. "They're like a wrestler's I once knew if you had more weight on you." His head inclined ironically. He had nothing to say.

All during the rest of the afternoon he relaxed in bed, waiting for his body to recuperate, wondering, pondering. Several times the lank man looked in, his face bloated by the contents of too many bottles emptied the night previous, and each time the Baron closed his eyes, simulating sleep.

Only one person could have attacked him in the attic. And that person was Blane, the Baron decided. Kerby, Caryl, the servants, were in the garden. Blane had wanted to go into the attic. That was it. It was as though the Baron had spent all the time until now collecting pieces of a jigsaw puzzle.

Constantly, as his mind ferreted into the dark grooves of the case, he would touch the shadowy figure of Tarn, the one person outside the house who could claim the Baron's attention. But the Baron was an obstinate man. He recognized that Tarn was jealous of Kerby. He knew that Tarn had reason to hate Lucille, had known "Dude", and was as familiar with the construction of the jail as anyone in Carmel. Tarn could possibly have bribed one of the three or four house servants in the Kerby residence or the gardener or the chauffeur to creep into the attic late at night and start the metronome which was gradually to drive Kerby frantic.

The Baron was too astute not to admit these points against Tarn. But as has been suggested before, the Baron was not only obstinate but often too proud for his own good. He had obtained the case by stating most flatly that

Tarn was not guilty of the ticking noises. And his puzzle would be completely disrupted if the mind that thought of the ticking noises was not the identical mind that planned and accomplished the murders. His reasons were substantially those he had given to Kerby: Tarn was a politician. Tarn's whole interest lay in his career. Tarn would not jeopardize his career by committing murder. And even if Tarn were willing to jeopardize his career, the crimes, as they had been executed, were far too subtle to have been conceived by the brain of a politician.

And possessing the majority of those jig-saw puzzle pieces in his mind, already he could sort out enough of them, as it were, work them together into a corner of that picture which would represent the activities of Blane. He considered each member in the house, catalogued their tangled jealousies, their fears, what hatreds and ambitions they had which would be of such nature to push them even unto murder. In that long afternoon, for the first time he had the opportunity to study the Tarn case from a distance.

Thus, as the afternoon came to a close, the Baron most complacently believed that he had satisfactorily eliminated Tarn. With Tarn eliminated, the pieces of the puzzle took form and the Baron was convinced that he had the solution. That he could give the name of the murderer of Lucille Tarn and "Dude" McKay.

Only one shadow of doubt was left in his mind. There was a fearful possibility that in the few missing pieces or facts, another person, or motive, might be hidden which could radically change the entire picture.

Sternly he told himself that this was an utter impossibility. Impatiently he refused to give rein to his imagination, his thoughts reverting to himself. Last night's exertions had served to stimulate him, to clear his brain of the lingering fog, or so he thought, and now he wondered why he was lying here in bed, permitting these two people to hold him as though he were a frightened imbecile.

Ach, hold the Baron von Kaz? Few prisons were built that could hold him. He had been a dolt to attempt to rush out of the house the night before. That was no way for a von Kaz to escape. First let him learn all he could from these people and then outwit them. Were they more clever, wiser than he was? And so confidence returned, joining with his anger at the treatment to his person.

Sally and the lank man entered the room to remove the oil lamp and lock the Baron in for the night. The lank man was preparing to turn low the lamp wick when he was surprised to hear the Baron ask, "And so? I am married?"

The lank man turned from the lamp to exchange a sly glance with the girl.

"Sure, you two are married," blustered the man. "Feelin' so you'd like to talk are you? Well, let me tell you this then; don't think you can escape with no clothes on, Baron. You'll freeze before you get a mile away up in this altitude. And we got your clothes in the other room so you won't get 'em and besides, I'm sleepin' in the next room with this." He lifted his coat, revealing a heavy forty-five strapped around his waist.

And as the Baron made no reply, his blue eyes coldly, reflectively regarding the man:

"Yes, sir. You married Sally here. You said you was a Baron and you was goin' to make her a Baroness. You stopped by here last week sayin' you'd been huntin' and when you got a few drinks in you I never saw a man make such vi'lent love to a girl. That right, Sally?"

Sally giggled, withdrawing to the door.

"Yes, sir, Baron. I told her you was foolin', but you had to have your way and you two was married by that Italian preacher down the hill, and lookin' bold and pretty to please yourselves, and you drinkin' all my corn and tellin'

Sally here what a fine lady she'd be. Now, if you're thinkin'
to change your mind, Baron, why you're mistaken. It'll
cost you money."

Wild stratagems wheeled in the Baron's head, only
again to be interrupted by the monologue conducted by
the lank person. "And what are you goin' to do?"

The lank man lifted the lamp. "Won't talk? All right.
That's okay with me, Baron. I got plenty of time. Come
on, Sally. Well let him figure for himself another night
and then tomorrow maybe he'll talk. Come on, Baroness!"

Superiorly the red-haired girl flung open the door; she
halted at the Baron's "Wait!"

This word was followed by a disgustingly lascivious
smile. He nodded, signaling for the man to leave the room
with the explanation, "Tonight my dear wife stays here."

"Why you—"

The man flushed with anger. He tore at the gun strapped
to his waist. Disgorging a little squeak, the girl grabbed
for the weapon and the lamp in the man's hand sent whirling shadows shifting about the room. The Baron leered,
hugely pleased by his histrionics. The girl thought he was
smiling at her. Fluently she swore, giving the Baron to
understand that she had thought he was a gentleman. Her
disillusionment impressed the lank man. He pushed the
girl out of the room, ordering her to keep *her* mouth shut,
and slammed the door.

Through the wood the Baron could hear tumultuous
invectives. The moonlight outlined the green umbrella
hanging on the poster. He reached forward, took it by the
handle. Then he adjusted the pillow behind his head so he
could rest comfortably sitting up. This done, he winked
fondly at the umbrella as though it were something more
than an inanimate object and waited, and while he waited,
his active mind reviewed and considered the facts he had
learned during the past few days.

From the conversation with the girl, plus the rouged lips he had noticed the morning he had returned to consciousness, the Baron held that he had indisputable evidence that he was still a bachelor, and that he was the victim of a hoax.

In the first place, he felt positive that even in these barbaric Northern States of America no woman who thought enough of her appearance to employ powder and rouge would bed herself for the night without cleansing her face and lips. That the red-headed girl *had* rouged her lips, and recently, would indicate strongly that she had not remained by the side of the Baron for the night but had climbed in during the morning hours, after she had awakened, after she had dressed, after she had noticed that the Baron gave indications of reviving. And in the second place, the Baron decided that the man's jealousy would suggest he had more intimate claims upon the girl's company than that of an uncle for a niece.

Having had no mathematical training whatsoever to destroy his confidence, the Baron privately considered himself as a miracle of logical deductions. He mistrusted his faculty, so often found in poets and those of Bohemian ancestry, of leaping far ahead in brilliant intuitive flashes. Accordingly he felt it necessary to follow up these lightning like flashes with a solid and almost always useless groundwork of argumentation. He was involved in the process of arguing out his convictions when he heard the door creak. His head lifted. For a moment he intently regarded the door, and then his head sunk again as though he were half asleep. The door was flung open. The lank man entered, placing the lamp on the table and declaring, "What you need is a good beatin', Baron, to unroll your tongue."

He put the key beside the lamp, turned unhurriedly, and when he saw the bulky green umbrella lying on the covers between the Baron's legs, he stopped, "Think it's goin' to rain?"

The man reached down to remove the umbrella, "What I want is a thousand dollars and quick if you're ever goin' to—"

The lank man never finished it.

The green umbrella had opened with a soft whirring crash and the man jumped back, reaching for his revolver.

The Baron threw the bulky umbrella at the man. The huge, round, green expanse wobbled into the air, confusing the man more than frightening him. He struck at the heavy green fabric with his gun and as the umbrella momentarily obscured his vision, the Baron slid off the bed and in his right hand was a thin blade of steel, three feet long, sharp as a razor, which had been hidden in the umbrella stick.

The lank man whirled, his gun lifted.

The steel passed through the right shoulder like a red hot pin through butter. The man's right hand spasmodically jerked. His whole arm and hand went numb and the gun dropped to the floor. The Baron's flat hand slapped him on the shoulder, spun him around. He began shrieking when the Baron withdrew; the steel, now crimson under the lamp light. The girl was frantically pounding on the door, "Herb! What's the matter? Herb!"

The man's right arm swung limply as he went for the Baron. The Baron moved agilely to one side, tripped him. The man plumped face down on the floor, tried to get up, felt a warning prick at the base of his neck. He didn't move after that. The Baron reached for the green umbrella and closed it. He eyed the man once, listening to the girl outside the door. He took time to wipe the blade on the covers before shoving it into the umbrella stick. Then he grasped the umbrella by the other end, brought the weighted handle down on the man's skull. The lank man groaned and was silent.

The Baron stooped for the gun, grabbed the key, unlocked the door, opened it, pushing the girl aside. The sight of this naked, panting demon grinning down at her was paralyzing. She cried out. He tossed the gun toward the far end of the room, kicking shut the door with his bare foot. She attempted to go for the gun. He pushed her and held her securely in a chair. "My dear Baroness—" he could not resist saying.

"I'm not your wife, you fool! Herb! What have you done to Herb?"

"Your dear uncle?"

"He's not my uncle—"

"Ach so. In two or three minutes he will bleed to death. It is such a pity."

The red-haired girl clawed at the Baron, covering his hard arms with scratches. "You smirking fool! Let me in there!"

"Do you wish him to bleed to death?"

She began to cry, to weep, and to kick at the Baron. Ruthlessly he demanded, "Who brought me here, if you please?"

"Mr. Blane," she admitted, sniffling, casting terrorized glances at the closed door. "Now let me get my husband—"

"And where am I, please?"

"Sur Chiquita. Oh, God, let me go to Herb."

"Sur Chiquita? Ach so. And where is that?"

In desperation she tore free from his grasp as she heard her husband groan weakly. The Baron barred her way. "Where, my dear lady?"

"Twenty miles from Carmel." She hit at him. He caught her wrists, the pain in his left palm now negligible. "We didn't mean anything. Mr. Blane said to hold you for two weeks. I'll give you the money. He paid us two hundred dollars. When we found you were a Baron we thought it'd be a joke to say you were married to me."

He regarded her steadily. "That marches better, dear Sally. You wish to save your husband? Quiet then. Raise your head. Close your eyes."

His voice was so dominating that dumbly she obeyed. Just below the ear he struck her, catching her before she could fall to the floor. He laid her gently on the rug near the kitchen table, without the slightest conception of having done that which was clearly against all the established rules of gallantry. He required an hour of freedom to escape from this house. It was quicker, more satisfactory in every respect to deal with the girl efficiently than to take the time to tie her up.

He thrust open the door of the bedroom, looked at the bleeding man on the floor. He tore several long strips of sheeting, spent four minutes tying a tourniquet above the clean wound. He let the man's head thump onto the floor, took his suitcase and the purple quilt and returned to the other room. It was cold in this house. He knelt, covered the girl with the purple quilt. Then he found his suit on the floor of the closet; it was the suit he had worn when Blane had brought him to Sur Chiquita.

Taking clean linen from his suitcase, he dressed, and started for the front door with the pigskin bag swinging from one hand, the green umbrella hooked over his other arm. One of the dogs growled menacingly. He shrugged, climbed out the back window, circled the house. He found a downward path cut in the mountain side which led to a dirt road. The girl, he knew from past experience in such matters, would recover in an hour or so; in ample time for her to take care of her man and get him to a doctor. The Baron didn't think that the pair would bother him. They were too involved to lay any complaint to the authorities.

The moon was high and yellow. The Baron grasped the handle of his green umbrella, swung the umbrella cheerfully, as he walked with springy steps through the night.

12

Raspberry Popping

Seven o'clock Sunday morning old man Pringle, as had been his custom for the past three years, left his daughter's ranch on the west side of Sur Chiquita, drove four miles until he reached the graded road at the foot of the mountain. Here at the crossroad was a small store, dried gray by the California sun. Old man Pringle parked his model T Ford in the rear under a tin roof projecting from the store, lifted out a pile of Sunday papers for which he had driven into Monterey Saturday night, made sure he hadn't left his pipe in the seat, and walked through the dust to the front of his store.

He first unlocked the single oil pump. Toward noon the folks from Carmel and Monterey would be driving this way and often they ran out of gasoline. Inasmuch as old man Pringle charged three cents more per gallon than was obtained in Carmel, twelve miles distant, often he gained as much from the Sunday tourists as he did during two or three weekdays selling supplies to the ranchers and "Portygee" farmers who lived in the neighborhood.

He unlocked the door of his store. From seven to nine o'clock in the morning, or thereabouts, were his hours of absolute freedom. His daughter, Marge, couldn't complain if he filled the room with tobacco smoke. He wasn't apt to be troubled by customers until the sun would lift above the dome of the mountain which he could see from out the door by raising his head from the newspaper. He cleaned his pipe. He selected a new package of tobacco from his shelves, pulled up the comfortable cane-bottomed chair and prepared to enjoy an unusually fine morning. He unwrapped the Sunday morning issue of the San Francisco *Chronicle,* lit his corn-cob pipe and was ready to resume his reading of the Lucille Tarn case, hoping that the paper would have a new sensation for its Sunday readers as thrilling as the murder of that Carmel negro. He got as far as two paragraphs into the story, reading that not even the San Francisco fingerprint experts who had been called in by Police Chief Watson had been able to uncover any fingerprints on the hammer which had crushed the skull of the negro.

He shifted his feet, having the uncomfortable feeling that someone was watching him. The nearest ranch was approximately two miles from his store and, after just reading the gory Sunday résumé of the two murders, it is understandable why he greeted the gentleman at the door with little tact. This gentleman had a dark, foreign face. He was carrying a dilapidated pigskin suitcase in one hand, and a green umbrella in the other around which was a filthy bandage. He was pale with fatigue. His clothes were covered with dust. During the night he had lost his way, walked over twenty miles, and only by chance had crossed the road winding along the valley between Sur Chiquita and the Big Sur range.

"If you please," asked the Baron, "permit me to use your telephone. I wish to call Carmel." The Baron deposited his suitcase on the porch and walked unsteadily toward old man Pringle, who promptly sprang spryly from the chair.

Old man Pringle was more than six feet high, stringy of build, and he spoke in a sour nasal whine. He thought that road tramps were one degree lower than coyotes and his manner indicated plainly that he held no truck with either species.

"Ten cents if you want to use my phone."

The Baron shifted his umbrella to the uninjured hand, explained with the utmost courtesy that he had gone for a walk in the hills, inconveniently forgetting to bring along money.

Old man Pringle had heard better stories and said so. "Ten cents if you want to phone Carmel. Ten cents, or out you go."

"Ach so?" asked the Baron mildly.

"You heard me." The storekeeper advanced upon the Baron and the club-like handle of the green umbrella swished through the air, deftly stopping at the base of the man's neck.

The Baron, who considered himself a peaceful individual, abhorrent of all bloodshed, dolorously sighed. He stepped over the storekeeper's body and examined the cash register. Somewhere it had been put into the Baron's head that American cash registers were an unfailing source of financial supplies. He grasped the umbrella, swung the handle again.

He felt sorry regarding the cash register. But lieber Augustin! What could he do? He was in such a hurry. Glass shattered under the impact of the umbrella handle. Springs and cogwheels fountained into the air, descending with mournful clackings upon the floor. He was in a great hurry. In ten minutes, in fifteen, easily he could have solved this fantastic American contrivance and opened it. However, any moment an automobile might arrive and demand petrol.

He selected a dime. The telephone operator put him through to the Hotel Della Vista in Carmel, where the invaluable Tivvits had registered. By now Tivvits would have returned from his jaunt to Los Angeles. As he waited, fondly the Baron imagined the joy with which the noble Tivvits would welcome the voice of his patron. Tivvits would rush from Carmel. In half an hour the Baron would again be at the Kerby residence. He would report to Mr. Kerby his solution of the ticking noises. The murders would be solved. And the Baron would receive his five thousand dollars. And he would take a nice long hot bath and perhaps ask Alice to have dinner with him at Del Monte . . .

"I wish to speak to Mr. Tivvits," he said when a woman's voice came over the wire. He spelled the name "Tivvits", adding, "If he is asleep, please wake him at once."

The woman's voice replied acidly that Tivvits was no longer at the hotel. Who was speaking?

"The—a friend of Mr. Tivvits. It is extremely urgent. Where is he?"

Tivvits was in jail, said the relentless voice. He had started for Los Angeles Wednesday afternoon and was arrested driving through Salinas at the speed of seventy miles an hour and wouldn't be released for a month and he still owed an hotel bill of sixteen dollars and if this were a friend of Tivvits the voice wanted to know if the friend didn't think *he* should pay for the hotel bill . . .

The Baron replaced the receiver. "Ach du lieber Augustin!" murmured the Baron. He thumped his forehead with his knuckles, repeated, "Ach du lieber Augustin!" He chose another ten cent piece from the change scattered upon the floor, inserted the second coin in the telephone and asked for the Kerby house in Carmel.

Caryl Kerby answered.

For a second the Baron was unable to speak. He could not believe that such abominable luck could persist. It was this country. This barbaric country.

He had difficulty in getting through to David Blane. This was due to the fact that the Baron immediately disguised his voice. When Caryl Kerby first lifted the receiver she thought that a Chinaman was speaking, then an Irishman, and finally, completely bewildered by the pyrotechnical array of accents, called the Englishman to the phone assuming it was one of his movie friends, very drunk.

As soon as Blane spoke the Baron said in his natural voice, "If you please, do not show astonishment if Mrs. Kerby is near. I disguised my voice when—"

"What?" the amazed Blane demanded. "Is this a joke? Speak so I can understand."

"Gott! This *is* the Baron. The Baron von Kaz. But now my voice is not at all disguised. One minute, please." Behind him, the storekeeper was getting to his feet.

Near the telephone was an ice-cooler. The cooler was empty of ice but filled with bottles of soda-pop. The Baron quickly grasped one of these bottles by the neck. Inasmuch as he was afraid that Blane would close the telephone connection, the Baron was forced to apply the bottle at once, without taking particular aim.

The bottle broke. The raspberry pop popped over the weather-beaten skull and face of the storekeeper. For one instant this stunned individual remained sitting upright on the floor. He resembled a lean stone Buddha who has been visited by an inexpressible indignity, the raspberry liquid painting the shiny dome, trickling down his face. His blank eyes regarded the Baron with an expression of total abhorrence. Then old man Pringle rolled slowly to one side where the Baron hoped that he would stay until the telephone conversation was completed.

The Baron returned to the mouthpiece. He menaced Mr. David Blane with prompt arrest. He menaced him with numerous lawsuits, grave scandal, if the Englishman should as much as let drop a word that the Baron was at the other end of the wire, and if he did not at once contrive an excuse to take an automobile and drive to the Sur Chiquita road. Here he was to proceed until he encountered a

roadside grocery store with the name—the Baron glanced
at the window, read the letters backwards, translated them
correctly into "Pringle's Ye Olde Chiquita Groceteria." He
had to give this name twice to Blane.

The call ended, the Baron shut and locked both front
and rear doors. He pulled down the shades. He dragged
old man Pringle behind the counter. When he leaned over
the old man, he ascertained that the storekeeper's heart
was stoutly beating. The Baron congratulated himself. He
seriously thought of keeping American pop-bottles in his
pockets for similar emergencies in the future.

However, the pop-bottle manufacturers lost a potential
customer when his roving eyes happened upon the first
page of the San Francisco *Chronicle,* spread upon the floor,
where it had dropped when old man Pringle had arisen to
throw out a dusty road tramp. He snatched at the paper,
his attention drawn to the story next to the recapitulation
of the sensational Lucille Tarn case.

BEN WARD IN CARMEL
TO SOLVE STRANGE DEATHS?

*When Questioned Famous Los Angeles Detective
Hints at Speedy Solution of Mysterious Tarn Case.*
Members of Carmel's exclusive literary and
art colony all professed their surprise when
they learned that Ben J. Ward, famous Los
Angeles criminal investigator, arrived in Carmel late yesterday afternoon to investigate
the Tarn case.

Mr. Ward smiled when interviewed, stating that he had been invited to Carmel by a
group of prominent citizens who have been
active during the past year in suppressing rad-
ical activities and who were interested in a
better civic government.

Arrest Near!

Mr. Ward claimed that he was not at liberty to reveal the names of these citizens. He added that he was in possession of, definite information which he was preparing to hand over to Chief of Police Lou Zachrisson Watson Sunday. This information, he believed, would lead to the arrest of the guilty party.

Mr. Ward has had a long series of successfully terminated cases. At present he is employed in a confidential capacity by Mr. Isaac Smith-Goldstein, president of Solar Pictures, Inc., who recently visited Monterey to attend a party given in his honor by his scenario chief, Mr. David Blane.

Although Mr. Blane is now in Carmel, when questioned Mr. Ward emphatically insisted that his presence had no connection with the scenario editor's visit. Mr. Charles Tarn, who left for Sacramento after the funeral of his wife Friday morning, was called by telephone but stated that he had no previous knowledge of Mr. Ward's arrival. Mr. Tarn said that he expected to return to Carmel Wednesday or Thursday of next week and if no progress had been shown by then toward solving the murder of his wife he would appeal to the governor, if necessary, to have government men placed on the case.

The storekeeper slowly reencountered this world, this barbaric world so many thousands of miles away from Vienna and civilization and stone walls where loyal but indiscreet monarchists were shot to death.

Old man Pringle dazedly found himself propped in a sitting position behind his counter. A determined maniac

was shaking a newspaper furiously in front of old man
Pringle's nose.

"Do you see that, my dear sir?" shouted this raving madman. "He has brought a detective from Los Angeles. But he
will not lose for me my five thousand dollars! He will not
trick me! Do you not comprehend, my dear sir? Ach!" Disgustedly the maniac pushed old man Pringle to the floor.
"Dolt!" cried the maniac. "Double and triple dolt!"

Tightly did old man Pringle close his eyes. He remembered that a mountain lion wouldn't attack a man playing
dead. Old man Pringle had reached that state where he was
willing to try anything, any experiment. The raspberry
pop trickled into his nose. He sneezed violently. Then he
remained very quiet, playing dead. If it would work on a
mountain lion it might work on a maniac.

After the passing of thirty or forty minutes he coura-
geously risked peering above the counter. His store was
empty. He placed a call to Monterey. When the police
arrived late in the afternoon they learned that although
the cash register had been broken, only two dimes had
been stolen. They departed from "Pringle's Ye Olde Chiquita Groceteria", solemnly promising to try to locate the
thief. They never did find him . . .

Quite disgusted with Mr. Pringle and his establishment, the Baron trudged gloomily down the road toward
Carmel on the alert for the appearance of Blane's roadster.
The Baron realized that his career in the Northern States
of America faced a crisis. If the great talents of the Baron
von Kaz were so little appreciated that an American detective was to be given the case, he decided that he would
not humble himself by returning with Blane to the Kerby
residence.

Bulwarked by his enormous conceit, the Baron would
not admit that it could be possible for Mr. Ward to find

the solution. What he would do, he decided, would be to stay away from the Kerby residence for a few days and then when his absence was missed he would descend in a dramatic blaze of glory and show these dolts the truth. Ach, that would be amusing. He smiled, thinking of this splendid revenge.

But then he angrily shook his head. He had no money. Unless he contrived to get funds he could not show his independence. Ach du lieber Augustin! If only he could secure a miserable two hundred or three hundred dollars! He stopped in the middle of the road absolutely oblivious to the impertinent remarks delivered by a blue jay perched on a redwood bough overhead. Now, if Mr. Blane has money with him? The Baron considered this, stroking his green umbrella. How easily dear Mr. Blane might be able to solve this miserable financial problem. Impatiently the Baron peered down the road.

Blane stopped the roadster a mile from the store. A dusty, disheveled Baron from Austria threw his suitcase and umbrella in the rumble seat and climbed into the car next to Blane.

Blane was frightened by what he had done. In a way, something which he hated to admit even to himself, he feared this strange foreigner with the elaborate manners, endless bragging, and the sinisterly courteous smile. He had conferred with Ward, the famous Los Angeles detective, regarding the Baron. Ward advised Blane that the Baron could sue for what had been done to him, suggested that Blane see the Baron alone and try to hush matters.

Knowing nothing of this previous discussion, the Baron prepared his attack, expecting staunch denials from the Englishman. Once in the car, when he asked Blane in a most innocent and guileless manner if a drug had not been administered to Gertrude the cow, the Englishman was unable to repress a gasp. That Wednesday night, when Blane had climbed into the attic to possess himself of the ticking noises, or rather of what made the noises, he had considered that his preparations had been planned perfectly and secretly.

He drove into a side road. Warily the Baron watched Blane. When the roadster halted between thick clumps of bushes, the Baron had one hand on the door, ready to leap over it. "I say." Blane lit a cigarette. "I think we should discuss this."

"By all means, my dear Mr. Blane. I have wondered what the newspapers would say should—"

"See here," said Blane hastily. "I can explain this. There's no need for any cheap publicity. I'm quite willing to admit that I was in the attic."

"Also," asked the Baron, "I believe you struck me, no? I do not like to be struck. Even in this country, I can receive just recompense for such a—ach—cowardly attack."

"Listen to me," said Blane. "Let me explain."

"As you wish." Carelessly the Baron opened the car door so that if necessary no obstruction would prevent a strategic retreat. "I have been resting for so long. If you do not mind, I shall stand."

"Well," began Blane, "Wednesday afternoon . . ."

Wednesday afternoon (according to Mr. David Blane, scenario editor of Solar Pictures, Inc.), he had walked into the rose garden, behind the Kerby residence. Blane had smoked a cigarette and then another in quiet contemplation, leaning against the lattice-work. This was so close to the house that his head rested against the stucco. As he smoked, he grew aware of a sound so soft that it hardly penetrated his consciousness.

He listened intently. And when he listened for it, he heard the sound most clearly; it came with insistent softness, as if water were dropping or a cricket rasping its legs.

As soon as he stepped away from the latticework, going into the garden, the sound was lost. And, strangely, when he approached the house from any other direction than toward the latticework, or moved from the latticework to either side, the noises promptly diminished, ceased. But the sound was there, present, apparently coming from somewhere in the house, hidden, malevolent.

Kerby had complained of the ticking noises. But Blane had attributed them to Kerby's nervous imagination. However, now that the Englishman was confronted by their reality, he determined to do something at once. Examining the house more closely, he noticed that near the plantain tree, a few feet below the tiles bordering the flat roof, there was a greenish colored metal grill placed in the stucco plaster. Presumably this metal grill served to ventilate the space between the second floor and the flat roof. Standing directly under this grill, Blane was positive that he heard the tickings with the most clarity.

Before lunch Blane had learned that the Baron von Kaz was a detective, hired to solve the ticking noises. This mystery, he decided, was entirely too complicated for a foreigner to solve. In addition, he had no confidence in the Baron's capacity as a detective.

Blane made up his mind. He took his car, drove to a Monterey drugstore where he could safely telephone by long distance to Ward, a competent and, close-mouthed investigator who was now working for his firm. Ward, when he asked him to come to Carmel immediately, replied that he was tied up in another case and could not possibly reach Carmel until Sunday morning or, by airplane, Saturday noon. Blane, knowing no other detective in whom he had confidence, reluctantly agreed to Saturday noon.

Blane was now determined to go into the Kerby attic that very night. To do this, he had to think of a way to distract the attention of the occupants of the house. He

stopped at a different drugstore, purchased a mixture of
chemicals which given in an overdose, he knew from experience, would drive a dog temporarily insane. He bought
enough, he hoped, to produce the same effect upon Gertrude the cow, and drove back to the Kerby home.

Here, unnoticed, he entered the stable and without
great difficulty persuaded Gertrude the cow to swallow all
ten capsules, a dose that eventually killed her after she had
demolished Caryl's garden. Blane reckoned that Gertrude
the cow would go berserk around dinner time. Her stomach, however, was more resistant, and not until appreciably later did she break loose from her stable.

When Blane heard Kerby and Caryl rush forth to save
the garden, he dashed out of his room and into the linen
closet. But here, instead of ascending into the attic at
once, he stayed in the closet hearing footsteps and voices.
Not until there was silence in the hall did he decide that
all had departed for the garden leaving him free to explore
the attic.

His astonishment was profound when, after locating
the ticking metronome, placed on a beam which supported that part of the ceiling over Kerby's bedroom, he saw
someone else entering the attic. Throwing the cigarette
lighter had revealed the Baron's identity. When the Baron
stumbled, Blane had thought that he had an excellent
opportunity to get rid of an unnecessary detective.

Blane hid the metronome under a pile of sheets in the
linen closet. Alice opened the closet door having heard the
commotion. Alice had a gun in her hand. Saying nothing
concerning the metronome, Blane stated that he and the
Baron had fought.

"In the attic?" Alice asked.

"The man's absolutely mad," replied Blane.

"He certainly is." Briefly she told how the Baron had
forced his way into her room, attempting to attack her . . .

(Here the Baron coldly interrupted the Englishman's explanation, remarking that Miss Rittenhouse was mistaken. "If required to," said the Baron, "I am most willing to go to court and protect my reputation. *I* am not afraid of scandal. I have been grossly injured. My feelings have been wounded. I am not mercenary at all, dear Mr. Blane. Not at all. But I do desire justice." He smiled significantly at Mr. Blane, rubbing his fingers over his palm, and Mr. Blane absorbed this information, looked at the Baron with increasing distaste and some relief, and completed his recital quickly.)

With the assistance of Alice, Blane managed to transport the senseless Baron to his own bedroom. As soon as the cow was captured, about half an hour before it died, Caryl and Kerby, exhausted, came upstairs to find two of their guests accusing the third.

Blane offered to take the Baron to a private hospital where the fellow, could recover and then be packed off without any possible notoriety. Kerby steadfastly refused. Blane then told Kerby that Ward was arriving Saturday and showed Kerby the metronome. Alice and Caryl had agreed that the Baron must be sent away, that Ward must be given a free hand. Kerby then had assented.

When this high-minded explanation had ended, Blane stepped out of the car, his mouth grim, his not unpersonable amount of chin most pugnaciously in evidence. "Now my good man, I've told you everything. It was my fault entirely. What do you intend to do?"

"Intend to do?" the Baron cried. "I shall complain to Mr. Kerby. Badly have I been mistreated, my dear sir. I would not think of demanding money for such mistreatment. Ach, no, I assure you, I wish satisfaction."

"All right." Blane reached in his pocket. "I see what you're driving at. How much?"

"Mr. Blane!" The Baron was shocked. He was outraged. He straightened his shoulders. "I would not consider money."

Blane counted out one hundred dollars.

"I will sue," said the Baron, refusing nobly.

"Two hundred then."

"My dear sir. Consider my wounds. My feelings. My— Five hundred dollars. You have that much, no?"

Angrily, Blane offered the sum mentioned to the Baron.

But now that the money could be his, he refused again. "And poor Mrs. Tarn?" he asked slyly. "And the blackman? And the reason why the metronome was placed in the attic?"

"All of your questions," said Blane, "have been answered."

"Ach—so?"

"Mr. Ward, I may tell you in confidence, knows who was responsible for the murders. In less than twenty-four hours he has established such definite proof for conviction that Watson is ready to make the arrest."

"So?" The Baron tried to hide his dejection. Ach, this country. In less than twenty-four hours an American detective discovers what it took the great and brave von Kaz days to learn? "And who will be arrested?"

"I think," returned Blane bluntly, "that Mr. Ward would prefer that you obtain all future information in the newspapers along with the others who seem to be interested in this lamentable affair."

The Baron shrugged. That was understandable. Without appearing to notice it, he held out his hand. The five hundred dollars were exchanged in silence. The two climbed into the car. Relieved to see the Baron counting the money, sticking it in his pocket, Blane started the roadster, wondering how he had once thought that Alice was impressed by so obvious a rascal. If it were not so important that the Baron be hurried away before he could change his mind and start more trouble, Blane would have liked nothing better than stopping the car, hauling the beggar into the street, ordering him to stand man to man and giving him the beating of his life for his abominable treatment of Alice. God! the man was a cheap cad. Trying to attack her.

By a roundabout route Blane drove skirting Carmel and on to Monterey where they reached the railway station. The Baron jumped out, withdrew the battered pigskin suitcase and the green umbrella.

He offered his hand. "I bid you a good day, my dear Mr. Blane."

Blane was so occupied in shutting the door that he overlooked the hand. "There's your train," he said. "And remember, I'm giving you this five hundred dollars with the definite understanding that you will trouble us no longer, that you will not return to Carmel!"

"But of course, my dear Mr. Blane."

13

Cat's Tricks

Monday morning the Baron awoke with a headache. Glumly he looked out of the window from his room in one of the most expensive hotels in San Francisco. After suffering through a cold shower he felt worse. He ordered breakfast in his room. He ordered champagne iced for precisely fifteen minutes, five slices of Melba toast, a small stone jar of bitter marmalade, and, as an afterthought, a glass of orange juice.

He had finished shaving when this breakfast arrived. He took the glass of orange juice and solemnly poured it out of the window. Then he sat down to the first civilized breakfast he had eaten since he had taken the boat for the Northern States of America. Even the breakfast, such as it was, failed to inflate his usually volatile spirits.

He had read the morning newspapers. The famous Los Angeles detective, Ben Ward, again was interviewed. He still hinted at an arrest in the very near future, said he had imparted his information to Chief of Police Watson, and refused to make further commitments. Police Chief Watson proved equally coy. "We believe we have indisputable proof as to the identity of the murderer," he was quoted as saying, but that was all he would say. When pressed for a reason for not closing the case at once, the police official replied evasively.

The Baron's imagination, never repressed, was stimulated when he reread these interviews. It was as though the two men, the policeman and Ward, were deliberately holding back, waiting for someone before striking the final blow. That seemed obvious, worried the Baron. But du lieber Augustin! why did they announce their purpose so transparently? Unless . . . And he hit the table with his fist.

Ach Gott! Was their trap empty? *Were they trying to bring the one whom they thought was the murderer to Carmel to entice into their trap?*

Did they hope that the murderer would be persuaded that the crimes had been planned so perfectly that it would be safe to come to Carmel? Would the murderer be trapped by the instinct to return to the scene of the crimes? Would the murderer wish to see whom these bunglers had selected as their victim?

If this were Ward's plan, the Baron confessed a certain reluctant admiration for the detective. The plan was clumsy to be sure, but it might work. He got to his feet. He paced the floor. He was convinced that he knew as much, if not more than Ward. He could name the murderer.

He realized that Blane had contrived to end Kerby's welcome; and deprived of a residence, and without money, the Baron was helpless. Now that he had money, now that he was convinced that he saw through Ward's plan, the Baron decided that he must hurry because if Ward should blunder then a third death hovered over that small group of people he had left, those whom he had once listed as suspects.

However, he must be absolutely certain.

He could risk no mistake.

He had accounted for everyone in the Kerby household. But Ward's attitude made the Baron cautious. Ward, evidently, was acting upon the theory that the murders were conceived and put into execution by someone outside, not only the Kerby house, but Carmel as well.

Otherwise, why should this famous detective wait so patiently, doing nothing, cheerfully broadcasting in the papers that he knew the one who was guilty?

More and more the question arose in the Baron's mind. *Had he inadvertently overlooked someone?* Could there be another motive for the killing of Lucille Tarn? For the scheme behind the metronome? Had Ward uncovered something that he—the Baron—had missed?

Never would he be able to hold up his head to the world, dramatically announced the Baron to himself in front of a mirror, if this American detective had beaten him. And the Police Chief—the official who had locked him in a cell—could it be possible that he could see a solution where the Baron could not? He watched the person in the mirror frown tragically; with one of his complete about faces of mood he winked at this tragic person and left the room.

If he had missed any person who might be connected with Kerby or with Lucille Tarn, he had one chance to find that connection. That chance brought him to the public library because here, as in any large city, he could locate files of newspapers for many years back. He set for himself the stupendous task of going through all the local newspapers in the hope of finding some item, something, connected with either Henry Kerby or Lucille Tarn that might point to a third person.

He was at the desk, about to ask for the Carmel *Seaweed* when suddenly he swore. The girl at the desk stared at him. He apologized. It had completely escaped his mind. He called for the entire series of Carmel directories instead of for the Carmel *Seaweed* file. As soon as these were brought to him, feverishly he started opening the pile of slim red books dating from the year 1891.

Not until he had leafed through twenty-one directories did he come across the first item:

"Kerby, Henry I(nnman). R. Carmel Inn. P. Author."

In the 1918 directory published five years later he learned that "Kerby, Henry I." had moved to 896 Ocean Boulevard. In the 1919 directory he found that which he had been seeking, that fact which Caryl Kerby had first told him in the garden and which he had almost forgotten:

"Kerby, Henry I.; Mrs. Frances R.: R. 896 Ocean Boulevard. P. Author."

This line remained unchanged until 1931 when again it was "Kerby, Henry I." alone. And in 1932 the line again changed:

"Kerby, Henry I.; Mrs. Caryl D.: R. 12 La Honda Drive. P. Author."

At the desk an excited, dark-faced man inquired whether or not they had filed the issues of the Carmel *Seaweed* for the entire year of 1919 and also for 1932. Yes, they had, the girl behind the spectacles thought. She was touched by the gentleman's gallant bow when she handed him the yellowing newspapers.

It took nearly four hours more to cover thoroughly the some seven-hundred-and-thirty issues of the Carmel paper. In these seven-hundred-and-thirty issues he located exactly five separate paragraphs which interested him; two of which appeared during the year 1919, and three during 1932.

The first was dated February 14, 1919:

Miss Frances R. Taylor, direct from Worthy & Holden, New York, announces the opening next Thursday of a new shop where will be shown exclusive women's sport clothes from Paris and London.

Frances Taylor. 16 Ocean Boulevard.

The second was inserted in the society column, August 30, 1919:

Mrs. Frank Rithburn Taylor of New York has announced the approaching wedding of her daughter, Miss Frances Taylor, to Mr. Henry I. Kerby, well-known Carmel author and humorist, to take place next Sunday . . .

The third was an advertisement. It was dated February 19, 1932:

CARMEL'S NEWEST SPORT SHOP

Summer suits, original and charming. Authentic models from Paris. Smart dress and cape combinations. Nippy Lelong Cashmere flannels. Gray, navy, brown, or black. Lowest prices. Paris-Hollywood Dress Shop.

Frances Taylor Kerby, Mgr.

The fourth, two months later, April 15, 1932:

PARIS-HOLLYWOOD CLOSING OUT SALE!

Frances Taylor is closing out her Paris-Hollywood Shop. Reduced prices. Sale starts Monday to last only four days . . .

The final item was headlined on the front page, October 4, 1932:

FAMOUS CARMEL AUTHOR WEDS
LOCAL GIRL IN SURPRISE CEREMONY!

Yesterday, Mr. Henry I. Kerby, nationally acclaimed humorist, and Miss Caryl Miquet were united in marriage at Reno according to reports received here via United Telegraphic Press. Mrs. Kerby is well-known in Carmel. Born in Carmel, after her parents died she studied in the East where she was awarded the Boston Academy Scholarship, returning here several months ago to paint the scenes so familiar to her . . .

Not a word could the Baron find in the circumspect Carmel paper concerning the divorce. These five items contained a whole story of heartbreak and romance, of lost and rediscovered hopes.

And what of this woman, Frances Taylor, who sixteen years ago had arrived in Carmel from New York, had married a promising author by the name of Henry Kerby? Could she still be in Carmel? The 1935 Carmel Directory listed no Frances Taylor. Until then the Baron had been sustained by the excitement of discovering a new lead. Now he groaned. Frances Taylor—Kerby's first wife—how could he ever hope to locate her?

In the half-light of the reading room he sat at the table, alternately striking his forehead and thumbing through the Carmel directories, all the while muttering to himself. A dignified and elderly gentleman shifted uncomfortably across from this dark-faced fellow. Talking out loud. Absolutely no manners. Good God! You couldn't find privacy any more.

Abruptly the Baron got up; strode the length of the reading room and entered one of the three telephone booths. When he opened the book to the "T's," he found not one but two addresses:

Taylor, Frances R.; r. 45 25th Ave., BAyview 8164
Taylor, Frances R. & Co. (sportswear); 239 Post, SUtter
2534

. . . and then he decided that at last his evil luck had broken and he would see if there were other pieces that could
fit into the murderer's place in his jig-saw puzzle of the
Lucille Tarn case.

It was four-thirty when the brave Baron von Kaz entered 239 Post Street and asked a young lady if he could
speak to Miss Frances Taylor. And why did he wish to speak
with Miss Taylor? "I am from New York." He bowed. "Five
months ago my wife purchased a blue sweater from Miss
Taylor. My wife requested me to stop in your so charming
little shop and ask dear Miss Taylor to choose a similar
sweater. But this time it must be, ah—mauve. Of a mauve
color."

The young lady appreciably melted. He was such a
helpless, diffident, man. And he had nice, candid blue
eyes. She sympathized with him. She realized how men
hated to shop for their wives. And here he was coming in
and asking for a mauve sweater. The poor dear. "Miss Taylor," she uttered sweetly, "has left for the day. If you could
come tomorrow?"

He was sorry but he couldn't come tomorrow. As soon
as he could he left the young lady who wished to show
him some just heavenly sweaters and made for the nearest
drugstore where, he recalled from Blane's conversation, he
could find a telephone booth.

The woman's voice at Bayview 8164 informed him that
Miss Taylor was not in. No, she wouldn't be in for dinner.
She was going to the opera and wouldn't return until late.

At the hotel the Baron learned that the opera should
end tonight around eleven-thirty. Having nothing to do

until that hour, he descended into the lobby, purchased several more shirts, handkerchiefs, silk socks, and other needed accessories. Returning upstairs, he sent his suit to be cleaned and pressed with the agreement that he would receive it before eleven o'clock. He took a long bath, shaved again, then went to sleep and did not wake until his suit was brought back. He ate a sandwich, drank a small bottle of fine Burgundy, reluctantly hailed a taxi-cab. Every time he saw a taxicab his conscience, or what served the Baron as a conscience, hurt. He would think of the admirable Tivvits, the trusting Tivvits, languishing in a jail in a place called Salinas . . .

Frances Taylor had removed her opera coat and was powdering her blunt nose when the doorbell rang. Frances was a brown-haired woman, somewhere between forty and forty-five, a trifle heavy in the shoulders and arms. They were the shoulders and arms of a woman who swam of-ten and well. She had a good-looking shrewd face above a fine, powerful figure draped in a black checkered evening gown which swished as she walked. The maid, Deborah, announced that a Mr. Brandenstein was waiting. "A who?" Frances Taylor asked. She couldn't place a Mr. Branden-stein. It was about a sweater his wife had purchased, Deb-orah explained vaguely.

"Tell him I can't see him at this hour, Deb. If he wants a sweater for his wife, for Heaven's sake tell him the shop isn't here and that we close at six."

Frances swept into her ornate salon, hung with thick plush drapes, cluttered with dark-wooded and heavy fur-niture. On the table was a small glass of rye, a larger glass of Perrier water. She sank into a red sofa affair underneath a large English sporting print, crossed her legs, lifted the evening dress the better to inspect them critically, decid-ing that they were still worth crossing. If she took care of herself and could find time to swim an hour instead of half an hour every day, she would be able to expect opera and dinner invitations for at least five or six years more from handsome bachelors. Oh, well! She mixed the rye in the Perrier water and drank it.

Deborah stood in the doorway, a well-shaped little mixture of timidness and brazenness. Deborah was mildly flustered. "The gentleman says he's leaving San Francisco tomorrow morning and must see you."

"Tell him I'm in bed."

"Yes, madam."

Frances yawned. She was bored. She didn't want to go to bed. She didn't have a damn thing in the house to read. She yawned for a fourth time when Deborah entered again. "He says—he says—"

"Say it then," demanded Frances with a beginning interest in this persistent stranger. "Don't stutter. Is the man an idiot?"

"Oh, my, no, Miss Taylor." The maid blushed. "He says so much the better if you are in bed. He says he's used to talking to charming ladies in or out of bed. What'll I tell him?"

"Tell him I'm old. I'm hideous. I'm tired. Tell him I've stopped talking to idiotic fools twenty years ago—"

"But dear, gracious madame, permit me if you please." The woman and the girl were both startled. The Baron stepped between the folding doors, flourished his hat, bowed with the most respectable and impudent courtesy imaginable.

He took Frances Taylor's hands. "Ach, I insist. You are charming—" He kissed her right hand and she indignantly snatched it away. "Charming," he repeated.

Frances waved at the maid. "All right, Deb."

Deborah hesitated. Deborah backed from the room in such a manner that she could watch the gentleman until she was out in the hall.

"Well!" Frances inspected the Baron and then, remembering, whisked the black, crinkling skirt over her knees. "Well!" this time there was an attempt at crispness which fell somewhat flat because of the man's quick smile at her gesture.

"Permit me?" Not attending for permission, he seated himself upon the red atrocity as though he were in his own home. He spoke with feeling of his dear wife in New York. He explained how delighted she had been with a sweater a friend of hers had purchased from Miss Taylor's shop. This sweater was a marvel, a miracle of hand weaving. His dear wife was determined to possess one. Only could Frances Taylor supply her with the desired sweater, the inimitable and clever Frances Taylor. "Yes, I will. Thank you," he said as the inimitable Frances Taylor reached into a cabinet, took out a clean glass and the decanter of rye, filled her glass with rye and offered him the empty glass and the bottle.

"And so," he concluded, "tomorrow I must depart for New York. And I promised to my beloved wife to return with a Frances Taylor sweater."

That evening, Frances Taylor was in the mood for adventure. It might be amusing to take this devoted husband down to her shop in her car. Devoted husbands were oddities. This one perhaps would prove interesting. The moon was full tonight, she remembered. "Have another?"

Mr. Brandenstein would be only too pleased to pour himself another.

"Now, I insist, gracious lady, that you deprive not yourself for me." And so saying, he also filled her glass half full. Frances laughed. By the time their second and third glasses were emptied, Frances was all for getting her car at once.

The Baron wavered in his conversation, trying to tactfully drive it to the locality of Carmel.

His new luck held.

Frances gave him the opportunity. When she entered the room, holding a sleek mink coat in her arm and wearing a sleek smile on her face, she inquired, "You haven't told me who your wife's friend is, Mr. Brandenstein? The one who bought the original sweater?"

Frances really didn't care who the friend was, but it made conversation while he assisted her with the coat. "Mrs. Brandenstein's friend? Ach, so?" This was a point that, until now, he had neglected. "Miss Rittenhouse. That is a beautiful coat, dear lady." He admired the coat. "Miss Alice Rittenhouse." Turning to gather his hat and umbrella from the red sofa, he was unaware of the strange expression sliding over Frances Taylor's face. "Miss Rittenhouse is in Carmel, I believe. She wrote to my wife that the only place in California to purchase splendid sweaters was your charming store."

He hooked the umbrella on his left arm, offered his right.

She was before the mirror, doing something to her hair, asking quietly, "Alice Rittenhouse? She wrote your wife?"

"Ah, yes," he replied blandly, thinking how clever he was. Ah, the great von Kaz! Someday Vienna would appreciate what it had lost. Four rye whiskies had rapidly replated his damaged self-esteem with a fine, new glitter. "It is a lovely night tonight, dear Miss Taylor."

"I thought your wife saw the sweater?"

"Saw it? Oh, no. No, dear Alice wrote my wife. She wrote that she had purchased a sweater from you. She wrote two or three weeks ago, before I flew to the Pacific coast. I suppose you know Alice?"

He had expected her to say "no." Then he had planned to ask Miss Taylor if she had customers in Carmel. A fashionable sportswear shop should have customers from Carmel. Her answer would be "yes" to that question. Next he

would casually, oh so very casually ask if she visited Carmel frequently. Her spoken answer would not be so important. It would be the way she replied. He would watch her.
He, the great and astute von Kaz, would observe her. And
what he did next would depend entirely upon her attitude
while answering that third question. He would penetrate
into her very mind. He had it all thought out.

Unfortunately, his new luck wobbled slightly; she replied yes, that she did know Alice Rittenhouse.

"Oh," he said.

She had greenish eyes. Now they bored into him. She
was removing her coat. As she grew unaccountably angry,
her eyes reminded him of that yellowish blaze you see in
a cat's eyes when you step on the creature's tail. He didn't
like cats. He was wondering seriously whether he liked
Frances Taylor as much as he thought he did a few minutes
before he had mentioned Alice Rittenhouse.

He edged toward the folding doors. "Ah, she is charming. When I think of her—'Vox faucibus haesit!'" He
looked at her with a modest little tilt of his head. "That,"
he said in the delightful manner of one who wishes to make
light of so much erudition. "That is Latin. It means—"

"Virgil, if my memory is correct," she replied, "But I
am rather surprised to hear you say that."

"Ach, it is nothing. Nothing at all, dear lady. And Alice?
Does she—"

"I mean, for you to admit that your voice *can* stop in
your throat. That's the translation, isn't it?"

"Translation, dear lady?" He smiled a trifle nervously.
"So. In a way. Yes. However, Alice—"

"In other words, Mr. Brandenstein: 'Stultorum infinitus est numerus?' That, I trust, is Latin, also."

"To be certain. And now, my dear Miss Taylor, does
Alice—charming Alice—often buy sweaters from you?" He

thought it had been very clever of him to give Alice's name. She *was* from New York. And now she was in Carmel.

Frances threw her coat on the red sofa without taking her eyes off his face. "And you do know Latin, Mr. Brandenstein?" she asked silkily. "I thought you would appreciate that little tag I gave you. It's so appropriate."

"Undoubtedly. Undoubtedly, dear lady." He smiled again. "As I said, does Alice—?"

"'The number of dolts is infinite.' You recognize its application, of course?" And as she examined him, his assurance fled. He wet his lips. He could think of nothing to say. He became angry. He wasn't here to exchange Latin phrases. That was the trouble with these Americans. They were without culture. If they knew a little Latin they became unbearable nuisances. The woman should be flogged. "Stultorum infinitus—" Lieber Augustin . . . She was asking, "Well, are you going to present me with the next question, Mr. Brandenstein? You claimed that was your name, I think."

"Next question? Pardon, my dear Miss Taylor, but I do not comprehend."

"Do you consider that I, too, am a dolt?" she demanded furiously.

He didn't care for the way she looked. Her eyebrows were suddenly heavy. The eyes held a queer light in them. He wanted to leave. The woman was insane. As soon as he had mentioned Carmel, she had changed. That was indication enough. He could learn no more directly from her.

"Aren't you going to ask me if I've been in Carmel recently? Aren't you going to ask me if I've talked to any of the servants at the Kerby house? Go on. Ask. I'm waiting."

"But I assure you—"

"You'll assure *me,* will you? That's what your friend, what's his name, Ward, wanted to know last Saturday

night. If Henry Kerby's been threatened by the same maniac who killed Lucille Tarn, you can't implicate me! Ward
may think he's very clever to look up the first wife. Or
perhaps Ward didn't think of it? Caryl suggested it? And
why? Simply because I hired Maggy when I was Mrs. Kerby
and she still comes to see me. Don't pretend to be so helpless, Mr. Brandenstein. *You* don't have to tell me anything.
But let me tell you this: I haven't taken any trips to Carmel. I haven't, do you hear? And I haven't been near Henry's
house for—for over a year."

Tightly he gripped his umbrella. His assurance, his bravado was so demolished that if she had advanced to attack
him it is quite conceivable that he would have thrown the
umbrella at her, forgetting that she was a woman apparently unarmed. And from a much greater distance than where
he was standing—from a distance as far as six yards—nine
times out of ten he could throw the weighted umbrella and
knock out his object.

"If you or your detective friend think one of Henry's
servants put that bomb, or whatever that ticking thing
was that Ward tried to be so evasive about, in the attic, it
wasn't Maggy. She's a good, honest housekeeper. And you,
Mr. Brandenstein . . ."

In his imagination, as fascinated he gazed at the greenish eyes, almost could that active, creative mind of his
detect a long furry tail swishing behind her in place of
the black checkered train of her gown. Almost could he
visualize sharp claws in place of the long, strong fingers.

"You, Mr. Brandenstein," she was saying, "You come
here, believing you can fool me with your story of a sweater, and work the talk to Carmel and get me to admit, without being aware of it, that I've been there recently. Well, I
know why Caryl's persuaded you and that other detective
to think I've been in Carmel. *I* know. And I haven't been
in Carmel!"

All at once her hoarse, angry voice subtly changed. It softened. It became like the purr of a cat. She swished past him into the hall, glanced over her shoulder with one of the bitterest smiles the Baron ever had encountered.

"Good night to you, my fine man. Caryl sent you here, I suppose, after the other man failed and paid you to try to ask the questions, and you've played your little part and I've been saved from boredom. Tell her that when you report to her. And tell her this, too: Tell her I read the papers. Tell her I'm going to continue to read them until I see her name in the papers and then I'll come to Carmel. I'll come to Monterey and I'll get a seat in the front row in the court house when she appears before the judge!"

With that, Frances Taylor passed through the other door and the maid materialized and followed the Baron to the entrance hall. She was a pretty little person with soft brown eyes and a knowing little mouth. He pressed her hand absently. Her cheeks grew rosy. When she opened her hand she saw a five dollar bill. "Oh," she protested faintly, turning the doorknob.

"The name, my dear?"

"Deborah, sir."

"Deborah? A nice name. However, one is not sufficient."

"Deborah O'Hara." Nervously she glanced behind. "You must go, sir. Miss Taylor, she'll—"

"Pooh!" He winked. "When does the charming little Deborah have free an afternoon?"

"Please, sir—"

"Another five dollars? Ach, what would it purchase?"

She blushed redder. "Do go, please."

"Twenty dollars?" he offered recklessly, because only the maid Deborah could tell him if Frances Taylor kept old-fashioned hatpins hidden away in her rooms. If anyone would know, this little maid would.

Deborah's face was crimson. She had attended too many movies not to appreciate what it implied when a gentleman gave a girl five dollars and promised twenty in addition. But for sixteen months she'd been working. And she knew just how many days of saying, "Yes, m'am," and smiling when people said the furniture wasn't properly dusted and pretending not to mind when gentlemen visitors pinched your arm, it took to save twenty-five dollars.

"Two o'clock tomorrow?" she whispered.

"Good. I will await in front of the Hotel St. Francisco. You will not forget?"

She shook her curly head.

After all, he was clean and had manners and acted nice. That was something. Recalling her past movie, she decided what to do. She raised her head. She languorously fluttered and shut her brown eyes, very tightly, however, because she was frightened. She'd never earned money this way before.

And when the door closed, she opened her eyes, bewildered, and then glanced at the money in her hand. It was five dollars. Lord! The bill was moist. Deborah didn't go to bed right away. She spent an hour pressing her yellow dress, the one that had taken her three months to pay for on Goldenberg's Easy Installment Plan.

14
Death Calls for the Third Time

When the Baron sat down to a light lunch on Tuesday, with a small bottle of chilled Liebfraumilch, he was certain that he had the only solution for this case which had started with ticking noises and progressed to two deaths, but this solution had no part in it for any motivation induced by the possible participation of Frances Taylor.

The first wife had assumed a position of great and unknown importance to the Baron. She represented an enigma. She was conspicuous by her total absence in his final theory which accounted for the solution of the Tarn case. Yet she had previously been interviewed by Ward regarding the probability of her presence in Carmel. And on Saturday night. Blane had said that the detective arrived Saturday noon. Someone—undoubtedly Caryl—had thrown suspicion on Frances Taylor in connection with the placing of the metronome in the attic and Ward had immediately left Carmel to interview Kerby's first wife. Therefore, Frances Taylor worried the Baron. If she had played a part in planning or originating the murders, then his theory crumpled. Because of that, before he could act, before he could again inject himself into the Carmel imbroglio and claim Kerby's interest, he had to substantiate or reject his theory by determining what place, if any, Frances Taylor held upon this human jig-saw puzzle board.

He was a few minutes late. Deborah was waiting in front of the hotel in her crinkly yellow dress. They ascended to his room together. The Baron closed his door, sat at the writing desk deep in thought, ignoring the girl, trying to outline his questions. It was necessary to question her adroitly. He must not awaken her suspicions, now that she was here, as to his real intent. He picked up a pen, dipped it in ink, slowly turned, said, "Deborah," and then—completely astounded—"Lieber Augustin!"

Deborah was carefully folding the beautiful yellow dress on the chair. "I don't want to get it mussed," she explained. In the movies, some of the heroines removed their stockings, others didn't. She had nice legs. She wondered if he would tell her what to do. When he stared at her in amazement, she reluctantly decided that she was supposed to take off her stockings.

"If you please," he asked, "is it so warm this afternoon that you feel more comfortable in—" He nodded briefly at her.

"I don't want to wrinkle my dress. It's nearly new."

"Ach so?" His manner changed. He lifted the dress. "It is very lovely, my dear Deborah."

"It cost twenty-one dollars."

"I think you will appear more charming with it on, no?"

"But—"

He dragged a chair close to the window. The window was half-way across the room from the bed. "And, if you are too warm. Ach!" He cheerfully unbuttoned his coat. "It is warm. I suggest you sit by the window and I shall ask you a few questions and then you shall receive your twenty dollars. Does that march, my dear Deborah?"

While she wiggled into the yellow frock, perplexed, he explained that he was a designer of dresses. He said this most suavely. He was planning to locate in Carmel. Miss Frances Taylor, so he understood, had a long list of

Carmel clients. He was willing to pay Deborah the total of twenty-five dollars for information concerning these clients which would help him to gain new business. She was listening so concentratedly that he had the sensation that he was swimming along splendidly with this credulous little maid. "Now," he said, "I presume she goes often to Carmel?"

"This is exciting, Mr. Brandenstein." She wriggled. "I've never helped a detective before."

"A detective—"

"You are one, aren't you? I mean, what else would you want to pay me the twenty-five dollars for, if you don't want—I mean—if I'm not to take off my dress?"

"Deborah," he accused gravely, "you listened last night."

"I did no such thing, Mr. Brandenstein. It isn't my fault you talked so loud I could hear you in the hall, is it? And, goodness! I'm not dumb. There was a man came last Saturday asking questions, too. He said Mr. Kerby's life had been threatened. They'd discovered something ticking up in the attic—a bomb, I guess. And one of the servants had probably stuck it up there."

"You were there when he talked with Miss Taylor?"

"Of course not. But I was in the next room same as last night. And besides, she was Mr. Kerby's first wife and, after all, she *did* go to Carmel once or twice just before the murders even if she said she didn't. And after hearing about Mr. Kerby I wondered why she went down there. She *said* to me, Mr. Brandenstein, that she was going to see one of her friends who used to work in her Carmel store, and I can tell you her name. Let me think." She placed her finger on her chin. She was thinking.

The Baron von Kaz waited resignedly.

Frances Taylor had visited Carmel twice before the murder of Lucille Tarn. She had driven there to see a Mrs. Echardt. The maid remembered the name because Miss

Taylor had left it with her should anyone call and try to
get in touch with her. After the news of the murder had
been in the newspapers, Frances Taylor had seemed upset.
She hadn't made any trips to Carmel after the murders.

The Baron silently considered this information. Finally
he asked, "Do you know whether Miss Taylor has old-fashioned—"

"Hatpins?" whispered Deborah excitedly. "Oh, yes she
has. Lots."

"Lots?"

"Four or five, anyway. She's kept all her old hats on the
top shelf of one of the closets and the hatpins are in them.
Leastwise, they *were* in them, Mr. Brandenstein, until
after the murders and then I peeked into the closet and
the hats were gone. I go to a lot of movies and I've seen
how the detectives do it in the movies and, after all, Mr.
Brandenstein, Miss Taylor *was* Mr. Kerby's first wife. And
he's in danger, the other detective said. And she hates the
present Mrs. Kerby just terribly." Deborah lowered her
voice. "But why should she have taken the hatpin to've
killed that beautiful movie star, Mr. Brandenstein? Why'd
you ask if she had any hatpins? I looked in the closet because I wanted one of the hats for the Police Masquerade
Ball. I didn't *think* of the hatpins then. O-oh! Was Mr.
Kerby maybe in love with the movie star? That'd be a reason, wouldn't it, for Miss Taylor killing her?"

The Baron closed his eyes. He had tried for a trickle
of information. He was overwhelmed by the torrent. He
made feeble gestures to stem it, but the maid went on with
faucets wide open.

"She was awfully jealous. I know, Mr. Brandenstein.
I was serving coffee last month to Miss Taylor and this
friend, this Mrs. Echardt I was telling you of and I heard
Miss Taylor say to her friend, she said, 'Henry's wife is a
cold-blooded minx'—Henry is Mr. Kerby—and then she

stopped when she saw me but I didn't forget. I have a wonderful memory, Mr. Brandenstein, and I'm just crazy about detectives. Everytime there's a movie that's a detective movie, I go and I've often thought with my memory that perhaps some day some detective might need a girl who can serve, like I do, who could act as a maid and get into a home . . ."

The Baron stood up. He counted twenty dollars and gave the money to Deborah, bowing. "You have been of invaluable help, my dear young lady."

"I'm awfully glad," she said breathlessly. "If you like, I could telephone Mrs. Echardt and imitate Miss Taylor's voice and maybe say I forgot what we talked about in Carmel and what was it?"

"That would be splendid," he assured her, taking her by the arm and imperceptibly leading her to the door. "However, you can be of greater assistance at present by doing nothing which will arouse Miss Taylor's suspicions. If you do—" he whispered, "one night you might have a hatpin plunged into your heart!"

The maid gasped.

"And I know that I can trust you—"

"Oh, Mr. Brandenstein," she said tremulously, "I wouldn't say *a* word! And you *can* trust me. I'll do anything for you, you've been such a gentleman."

"Thank you. Thank you, my dear Deborah." He opened the door for her.

She held back. "You don't need me any more?"

He bowed. "I am afraid I have taken too much of your time already. Good day, Deborah."

"Mr. Brandenstein," she said dubiously, the bills clenched tightly in her hand, "Mr. Brandenstein, I've all afternoon free and—"

"Splendid." He took her elbow and ushered her through the doorway. "It is a lovely day, Deborah. Enjoy yourself."

"But Mr. Brandenstein—"

"Good day, my dear Deborah." Quickly he shut the door.

He took the two forty-three train for Monterey, making it with one minute to spare. On the train he read the San Francisco *News*. There was a paragraph on the third page which he studied for a long time. The paragraph was short. The *News* reporter had learned that Mr. Charles Tarn was expected to arrive in Carmel late Tuesday afternoon, cutting short his stay in Sacramento by a day. It was conjectured that Mr. Tarn was returning to attend a meeting with Chief of Police Watson and Mr. Ward and that by Wednesday or Thursday the Tarn case would be closed.

Mrs. Echardt had an attractive curio shop two blocks from the Carmel jail. She was a large, blonde woman in the early fifties and was considerably impressed by the customer, a medium-sized, dark-faced gentleman of elaborate manners, who had entered her store. He introduced himself as "Mr. Kirschfeld," saying that he was traveling through Carmel and wished to purchase presents for two charming nieces of his who lived in New York City. There were no other customers in the store at the time; indeed, no one had entered the store since mid-morning until the arrival of Mr. Kirschfeld and Mrs. Echardt was determined to complete a sale. She showed him handsome hand-made Indian moccasins, intricately decorated abalone shells, and a box constructed of real redwood with a picture of the Carmel mission burnt into the top, just the thing for trinkets, Mr. Kirschfeld, and so tremendously practical as well as beautiful.

"Miss Taylor, Miss Frances Taylor is a friend of my wife," he introduced the name most casually, "and I remember Miss Taylor said that you had delightful—ah—" His eyes searched the shelves. "Delightful lace. Perhaps I could see it?"

"You know Miss Taylor?"

"Very well; oh, very well, Mrs. Echardt. It was she who suggested that I drop into your charming little store."

"You knew her in New York or San Francisco?" Mrs. Echardt draped the lace over her ample arm.

"Both in New York and San Francisco. I assume, my dear Mrs. Echardt, that the lace is expensive?"

Mrs. Echardt said that it wasn't expensive at all, considering that it had been imported from Brussels and the import duty being what it was. "It was so sweet of Frances to tell you about the lace," she cooed. "She is a darling. Have you seen her recently?"

"Two weeks ago, dear Mrs. Echardt. You see her frequently, no doubt?"

"Hardly ever any more."

"Uhm . . . and what else have you besides the lace? I do hope I am not intruding on your time, dear Mrs. Echardt?"

"Not at all, Mr. Kirschfeld. If you will wait a minute, I think perhaps I have something in the rear of the store which would interest you."

While Mrs. Echardt bustled into a back room, the Baron lit a cigarette, congratulating himself upon the astute way in which he had handled the conversation so far. After such disastrous results with Miss Taylor and Deborah he began to appreciate that these American women possessed a certain amount of native wit. It was essential to approach them with cunning and not address them as you would the peasant and shopkeeping types in Austria. However, the brave Baron von Kaz was nothing if not adaptable; a lesson learned was a lesson for always remembered with him.

He was complacently puffing his third cigarette when Mrs. Echardt returned.

"Mr. Brandenstein," she said heavily, "Frances is on the phone. She insists on speaking to you—"

"But dear lady," his cigarette dropped to the floor.

"Don't *you* 'dear lady' me!" she threatened. "Trying to tell me that Frances had mentioned this lace when it only arrived two days ago." She placed her hands on her hips. "Are you going to speak to her or not? If I had my way, I'd call the police."

"Hello . . ." The Baron hardly recognized his own voice when he spoke into the receiver.

"Mr. Brandenstein," Frances said crisply, "I want to tell you this, and then if either you or that other detective person bother me again, I'll go to the police. I've been to Carmel twice recently. I don't see what business it is of yours or that Mr. Ward's, and even if my former husband's life is in danger, I don't like the way you two came sneaking around trying to trick me into admitting something which I would have told you if you had asked for it outright. My chauffeur drove me down to see Emma Echardt both times. Emma and my chauffeur can testify that I only saw her, returned to San Francisco directly. I suspected you got your information from that little fool, Deborah. I wish you'd leave my maids alone. If you have questions to ask regarding hatpins, and whether or not I have any, henceforth please ask me. Last week, I sent all my old hats to the San Francisco Charity League because the girls there think they can learn the millinery trade and they need old hats to remodel. My hatpins went with the old hats. You can verify this by telephoning the Charity League. If you or anyone else troubles me again, I shall call my lawyer. Good-by!"

Very shaken, he left the shop owned and operated by Mrs. Echardt. It was close to six o'clock. Not until he was opposite the jail did he realize where he was.

He stopped, curiously. A long, green car that he had seen before was drawn up by the curbing. As he contemplated this Mercedes, a stubby blue-black police automobile roared out of the alley and sped down Ocean Boulevard. In the police car, the Baron saw that Police Chief Watson was driving. Sitting next to him was a broad-shouldered man in civilian dress.

Blane ran down the steps of the jail. Not pausing to open the Mercedes' door, he leaped over it. He inserted the ignition key in the lock and was turning it when he heard a voice say, "Not dear Mr. Blane?"

For the second time in his life, dear Mr. Blane nearly fainted from a shock. "You?" He stared at the sardonic, smiling face. "What in hell are you doing here?" He stepped on the starter. "I can't argue with you now." A hand grasped his wrist. The man had slid into the empty front seat as easily as running water slides through a crack.

"If you please—"

"If I please!", blazed Blane, freeing his hand. He had no time for fighting now. Otherwise, no other prospect would have suited him better than inviting this cad into the alley where he would have enjoyed beating the fellow to a cringing pulp.

"Get out or I'll throw you out!"

The man's fingers seemed to be made of steel. Blane's wrist went numb as the Baron's hand tightened. "One minute," requested the Baron mildly.

"One minute? For God's sake, they'll be there—"

"They?"

"Tarn's already at the house. That was the plan. And Ben Ward and I came for the police as soon as Tarn telephoned he'd come. Get out!"

Two boys on the sidewalk paused as they saw a tall blond-haired man apparently attempting to throw an inoffensive, medium-sized individual out of the car. The medium-sized man resisted only passively, holding the other's wrists. "I comprehend. Your formidable Mr. Ward has been told then that Mr. Tarn urged his wife to go onto the stage?"

Blane was on his knees, violently pushing at the Baron. "Damn you, I'll break every bone in your body!"

"And Mr. Ward also knows that the negro once worked for Mr. Tarn?"

"What are you driving at?" Momentarily, Blane halted, breathing hard.

"And Mr. Ward, the astute Mr. Ward, has not arrested Mr. Tarn as a matter of safety? No? He has not permitted Mr. Tarn to go to the house before getting in touch with the police? Gott! You are stupid."

"Tarn's calling on Henry. That's part of the scheme. I warn you, Baron, if you persist in—"

A hand clasped Blane's coat collar. A force lifted Blane from his seat and tumbled him over the side of the Mercedes. Blane stumbled to his feet as the Mercedes gave forth a loud whoosh. He started running after the automobile, crying, "Stop him! Stop him!" The Mercedes careened down Ocean Boulevard as if driven by a man who had either lost his mind or all sense of caution.

The Mercedes skidded into the Kerby driveway, ramming into the police car. With one bound, the Baron sprang from the Mercedes. Holding the green umbrella handle foremost, ready to throw, he hurled himself through the front door.

In the hallway, Police Chief Watson was kneeling next to the detective imported from Los Angeles. Watson whirled around jumping at the intruder as the Baron leaped into the hallway. The Los Angeles detective whispered agonizedly, "Ah-h-h! For God's sake, no noise now!"

And from Kerby's study, a lean, spare man backed out. This man was oblivious to the commotion a few yards behind him.

His face was ghastly white.

In his hand was a gun. "You can't say that to me, Henry Kerby!" he was shouting, his voice spiraling. "I'll kill you for saying that Lucille—"

"I'll say it again, Charlie." Kerby's beard glowed red in the late afternoon sunlight streaming into the hall. "You killed Lucille. You killed 'Dude'. But by thundering God! Charlie Tarn, you haven't the courage to kill me. We've proof that will hang you. Now give me that gun you grabbed or I'll take it."

The living room doors parted. In the doorway was framed Caryl Kerby. But Charles Tarn heard no noises of doors opening, no sounds of three men scuffling on the hall floor. He heard nothing except that great, booming voice in front of him coming from a man he hated with such mounting ferocity that nothing in the world mattered except to extinguish that voice forever.

The red beard was a burning target.

"Henry!" warned Caryl. She ran forward. The Baron jerked loose from the two men, tripped her, and she fell. Watson grabbed the Baron by the left arm.

"Give me that gun," ordered Kerby.

"If you move a step, I'll kill you."

"Kill *me?*" At that moment, Henry Kerby laughed. He laughed as a man who has never known what fear is and reached for the gun.

The Baron shook himself free of Watson, sent the Los Angeles detective sprawling against the police official. The Baron grasped his umbrella by the silver tip, lifted it over his head, ready to send it whirling as he had done so many times before, so that the weighted handle would strike Tarn's face with the full force of the throw plus the added momentum gained from the end-over-end revolutions in mid-air.

Kerby's laughter roared through the hall and Tarn lifted his gun and Watson threw himself once more upon the Baron.

Tarn lifted his gun and he aimed at the great red beard.

In the narrow confines of the hall the explosion reverberated and washed away the laughter as a huge green wave pouring upon a small ship and engulfing it and sweeping all life from the decks with the thunder rolling in the skies long after the ship has disappeared. Kerby's knees slowly bent. His hands went to his face and beard. He rocked forward, dropped to his knees, then twisted sideways and in the space where the two had been only Tarn was standing.

With one glance the Baron saw all that he needed to see. He dropped his umbrella. Too late Watson turned his head toward the Baron. Something struck him on the nose and he reeled, again lightning streaked before his eyes and his whole face felt the jar and impact for the second time and he went back upon his haunches.

"Dolt!" exclaimed the Baron mercilessly. "Quadruple dolt!"

15

Mr. Ward Explains

Caryl rushed to her husband. When Watson sat up, wiped his face with his hand and saw that it was smeared with blood, in his confusion he thought that *he* had been shot. He murmured bravely amidst the disorder, "Don't mind me, boys. Get Tarn first," and limply sank back to rest against the table.

Alice Rittenhouse ran downstairs crying, "What was the shooting?" At the foot of the stairs she stopped. "Oh, God!" She kneeled, pushing Caryl away with one frenzied hand. "Oh, God! Henry! He's dead. Oh, my darling." She took his head in both hands, sobbing. Slowly Caryl regained her feet. At that moment the Baron thought he had never seen so much dignity and breeding show in a woman.

"Tarn!" ordered Ward in a dangerous, flat voice. "I'll plug you if you move. Mrs. Kerby call the doctor. We'll take care of Tarn."

Caryl told the Los Angeles detective, "I'll get a doctor at once." Without glancing at the girl kneeling over her husband, Caryl vanished.

On Tarn's pale brown tweed suit was a round, smoke-blackened stain as large in diameter as a stove lid. Even as the Baron watched, the black stain changed slowly to scarlet and Tarn wearily leaned on the wall, staring

225

unbelievingly at his suit. The shattered gun dropped from his hand. Tarn placed his hand to his chest and the Baron saw that the hand was mangled and red, as though Tarn had dipped it up to the wrist in red paint, and where the thumb should have been was a sodden flap of flesh from which something dripped to the floor, spattering upon the dark, waxed wood.

"Up with your hands," shouted Ward, thrusting his gun at Tarn. "Do you hear?"

But a greater thing than a gun held Tarn's attention. Dazedly he drew his hand away from his chest. The feeling had gone out of his hand. He stared fixedly at the hand, seeing the red and then again touched the scarlet which was spreading down his suit. Then the numbness departed from his body and from his hands, quickly, without warning. The fire, seizing his nerves, flooded his body so rapidly that he could not consider such agony possible. Hold still. It will pass. The pain cannot last. But the fire spread from his chest and his hands, leaping before his eyes and blotting out all sight, roaring into his ears, crumpling ear drums and grinding into his brain and then he knew that it was death. All at once he shivered. He jerked as though his legs were twitched by hidden wires, bloody spume smearing his parted lips, his mutilated right hand twisting horribly to his chest and the Baron, who was a brave man, shut his eyes.

Ward thought that Tarn was attempting to escape. He shot twice. One little blackened hole followed another in the white forehead before it thumped upon the floor and Charles Tarn lay still and quiet, pain and terror extinguished as quickly as they had come. No longer would Charlie Tarn worry whether or not the Democrats would find a strong candidate for governor.

"You have wasted two bullets," observed the Baron without emotion, turning Tarn over on his back, wrapping

Tarn's gun in his handkerchief and examining it. "The hole in the man's chest is as large as my fist." He unbuttoned Tarn's sticky coat. "Larger. The breach of his gun exploded. Somehow the bullet must have stuck in the barrel."

Ward snatched the gun from this stranger. "Who the hell are you? Watson!"

The Chief of Police opened his eyes. He was very calm. "Tell them I did my duty, Ben." He closed his eyes.

Ward shouted, "Get up, man! What's the matter with you?"

"I think Mr. Watson's nose has been damaged," said the Baron. Alice began screaming at the top of her voice, diverting attention from the police officer. Ward lifted Alice, dropped her on the wooden hall bench.

"Keep quiet, sister. Everything'll be all right in a minute. Keep quiet, I say. Oh, for God's sake. Can you shut her off?"

The Baron supported Alice's head and she clung to him. She would have clung to a hatrack at that moment.

The head of the Carmel Police Department inspected himself in the hall mirror. He felt his nose. It didn't feel broken. Thereupon, he became very busy, filled with authority, hoping that his heroic conduct when under the delusion that he had been shot would be forgotten by everyone concerned. Watson kneeled beside Kerby. While his fingers investigated the writer, trying to discover where he had been wounded, the Police Chief's mind was still puzzling with the matter of his nose. The gun had gone off. Something had twice smacked him with tremendous force in his face. It had all happened so quickly. Perhaps it was from fragments of the shattered gun.

He advised Ward, "Henry received part of the explosion in his face. Yes, sir, and you can see where it burnt his whiskers. Can't find any wounds."

Caryl appeared, saying that the doctor was on the way and that she had telephoned for more police and an ambulance.

"Good girl!" said Ward without intentional lack of respect. He stood, wiping the blood from his hands after examining Tarn. "I'm sorry, m'am," he told her simply. "I warned Mr. Kerby that your gun was too old to protect him in an emergency. When Mr. Tarn grabbed it from Mr. Kerby and then pulled the trigger, the blank cartridge inside must have busted the breach." He gathered a few metal pieces scattered on the floor. "The metal exploding from the gun didn't strike Mr. Kerby, did it, Watson?"

"He's breathing. Shock and concussion knocked him out, I guess. You're getting Doctor Roth?"

Caryl nodded. Ward sighted through the twisted muzzle of the gun. "That's what it did, m'am. You can see the lead accumulation from the previous bullets clogging the muzzle." He faced Caryl. "We had it all planned, m'am. We had Mr. Tarn cornered just as you suggested—"

"As I suggested?"

"Mr. Kerby was to accuse Mr. Tarn while we hid. And then this fellow—" He scowled at the gentleman who was soothing Alice by the simple procedure of clamping his hand over her mouth in order to forestall extraneous sounds that might prevent him from hearing the Los Angeles detective's explanation. "He upset everything, m'am. We didn't figure on Mr. Tarn snatching the gun. If it hadn't exploded—" Again that scowl was directed at the Baron. "It's your fault, my man, if Mr. Kerby dies."

The Baron forgot that he was commissioned to hold off Alice. "Pardon. You stated that the gun was for blanks only?"

Alice squirmed from the bench, threw herself on the recumbent and unconscious Mr. Kerby, unloosening an assortment of shrieks and sobs. Ward was fast losing his patience. There was a dead man on one side of him, a man perhaps seriously wounded on the other, a policeman with a bloody nose, a stranger from God knows where, a yelling girl, and a wife who was eyeing him as coolly as if she were coming in from a tea party.

Something was wrong. All his plans were going to hell. "M'am," he pointed at Alice, "is she a relation? No? Watson take that girl out of here."

Sullenly Alice got up. "It's a miracle Henry wasn't killed," she told Caryl, who remained silent. "You *know* it was."

Now what the hell did she mean by that, wondered Ward. And where was Dave Blane? Blane was to have followed in the Mercedes. The Police Chief came from the living room, wiping his bloody nose. "She's got hysterics," he said sadly. "She's got them bad, too."

The Baron murmured that he would be delighted to take care of Miss Rittenhouse, passed into the living room after receiving a vague smile of thanks from Caryl. Maggy was already administering to Alice.

The Baron wandered into the dining room, returning with a decanter of brandy. Alice saw that it was the Baron who was offering her a glass of brandy, promptly buried her face in Maggy's large bosom declaring that she didn't ever, ever want to see the Baron again and that he and Caryl had tried to kill Henry.

The Baron repaired to the dining room. Here he sat down at the head of the table, splendidly aloof from the world, and proceeded to drink numerous glasses of brandy. His plans, too, had gone all to hell and his opinion of the inhabitants of the Northern States of America had attained a new low.

Meanwhile sirens shrieked. Five motorcycles thundered into the driveway ahead of the ambulance. The doctor followed the ambulance. The unfortunate Mr. Blane had been passed by this cavalcade as he was nearing the Kerby residence in an antique delivery truck which refused to be pushed above thirty miles an hour.

When he entered, the late Mr. Tarn had been deposited in the ambulance. Doctor Roth had moved Kerby to the couch in the study, ascertained that the writer had been stunned by the concussion, suffering from nothing more serious than a bruised face and badly singed whiskers.

Upon returning to consciousness, and being informed of his narrow escape, Kerby refused to be sent to bed, saying that he was all right, or would be all right in a few minutes. His wife sat beside him. He took her hand, holding it tightly. She passed her other hand over his forehead. Blane was comforting Alice in the living room.

The reporters arrived before the ambulance could take the body away. This increased the confusion. Photographers adjusted their tripods. Bulbs flashed in the hall. Men crowded into the study. "Right here, Mrs. Kerby," requested one. "And Mr. Ward, if you will stand at the left, with Mr. Kerby in the middle—"

"Almighty hell," rumbled Kerby as the doctor finished dressing his bruised face. "No pictures! I've had enough for one day. Dave! Caryl get Dave to clear this house, will you?"

David Blane deserted Alice. Urged the reporters to leave. They wouldn't go. They wanted the whole story at once. They could make the extra editions in San Francisco. The *Call-Bulletin* man and the *Examiner* man were struggling for the telephone in the study. The *Chronicle* reporter had yanked the hall phone off the stand, already had his paper on the line and was sticking his head through the door, pleading with Ward for the facts.

"If Ward will explain quickly," Blane finally suggested to Kerby, "it's the best way to get rid of them. Otherwise, God knows when they'll leave." When Ward began his explanation, no one noticed the gentleman who approached the doorway, more or less shielded from view by the reporters crowding about Ward and Kerby. This leering gentleman who had attained the relative shelter of the doorway, every now and then lifted a decanter of brandy, drank from it, wavered, and clutched the edge of the door, waggled his head in a most saturnine fashion.

"To be brief," commenced the eminent Los Angeles detective, "I knew that Mr. Tarn was the only man who could have committed the two terrible murders for the following reasons. First, he was intensely jealous. He completely misunderstood the harmless relationship between his wife and Mr. Kerby, a business relationship, I might add."

And then Mr. Ward spent ten minutes explaining to the reporters that Lucille Tarn was planning to return to Solar Pictures. Both Mr. Kerby and Mr. Blane were interested in Mrs. Tarn's talents as an actress, and in the scenario which they are now writing for Solar Pictures, they had a part for her. Mistakenly, perhaps, Mrs. Tarn had insisted upon meeting the two collaborators—by so adroitly bringing in both writers, Ward succeeded admirably in the inference that these meetings were innocent. And if the eminent Los Angeles detective exchanged glances with Blane at this point in his story, the reporters were too occupied with their notebooks or with the questions they wished to ask to notice the byplay.

At this point he piled sensation upon sensation by stating that Mr. Tarn for some time had been making an effort to drive Mr. Kerby to suicide. Ward, very concisely, told the gaping reporters how Mr. Blane had found a metronome cunningly placed in the attic above the writer's own bedroom. This metronome, it was presumed, had been placed there surreptitiously night after night by one of the servants in the Kerby House who had been bribed by Mr. Tarn. Although the servants had been severely questioned, now that Mr. Tarn was dead, Ward doubted whether he would be able to prove which servant had acted as accomplice. "However," he continued efficiently, "that is a minor point. Off the record, I have no desire to disrupt a household by further investigations. I am positive that Police Chief Lou Watson will be able to give you the name of the servant in a few days."

For an instant Ward smiled handsomely while a photographer took another picture, then resumed:

"To return to Mr. Tarn. Therefore, as I have said, misunderstanding these business meetings, Mr. Tarn brooded over them. Mrs. Tarn should have told her husband that she was intending to return to the screen, but she concealed these meetings, rather, tried to, because she was afraid that her husband would forbid her to act in pictures. Thus, through the lamentable misunderstanding between husband and wife, Mr. Tarn grew jealous. Madly jealous. Therefore, I think it is quite obvious why the poor fellow wished to kill his wife and Mr. Kerby.

"You all have been told how the negro managed to kill Mrs. Tarn." He waved at the Police Chief. "Mr. Watson deserves great credit, gentlemen, for determining that the negro killed Mrs. Tarn by thrusting a poisoned hatpin through the ventilator when the elevator was descending. He—what?" Ward looked around. Unable to perceive the gentleman sagging against the door, the detective decided to overlook this raucous sound from one of the reporters and proceed. Caryl Kerby also heard it. Sitting near the end of the couch she had a better view of the door. "The question," declared Ward, "after it was established who it was who killed Mrs. Tarn was then, *who* hired 'Dude'? Inasmuch as Mr. Tarn was the only person who had a motive—at least, let us say, a motive which he fancied was real—for killing Mrs. Tarn, immediately I inquired whether or not he had an opportunity to hire 'Dude'. I learned that 'Dude' had worked for Mr. Tarn as well as others. Furthermore, I established this fact: 'Dude' himself, knowing that Mrs. Kerby was in charge of the charity show, said that he had heard that the magician required an assistant and asked if he could have the job. Is that correct, Mrs. Kerby?"

"That is correct, Mr. Ward," she replied in a low voice.

"Thank you, Mrs. Kerby." Mrs. Kerby quietly slipped between the reporters and when the Baron paid no attention to her whispers, she ran out of the house toward the garage, for the chauffeur.

The third point, according to Ward, establishing Mr. Tarn's guilt, was that he was well acquainted with the construction of the Carmel jail and realized how easy it would be to kill 'Dude'.

"I think it is clear to all of you gentlemen why 'Dude' was murdered. His death eliminated the possibility of any revelation of who was the real instigator of the crime. Also, as I have indicated, Mr. Tarn tried to molest Mr. Kerby—tried, certainly, to drive him to suicide or at least insane by the monotonous, regular tickings of the metronome which came into his room from the attic above. You gentlemen can decide what effect a steady tick-tick-tick at night would have upon the nerves and imagination of a man as sensitive as Mr. Kerby. Knowing all this, it was merely a case of trapping Mr. Tarn and forcing his confession. I took advantage of a suggestion offered by Mrs. Kerby. That was to have her husband call Mr. Tarn and request him to come here for a conference. Meanwhile, the newspapers cooperated with me. I announced that I knew the name of the murderer, doing this deliberately to frighten Mr. Tarn. He had departed for Sacramento. Gentlemen, I expected him to flee the state. However, he was an astute criminal. He made no obvious attempt in this direction. I think that he thought we had some other suspect in mind. When we called him at Sacramento, asking for the conference, he accepted, partly out of curiosity, partly because if he refused, from his point of view, it would have appeared that he was afraid to come. Have you got that down, gentlemen?"

The *Examiner* man wanted to know why Tarn was asked to come.

"Simply because," replied Ward promptly, "we as yet had no *actual* evidence. Our entire plan was constructed in order to force Mr. Tarn to admit his guilt. We trusted that our tactics had, so shaken him that once he was accused, the man would collapse. We were right. That was what happened. I might explain at this point, that Mr. Watson again deserves high praise. Although we kept in close touch with Mr. Watson, neither Mr. Blane nor myself wished to risk bringing in the law as represented by the Police Chief until we believed that we had Mr. Tarn.

"Mr. Tarn telephoned us, an hour or so ago, that he had arrived in Carmel and would be over shortly. Mr. Blane drove me to the jail to get Mr. Watson as witness, who, as soon as the plan was explained, at once appreciated it and came."

"But the revolver?" demanded the man from the *News*. "That exploded—"

"In order to protect Mr. Kerby during this hazardous interview, I tried to get him to take my revolver. However, Mr. Kerby showed us an old revolver belonging to his wife and insisted that I retain my own, saying that he would be amply protected. Mrs. Kerby's revolver wasn't a true revolver at all; it was one constructed for shooting blank cartridges. You have heard all the rest, gentlemen. Our plan worked exactly as I had planned it except that Mr. Tarn snatched the revolver. Even then, if it were not for an unfortunate interruption by a busybody—"

A voice came hollowly from the doorway. "My dear sir. I do resent that."

"A busybody," repeated Ward loudly, at last divining the origin of those annoying interruptions. "A busybody who almost brought our plan to a tragic end. If that fellow—"

As a man, the reporters turned. They gazed upon the leering visage of that fellow who was clutching an empty brandy bottle with both hands. "If that fellow," shouted Ward, "hadn't deliberately attacked myself and clouted Mr. Watson on the nose, I say to you that there would have been no accident and Mr. Tarn would have lived to hang because we would have interfered before he could have pulled the trigger."

Police Chief Watson had plowed through the reporters. "*You* smashed my nose?" he bellowed. "You did it?"

Caryl returned with the gardener and chauffeur, imperiously ordering them to throw the Baron von Kaz out of her house. The doctor refused to permit Kerby to leave the couch. "Dave!" Kerby called, "What the hell is Franz doing here? I thought you said he'd gone?"

Watson was apoplectic. "Arrest that man. Arrest him for drunkenness, for attacking an officer of the law, for conniving to interfere with the due process and—arrest him!"

This was an anti-climax. In the hall the reporters crowded around the dark-faced man holding the empty brandy bottle. He was very drunk. His face had lost its color. The scar on his cheek flamed vividly. But drunk as he was, he apologized to Caryl Kerby for causing her trouble. His speech was not incoherent. His blue eyes were only colder, more distant in their regard.

One of the policemen grasped the man, to eject him. Not one of them crowding and jostling the man, shouting questions at him, laughing at him, saw how it happened but somehow the policeman became entangled in his own feet, stumbled, sat down abruptly, and in his fall smashed one of the cameras. "Here," said the Baron. He shoved the brandy decanter into Watson's gesticulating hands. "I am finished with it, my dear sir."

"Why damn your lights!" shouted the Police Chief. "I'll—" he lifted the decanter.

"You'd better not," advised the Baron, smiling strangely. The Police Chief lowered the decanter hesitantly, venting his wrath upon the policeman who was lamely getting up.

"Can't you stand on your own feet?"

"He tripped me—"

"He tripped you? Why, you lummox, you fell. Lock him up."

In the midst of the tumult, the Baron grew more frigidly calm. "I desire to speak to Mr. Kerby," he stated distinctly.

"I say," Blane took the man by the arm. "Will you leave and stop troubling us?"

"I wish my five thousand dollars."

"He's mad," said Caryl. "Utterly mad."

"I will not depart," insisted the Baron obstinately to his audience, "until I receive my five thousand dollars."

"Franz," shouted Kerby from the study. "What the devil's the matter with you? They won't let me up. Come here, will you?"

"Excuse me." The Baron had the audacity to shove the stupefied Watson to one side. "Mr. Ward is wrong. Dreadfully wrong. I can show Mr. Kerby why he is wrong and why I can collect my five—"

This was too much for David Blane. He had suffered too much from the Baron to permit the man to interfere any longer. He stepped in front of the Baron, grasped him by the coat lapel, struck him in the jaw. This blow, combined with the brandy, laid the brave Baron Franz Maximilian Karagôz von Kaz upon the rug.

16

The Baron Also Explains

During Wednesday and Thursday, Chief of Police Lou Zachrisson Watson diligently examined into the past of the Carmel jail's newest guest.

This worthy police official had been extremely suspicious of the Baron ever since this latter had embroiled himself by the disclosure of the negro's murder. And now, although detective Ward had satisfactorily unraveled the Tarn case and departed to other glories, the Police Chief remained convinced that somehow the Baron had become involved in this case which was officially closed.

Watson, therefore, resolved to absorb a little honor unto himself by investigating this guest of his. He opened the Baron's pigskin suitcase. He found, the thief's tool. He sent a number of wires to Sacramento and to San Francisco, and then to Washington. During these two days the Baron philosophically accepted his fate, suspecting that the Police Chief was searching into his identity. Whatever thoughts he had during these two days were concealed beneath a manner which was strangely taciturn for him.

He had made only one request, and that was when he was brought to the jail. Of the two rows of cells, he had requested that he be placed in a cell of the inner row, with no window. "Afraid of too much sunshine?" asked the jailer sarcastically. "Well, in this country, prisoners don't select their cells. They go where we put them."

"Ach so? And do you wish them all to be murdered, as was the blackman, my dear sir?"

The only other prisoner, a Mexican convicted of chaining his eldest daughter to a bedpost as a fatherly means of inducing her to a desired marriage, had been removed to the safety of the inner row. Dacrokoff the magician had been released by the Police Chief Tuesday night and conducted to the station where he was warned not to set his person inside the boundary line of Monterey county again. That was the last that Carmel, and California, ever saw of the magician. It was supposed that he had taken a Japanese boat for the Orient . . .

Friday afternoon, backed by the husky jailer, the Police Chief entered the Baron's cell in a triumphant and thoroughly irritating fashion. In his hand he held a sheaf of papers. Without preliminaries, he demanded, "You admit that you are the Baron Franz Maximilian Karagôz yon Kaz?"

The Baron nodded.

"Sixteen months ago you escaped from Austria?"

"I departed from Austria sixteen months ago, my dear sir."

"You had been arrested in Vienna after being dismissed from the Department of Special Investigation attached to the Viennese police, the department of which you were in charge? You were sentenced to death? You were accused of treason? Accused of assisting the Monarchists in a plot for the restoration of the Austrian Empire?"

A faint smile illuminated the dark face.

"And, if you return, you will be shot?"

The Baron bowed.

The Police Chief significantly glanced at the jailer, turned a sheet of paper. "You entered Switzerland. There you remained until some two months ago when, according to these reports, you nearly killed a German because of a political argument?"

The Baron showed momentary annoyance. "Ach, then he did not die? A pity."

"Again you were forced to escape. You entered the United States illegally through the connivance of your friends in France. I have orders to hold you until tomorrow noon when the immigration men will arrive to see that you are sent back to Austria. What have you to say?"

"Ach, my dear sir. If you knew how tired I am of this country. This strange country where it is believed that a man who desires a high public office will so stupidly murder his wife."

"Eh?" Watson uncomfortably eyed the jailer, who was breathing hard, listening with great interest. "What do you mean?"

"And this servant which the astute Mr. Ward believes was bribed by Mr. Tarn? You have decided what servant it was, no?"

"Not yet. It might have been the chauffeur."

"Might have been?" asked the Baron ironically. "He who was domiciled over the garage could prowl through the house at night?"

"The housekeeper, then. She knew her way around better'n anyone else."

"So? The good Maggy who has been how many years with Mr. Kerby? Who is devoted to him?"

"You know so damn much? Well, why don't you come clean?"

The Baron glanced significantly at the open-mouthed jailer, hunched his shoulders in a stubborn posture, and remained silent.

"Karl," Watson took the jailer to one side. "You don't have to stick around. I can handle this." He returned to the Baron when the jailer had closed the door, said anxiously, "Now see here, Baron von Kaz. I don't want to be hard on you. I've got friends. I knew Tarn well. Worked with him. He'd rather have been governor than—well—there's still something fishy about this case. You've learned something? If you'll come clean I'll try to fix it with my friends so you won't be shipped to Austria."

The Baron smiled. He said he'd think it over. He wanted time, until next morning.

"Tomorrow morning? No, sir. The immigration men will be here by noon. If you've got anything to say, you'll have to say it now."

The Baron protested. He desired time to think. His conduct in front of the Police Chief became secretive and worried. The more the Baron protested, the more convinced was the Police Chief that he was on a trail of importance.

"My dear sir," whispered the Baron darkly, dramatically, "I am afraid. Ah, fearfully afraid."

"Nonsense man," urged the Police Chief, unconsciously lowering his voice. "You're absolutely protected. Now, honestly," he asked cunningly, "you haven't really anything to tell me, have you? After all, Ward *is* a very smart detective."

"Very, my dear sir."

"Come now, you don't *know* anything, do you?"

The Baron shrugged. "Perhaps not. Who does know?"

Watson grew confidential. "Now, see here, that's no way to act. Why, I *want* to help you. Yes, sir, just because I'm an officer of the law doesn't mean I'm not your friend. Why, I'd be glad to help you. You don't think I want to see you shot, do you?"

The Baron crossed his legs, placed his hands behind his head, and gazed at the ceiling. Anyone could see that he was holding something back. The baffled Police Chief began to sweat. He thought of what the papers would say.

"Carmel Chief of Police Cleverly Outwits Criminal and Opens Up Tarn Case." Ward would grow green with jealousy. . . .

Watson sat hopefully on the bed. "Yes, sir, Baron, I want to help you. You can trust me. In Carmel they'll tell you that you can trust Zack Watson."

The Baron darted to the cell door, gazed through it, returned, trembling magnificently. "What's the matter?" Watson started for the door.

"It is nothing." The Baron sat on the stool, far enough away so the Police Chief couldn't continue to clap him on the knee with so much friendliness.

"Nothing?" Watson peered between the bars of the door. The jailer with the keys was at the far end waiting. "You don't have to get scared. Karl's the only one out there."

"I dare not tell. Think of the poor blackman. Not now in any case. It is so hideous. So hideous! Perhaps tonight. I must have six or seven hours alone to consider, to decide first."

"Tonight?" eagerly asked Watson.

"Ah, should we be overheard—" The Baron shuddered.

"No one'll hear us, Baron. I'll see to that. I'll come alone. You go to sleep now. You get your rest. I'll come in here about midnight. No one'll even suspect you told me. How's that?" The Baron turned his face away. "And I'll promise this. If you know anything. If you're not kidding me, I'll—well," he said importantly, "I've got influence. I'll *talk* to those immigration officers."

He called the jailer. When the Police Chief was outside the door he declared loudly for the jailer's benefit, "If that's the way you feel, don't talk. He's faking, Karl. He hasn't a thing on the case. Just bluffing."

And as Watson departed behind the jailer, he winked at the Baron.

He didn't want the foreigner to think he was being let down. No sir, thought Watson. Why, good God! he had

that foreigner in the palm of his hand. He'd learn what the
foreigner was holding to himself; and, if it were important, there'd be enough publicity and comment to make it
worth while running for the state assembly.

When the steps of the Police Chief and jailer had died
away, when the silence was only broken by the Mexican's
weeping, the Baron stood up, stretched restlessly, sat again
on the stool, placing his finger by the side of his nose,
frowning thoughtfully.

He was right. He was positive he was right. There could
be no other solution. No other possibility to mislead his
imagination. And there was only one way to prove it and
claim his five thousand dollar fee.

Ach, these Northern Americans. They were a terrible
people.

That night Kerby and Blane were working late on the
scenario. It was past one in the morning when the front
doorbell rang. It was the Baron. He had his green umbrella
and his disreputable suitcase. He had been released late
this evening, he explained amiably. Now it seemed that
he had been called to Canada rather suddenly and before
departing had come to collect the five thousand dollars.

"For solving the ticking jeopardy, my dear sir," the Baron said as Kerby's face went blank. The Englishman declared the Baron completely insane and then remembered
his five hundred dollars and demanded that as the bargain
had not been kept, his money be repaid. Icily the Baron
stared at the Englishman.

The telephone rang in Kerby's study. "Dave, give Franz
a glass of brandy." Kerby lifted the receiver. "Henry Kerby speaking . . . what? Why, yes, as a matter of fact, he's
here. He's . . ." There was a longer pause. "No? Thunder
and damnation! He did? On the nose again? On the chin?

. . . Oh, my Lord! I guess so. I'll try to, Zack, but he's a violent man. He may escape . . . All right."

Kerby replaced the receiver, stared accusingly at the Baron.

The Baron smiled.

"By thunder, Franz! I never saw the like. Never—"

"What's the matter?" Blane asked.

"Matter? The Baron here managed to trick that blundering jackass, Zack, into his cell, smashed him on the nose, and escaped in Zack's car."

Blane promptly stepped in between the door and the Baron, barring the latter's way. "Quick. Call the chauffeur. We can hold him."

"Hold him?" Kerby laughed. "After he's gone to all that trouble? Zack took a chance and called to see if you stopped here, Franz. Why in hell did you ever take such a risk?"

"If you please—"

"You beat me. I don't know what to do with you. Zack will be here in ten or fifteen minutes."

"I say, my man." Blane suddenly sat down, pointed to the door. "Why not be sensible about it? You're right, Henry. After all, I'm sure the Baron hasn't meant any intentional harm. Go on and escape, Baron, while you've got the time. We'll tell the police you headed east, won't we, Henry?"

"The agreement was that I would receive five thousand dollars if I solved the mystery of the noises, my dear Blane. The noises were originated by the murderer. And the murderer was *not* Mr. Tarn."

"Not Tarn?" queried Kerby, his beard swinging back and forth. "Who the hell was it?"

"I say," shouted Blane, "this fellow's mad. Give him a thousand and pack him off. He'll simply create more trouble. He's just—just insane enough to threaten us by saying one of us did it after an expert has already satisfactorily proved Tarn was guilty."

The Baron sat down, crossed his legs, folded his hands on the green umbrella. "An expert? Ach so? The gentleman *you* engaged, my dear Mr. Blane."

And after that statement, as though holding to a preconceived plan, he refused to budge despite the threats produced by the outraged Englishman. Watson accompanied by two policemen roared into the driveway, followed by two others on motorcycles, and stamped into the house. The noises brought an indignant Caryl Kerby down to remonstrate at this new disturbance. Alice trailed behind her, her blue pajamas showing beneath the Mandarin coat the Baron remembered so well.

"All right," decided the Police Chief after hearing the Baron's claim. "What've you got to say? Be quick. Take it easy, Blane," he nodded at the white-faced Englishman. "I'll handle this."

The Baron said, "Thank you, my dear Mr. Watson," and added that he would talk as soon as the check was written out for him. That is, with Mr. Kerby's permission. The Police Chief completely lost his temper. "Write it, Henry. Anything to make the man talk. He can't get away with the check." Kerby stepped to his desk.

"There!" He laid the check on the blotter. "Go to it, Franz. If you can get us to believe you, it's worth five thousand dollars."

The Baron bowed. "First, motive of jealousy. Correct. We have assumed Mr. Tarn arranged to have his wife killed, next killed the murderer to close his mouth. But if you please, Mr. Tarn was of that type who thinks too much of a career to jeopardize it by killing. Notice that the entire case against him was built upon the supposition that he *knew* his wife was unfaithful. I shall prove that he did not know."

He leaned on the green umbrella. "Could not someone else be jealous? Ach!" He indicated Mrs. Kerby. "Like all geniuses her husband has—ah—unstable affections. And did a woman do these horrible murders? Does not a woman think of a hatpin? Did not Mrs. Kerby accompany her husband to the party where first she saw Dacrokoff? Next, did she not bring Dacrokoff to the Carmel Theater? Did she not employ 'Dude'? Was it not her metronome that was placed in the attic and discovered by the admirable Mr. Blane? And why did he find it? Because it was set on a beam near the grill under the eaves; and when Mr. Blane was in the garden, the beam acted as a sounding board. Whoever was in the garden could hear the tickings as well as whoever slept in Mr. Kerby's bed."

Calmly he stood, requested a flashlight from the Police Chief, and led them all into the garden to show them the grill opening beneath the roof. They looked, trooped back after him with Alice complaining that she had gravel in her bedroom slippers. The Baron resumed his seat, continued:

"And so Mr. Blane poisons the cow to provide a diversion while he explores the attic." He pointed at Blane. "Did you not believe, dear sir, that you knew who perpetrated the ticking? You hired the detective *before* you found the metronome. Was that not why you said nothing when your brilliant Los Angeles expert declared that blank cartridges had left a lead accumulation in the barrel, forgetting that blank cartridges do not have lead bullets? Did you not think that Mrs. Kerby had deliberately poured a few drops of lead in the gun, hoping it would explode and kill her husband—"

One of the policemen grasped the Englishman by the wrists. "No you don't. No rough stuff." Watson regarded Mrs. Kerby who stood proudly, her lips dry and white. "Go on!" Kerby went to his wife.

"And finally," said the Baron with a strange smile in her direction, "did Mrs. Kerby not attempt to throw suspicion on Frances Taylor, Mr. Kerby's first wife, and was she not familiar with the jail, her landscaping committee having planted roses in the alley?"

A deathly silence hung over the room. Watson broke it by coughing nervously. He approached Caryl Kerby. "I'm sorry, Mrs. Kerby, but I've got my duties."

"You blasted fool!" roared Kerby. Then he leaped to the desk as the Baron pocketed the check.

"Caryl didn't do it! You know damn well Tarn did it. Give me that check."

"She didn't do it?" The Baron opened his eyes innocently, his hand over his pocket. "Who did then?"

"Tarn."

"Mr. Tarn placed your wife's metronome in the attic?"

"Certainly."

"And how did he know I was going to search for the ticking noise the night he placed it in the attic?"

"What d'you mean?"

"On the night you thought I was not going to look into your room I *heard* no ticking. Evidently no one in the garden heard it that afternoon or evening. On that night, dear Mr. Kerby, the night 'Dude' was killed, you were not in your room. Was it you who departed to murder 'Dude'?"

"Oh. So that's it?" Kerby leaned on the desk. "What else?"

"I forgot to say that on the same night the blackman was killed, Mrs. Kerby *was* in her room." Watson started toward the Baron. Alice gave a little yelp.

"You're crazy, Franz," said Kerby calmly. "Crazy. Why should I want to murder Lucille? Zack, the man's absolutely crazy—"

"Motive you wish? Ach, so. . . . You murdered Mrs. Tarn, for you could not otherwise rid yourself of her. She desired to marry you. She was so desperately in love with you, my dear sir, that she was determined to divorce her husband to marry you. That she told me. But you—you did not wish to marry this woman. Alice has arrived from New York. You are a little tired of poor Mrs. Tarn, no? She is too insistent. And so you think of something to frighten her. You tell her that you hear ticking noises night after night. That is very good, my dear sir. You say that Mr. Tarn is causing them. That he has learned of your relationship with Mrs. Tarn. If he knows, should she attempt to divorce her husband there will be a scandal. And a scandal will ruin her chances to return to the cinema and may harm your sale of the important script. These imaginary noises, they are so bizarre that, paradoxically, dear Mr. Kerby, they impress Mrs. Tarn more than an ordinary lie. No, those noises were admirable as an excuse. She worries. However, you are unsuccessful in persuading her to relinquish the idea of marrying you.

"She will wait only until you finish your script for the pictures. Then she will divorce her husband, and you will be forced to divorce your wife. And you had never planned upon divorcing Mrs. Kerby. Ach, no, it was too convenient as it was. She was too proud to let you know that she saw through your sham faithfulness, that she was aware why dear Alice Rittenhouse had arrived. And what then is your program? To rid yourself of this poor Mrs. Tarn who takes an affair that was to be casual seriously? Yes, you decide to murder her. But unfortunately, my dear sir, you have so worried Mrs. Tarn that she requests me to come to San Francisco. That might trouble an ordinary man to delay the murder, but not you, you are infallible, and besides your time to dispose of Mrs. Tarn is short. I arrive on the day you intend to kill her. You have to see me or she will be suspicious. I am a foreigner. The great von Kaz does not impress you. I, you decide, will become an asset. If necessary, you will arrange ticking noises for my benefit."

"I'm listening," growled Kerby.

"I am engaged as a detective. Whatever I discover I must report to you. You will now prove to me that there is a ticking noise. And on the night I tell you I shall seek it, miraculous! There is a ticking noise. However, my dear sir, are you disturbed? Do you toss in anxiety? Ach, no. You are worn out. The night before when I heard no ticking noise in your empty bedroom, where were you? You were walking to and from the Carmel jail with death slinking by your side. So on the next night you are tired; you sleep and the metronome ticks above you. You are asleep, dear sir, *because it does not frighten you!*

"The hatpins? Again they betray you. Your bravado tempts you to leave your calling card with the blackman. Where did you acquire them? Perhaps during your visits to San Francisco you bought them. The poison on the first hatpin? Again anyone could have purchased it. That is not important."

"Important?" Kerby swung his head to those staring at him. "What else?"

"What else, my dear sir? Lieber Augustin! In this very room Mr. Watson heard Mrs. Kerby admit that the negro came to her, asked her for the position as Dacrokoff's assistant. And why should the negro come to her, instead of directly to Dacrokoff or the manager of the theater, unless he had been *sent* to her by that relentless and bizarre brain which had devised the plan of the murders? What else? Ach, so. . . . You were as familiar with the jail as was your wife. Everyone in Carmel was interested in this so beautiful jail and in the warm weather the prisoners were always locked in the cells with windows. More? If you so wish." He addressed Mrs. Kerby with dignity and courtesy. "Permit me, gracious lady. Was it your suggestion to trap Mr. Tarn? Was it *your* revolver?"

Hardly audible was the faint reply, "It was my gun—"

"So! But *his* idea, no? It is finished, gentlemen. My *dear* Mr. Kerby—" And there was something so ironical and sinister in his blandness, that Kerby felt as might a huge confident boar of the jungles who irritably brushed aside a harmless vine and then realizes too late, as slippery coils slowly crush around him, that it wasn't a vine, that it wasn't harmless. With an effort, his hands fumbled at the drawer, unable to remove his eyes from that terrible smile. "My dear Mr. Kerby," requested the Baron with utmost politeness, "You, yourself, may wish to offer us the final proof that Mr. Tarn did not know his wife was unfaithful. And if Mr. Tarn did not know, where is your case against him? Who was it, if you please, who deliberately drove the unfortunate man into a murderous rage by first giving him the news of his wife's deception? Hein?" Sadly the Baron smiled, glancing, however, out of the corners of his eyes to be sure his breathless audience was affected by this revelation. His voice dropped tragically. "Gott! So easily do we forget Mr. Tarn's cry as he backed from the study, 'You can't say that, Henry Kerby. I'll kill you for saying that Lucille—' And what did you say, sir, to Mr. Tarn instead of accusing him of murdering his wife that could make him wish to kill you and—ach, no. No!"

As a man possessed, Henry Kerby had jerked open the desk drawer, grabbing from it a shiny new automatic.

A green umbrella handle struck Henry Kerby at the base of his head. A policeman had leaped upon him as he fell, going to the floor with him. Frozen by horror, Caryl looked on, powerless to move. Alice, more practical, conveniently fainted. The Englishman sat down in a chair, swearing softly without appreciating that he was swearing.

The Baron picked up his pigskin suitcase, tucked his green umbrella under his left arm, and stopped near the doorway in front of Caryl.

That man on the floor, who had confounded the wild
and bizarre dreams in his head and confused them with
reality, whose existence was lived in a curious world of
his own where wild laughter was heard through the trees,
where his desires and his wants sprang from his thoughts
to white paper and from this paper to the illusion that
even the living were but flesh and blood puppets to laugh
with him and to give him endless pleasure until he tired
of them—that man on the floor, his tragedy must not be
permitted to ruin the rest of her life.

Her love must be sheared. And quickly.

He bowed over her cold hands, kissing them in fare-
well. "Have no more fear, gracious lady. It is not you who
will die next."

Police Chief Watson walked with the Baron to the
driveway. "Don't apologize, Baron. You don't need to. That
clout on the chin tonight was the luckiest thing that ever
happened to me. Good Lord! Suppose you hadn't knocked
me out and swiped the keys? Suppose Karl had been awake
when you went into the office for your damned umbrella
and bag?"

The Baron climbed into a small car. Watson leaned on
the car. "With luck you can reach Mexico. I'll say you
headed north if it costs me my job. And I'll talk to the
immigration officers tomorrow. Maybe I can fix it so you
can return."

There was only one country, only one city, to which
the Baron ever wished to return. That country was not the
Northern States of America. Nor was that city a little town
on the coast of California.

"Well—" Watson grasped the Baron's hand.

"Good luck. You're sure there's nothing I can do for
you? You don't realize how I feel, not being able to stop
those damned immigration officers."

"If you please, have you influence outside of Carmel?"

"Have I—what do you mean?"

"Do you know where Salinas is?"

"Salinas? That's only twenty miles from here. You turn off at Salinas to get to Los Angeles and when you're there you'd better hide out and cross the border at night. Wire me after you're located."

The Baron listened patiently, then asked, "Could you persuade the policemen in Salinas to release my chauffeur? I sent him on an errand for me. He aided me materially in solving the case. That is, with your splendid collaboration, my dear sir—"

"Your chauffeur?"

"He was arrested for driving too rapidly. He was acting entirely on my orders."

"Sure. I'll fix it. What's his name?"

"Tivvits." The Police Chief rode with the Baron until the car reached the road, where he jumped off the running board. "Wait!" He ran after the car, jumped on again. "Have you plenty of money?"

"Money?" The Baron applied the brakes. "Dear Mr. Blane offered me ample until the check is cashed. And that reminds me, my dear sir, of another favor with which you could oblige me."

"I'll be damned," the Police Chief swore. He had forgotten the check for five thousand dollars. Even though Henry Kerby eventually would be hung by the neck until pronounced dead, his check was good.

"If you please," said the Baron. From his pocket he withdrew three hundred and some dollars remaining from the sum paid to him by Blane, divided it in half under the light from the dashboard. "When Tivvits is released, give him this from the Baron von Kaz."

"Sure." Watson took the money. "Say," he asked conversationally, "what won't Ward do when he hears how I solved the Tarn case?"

"Pardon? When he hears that you solved the Tarn case?"

"He'll go wild," said the Police Chief happily. "What do you think?"

The Baron began, "'Infinitus est—'," asked suspiciously, "Do you understand Latin?"

"Only Spanish. When I write Ward—"

"'Stultorum est numerus est—est—' Never mind." He stepped hard on the clutch as though all of this barbaric country could be pressed out of existence. "That is Latin. It translates, 'The number of dolts is infinite'."

As the car moved, the Police Chief complacently advised, "Don't be too hard on Ward, Baron. Remember, those people from Los Angeles haven't the brains we've got." The car lurched forward with a jerk.

Feeling a surge of reluctant admiration, Chief of Police Watson remained in the middle of the road watching the brave Baron Franz Maximilian Karagôz von Kaz drive off into the velvet, star-sprinkled darkness of a California night, along that road first laid out by men from Spain. Then the Police Chief turned toward the Kerby residence.

A policeman ran from the house. "Kerby's having fits of some kind, Zack. We've called an ambulance. Look!" Wildly the policeman pointed to the driveway. "Where's your car? The one the Baron drove here in. It's—gone. He didn't swipe it again did he?"

"My car?" The police official somberly awoke from a reverie of future glory when upon the morrow the, reporters from the city papers would interview him. His car gone? For the second time that night he stated that he would be damned.

The policeman jumped on his motorcycle. "I'll stop him, Zack. Which way did he go?"

Stop him? Stop the Baron? Have him sent to Austria? To a bleak stone wall in Vienna that was pitted by bullet

marks? No, not the Baron. He was not one to allow himself to be stopped. Not as long as he could hold the car on
the road. Not as long as ahead he could see unwinding that
road to freedom . . .

Something of this the Police Chief must have vaguely
sensed.

And, besides, the reporters would be coming soon. And
even if the Baron were successfully stopped and brought
back to Carmel, you couldn't ever trust him. The reporters
would want to see him. And he was so damned conceited,
he might say anything to them. He might even claim he
solved the Tarn case.

"Get into the house, Caleb," virtuously ordered Mr.
Watson. "I suppose you're going to tell *me* I can't lend a
gentleman my own car?"

THE FEATHER CLOAK MURDERS

The Second Adventure of the
Brave Baron Von Kaz
in the Northern States of America

To James W. Poling

*as a poor substitute for a certain bottle of brandy
duly promised and lamentably forgotten*

1

Sprouting Feathers

The man was saying something. The wind lifted tattered sentences, torn fragments from his speech, and hurled the words around the corner of the deck.

"I'm not double-crossing you. . . . I'll prove it. The assistant manager of the club's a friend of mine . . . he sent me the radio . . . this afternoon. He saw the letter from . . . San Francisco. And they're mailing it to her in Hawaii. That's God's truth. . . . He didn't say, but it ought to get there soon. We can watch her mail . . . know it's coming and can wait and get it and . . ."

Then the man began to laugh. It was a heavy laugh. The other person with the laughing man would speak in a low voice and then this laugh would come, huge and hearty, carrying over the rush of wind, over the wash of waves, as the *Kohala's* streamlined prow cut through the dark water.

It was past midnight. The great Pacific liner raised up and down easily, like a luxuriously appointed lady with one cocktail too many who still retains all her dignity. The motion became a long, slow, rhythmic weaving into the waves. It was warm. The clouds rolling across the moon were thick and bluish, as though they had been rinsed in too much bluing and stuck up there to dry against the soft, star-sprinkled velvet of the night.

Tomorrow morning the *Kohala* would be in Honolulu. Down below, in the bar, in the ballroom, and in all the cabins, from the expensive Lanai suites on B deck to number six-twenty on D deck, into which the two chorus girls had wangled the two evaporated milk salesmen, the passengers were celebrating their last night before reaching Hawaii.

They were happy, drinking, dancing, and the music floated up through that powdery tropical night to the sports deck.

The laughing man and his companion were standing on the trap-shooting platform at the rear of the sports deck. The platform projected several feet beyond the side of the ship, a sheer drop of fifty some feet to the curling streaks of water creased with shimmering strips of foam. The man continued to laugh. The laugh sounded as though a number of small paper bags were being exploded in a series of three and four at a time.

The laughing man leaned on the railing. Behind him, his hands rested on its salt-roughened wood. His head was back. His big, wide, drunken mouth was opening and closing and letting out the laughs, his eyes wrinkling when they shut. When he laughed his whole body would move. His coat would part. His stomach was big. His stomach would contract as if the laughter were something hard and solid which had to be shoved out, and then the stomach would relax and flow over the belt again.

The other didn't speak very loudly. The other watched the man's big stomach expand and contract and stepped closer to this stomach and quickly, with a single motion, drew an object from a holster placed flat against the chest under his coat. The man was still laughing when he felt that hard, shiny thing dig into his stomach, go creeping upward to his heart.

All at once the laughter stopped.

It stopped with an odd fluttering squeak. The laughing man wasn't drunk enough not to know what was in his friend's hand. The night, and the hazy light from the clouded moon and the stars, curiously exaggerated the form of the revolver. The light touched on the barrel of the weapon. It was a long barrel. Twice as long as the barrel of an ordinary revolver. The front half of the barrel was slender. The latter half was swollen, bulbous in outline. The mouth which had been laughing was open, but no sound issued forth, and the eyes sighted down at that cold swollen thing pressing at his heart, and hazy thoughts, clumsy ideas, flashed through the man's head.

From the steel barrel of the elongated revolver came a hissing sound, as faint as any tremulous sigh of the night.

As the big body pitched forward, the barrel was rapidly withdrawn.

The big man fell limply. He went down on his stomach. A fraction of a second after the stomach squashed onto the wood, the head smacked the deck hard.

One of the hands crumpled unnaturally under the soft, bulgy stomach, as though in that instant before he had finally gone off into death he had wished to feel that feathered dart which had struck into the flesh covering his heart.

The other arm had hit the deck, remaining there. His body was rolled to one side. A hand plunged into his inner pocket. A shadow passed along the body. And then the body was alone on the port side of the deck, moving sluggishly with the lift of the ship. . . .

Listening to those words whipped to him from the other side of the deck, listening to them without paying attention to them, the brave Baron Franz Maximilian Karagôz von Kaz, formerly of Vienna, looked irritably at his watch for the fifth time.

It was twelve twenty-eight. He had been on A deck since midnight, expecting Caryl Miquet. He lit his seventh cigarette, placed his elbows on the railing and moodily gazed out into the night. Ach! he firmly decided; five minutes longer shall I wait. Only five minutes.

He could hear the nostalgic refrain of the Viennese waltz which the orchestra was playing below. It brought him memories of Vienna. He had been away for three years. Lieber Gott! In a few weeks he would be in Vienna, and no longer would he hear this barbaric American language spoken; no longer would he have difficulty in making it clear to stupid waiters that it was champagne he wished for breakfast and not curious fruit juice concoctions. He sighed and looked at his watch again. Twelve thirty-five. Perhaps it was that imbecile laughing on the other side of the deck who had frightened her.

The music ceased. He lit another cigarette. He would give her five minutes more. No one could say that he, the great Von Kaz, cared whether she came or not. Miti Klingefass was still in Vienna. The Baron lit the cigarette as the laughing blown by the wind from the other side of the deck stopped. The Baron flicked his cigarette overboard. He was in vile humor. He would telephone Miti Klingefass as soon as he arrived in Vienna. He would keep her waiting. He would telephone Miti and Rachel von Freiden and the Countess Polakj; then they all could wait for him.

He took his watch out of his pocket and then, coming to a firm decision, clapped it back into his pocket, pulled his felt hat low on his forehead and, with the air of a man who is far superior to the idiotic vagaries of women, especially barbaric American women, walked around the wireless cabin toward the trap-shooting platform. Halfway around he stopped, peered hopefully down over the railing toward the lower deck. He rubbed his nose, muttered to himself. He glanced at his watch. It was eighteen minutes to one. Also, he savagely promised himself, he would telephone Vilma Hobraz and Clara Schonfeld, if they were in Vienna. He would keep them all waiting. Every one.

He passed the wireless cabin, wondering if it could be possible that this American woman had misunderstood the time. Ach, no. That could not be. There must be some other excuse. Thus reassuring himself, he was so occupied by anointing his grievously speared pride that it is conceivable that he might have stridden the full length of the ship and into the Pacific, such was his preoccupation, had he not stumbled.

His foot struck a dark massive shape stretched on the deck. The Baron pitched forward. He landed on his knees and hands like a cat, jumped up, balancing on his toes. All thoughts of the fickle Caryl Miquet vanished from his mind. Head cocked to one side, for a moment he stood over the body looking at the thing rolling back and forth on the grilled wooden platform with every rise and fall of the ship.

The Baron von Kaz had eyes which were remarkably sharp, even at night. The upper deck, as far as he could see, was empty, deserted. Suddenly he stooped, turning the body on its back. By the flickering gleam of his cigarette lighter he examined the face. Something puzzled him about this death, and then he knew: He had heard no shot. There were only two types of guns which could kill noiselessly; the revolver with the silencer or the air pistol. The revolver bullet left a clean hole when shot close, always with powder marks. The silent air pistol shot mushroom lead pellets which made, jagged wounds, or slender tufted steel darts. He placed the cigarette lighter near the small, bloody puncture above the heart. Then he saw gleaming, in the bright blood, two hairlike bluish strands.

He lifted the coat a few inches from the white shirt, touched the blood, then placed the tip of his finger beneath the cigarette lighter. The blue shreds from the tufted or feathered steel dart clung to his finger. The tufts or threads or feathers placed in the darts to guide their flight were often loosely inserted, easily detached and ripped away. He wiped his fingers with his handkerchief. The man, whose body was still warm, had been killed by an air pistol. Not a toy pistol, but one of the German pistols, because only in Germany were air pistols made with sufficient power to be used for killing small game . . . or human game at close range.

He threw the handkerchief overboard, watched it flutter, a pale white square, into the night and disappear. After once more regarding the dead man he rapidly ran forward. Amidships was a door which he opened. Entering the stair hall he impatiently glanced at the elevator indicator, saw that the elevator was between B and C decks, plunged down the stairs to B deck, where he found himself in the amidships hall, decorated with mirrors and gold furnishings and two or three women sitting upon the blue-and-gold chairs waiting for the elevator to rise, their escorts in evening clothes smoking and commenting on the fine weather you always have when you begin to near the Islands.

The Baron von Kaz went right, turned, passed through the library and smoking room, entered the corridor leading to the Lanai suites, the cabins de luxe of the *Kohala*. Three times he rapped on the paneled door of suite number four, and he heard someone move softly inside, and a suspicious voice came through the wood: "Yes?"

"Von Kaz."

The door opened slightly. For an instant before the door swung sufficiently wide for him to squeeze in, a face stared at him. The Baron shut the door behind him, leaning against it, peering about the room. In impeccable dinner attire, Mr. Hiroshita twirled the stubby little automatic he had been holding in his right hand. "You have greatly pleasing visit, Baron?"

Silently the Baron reached the door separating his stateroom from Mr. Hiroshita's suite, opened the door and peered into his own quarters. The cabin was empty. "If you please, my dear sir," he asked casually, returning, "did you enjoy the music of the dance?"

"From here one cannot listen to music."

"Ach!" The Baron showed his surprise. "But on such a lovely night you did not go for a walk on deck, no?"

Mr. Hiroshita sat down. "Not safe to do so." He watched the Baron restlessly pacing the width of the stateroom. "You have greatly pleasing visit with Miss Miquet?" he repeated.

The Baron snapped his fingers. "Naturally." He glanced at his client. "Naturally," he said more loudly. He walked to the telephone. "You were here all the time, my dear Mr. Hiroshita?"

"All the time. Why asking?"

The Baron lit a cigarette, slyly squinting through the smoke at his client. "Our dear friend," he stated with deliberate bluntness, "has been murdered."

"Please?" Air hissed from Mr. Hiroshita's yellow teeth. The long head completed a quick, startled motion.

"Mr. Kohler is on A deck. Dead. He will trouble you no longer, my dear sir."

After a long pause Mr. Hiroshita nervously produced a smile. "So very sorry dead." He placed knuckles to his temple where the veins showed blue under the parchment skin. "You are certain?"

"Do you presume, my dear sir, that the Baron von Kaz could be mistaken? He is dead."

"You have told anyone else, please?"

"No one. I came to you first."

The two men eyed each other. "Very clever man," said the Japanese at last. "However, poor Mr. Hiroshita in stateroom all evening."

"Ach." The Baron shrugged. "I wished to be sure." Briefly he explained that he had walked up to A deck for exercise and stumbled on the man lying dead on the trap-shooting platform.

"Miss Miquet not see the lamented Mr. Kohler?"

For a moment the Baron stared at the Japanese, then said coldly, "No," paused, concluded as though Miss Miquet's name had never been pronounced, "Air pistol. He was killed by an air pistol. The German Haenel pistol employs feathered darts. That is why there was no noise. 'Abyssus abyssum invocat.' That is Latin," he explained gravely. "It translates, 'One fault—'"

But Mr. Hiroshita was not properly impressed with this display of superior erudition. While talking, the Baron had lifted the telephone receiver, and the Japanese sharply interrupted, "Who telephoning?"

"Hein?" Sadly the Baron dismissed his Latin, resignedly explaining that it was wise to telephone the Captain, inasmuch as Mr. Hiroshita apparently had not left his stateroom to kill Mr. Kohler.

Mr. Hiroshita accepted this stolidly, showed his teeth again. "Must deny having pleasure to kill poor Mr. Kohler. Have suggestion, please. Greatly better to see Captain Anderson in honorable person."

"So?"

"Who knows who listens with telephone? I remain here with door well locked."

The Baron shrugged. "I will call the Captain."

"Greatly better to talk in person."

"But, my dear Mr. Hiroshita, is it wise to leave you alone again?"

"Wise?" Mr. Hiroshita dropped his right hand to his pocket. "Please to tell me what is 'wise'? You speak to Captain, Baron. In fifteen minutes, if you are not returned, Mr. Hiroshita rings for kindly steward, inviting him for game of poker which extends to your arrival."

"The steward will not play—"

The Japanese made motions of counting out money.

The Baron smiled, unlocked the door. "With someone in the cabin you should be safe."

"Honest man always safe," softly stated Mr. Hiroshita.

The Baron believed that he knew all there was to know concerning boats. Had he not crossed the Atlantic, penetrated through the canal to the Pacific? Accordingly, when he approached a steward in the B deck lounge and demanded where the Captain could be located and the steward said somewhere in the stern, the Baron marched forward.

The steward ran after the Baron. "In the stern, sir—"

"Exactly," said the Baron. "I understand both the American and English languages perfectly, my dear man."

The steward mumbled protestingly, but the Baron was already out of hearing.

Approximately fifteen minutes later the brave Baron again passed through the B deck lounge and in passing the steward remarked in a saber-edged voice that the Captain was supposed to be in the bar and consequently was not in the stern.

Captain Anderson was sitting with three other men at a table in a deserted corner of the bar. An elderly and liberally rouged woman was rattling the slot machine while three or four girls and their mildly drunken escorts were cheering her on.

Captain Anderson put down his glass of lemonade as, back stiff, feet clicking, the Baron bowed. "Pardon me, my dear sir. I wish to speak to you."

"Sure," said the Captain genially. "Pull up a chair. Feeling better?"

Neither the brave Baron von Kaz nor Mr. Hiroshita had departed from their staterooms for more than a few minutes at a time during the entire voyage. Both had explained to their stewards that they were very ill. Inasmuch as the *Kohala* rocked in normal seas about as little as an express train over a ballasted track, when the Captain had heard of the preposterous behavior of the two passengers in the exclusive Lanai section he had dropped in upon them to assure them that a brisk walk around the deck was all that they required to feel fit. He had found them playing cards, surrounded by a choice collection of brandy and whisky bottles and determined not to brave the elements.

As a result, the Captain had decided that these ill-assorted travelers—a Japanese and an Austrian—were merely utilizing the trip to drink themselves to death. While the Captain didn't mind a drink now and then, he disliked sots who preferred to drink in their staterooms and to issue calumnies concerning the seaworthiness of his ship.

"Thank you," replied the Baron. "I am better. I wish to—"

"Fine." This was the last night, and the Captain felt fine himself. "Baron von Kaz," he waved to the three men, "Mr. Preacher, Mr. Sargent and—"

The third one, sitting at the end of the table, said, "Bolton." Jeffrey Preacher, next to the Captain, was thin and youthful, about twenty-seven, with wheat-colored hair. John Sargent was stockier, with broad shoulders and a tanned face. "Bolton," concluded the Captain. "This is Mr. Bolton."

Despite his haste, formally the Baron bowed to each one in turn. The Baron had been reared in a land of rigid rules and manners; in Austria, when you were introduced to an individual, there was a proper way of acknowledging this introduction, a formula which must be gravely followed through even though it might be necessary to make death wait. . . .

Jeffrey Preacher raised his glass. "Aloha! Better have one with us."

John Sargent folded his arms on the table. "My fiancée's cousin, Miss Miquet, has mentioned you, I believe."

And Bolton's thick colorless lips rolled into a grimace. The lips remained pressed together during the smile. Bolton was fat, but the fat was hard and solid. Above his pudgy cherubic face pale brownish hair was brushed forward to hide the bald spot.

The Baron's glance passed over John Sargent as he again turned to the Captain. "If you will permit me, my dear sir?"

"Oh," grunted the Captain. "Want to see me alone?" He addressed the three men: "You'll excuse me?"

He and the Baron withdrew to one side. The Baron whispered.

The others saw the Captain frown, shake his head, then give a forced laugh. "See here, my friend," he stated, forgetting to lower his voice, "no one's shot. Besides, you can't shoot a person dead with an air gun." He clapped the Baron on the arm. "I tell you what, you run off to bed like a good fellow. You've had one too many."

The Baron again started to whisper.

"Yes, yes," said the Captain with an attempt at good nature, "Don't you worry . . . Of course he's shot. No doubt about it. Now you go on to bed and don't worry." He gave the Baron another clap, walked away, and sat down, looking wryly at his companions, The Baron stood in the corner, philosophically reminding himself that in a few weeks no longer would he have to suffer the company and the stupidities of the North American barbarians. . . .

"Who's shot?" John Sargent shoved the glass of lemonade toward the Captain.

"Shot?" Nervously the Captain glanced around, uncomfortably aware of a darkly sardonic countenance regarding him pityingly from the corner. "Nobody, Mr. Sargent. Forget it." He wiped his mustache after the drink, resisting the temptation to look over his shoulder at the foreigner. "See Carl Kohler this evening? You know him, don't you?"

"Carl?" John replied vaguely. "Saw him early this evening. Said he was going to bed after a dance or so. Why?"

Captain Anderson nodded in satisfaction. "Sometimes these passengers of mine get a little too much to drink. The foreigner over there— Don't notice him. He'll go to bed in a minute. He thinks he saw Kohler up on A deck. Says he was shot with an air gun." The Captain replaced the empty glass on the table. "An air gun. We'll be having sea serpents next."

The people around the slot machine were already looking curiously at the Captain's table, sensing that something unusual was taking place. The Captain left his chair again and took the Baron by the arm. "Go on," he urged. "You need your sleep, old fellow."

"Captain." Bolton had oozed out of his chair and was facing the two. "The man may be so drunk that he's really killed someone. Do you want me to go and see if anything *has* happened to Mr. Kohler?"

Bolton's face was more cherubic than ever.

Those at the slot machine heard what Bolton had said. Jeffrey Preacher and John Sargent stepped forward. "How about all of us taking a look-see, Captain?" asked Jeffrey. "This hasn't been such an awfully exciting trip so far."

"And it isn't going to be, if I can help it," stated the Captain grimly. "I'll go, if it's necessary. Come on, Baron. The rest of you stay here. Baron von Kaz has—these tropical nights are rather stimulating to the imagination." He grasped the Baron's shoulder forcefully, gave him a little jerk, not angrily, but indicating that he wasn't going to tolerate any more nonsense.

"If you please, my dear Captain," murmured the Baron politely as he lifted the other's hand from his shoulder. He smiled pleasantly. "I am able to march without assistance."

The Captain opened and shut his right hand until feeling was restored into his fingers, staring at the foreigner in bewildered surprise. The dark face smiled at him; the eyes were uncommonly innocent of all malice.

At the same time a brown-haired girl in a flowered evening dress ran from the bar to the table. "John, who's killed?" She pointed at the fat man who was lighting a cigar. "I heard Mr. Bolton say that Carl Kohler had been—"

"Come, come, Miss McKay," soothed the Captain. "No one's been hurt."

But the damage was done. The old woman let loose a scream. The girls with brightly painted lips clutched at their escorts, and Bolton continued to puff the cigar, his cherubic countenance as expressionless as a rubber doll's with all the features worn away. The Baron wondered if this Mr. Bolton had deliberately spoken to the Captain in a voice loud enough to reach the slot machine. And above the questioning voices Jeffrey Preacher cried hotly, "I won't, Bolton. I won't go to my room." He looked ashamed, embarrassed by the quick silence. "Sorry to yell. But Bolton's been ordering me about so long that he forgets I'm not fifteen years old now."

Bolton's thick lips twitched; the rest of his face was stolid. The Captain, deciding on the only means by which to calm his passengers, called to the Baron, "Let's go."

Jeffrey Preacher, John Sargent, and the brown-haired girl in the flowered dress followed them along with several others. At the entrance to the empty ballroom the Captain instructed them to wait in the bar. "No one's been hurt.

I'll be right back. The Baron's probably been dreaming of some child's popgun."

Ach, thought the Baton. A child's air gun. In Germany he had seen the Haenel air pistol shoot through three inches of seasoned oak.

Bolton was finishing his drink when the two men and the girl returned. Jeffrey said cheerfully enough as he sat down, "You are a fool, Bolton, shouting like that to the Captain."

Bolton's slate-gray eyes raised, looked at the young man.

"And why the devil couldn't I have gone with the Captain?" Jeffrey dropped his elbows on the table. "I'm getting tired of being ordered by you all the time."

Bolton stood up. Ignoring Jeffrey's rebellious complaint, he removed the cigar to say quietly to the other young man, "I don't like this, Mr. Sargent. I think I'll go and see what the trouble is." Jeffrey started to leave the table, saw the expression on the pudgy face and sat down again.

"I'll go with you," decided John. "You two stay here."

Mary McKay shook the ice in Jeffrey's glass and after a few minutes asked, "Why don't you get rid of Bolton? Every time I look at him he gives me a funny feeling."

"Don't be silly. He's all right. Only he likes to boss me as if I were still a kid."

"I don't like him."

"John seems to. What do you want to drink?"

"Chartreuse. He used to be a wrestler, didn't he?"

Jeffrey called the steward, ordered a Chartreuse and another scotch-and-soda. "He told you?"

"He told John. I don't see why John likes him."

"Bolton's been with me so long, I wouldn't hardly know how to tell him I didn't need him any more. That's the trouble. Mother took me to Paris because she had a mania about kidnapers. Bolton was physical instructor at an American boys' school outside of Paris when she got him. And since she died he's been so damned loyal I don't know what the devil to do about him."

"Well," declared Mary decisively, "if John thinks he's going to get Bolton to take charge of Billy, I won't have it."

"Oh." Jeffrey opened wide his eyes. "You're not luring him—"

"Certainly not," Mary said. "And John's marrying me, not Billy. Billy doesn't need anyone to look after him on the ranch."

"How old's Billy?"

"Nine, and he's swell, Jeff, even if he is my brother. . . ."

The Baron von Kaz and Captain Anderson had climbed the outside stairs to A deck. Above them the tall slender masts swayed in the night, and ahead huge funnels jutted toward the stars like massive cliffs. "This way," said the Baron. "He was lying on the trap-shooting platform."

The Captain walked past the wireless cabin, reaching in his pocket for his flashlight. The beam picked out the grilled wooden floor of the trap-shooting platform, but there was no body upon it.

Angrily the Captain swung his light on the grilled floor, then up and down the deck. "Are you satisfied, Baron?" he asked grimly. "There's no body here."

"So? However, Mr. Kohler's body *was* here, my dear sir."

The Captain sighed. It was part of his duty to be patient with his passengers, but mortal man has limits to his endurance. "Come on, Baron. What you need is sleep. I'll help you to your stateroom." The Captain silently told himself what he thought of these drunks, these damned drunks going and upsetting everyone in the bar by their silly talk.

The Baron was on his knees. Assuming that the foreigner had collapsed, the Captain resignedly reached to haul the man to his feet when the Baron's voice came, metallic, precise. "Here! If you please, your flashlight. He was here. His body was here."

A white beam of light splashed on a small, reddish stain. "See here, Baron, that's paint," explained the Captain. "Red paint."

The Captain even condescended to place a finger on the stain to prove to this foreigner that it was red paint. "Certainly it is. You come along to bed and— God Almighty! It's *blood!*" He had put his finger to his tongue.

Now he choked, feeling a queer rush of nausea. Frantically he wiped his fingers on the white dress coat, spat over the railing.

"So?" The Baron stood.

"You're right." Only for a moment did the Captain hesitate. Then he ran to the wireless cabin, knocked on the door. "Baron," he called, "will you wait in the wireless room?"

The Baron hadn't foreseen this. The Captain was issuing orders to the two wireless operators. One stepped out, hastily buttoning his coat. "He wants you in there, sir." Realizing that if he refused he would cast suspicion upon himself and thus risk involving his client, the Baron von Kaz bowed slightly, entered the cabin where the Captain had the chief purser on the telephone.

When John Sargent and Bolton, followed by several other curious passengers, reached A deck, they were stopped by a polite but firm wireless man.

"Sorry," he said. "There's been a slight accident. This deck will be closed for at least half an hour."

The lights were shining through the wireless cabin windows. At one of the windows Bolton saw the Baron's head, nodding vigorously, as if explaining to the officers in the room what might have occurred.

A few minutes later Bolton sat down next to Jeffrey. "They've got the Baron up there, and they're closing the deck for half an hour. Something's doing, all right. I think you'd better go to your room." And as the younger man didn't move Bolton's voice pitched higher, "Do you hear, boy? Get to your stateroom."

"Don't be so excited, Bolton." John gave the fat man a friendly glance. "Take it easy. I've managed too many Mexicans doing geological work to get excited when I'm giving orders."

"I'm never excited," contradicted Bolton flatly, unemotionally. "I am a plain, humble man. Mr. Sargent, my job is to protect Mr. Preacher. For fifteen years I've made that my job—"

"Oh Lord!" said Jeffrey wearily. "Let's not go into that again. Who the hell's going to kidnap me on a boat? I'm not going to my room. I'm staying here with Mary. And John," he added as an afterthought.

Bolton pushed back his chair, his colorless lips twitching. He got up and walked out of the bar. There was a long, awkward pause, and Jeffrey said finally, "He always gets sore if I don't do what he says. I guess I'd better go after him and tell him I'm sorry."

"I've got to go down for cigars," the geologist announced as Jeffrey stood. "They don't sell any decent ones here at the bar. I'll go part way with you. Coming, Mary?"

"I'm staying. *I'm* finishing my drink."

"Good," he said, oblivious of her frown. "I'll be back in a few minutes."

During the twenty-odd minutes that he was in the wireless cabin the Baron repeated his story, telling how he had discovered Mr. Kohler's body, to at least four ship's officials. He did not mention Miss Miquet. He merely said that he'd wandered to A deck to smoke a cigarette before retiring.

During these twenty-odd minutes the stewards had been notified by telephone unobtrusively to search the *Kohala* for Mr. Kohler. And Mr. Kohler was not located. Very little more could be done. There was some hope that he might be sleeping in another passenger's cabin. It was obviously impossible for the stewards to rouse every person on board. Captain Anderson thanked the Baron, apologized to him for disbelieving his story at first, and said he was quite free to return to his stateroom.

The Baron descended to B deck at once. For a few minutes only he stayed outside the ballroom on the promenade deck overlooking the tourist quarters. Like tiny flashlight bulbs, the stars went on and off in the midnight sky, and the wake of the ship curled toward the rear, luminous and vague.

Thoughtfully he lit a cigarette. Mr. Hiroshita had been afraid of Mr. Kohler. And now Mr. Kohler had been shot in the heart, and his body had in all probability rolled off into the sea unless . . . unless it had been deliberately pushed off after the Baron had departed. Ach! thought the Baron, that is not pleasant. He wished that he were certain Mr. Hiroshita had been in his stateroom during the time taken to wait for Miss Caryl Miquet.

The Baron absently considered the fiancé of Miss Miquet's cousin. He hadn't met him before on board. As he flicked his cigarette into the water, in the shadow under one of the lifeboats he saw a rounder dark blob. It was Mr. Bolton. This gentleman puffed at his cigar, giving no sign of recognition. The Baron had no idea how long the man might have been there, or even whether he had confined himself to B deck or had followed to A deck. Quickly the Baron went through the empty ballroom, from there into the bar.

Half an hour ago nearly deserted, now there were at least two dozen men and women excitedly clustered around

Mary McKay. "I heard the Captain say it," she was assuring them. "He said Carl was killed."

"Where's the body, then?" a man wanted to know. "Are you sure Carl was shot?"

"Right in the heart with an air gun. They've gone up on A deck to find the body now. Isn't it *awful?*"

"Mary!" John Sargent's big shoulders easily thrust through the throng collected at the bar. "I'm turning in. I'll walk with you to your room."

Mary's drink slopped on the bar as she saw the Baron standing near the slot machine, his dark face impassive. "There's the man now!" she cried, and would have run to him if John hadn't taken her by the arm. Anxious to reach his client, afraid that he had been too long away as it was, the Baron heeded none of the questions thrown at him as he passed out of the room.

The Baron rapidly walked down the hall toward the Lanai suites. Not until he had twice rapped three times on number four did he wonder if something were wrong. He stepped back from the door, his face sharper. A light leaked under the door into the hall. "Mr. Hiroshita!" he called, again rapping three times. "Mr. Hiroshita! It is Von Kaz."

There was no reply.

He darted to his own door, next to Mr. Hiroshita's suite, unlocked it with his key, switched on the light, ran to the intervening door, smashed it open on the third attempt.

Mr. Hiroshita was on the bed. Mr. Hiroshita was lying on the bed with his eyes closed and a bloody welt stretching across his yellow forehead.

2

The First Green Lion

The Hawaiian woman standing next to the bandmaster in Aloha was singing, her brown friendly face, shining like a well-oiled poi bowl, was raised to the passengers massed against the railings of the *Kohala*.

Two newspaper men finished taking photographs of a congressman from Louisiana on his way to Japan to view with alarm the yellow peril at first hand; the newspaper men elbowed through the passengers squirming self-consciously under masses of scented leis and grabbed Mr. Hiroshita.

"No, no, gentlemen," protested Mr. Hiroshita. "No pictures."

A dark-faced gentleman appeared from behind Mr. Hiroshita and accidentally bumped into the cameraman, and somehow the cameraman slipped and fell. The Baron von Kaz apologized for his clumsiness; butter would have melted in his mouth. When the cameraman got to his feet Mr. Hiroshita was going down the gangplank, the hat perched on his bandaged head. "To hell with him!" said the cameraman.

In the cool vaulted arches of Aloha Tower, the Baron and his client worked their way through a friendly people. The Baron was aware of white faces, brown faces, and those of various shades of yellow; a conglomerate of Oriental and Caucasian races under one flag and under one government and now for the moment united for the single purpose of welcoming these travelers from a land below the horizon.

The Baron was alert, watchful, suspicious. But the two men safely gained the exit, crossed the street away from Aloha Tower to the green park. Purple mountains lifted jagged sharp peaks above the buildings, and from the sun, hot, although it was only a few minutes after ten, poured a white radiance which shimmered in a blue, an eternally blue sky.

"This way, please," said Mr. Hiroshita, leaving the park. "I cabled automobile to wait for us at Bishop Street and Alakea."

As they walked beneath arcades of the old buildings, heavy, square, built of stone which had come from New England, the Baron glanced behind. The two Japanese sauntering half a block distant were examining the contents of a shop window.

The Baron grasped his green umbrella more firmly, increased his pace, but his client refused to be hurried. The Baron was forced to slow down.

At the corner of Bishop and Alakea a man jumped out of a big car and stepped in front of Mr. Hiroshita. The Baron reacted instinctively. Mr. Hiroshita uttered, "Umph!" as a hand struck him on the chest, shoved him to the stone wall. The umbrella handle gently stopped just below the other man's chin. "You wish?" asked the Baron with cold politeness.

Mr. Hiroshita recovered, sidled between the two men, laughing without humor. "Very sorry. This is George. Mr. George Tuung." Like a machine gun going into action, Mr. Hiroshita spoke in Japanese. George Tuung's mouth opened, and teeth three times too large for his triangular face shone brightly.

"How are you, Baron?" he inquired without the slightest trace of an accent. "Okay," he said as the Baron, realizing his mistake, bowed stiffly. "Don't apologize. I shouldn't have jumped at you so suddenly." Then he addressed Mr. Hiroshita in Japanese as he opened the rear door of the automobile.

"Only two?" For the first time Mr. Hiroshita looked over his shoulder. One of the men following them was lighting a cigarette. His companion was gazing at the sky. "Please." Mr. Hiroshita dismissed the two men, hissed liquidly at the Baron, "Please to get in, Baron."

For the first ten minutes of the ride the Baron said nothing, thought a great deal. From time to time Mr. Hiroshita slyly glanced at the dark-faced Austrian. "Have successfully evaded reporters, no?"

"Very successfully."

And abruptly changing the subject, "You thinking of poor Mr. Kohler? Body perhaps not rolled overboard?"

In the month he had been with Mr. Hiroshita the Baron had accustomed himself to the unpredictable leaps of the little man's mind. From the back window he saw the yellow taxi trailing them, and even as he replied he placed the green umbrella between his knees. "Ach, the great Von Kaz can not answer that question, Mr. Hiroshita. The body *could* have rolled overboard. I was stupid. I should have removed the body to a safer place, but I did not wish to touch it."

Mr. Hiroshita's eyes became half moons in a yellow square. The Baron looked out of the window again, placed his hand on his client's shoulder. "If you please, sit lower in the cushions. Your head is exposed, my dear sir."

The big automobile turned into a narrower street. Here the houses were smaller, newer than those huge cool buildings of stone in the center of Honolulu, but shabbier, dirtier. The sweet perfume of flowers, exotic and fresh, had vanished. The Baron sniffed delicately. The smells were sharp, sour. Dried fish hung in red strips from shop windows, and rancid vegetables and pickled beans; strange spices and condiments gave forth their own particular odors. The people in this narrow street were smaller. Old women clopped by in sandals. Their heads were nearly bald, wrinkles tracing their faces as if the flesh were covered with a coating of almond paste which too soon had dried in the bright flood of sunlight.

The big automobile coasted to a halt in front of an orange and purple painted store, three stories high. The windows were dusty slits. Above the drab-colored door was a sign: AKIA HIROSHITA, IMPORTER & GOODS OF NOVELTY. George Tuung opened the door. The Baron stepped out first. The yellow taxi slowly passed them. In the back seat the two Japanese were lounging, seemingly half asleep. George Tuung walked with the Baron and Mr. Hiroshita to the entrance of the building, spoke to the latter in Japanese. Then he waved cheerfully to the Baron, said, "I'll be seeing you."

There were little nods and murmurs of greeting from several yellow-faced men, who, almost as if by accident, found themselves in front of Mr. Hiroshita's store at the exact moment of his return. Suspiciously the Baron watched these people who were so small and suave, so oblivious of his own presence. And when Mr. Hiroshita had completed his hissing and his smiling and his bending up and down as though his head were attached to a pump handle, he ushered the Baron into a long, musty room with two counters on each side. In the greatest confusion, toys, knickknacks, bolts of cloth, a heterogeneous collection of objects, were piled upon the shelves and along the counters.

An oldish person, resembling a polished stone Buddha dressed in a dirty silk nightshirt, stepped over a rusty child's tricycle and advanced, making sounds like a leaky teakettle. When another stretch of Japanese backfiring was ended, the two almond eyes of the Buddha turned upon the Baron.

"Mr. Ukio," presented Mr. Hiroshita, "the Baron von Kaz I have greatly honored you writing about."

"So happy, Baron von Kaz." The Buddha inclined, the silken robes rustling at his arms.

Mr. Hiroshita continued toward a door at the rear of the store. The Baron regarded Mr. Ukio, considered the contents of the store and effectually concealed his enormous surprise. He had understood that his client was a man of great wealth. But this place—so shabby, so musty. . . . He smiled cheerfully at the impassive Buddha, caught up with Mr. Hiroshita, his eyes roving restlessly from side to side. This did not march so well, he concluded.

Beyond the door two flights of stairs led to a large sunny room. Here were cool gray walls and bright yellow mats on a polished floor, and waxy flowers waving on slender stalks cunningly arranged in red and yellow porcelain bowls. "Enter, please," said Mr. Hiroshita, stepping aside for the brave Baron, and this gentleman's umbrella dropped to the floor. Mr. Hiroshita leaned down to retrieve it, but the Baron said he was such a dolt and had the umbrella between his fingers before the Japanese's arm had reached the floor, and somehow, when all of this was accomplished, it was the Baron who was behind his client.

"Ach!" declared the Baron, obviously so entranced by the room that in his eagerness to enter he pushed his client into it ahead of him. "It is lovely!" The Baron, however, advanced in a slightly curious fashion; he came in crabwise, sideways, rubbing the green umbrella between his hands, and his eyes darting four ways at once, a great feat but not impossible to a man spurred by the vivid imagination of the Baron von Kaz. He was a brave man, to be sure, but it was extremely easy for him to imagine the paralyzing sensation of a feathered dart striking into his back.

"Most beautiful," commented the Baron, proceeding in his curious manner.

"Be seated, please," requested Mr. Hiroshita, ignoring the fine compliments. "No person here but us."

"My dear sir," protested the Baron, very pained, "I assure you, you misjudge, I desire merely to examine this admirable room. It is charming."

"Yes, yes," said Mr. Hiroshita, sinking into a green leather chair. He placed his hand on his bandaged head, relaxing for a moment with the pain flaring in his eyes. "Head persists in punishing poor Mr. Hiroshita, So sorry; have great deal to say, Baron. Please forgive if words come not quickly in present state."

With this he appeared to withdraw into the tenuous fastness of his own thoughts. The Baron sat down, continued to float a polite smile upon a foundation which was not so unconcerned as it seemed to be.

In Mexico City, and until last night on the boat, the Baron had believed that he was being paid one thousand dollars to guard a wealthy Japanese importer who was bringing a valuable jade piece to Hawaii. There were no complexities in that task; it was a simple, straightforward engagement.

Enormously confident of his abilities, the Baron had convinced himself that this frightened Japanese could be protected without complications which might interfere with the voyage on to Austria. An opportunity to collect a thousand dollars en route to Vienna does not come every day; the Baron could not resist it. He had accepted the engagement. But now the Baron felt a stir of annoyance. It was as though he had been gazing over a calm sea and suddenly sighted unsuspected depths from which loomed treacherous and hidden reefs, dangerous and obscure. . . .

As the silence began to stretch and wrap around the Baron and squeeze into him he tried to relieve this uncomfortable presentiment of future disaster by prodding the man opposite him into conversation. "Do you know, my dear sir," he asked with the most deceptive casualness, "I reproach myself severely for not remaining last night in your cabin with you?"

Mr. Hiroshita stirred slightly. The eyes turned to the Baron. "Happy to claim fault as mine. Insisted brave Baron locate Captain in honorable person. When hearing knock on door, made mistake to think my trusted friend desires re-entrance. When door unlocked, unhappy head struck. Awake to find Baron soothing inglorious head."

The Baron Franz Maximilian Karagôz von Kaz wasn't interested in anyone's inglorious head. He was interested only in obtaining his fee of a thousand dollars and departing. Unfortunately, the tenets and customs of that select and aristocratic Viennese circle upon which his habits and manners were molded included no formula permitting him bluntly to demand his fee.

In Hungary there are still a few surviving members of the Karagôz gypsy family, and they would have had no hesitancy in bluntly demanding their money and, if necessary, in slitting a throat or two to get it. But the Baron always firmly considered himself as a Von Kaz. In his innermost soul he deeply regretted the fact that his distinguished if erratic grandfather had ever wandered for a summer with a gypsy family. Now and then that wild, hot-headed Karagôz impatience with all order and rule would blast through his glacial Von Kaz polish. The results were usually so lamentable, not only to his dignity but to anyone who was present during the explosion, that each occasion only served to make him more determined to hold to the fond ideal of a pure Von Kaz.

And so, despite his growing impatience, he stated with the suavest of tones, "With dear Mr. Kohler dead, does not your attack indicate that someone else on board desired your valuable Green Lion?"

Mr. Hiroshita again wearily looked at the Baron.

"And why, my dear sir, did they not find it?"

Mr. Hiroshita blinked; he didn't know why they had failed to locate the Green Lion. "Already had pleasure to confirm Green Lion still secure in pocket."

"Ach, so," murmured the Baron blandly. Whoever had attacked Mr. Hiroshita certainly would have examined the man's pockets. The Baron raised his shoulders. "You are here," he suggested delicately. "My duty is—uhm—terminated, my dear sir." Mr. Hiroshita merely blinked. "You are aware that we were followed?"

The bandaged head inclined.

"I advise you to see the police at once." Mr. Hiroshita said nothing. The Baron's show of calmness appreciably diminished.

When he had accepted Mr. Hiroshita as his second client in the Americas, the Baron had faithfully fulfilled his obligations until the last night on board. Then his client had been injured, but this was not the Baron's fault. True, he had wished to see Miss Miquet at least once before the boat entered the harbor, but it had been his client who had suggested that he telephone her and ask for a midnight appointment. He was never guilty of mixing business and affairs of the heart. . . .

Mr. Hiroshita speculatively regarded him. "No, absolute proof not seeking Green Lion." He opened his wallet, extracted a round stone piece approximately two inches in circumference. It was greenly opaque. Upon one side, delicately carved, was traced the outline of a crouching lion.

This was the first time the Baron had seen it. "So? It is beautiful although I must admit I would not pay one hundred thousand dollars to possess it."

Mr. Hiroshita held the Green Lion to the light. "Not pay one hundred thousand dollars to possess?" The Baron wondered if there was a mildly ironic note in the inflection. "Note very cunning workmanship, Baron. Perhaps brave Baron lacks artistic background to appreciate true worth?"

"Artistic background? My dear sir! In Vienna, I inform you, no one appreciated art as did the Baron von Kaz."

"Excellent." Mr. Hiroshita tossed the carved stone to the Baron, who was so astounded at the sight of one hundred thousand dollars flying through the air that he almost failed to catch it. "Can be nice neckpiece for lovely lady, no?"

The Baron didn't reply. He turned the Green Lion around in his hands. On the rim were engraved the words, not in Japanese or Chinese characters, but in Spanish: *No Pidas De Grado Lo Que Puedes Tomar Por Fuerza*. As the Baron slowly translated the Spanish into English his dark face grew perturbed:

"'Do not ask as a favor what you can take by force.' Lieber Augustin! This is not at all Chinese jade!"

"Not Chinese jade?" Mr. Hiroshita inserted a cigarette into his long holder.

"It is soapstone! Ach, Mexican soapstone such as can be purchased in any market place."

"Not market place, Baron."

The Baron placed the soapstone upon the table. "If you please, why have you told me that you purchased a green jade carving which you had negotiated to sell to a wealthy American for one hundred thousand dollars? Did you not tell me that you required a brave detective to guard you in anticipation of being set upon en route to Honolulu?" Mr. Hiroshita closed his eyes. "One hundred thousand dollars. Ach! One hundred dollars would be—"

"One hundred twenty-four dollars, American money," said Mr. Hiroshita, opening his eyes. "A humble gift to brave Baron von Kaz. Ignore stone but study carving—"

"I have it? And my fee—"

From the same wallet Mr. Hiroshita counted ten one-hundred-dollar bills, laid them on the table beside the soapstone tablet. "One thousand dollars."

The Baron recounted the money.

"Do not forget Green Lion." Mr. Hiroshita handed it to the Baron. "Words are translated. But meaning? Maybe then would value insignificant gift more." Mr. Hiroshita's pink fingernail touched the rim. "Please permit slight demonstration." He took the Green Lion, held it between the palms of his hands. He twisted it, showed his hands with a round half of the ornament in each hand. The left half had a small cavity. Mr. Hiroshita screwed the two parts together, returned the stone to the amazed Austrian.

"When planning departure from Honolulu, please?"

The Baron said that he was taking next week's boat to Australia and from there an English boat to Italy. Landing at Naples, he would fly to Vienna. This did not please Mr. Hiroshita. He squeaked, "And Miss Miquet, please? Miss Miquet accompanies brave Baron?"

The Baron leaned on his umbrella. After a second's hesitation, while his face turned very dark, he said, "I do not expect to see Miss Miquet."

"Not see her?" The little man left his chair to come close to the Baron, squeaking a number of excited words to the effect that the Baron had persuaded him to delay departure from San Francisco by an entire week in order to be on the same boat with her.

This was true. However, at the same time, the Baron had been most casual in speaking of Miss Miquet, saying that a friend of his was to sail on the *Kohala,* and, all things considered, it might be wiser to cancel the reservations on the *Lohaala* and take the later boat instead. Then, if Mr. Kohler had heard they were departing on the *Lohaala,* they might be able to escape him more successfully.

But now Mr. Hiroshita was greatly disturbed that the Baron was not planning to see Miss Miquet. He explained to the Baron how greatly his services had been appreciated. Mr. Hiroshita's teeth showed in a smile. "As indication of high regard engaged room for you at Imperial Hawaiian, Baron. Gladly honored to pay fifteen dollars each day for brave Baron to stay long as desires. One week? No, please, two weeks. Three weeks, even. Three weeks, yes-s-s." Mr. Hiroshita hissed happily at the thought of the Baron staying three weeks as his guest.

"Then must meet Miss Miquet. Will recount greatly frightened client proved very large trouble on *Kohala* not permitting brave Baron—"

Above the door a bell rang. Mr. Hiroshita lifted the speaking tube, listened, replied rapidly in his native tongue. When he was finished, he rubbed his hands, addressed the Baron. "Greatly disturbed, Baron. Greatly sorry to state two police arrived here wishing to question you. Greatly sorry. Have much of importance to say, please. Tonight in Imperial Hawaiian at seven." He tittered. "Police here very curious. Please do not mention engaged by Mr. Hiroshita."

Christian Jameson, chief of detectives of the Honolulu Police Department, sat at a desk of kola wood, fumbling with his silver-rimmed glasses while he examined the sheaf of papers before him. "That's all, boys," he told the two policemen who had escorted the Baron to the police station.

The swinging doors shut. Above on the ceiling green lizards scampered across the whitewashed surface, and the Baron nervously moved his chair to the left, afraid that they might fall upon him. Jameson was an old man. He had a missionary mouth, puckered and dry as though he had just bit into a green passion fruit. He raised his head, speaking with the soft, archaic inflection of the islander who has generations of New England ancestors behind him:

"Baron, you've caused us a lot of trouble. We wanted to question you about the murder—the presumed murder—of Carl Kohler. But after we got done talking with Cap Anderson and got the facts from him and tried to find you, we discovered you'd already left the ship."

The Baron politely informed the chief of detectives that he had been in a hurry.

"In a hurry, hey? Well, well. Let me see your passport."

The Baron showed it to Jameson.

"Been in Mexico City? Well, well. This is a new one, ain't it? Dated February nineteenth. Lose your old one?"

Over three years ago the Baron had escaped from Austria. In Vienna he had been in charge of the special investigating division of the Viennese Police until he was arrested along with others who had plotted for a return of the monarchy. He had escaped to Switzerland, and from there to the Northern States of America where he had hoped to make his fortune.

After an experience in Carmel, California, where he had met Caryl Miquet, the immigration officials learned that he had illegally entered the United States, and he was forced to flee to Mexico. Here he had hidden a few months with a compatriot, that Braunback who had originally introduced him to Mr. Hiroshita at the Cosmopolitan Club in Mexico City, until he learned that the former socialistic government in Vienna had been wiped out. With a new regime, the Baron's powerful friends, now restored to power, arranged to bring him back, having a need for him, and had issued a passport.

Something of this he told Jameson. When the Baron was silent Jameson tapped several papers. "If we'd seen you a couple of hours ago you'd have saved us a lot of trouble, Baron. We wondered why you ran off, and while the boys were tracing you I telephoned the San Francisco police. They got hold of your embassy in Washington. Guess you're a pretty important feller after all, eh?"

The Baron modestly stated that he was the greatest detective in all Austria.

Jameson removed his spectacles. Without them his face looked harder. The near-sighted eyes were small round holes. "Well, well, Baron. We folks here don't think we need much detective work. We don't have much crime. Islands too far from any place for a criminal to escape." He polished his glasses. "You cost us a lot of money with all this telephoning. One of the reporters said you'd left with Hiroshita, but we didn't think to look there until we'd checked all the hotels. Wonder if your friends in Austria know you're so companionable with a dope smuggler, eh?"

The Baron grunted as though he had been kicked. His head swung from right to left. The Baron was a vain man. Accordingly it was his habit to conceal as far as possible his prognathous jaw, his single heritage from that distinguished grandfather of his, by compressing his lips, thus minimizing the major defect of a darkly aquiline profile. But now, in his astonishment, the jaw and lower lip thrust forward the full Hapsburgian length. "So?" he uttered unbelievingly.

"Well, maybe I shouldn't say that right off. We haven't had a complaint against Hiroshita for several years. How'd you know him?"

The Baron, recovered from the first shock, explained coldly that he had been introduced to the Japanese by a mutual friend in Mexico City. Hearing that Mr. Hiroshita was to sail for Honolulu on the *Kohala,* and as he was returning to Vienna via Hawaii, he had gone with him.

"Well, well," said Jameson. He handed the Baron a radiogram. "This came half an hour ago. Maybe you'd like to read it?"

> JAMESON CHIEF DETECTIVES HONO-
> LULU POLICE
> CHECKED WITH OCEANIC NAVIGA-
> TION COMPANY STOP CLERK DIS-
> TINCTLY RECALLS VON KAZ CAME IN
> DAY BEFORE KOHALA SAILING STOP
> ASKED IF MISS MIQUET HAD RESERVA-
> TION STOP CLERK POSITIVE WAS VON
> KAZ STOP REMEMBERS PHOTOGRAPHS
> FROM CARMEL CASE WHEN IN PAPERS
> STOP TELEPHONED AUSTRIAN EMBAS-
> SY AGAIN STOP THEY INSIST BARON
> OKAY AND ON WAY HOME STOP WE
> HAVE NOTHING AGAINST BARON HERE
> STOP ASSISTED US GREATLY IN CARMEL
> CASE STOP EXTEND ALL COURTESIES
> TO HIM
> LINN SAN FRANCISCO CHIEF POLICE

When the Baron returned the cable, Jameson didn't refer to it. "Cap Anderson says you were the man who found Carl Kohler dead. What d'you know?"

In five minutes the Baron had given all the details, saying that he had gone to A deck to look at the stars, happened to stroll to the port side, stumbled upon the body, went down in search of the Captain.

"You wanted to tell the Captain first?"

"Ach, my dear sir, he was the man in charge."

"Sure, and while you hunted him the body disappeared." Jameson lit a long dry cigar, puffed it reflectively. "You didn't know Carl, did you?"

"Mr. Kohler? I saw him once or twice on the boat."

"You didn't get out of your stateroom very often, the Captain says. Just happened to bump into Carl, hey, and introduce yourself?"

"I am a poor sailor. However, every day I would leave my cabin for a short walk on deck. I remember stopping in the bar and noticing this Mr. Kohler talking loudly. I heard his friends call him 'Kohler.'"

"And you recognized him on A deck at night?"

"There was the moonlight." The Baron added carelessly, "And I have a phenomenal memory, my dear sir."

Jameson coughed and eyed the Baron sharply, but the Baron was perfectly serious. He *had* a phenomenal memory.

"Well, well," said Jameson, biting hard on the cigar. "You haven't any idea what could 've happened, hey? Carl was a hard drinker. He could 've got drunk and fallen overboard, but your talk of an air gun makes it mighty confusing. Sure you weren't drunk too?"

"Pardon," the Baron informed him kindly. "Never does the great Von Kaz become drunk." He smiled.

"The great—" Jameson got up and went to the window. He took several deep breaths, walked back and sat down again. "Excuse me, Baron. You haven't any ideas, then?"

The Baron shook his head. "All right. Don't go around talking about that air-gun business. We've arranged for the papers to say Carl fell overboard. He fell overboard all right. When we examined the trap-shooting platform we found paint scratched away on the lower railing and a shred that was torn from his tie. We'll find out who killed him, but if there was an air gun we'd just as lief let the murderer believe we think you're lying." He stood. "As for

you, Baron," he said unwillingly, "you're cleared, I guess.
But let me tell you something before you go: We folks
here like to have people visit us. We don't aim to cause
trouble to them as long as they behave themselves. And
this is what I'm getting at, Baron. Most of us on the Islands sort of stick together. Maybe you don't know it, but
Caryl Miquet's got good friends here. Her uncle, Louis
McKay, came here fifty years ago from France; he bought a
ranch on the island of Hawaii and changed his name from
Miquet to McKay, so it'd be good American."

Jameson relit his cigar, puffed at it while the Baron remained silent. "He married a Lorring girl, and *her* family,
Baron, goes a hell of a ways back. Both are gone now. But
their daughter Mary McKay's well liked here. And someday
Billy McKay's going to grow up into a fine young feller—"

"Pardon!" The Baron leaned forward. "If you please,
who is Billy McKay?"

"Her brother. And as I was saying, Mary McKay and
her cousin Caryl Miquet've come here, and I'm not going
to have anything cause either of those girls trouble. You're
to leave Caryl Miquet alone."

The Baron was on his feet now.

Jameson waved his hand. "No need of you looking like
you were wishing to put a knife in my throat, Baron. You're
not in Austria now. And I can lock you up so damned
quick if you start anything that you won't realize what
happened. There's a boat leaving tomorrow for Australia.
You take that boat and get to hell out of here."

The Baron bowed.

He left the building in a ferment of indecision. The
uneasy feeling which had first oppressed him last night,
had increased. Something, he knew, was not marching.
Ach, no! Whatever it was, he assured himself as he walked
down the steps, was none of his concern. He was out of
it. He had intended to depart from Honolulu without ever

seeing Miss Miquet. She was as nothing to him. He had waited nearly an hour for her on the ship, and she had failed him; she was merely another barbaric American. He stood on the curbing, clutching his umbrella, absorbed and worried. Lieber Gott! why was it that Mr. Hiroshita had desired him to stay just to see her? And now this American police official had brought her name into the conversation. That was coincidence, perhaps. Naturally.

Impatiently he started to cross the street, trying to rid himself of that queer onerous feeling, and then someone was shrieking behind him, and the long gray car lunged forward, at him. It would have struck him and smashed him senseless to the pavement had he not reacted entirely by instinct.

Those muscular legs of his had not been inherited from the Von Kaz side of his family; and now they lifted him from the path of the car. They leaped, coiled springs suddenly released, and he landed on his shoulders in a most undignified and disgraceful position.

Automatically he raised up and saw a face peer down at him from the car. It was a rubbery, cherubic face. And the face was already starting to pout in disappointment as the automobile swept on, gathering speed. The Chinese woman rushed to him. "You neahlly killed."

"Hein?"

"You neahlly killed. Velly neahlly killed."

"Ach, so? Nearly? I see." He smiled mechanically, brushing his clothes. "Did you get the license number?"

She didn't understand. The man had been nearly run over, and she was excitedly trying to tell him how close had been his escape, and he didn't seem to care at all.

He wasn't listening to her.

He was peering down the street, but the gray car had vanished and with it Mr. Bolton.

3

Under the Yellow Umbrella

As he walked through the lobby of the Imperial Hawaiian the Baron bought a copy of the afternoon *Honolulu Star-Bulletin,* continued out to the terrace, where he ordered lunch. Carl Kohler's death filled two columns on the second page. Nothing in the story indicated that he had been killed. Nor was there any mention of the brave Baron von Kaz in the account, an oversight which caused this gentleman a slight amount of irritation because he enjoyed seeing his name in the paper.

According to the circumspect narration, Carl Kohler presumably had imbibed too freely and in some undisclosed way had fallen overboard. The police had investigated, and found on the trap-shooting platform marks where something heavy had passed under the lower railing. The police had also found blood spots on the wood, but this was another fact that was withheld.

Mr. Kohler's biography was short. He had been born on the Islands, graduated from the University of Hawaii, entered the plant research department of one of the pineapple companies. Nine years ago he had gone to the island of Hawaii as manager of a sugar-cane plantation. Five years ago he had accepted a position as assistant manager to the great Preacher Ranch in North Kona, three years later went to the McKay Ranch, which was next to the

Preacher Ranch, as manager when old Louis McKay died. He had stayed on the McKay Ranch about a year, then had resigned, according to the *Star-Bulletin* to handle his own affairs. During the past year he had taken several trips to Mexico in an effort to start a pineapple plantation there. That was the sum and total of Mr. Kohler's existence. The Baron folded the paper, completed his lunch. He looked at his watch. It was one-thirty. In five and a half hours he would see Mr. Hiroshita, and then he hoped to have the mystery of the soapstone Lion and how it involved Miss Miquet cleared. He signed the chit, wandered over to the low wall separating the white sands of Waikiki from the green terrace of the hotel.

Waikiki was disappointing in size. From what he had heard the Baron had expected a beach practically as long as the island of Oahu. But the green sea, translucent and dazzling under the sun, with flying manes of white surf, had such a regular lunge and roar that it made up for the smallness of the beach. Far out brown bodies on surfboards were waiting for the next big swell. Diamond Head loomed behind Waikiki, a backdrop for the bathers, fringed along the base with palm trees half hiding white and pink homes. The sand was covered with varicolored beach umbrellas and men and women doing their utmost to expose the legal limit of flesh to the rays of the tropic sun.

All at once the Baron's mildly scornful expression changed. Twenty feet or so away he noticed a bright yellow beach umbrella. It was tilted so that part of the rim rested on the sand. And extending from this umbrella were two legs. They were bronzed legs, marvelously and smoothly shaped. Even from where he was standing he could see that they were uncommonly attractive legs. Others also had discerned this fact. At frequent intervals gentlemen passing by the yellow umbrella would pause in complete and happy astonishment at the display. From their undisguised admiration the Baron gathered that the possessor of these legs was sleeping, unaware of the havoc her property was creating.

And as the Baron stood there idly, enjoying the sheen of water and the huge bulk of Diamond Head and the two bronzed legs outstretched upon the white sand, he saw a man and a boy walk toward the yellow umbrella.

The man was fully dressed, his face cherubic, and from the thick colorless lips protruded a large black cigar. The boy was in a bathing suit, black haired, with a smudge of freckles across a small tilted nose. The boy would run ahead, bouncing a rubber ball, and then wait for the man. The man sat down on the sand, a few yards from the yellow umbrella, glanced once without interest at the two bronzed legs near him while the boy began to dig.

The Baron circled back to the terrace, approached the sea wall in another direction. After a time he noticed that Bolton's gaze was directed to one particular stretch of water. Far out were three black spots, and when a green rush of surf flowed in from around Diamond Head these three black spots, along with others, were picked up. A little later Jeffrey Preacher, Mary McKay and John Sargent floated in upon their surfboards. Jeffrey's wheat-colored hair was glistening. Mary stood in the water, snatching off her red bathing cap, shook the brown curly hair, laughing. John Sargent pulled the surfboards high on the beach, waved to the fat man sitting there so quietly with his back to the wall.

The Baron hurried to his room, changed into a black bathing suit.

Ten minutes later the boy disgustedly destroyed the sand walls and commenced again to build. A shadow passed on the sand, and a voice above him asked amiably, "What is that, please?"

The boy frowned importantly. "A castle, can't you see anything?"

The man in the black bathing suit and striped bathrobe dropped to the sand. "Ach so, a castle? But it is a very poor castle, no?"

The boy's great gray eyes scornfully contemplated this intruder. The boy decided to ignore the man. But the man imperturbably rubbed his nose for a second, then poked his finger into the sand. "Now I should have a barbican here, and here will be the fosse defended by two guard-rooms. So?" He smiled.

In amazement the boy watched the man swiftly pat a small mound of sand, poke windows and doors into it, then efficiently mark off a large square.

"What's—what's a—" The boy pointed. "That thing you said."

"Ach—a barbican?" The Baron nodded. "The ante-mural. That comes from Latin. When I was your age I had to study Latin very much. It means in your language, 'the place before the wall.'" He said seriously, "I think for this castle we shall have five hundred soldiers, no?"

"Why, you know all about castles!"

"I lived in one many years ago," the Baron said as he scooped out the center of a pile of sand. "Here will be the inner bailey. Do you understand what that is?"

The boy shook his head.

"The courtyard. What is your name?"

"Billy."

"So? Billy what?"

"Billy McKay. Do you have soldiers in the—the ante-mural too?"

"Fifty, my dear Billy."

"What's your name?"

"Franz." He stood. "It is very simple, no? Now if I had a knife I would carve a portcullis."

"I've got a knife upstairs!" exclaimed Billy excitedly. "What's a porkillis?"

"Boy!" Bolton came up from behind. "It is too hot. Go to your room—"

"Gee, Mr. Bolton, Mary said I could stay—"

"Do you hear—" Bolton removed his cigar when he saw the face of the man in the striped bathrobe; it was a dark face with a projected jaw. The man's hair was dark brown, cropped short in the manner favored by German officers whom Bolton had seen in prison camps during the war. No emotion appeared upon the cherubic countenance of Bolton. He said, "Hello, Baron. I've been looking for you," and turned to Billy, absently caressed the boy's bare shoulders. "Get to your room, Billy."

"Aw gee, Mr. Bolton—" Entranced, Billy stared at the castle builder; a baron, Bolton had said! It was almost like seeing a prince. Or a king.

"We'll construct a better castle some other day," smiled the Baron.

Reluctantly Billy started toward the hotel, paused, asked shyly, "You're a real baron? Have you killed people? My tutor told me how the robber barons killed hundreds of people."

"Ach, my dear Billy. I have killed thousands," said the Baron.

Billy's gray eyes opened their widest, and Bolton looked furiously at the Baron, reminding the boy that he was supposed to be on his way to his room.

After the boy had vanished, Bolton said, as though there had been no interruption, "I've been looking for you, Baron. I've been so shaken."

"So?"

"I can't tell you how I feel, Baron. I was driving down King Street on an errand for Miss McKay. I was driving, and I'm afraid I was in a hurry, and then when you stepped in front of the car I lost my head completely." Bolton shuddered. "What if I should have killed you? It would have been terrible. I could never have forgiven, myself for such a terrible tragedy. Never!" His eyes watered at the thought. "By the time I had collected myself and returned you were gone."

"My dear Mr. Bolton." The Baron was frank and candid and puzzled. "Ach, I do not comprehend. I have not seen you since last night."

"You have not seen me?"

The Baron smiled, "I assure you, no. I have been in no accident."

"You— I've made a mistake. I'm sorry. But I thought it was you, and I wanted to see you to apologize."

"You are most kind, my dear sir. However, your near victim was not me." The Baron took his cigarette lighter from his bathrobe, lifted it to Bolton's cigar tip. "Permit me. Your cigar is out."

Bolton sucked on the cigar. "Thanks. Nice day, isn't it?"

"Marvelous, my dear sir." The Baron dropped the cigarette lighter into his pocket. "I see that the *Star-Bulletin* states that poor Mr. Kohler was so inebriated last night that he fell overboard."

"That's what I read. You thought he was killed, didn't you?"

The Baron lifted his shoulders. "It is so easy to be mistaken."

"I thought that silent air-gun story of yours sounded funny, Baron. I'm just a plain, ordinary man, but last night I couldn't figure how an air gun could kill someone." Bolton puffed impassively on his cigar.

"Ach, on the last night it is so easy to drink in excess." The Baron winked, but Bolton's face didn't change. "When

I read that he had worked on Mr. Preacher's ranch I felt that I should offer my condolences to Mr. Preacher, no?"

"Mr. Preacher didn't know him." Bolton flicked the ashes from his cigar. "Neither did I."

"So?" The Baron was surprised. "You didn't meet him on the boat?"

"I never permit Mr. Preacher to meet strangers on a boat or elsewhere," said Bolton in his hard, flat voice.

"Then Mr. Sargent had met Mr. Preacher before embarking on the *Kohala?*"

Bolton looked at the Baron, took the cigar from his mouth. "Glad I didn't run over you, Baron," he said, shoved himself to his feet and walked off, his shoes crunching in the soft sand. . . .

Under the yellow umbrella, about twenty minutes later, Caryl Miquet awoke. She yawned, stretched, then frowned severely at two male creatures who were staring at her. When they were immediately possessed of the desire to dive into the limpid Pacific she smiled to herself with satisfaction, unscrewed the top of a bottle of oil and commenced to rub her legs.

Her skin was very brown, and there was little of it unexposed. A white bandeau, tied beneath her arms and at her neck, was divided from the white shorts by an expanse of rippling skin. Her hair was midnight black, darker than the long eyes which maliciously followed the two males who were so hastily plunging into the ocean. She was a well-designed piece, even for Waikiki, and what's more, in her arrogant way she knew it.

"Damn!" she said when she accidentally upset the bottle, and as she moved lazily to retrieve it, her hand encountered another. The gentleman bowed, offered her the bottle.

"Good-afternoon," announced the Baron in what he hoped was a gallant and yet casual fashion. "Ah—good afternoon, my dear Miss Miquet. Ah, I cannot tell you how charmed I—"

"Please don't bow again." She applied the oil to her legs.

The Baron sat down. "I assure you, Miss Miquet, that my manners—"

"Your manners?" She rubbed vigorously. *"Your* manners. I know all about your manners, Baron von Kaz." Her legs shone.

"If you please," he suggested mildly, "you will remove all the skin."

"Oh!" She faced him. "I don't want to talk to you. I don't want to see you. Considering what took place in Carmel, I should think you could understand that!" The scarlet lips closed firmly.

He nodded humbly.

"Go away, then."

"But you consented to meet me last night."

"I consented to meet you?" Her voice was low but furious. "I was curious to know what you'd have to say. I wanted to know why you followed me. What are you doing here? Fortunately, I told John—my cousin's fiancé. He advised me not to see you—not to let myself be troubled by you."

"So?" He stood, bowed formally. In the bathing suit such a bow was somewhat ridiculous, but the Baron was entirely too vain to believe that anything he could do would be ridiculous. "I only wished to offer my deep regrets, Miss Miquet. I only wished to tell you . . ." What could he tell her? Against that flamboyant pink background of the hotel, here among her friends, where she was known, secure, his fears of this morning were out of place, unreasonable, the grotesque worries of a man who is so accustomed to intrigue that in any occurrence he reads danger. And was he to admit to this scornful creature that he, the great Von Kaz, beloved of the ladies of Vienna, was in love with her, an American nobody? Was that his message? He could see her eyes, ironic and amused as they regarded his discomfort.

He was not inured to this treatment. His back stiffened, "Tomorrow I depart for Austria. I bid you good-by."

"One question before you leave, Baron." She was imperious. She stood, tall and slim. She wasn't afraid of him. She wasn't afraid of anything any more, she had assured herself. "Before you go, Baron, will you tell me just why you opened my mail this morning?"

"Hein?"

"Why did you open my mail? What right had you to open my mail?"

"Mail?" he stammered. *"Mail?"*

"When they brought the letters to my room this morning, at the hotel, I found that all the envelopes had been obviously opened and clumsily restuck together."

"Please," said the Baron and put his hand on her bare shoulder, and under the weight of that firm hand she was forced to the sand. "Not so loudly. Excuse me, but I must comprehend." He crossed his legs, said very deliberately, "My dear Miss Miquet, this I do not ask you to believe. Nevertheless, I can prove it. This morning I left the boat with a friend—an acquaintance. I have reliable witnesses that will testify that not until after twelve o'clock did I enter the Imperial Hawaiian."

"Who else would open my mail?" she asked angrily, because she did believe him. "You've followed me. The man who made my reservations on the *Kohala* told me that you had asked about me. What have I done to you?"

"Attention!" The Baron smiled and began to tell her how beautiful it was and how pleasant Waikiki was, and then Mary McKay reached the yellow umbrella, dripping wet and a little out of breath.

"Hello, Caryl. You're awake at last." She glanced at Caryl, and then at the dark-faced man, thinking she had seen him before somewhere.

"This is the Baron von Kaz—my cousin, Miss McKay," Caryl heard herself saying.

Chivalrously the Baron bowed over Mary's hand, kissed it, and as he did so Mary winked at Caryl. Mary's grimace unaccountably irritated Caryl. When the Baron turned to her she gave him her hand very gracefully.

"The dancing commences at nine tonight," he murmured. "I hope I may be honored." His back was to Mary.

"I'm sorry." Caryl was aloof. Then some quality, something in his expression, caused her to add lightly, "But we can have a cocktail together at seven, if you like."

"At seven," he said, inclined slightly to Mary and departed. Caryl watched him go, wondering why she had ever mentioned cocktails at seven. She hadn't intended to. She had said it impulsively, without thinking.

"Did I hear you invite him?" Mary helped herself to the bottle of oil.

"He's impossible. I don't know why I even introduced him to you."

"So that's the way you feel?" asked Mary shrewdly, and they were both laughing when Jeffrey and John joined them a few minutes later.

Jeffrey sat next to Mary. "Stick your legs in my direction," he ordered, "and I'll show you how to put oil on them. Not too much. I learned that trick on the Riviera."

John Sargent took the bottle of oil, said gruffly, "You're not on the Riviera now, Jeff."

Jeffrey grinned. "You know sometimes, John, I forget you and Mary are engaged. How the devil did a cantankerous geologist like John ever get you to give in, Mary?"

Mary laughed, tossed her pretty head. Caryl looked at the two men. "John," she said quietly, "don't spill all the

oil over her legs. I need a little. Jeff, you can be my man-
servant."

"If you put more oil on those legs of yours they'll take
you for a Hawaiian," said Jeffrey.

John poured oil in his hand. "With that yellow hair of
yours, Jeff, no one 'd think you—"

"John!" Caryl interrupted quickly.

"Hell, don't mind John," Jeffrey said easily, stretching
full length on the sand, his bare arm touching Mary's.
"I'm a royalist. I've got just enough Hawaiian blood in me
to wish I were a king sometimes." His head moved lazily
toward John. "If I were king, do you know what I'd do?
I'd cancel your engagement to Mary and send you back to
Mexico. Then you'd be good and sore, wouldn't you?"

The Baron found Mr. Hiroshita's name in the telephone
directory. He was finally put through to this gentleman,
informing him that a most important engagement prevented him from seeing Mr. Hiroshita at seven o'clock. Nine
o'clock would be more convenient. Mr. Hiroshita protested. The Baron was firm. Mr. Hiroshita agreed to be at
the Imperial Hawaiian at nine o'clock sharp and clicked
the receiver. There was a ripe pineapple on the table. It
was the custom of the Imperial Hawaiian to welcome their
guests with this traditional fruit of hospitality. The Baron
tasted the pineapple, approved of it. When he had finished
it he took a hot bath followed by a cold shower.

Then he shaved and changed to immaculate gray flannels. He wondered if he should wire his friends in Vienna
and inform them that he might be delayed a few days.
He had promised to be in Vienna by the middle of May.
The government in power officially was neither friendly
or unfriendly to the monarchist element. It was a stopgap
affair, containing Nazis, monarchists, and those who believed that Austria would be better off without an emperor

or a Nazi dictator. The Baron's friends had scheduled their monarchistic attempt for the end of May, and the Baron was to help them. Despite his faults, they needed him. They were well aware of his pride, now so prodded by his supersensitiveness to his dubious ancestry that it had grown almost to demoniacal dimensions. He was a baron, to be sure; but that meant little to the august class in Vienna who still recalled the scandal resulting when his grandfather fell in love with a gypsy dancer . . . who in due course of time became his grandmother. And his friends deplored his impulsiveness, his erratic methods, his colossal assurance, and above all his volatile imagination. However, they admitted that no one else in all Vienna had his peculiar ability, amounting in fact to genius, in ferreting through an involved intrigue or counterplot. With him in Vienna, they believed they could proceed without being tripped up unknowingly by the opposition.

With his usual optimistic confidence the Baron decided that there would be no need to cable, that by tonight he would pierce through this mystery: He would discover why Mr. Hiroshita was so interested in Miss Miquet; he would learn why her mail was being intercepted.

He went to the elevator, already anticipating his meeting with Miss Miquet. He would be most firm with her; he would demand an apology from her for permitting him to wait on A deck. That was exactly what he would do, he had determined by the time the elevator deposited him on the lobby floor; he would suffer no more nonsense from her. She would know with whom she had to deal. . . .

When it was necessary to his own ends the Baron could be damnably engaging; he knew how to smile, his blue eyes would become candid and guileless, and he could listen in a way that indicated that no one else in the world could say such interesting and amusing things. Now he listened to the desk clerk, his head cocked attentively to one side, the two lines on each side of his lean face deepening in his swarthy skin as he nodded with utmost amiability.

The majority of the guests in the hotel were either napping or on the beach. The lobby was deserted. The clerk had been bored until this distinguished foreigner had questioned him regarding the island sights. The afternoon drowsed by. Butterflies alighted on the yellow coconut fronds arranged on the big table. The Filipino boys squatted behind the folding doors and nodded. And the clerk leaned on his elbows and told the Baron about the burial caves on the island of Hawaii, the blue clouds at night, the half-million-dollar feather cloak worn by King Kamehameha I which could be seen in the Bishop Museum, about the night-blooming cereus, the crater of Kaleakala in Maui, and when the clerk at last paused for breath the Baron thanked him politely.

The clerk had only just started. However, the Baron's attention had been drawn to the cluster of mail boxes behind the desk. "No," informed the clerk, "no, you haven't any mail, Baron. The *Kohala's* mail was sent in this morning, and we don't expect more from 'outside' for three days."

The Baron frowned. Now this was strange, was his mild complaint, because he had been given to understand that one of his shipboard friends was writing to him here an address of considerable importance.

"We sent all letters to the guests' rooms between ten-thirty and eleven," insisted the clerk.

"Ach!" The Baron pondered. "No one then is permitted to take it from the desk?"

"Sure, if you're here."

"Perhaps one of your other guests would have taken my mail by mistake?"

"Hardly." The clerk pointed to the boxes. "We keep the letters sorted for the various rooms. This is wing seven B.

We couldn't make a mistake. There are only six rooms in this section—"

"And you delivered all the mail to my wing, my dear sir?"

"Sure. I handled it myself. No, wait a minute." The clerk hurried to the door at his left, stuck his head through the doorway. "Say, Chuck. Didn't someone in Miss Mc-Kay's party call for the mail this morning?"

The clerk returned. "I'm sorry, Baron. Mr. Bolton stopped by for the mail. There are five of them with rooms near yours, Miss McKay and her friends. Mr. Bolton got the mail for them. He might 've taken yours too. I'll see if he's in his room."

"Ach! Donnergott!" The Baron struck his temple. "My dear sir, I am so stupid. I am most stupid."

The clerk dropped the room telephone.

"Do you know, my dear sir, I now have just remembered? My friend, he has promised tomorrow to mail me the address. One thousand pardons!" In his agitation the Baron retreated, and the clerk sat down again to his magazine. All these foreigners were nuts.

Upstairs again, the Baron stopped in front of seven thirty-two, the room next to his own. Each room was closed by two doors, one copper screened, and a second one of wood. The locks were simple. It would be a matter of a few minutes to open both doors. He was greatly tempt-ed, but the three elevators passing up and down his floor every minute or so made the act too risky. The elevator boys might know what room he should be in. Or one of the other guests in this wing might appear. No, he thought, not now. It is not worth it. He entered his room, locked the door with the screen and left the wooden one partly open to keep the room cool. It would have been cooler to leave it wide open, but the door shielded his bed. The brave Baron had not forgotten the silent air gun. He took out his watch. It was three forty-five. He threw himself

on the bed and in five minutes was asleep. He awoke at
six-thirty, verified the time by his watch, complimented
himself on his faculty for awakening at any time he so
desired, as if such a miracle were usual only to the Baron
von Kaz. . . .

"*You* are charming." He bowed over her hand. She was
one American woman who could give her hand graciously,
casually, as though she were accustomed to homage.

The ash-rose taffeta emphasized the warm olive color in
her cheeks. She did look charming; unfortunately she also
looked perfectly possessed, entirely too assured. She scrutinized him from under those level brows of hers, thinking
that he would appear very creditable indeed if he would
only let his hair grow long instead of cutting it short in
that ridiculous fashion. And so they faced each other at
the small table, with the perfumed breeze blowing in from
the terrace, and the parrots contributing clattering noises,
and the oiled Filipino boys pattering on the woven mats.

"Well?" There wasn't any need for her gesture of brushing her hair back from the wide olive forehead. The black
hair was perfectly arranged, parted in the middle, the
comb marks glistening. He told himself that this was the
time to be firm. This woman was but another North American barbarian. He was doing her a favor, ach! a great
favor. He called one of the boys. Caryl requested a long
cool drink. Something with rum in it, please. He ordered
a brandy-and-soda. Two of brandy instead of one.

"My dear Miss Miquet," he cleared his throat, sitting
very erect, "I wished to see you."

"So I gathered." She was equally impersonal. "And *I*
wished to see you to inform you, Baron von Kaz, that I
don't ever care to see you again."

"Excellent." He nodded. Women were always difficult,
and he had handled those who were more difficult than

this young person with the deep black eyes. "Tomorrow I will be on my way to Australia, thence to Austria. And so I desired to tell you that I did not touch your mail."

"You didn't?" The long smooth fingers tapped nervously on the table. "Who did, then?"

"Were all the letters opened?"

"No." Then she closed her lips firmly as though she had decided not to speak. He waited. She said, "Only two."

"Ach so. Small or large?"

"What difference does that make?"

He shrugged.

"They were large ones. They were on the door waiting for me. Mr. Bolton brought them up. I asked who had. John—Mr. Sargent said that Mr. Bolton had brought up all our mail."

"On the door?"

"Attached to the clip on the outside. Oh," she declared angrily, "you think you're very clever, getting me to talk!" The Baron wondered what she would do if he took one of those firm brown hands of hers. He relinquished the thought after looking at her face.

"Then anyone passing by could have taken them?"

"Any— Good evening, Mr. Bolton. I didn't see you."

She glanced at the man and, beneath the table, kicked at the Baron's shin for stepping on her toes and warning her as though she were a conspirator.

Bolton hadn't changed for dinner. He was in a colorless, formless business suit. "I'm not interrupting, Miss Miquet? Miss McKay was asking for you. The Rogers' are on the beach in their new sail canoe, and Miss McKay says they're all going in for a quick swim and for you to hurry, please." He thrust out his hand affably. "Glad to see you, Baron." It was soft and pulpy, and thick black hair grew on the wrist, creeping over the back of the hand.

When Bolton had departed Caryl uttered, "Damn! After I've changed, too."

The Baron smiled sympathetically. With a wistful air he suggested that she remain long enough to finish her drink, and he told her how he had waited on A deck for her. Instead of being sorry, she said that it served him right for delaying his invitation until the last night.

The Baron swallowed, recovered, and with some acidity asked her if she had been dancing while he was catching cold on A deck.

"Don't be silly. It was too warm for anyone to catch cold last night."

"So?" he asked quietly. "You were dancing while I—"

"Not at all, my dear sir," she mimicked him. "This cross-examining as to my actions last night can hardly have a bearing on my mail—"

Bolton was beside her again, hoping they would forgive a plain, humble man for intruding, but the others were on the beach, and they wanted Miss Miquet to come at once. They were going to sail toward Diamond Head in the new canoe. It wouldn't take over fifteen minutes, and Miss Miquet would have ample time to dress again for dinner. "All right," he said, and Bolton smiled.

The ash-rose dress rustled as Caryl stood. The Baron informed her that he would go upstairs with her; his room was on the same floor. In the elevator she remarked that it was quite a coincidence, wasn't it? The Baron answered that it was, undoubtedly.

He bowed, pressed his lips to her hand as she impatiently stood by her door. "Ach," he exclaimed, as an afterthought. "An acquaintance of mine on the boat said he had met you, a Mr. Hiroshita. I had—"

"Mr. Hiroshita? I don't know him."

"He is an importer. I had hoped tomorrow we could go to his establishment."

"Sorry." She shook her head, "Don't forget where you're going tomorrow. Run along to Vienna and have a nice time."

Her door closed.

He went into his room, slamming his door. "Run along to Vienna!" he bitterly repeated; ach du lieber Augustin, so that is how she dismisses forever the great Baron Franz Maximilian Karagôz von Kaz? He sat down at the desk to write a cable to his friends in Vienna, informing them that he might have to take a later boat.

Then he remembered the Honolulu detective's command to leave and tore up the half-completed cable, leaned back in his chair, folded his arms, shut his eyes and pondered on what was rounding into a most disturbing and intangible case. He assured himself that he was being a dolt: What affair of his was it if Mr. Hiroshita's Green Lion was of soapstone? If Mr. Kohler had been killed on A deck? If Caryl Miquet's mail had been opened? His duties to Mr. Hiroshita were completed. He had received his fee. He was to embark for Australia on the next boat—according to Mr. Jameson.

Abruptly he decided that he required a drink. Several drinks. And so headed downstairs toward the bar.

4

The Second Green Lion

Half an hour later, when the Baron ascended to the seventh floor, lights showed in other rooms. He paused at his door. There were voices and laughter coming from the room next to his, and one of the voices was Caryl's. The door at the far end of the hall opened. John Sargent came out, the white monkey jacket making his shoulders appear even broader.

If he recognized the Baron, John didn't give any indication; he knocked on the door next to the Baron's. "You can't come in," called a girl's voice. "Caryl isn't ready yet. We'll be down in ten minutes."

The Baron closed and locked both his doors. He switched off the light in his room and went to the balcony. Dusk had not yet vanished. The horizon was tinged with Vermilion, shading into pinks and then into purples, and the endless surge and ebb of the surf came to the balcony. Below on the terrace colored lights twinkled around the wooden platform for the dancing, and people were being seated for dinner. He wasn't hungry. He didn't wish to eat alone. How pleasant it would be if Miss Caryl Miquet enjoyed dancing and had accepted his invitation this afternoon. He sighed; in a few weeks he would be in Vienna. There, hundreds, ach! thousands of lovely ladies would offer to dine and dance with the great and brave Baron Franz Maximilian Karagôz von Kaz.

He leaned on the railing of his balcony. The balcony to the adjoining room was separated from his by a scant five feet. A huge mass of bougainvillea obscured most of Caryl Miquet's balcony. However, he considered, it would not be difficult for him to swing out and grasp the vines and climb over her railing. He would rap at the door. She would be there. "Dear Miss Caryl," he would inform her, "tonight is my last night in Honolulu." And she would open her arms. "No, my dear Miss Caryl. Not after such abominable treatment. No!" He would sternly fold his arms. She would cry. He would relent.

And then from the bathroom window, above and between the two balconies came her voice, "Mary, be a darling and hand me a dry bathing cap."

And Mary McKay replied, "For heaven's sake, take a quick shower." And, with this second voice the Baron sighed again, his dreams punctured. How could he capture the lovely Miss Caryl Miquet with her cousin in the same room? Lieber Gott! And this was his last night. Sadly he shook his head. The blind was drawn in the bathroom window, and a dull yellow glow penetrated the blind. He could hear water splashing as Caryl took her quick shower, while that cousin of hers from time to time would unfeelingly cry, "Caryl! Will you hurry?"

He shut his eyes, and the soft fragrance of Hawaii was in his nostrils, and he could visualize that cool slender bronzed body with the water dashing on it, and it was quite too much for him. He pushed into his own room, turning his thoughts upon all those charming women he had loved in Vienna: Magdi Klei, and red-headed Herecia von Buhl, and the little opera singer, Fräulein—what was her name?

At eight forty-five he called himself a quadruple dolt for the eighteenth time. Caryl and her cousin long since had departed. He washed his face in cold water, went downstairs into the lobby to wait for the arrival of Mr. Hiroshita.

As he was lighting a cigarette, standing near the entrance by the public telephone booths, someone said, "Hello," and he saw Mary McKay sitting on one of the big wicker chairs.

He approached her, bowed formally. She informed him that she was waiting for her fiancé, who was telephoning, and then said, "You made quite a hit with my brother this afternoon."

"Pardon. Your brother?"

"Billy. The boy you built a sand castle for." Mary smiled. "However, you really shouldn't tell him you've killed a thousand men, Baron. He's just at the age where he believes everything you say."

"A thousand?" The Baron's attention returned to this pretty little cousin of Caryl's after glancing to be certain that Mr. Hiroshita wasn't in the lobby. "But, my dear Miss McKay," he stated blandly, "as a matter of fact, I have killed two thousand men. I simply did not wish to frighten him by the truth." He peered toward the terrace. "It is so lovely this evening, dear Miss McKay, that it is a pity your cousin does not indulge in dancing."

Mary didn't understand. She said that Caryl did dance; and right now she was probably dancing with that Rogers man. "Want me to tell her that you'd like a dance when John and I go back to the table? Or don't you dance?"

The Baron informed her that he had been taught the most intricate steps by the greatest of French masters in the cadet school in Vienna; he coldly informed her that Mitti Schlossfeld, the loveliest danseuse in all Europe, always desired to dance with the great Von Kaz. However, he explained, tonight he did not have the inclination to dance with an American woman; besides, he had an important engagement with a prominent Honolulu business man, a powerful political figure, a descendant of one of the finest families. With that he bowed and left Miss McKay sitting there, and a little later, when she saw him greet the Japanese gentleman with whom he had traveled on the ship, she giggled. She was still giggling when John emerged from the telephone booth; and she told John, and at the table that night she had to tell them all how the funny Baron had tried to impress her with Hiroshita. A little later, during an intermission, Caryl glanced up toward her own room, and outlined in the French doors of the room next to hers she saw two men drinking, and her conscience hurt her a little that she had refused the Baron. . . .

Mr. Hiroshita wanted to go for a ride and to talk in his car. The Baron explained that it would be perfectly safe to discuss matters in his room: the others in the wing were eating and dancing.

The Baron locked both doors into the corridor. It was still warm, and the two men sat near the half-opened French window with the brandy and soda water on a table between them. Palm trees scraped gently together below the Baron's room. The orchestra was playing softly, and the faint scent of the night-blooming cereus was wafted in by a languorous breeze from the ocean. The Baron told his client that the police had questioned him about the finding of the dead body.

"Believe body pushed into water?" asked Mr. Hiroshita.

"Ach, my dear sir, that has little significance. What is of interest to me is that on the *Kohala* someone else, in addition to Mr. Kohler, wished that which you have." Mr. Hiroshita tried to speak, but the Baron said, "Pardon. Permit me to finish. This morning I said nothing to the police concerning my engagement as your—uhm—" He didn't like the word "bodyguard." The great Von Kaz never would condescend to become a hired bodyguard.

"As valued collaborator?" suggested Mr. Hiroshita.

"However, I inform you, my dear sir, unless you wish to explain several curious details, it will be my duty to divulge to the police tomorrow all that I know before leaving."

"Leaving?" squeaked Mr. Hiroshita.

"Exactly."

Mr. Hiroshita asked permission to pour himself a drink, which was granted.

"There exists too much of coincidence in the murder of Mr. Kohler, your anxiety for me to meet Miss Miquet at midnight, and the fact that during my absence, when you insisted I speak to the Captain and not telephone him, you were attacked and your room searched."

"Baron considers poor Mr. Hiroshita kills Mr. Kohler?"

"No, not at all. Mr. Kohler was laughing before he was shot. In your own language, my dear sir, you may be extremely humorous. But I do not believe Mr. Kohler would have laughed so pleasantly at what you could have said to him in English. Did you telephone Mr. Kohler yesterday on board ship?"

"Why inquiring, please?"

"You had the opportunity in the afternoon when you suggested that I take a nap or go for a walk. Or when I was dressing. If," the Baron said slowly, "you telephoned Mr. Kohler, or established contact with him, that might explain his death and why you were anxious to have me out of your stateroom at midnight. My dear sir, you *must* have spoken to Mr. Kohler."

Mr. Hiroshita touched the tips of his fingers to his cheeks, patting the skin softly, sucking in his breath. Finally he got the smile back on his face. "Baron clever man. Very clever man. Most astute. Now poor Mr. Hiroshita speaks only truth. Yesterday afternoon while Baron sleeps very soundly Mr. Kohler telephones. Asking appointment at midnight. Unfortunate Mr. Kohler states unearthed matter greatest importance. Claims approached by person determined to possess Green Lion—"

"If you please, I will not—"

"Two Green Lions, Baron. Explain at once. Being greatly fearful for own life, Mr. Kohler offers name of person seeking Green Lion. Arranged to deliver name at midnight. Necessary brave Baron absent from cabin at midnight, Mr. Hiroshita thinks of beautiful Miss Miquet."

The Baron stood, glanced out of the French window at the couples on the dance platform, the colored lights blending the couples into whirling particles of a musical kaleidoscope. He turned to Mr. Hiroshita. "Ach, Mr. Kohler was careless. He permits himself to be overheard or is intercepted going to your room. And this unknown person takes him to A deck because it is deserted. And he is shot. My dear Mr. Hiroshita, Mr. Jameson told me that you are suspected of dealing in dope. So!" He lifted his hand. "In Mexico City you engaged me to protect you. That is ended. Now at the hotel you take for me a room adjoining Miss Miquet's. Why are you interested in her? And what is this second Green Lion?"

"Baron, this morning hoped to reveal truth. Police intruded. Now poor Mr. Hiroshita tells all." According to a suddenly glib Mr. Hiroshita, a year ago a compatriot of his had accidentally located a lost Aztec city in the jungles of Mexico north of Acapulco. In this city was hidden a fabulous wealth, solid golden ornaments, priceless relics. After obtaining the location of this city, Mr. Hiroshita's friend had managed to escape from the small remnant of this ancient people who still held the secret of their ancient city, and had arrived in Honolulu stricken by fever brought on by exhaustion.

Before dying, the friend had given the map showing this city to Mr. Hiroshita. At first Mr. Hiroshita had assumed that this lost city was part of the fabric of his friend's feverish ravings, but after conducting research on the subject he had learned that a few early Spanish explorers had mentioned such a city. Finally, Mr. Hiroshita approached seven of his Japanese friends with the proposition that they gamble enough money for him to take a trip to Mexico. Mr. Hiroshita had spent eight months in Mexico, and became convinced that the map which he held could direct him to this lost city.

Returning to Mexico City, with a map which was now worth because of the knowledge it contained at least half a million dollars, Mr. Hiroshita was ready to report to his friends in Honolulu and obtain funds for the subsequent exploration when he noticed that he was the object of interest of an American by the name of Carl Kohler, who also lived in Hawaii, and who had presumably been traveling in Mexico for the purpose of buying lands upon which to establish pineapple plantations. Mr. Kohler had also been in Acapulco, there had learned, through a Mexican prospector, that Mr. Hiroshita had visited Acapulco where he had inquired so very cautiously about a lost city.

Mr. Kohler thereupon visited Mr. Hiroshita in his suite at the Cosmopolitan Club. In telling of this visit Mr. Hiroshita grew most indignant:

"Greatly fearful of Mr. Kohler, Baron. Knowing poor Mr. Hiroshita had priceless map, Mr. Kohler denied right to property, insinuating dear friend, who very honest and poor importer Japanese novelties, had stolen map. Greatly impertinent Mr. Kohler stated for many years had been seeking same map."

"Ach, so?" The Baron nodded commiseratingly, giving no indication that he suspected that there were no jungles north of Acapulco, and that in his casual reading about the

Aztecs he could recall no indication that their civilization had extended farther north than Mexico City, at least to the extent of building a fabulous city which in later centuries could be conveniently lost. Still, the Baron admitted to himself, that he was not an expert on Aztec history. Mr. Hiroshita was encouraged by the Baron's grave interest.

"Mr. Kohler suggests relinquishing map for considerable sum. Mr. Hiroshita very innocently informs him kind offer impossible as has no map. Next day poor Mr. Hiroshita's rooms ransacked. Day following, upon leaving for lunch, automobile inconsiderately attempts to end poor Mr. Hiroshita. Mr. Kohler obviously very determined man—"

"Why did you not report to the police?"

"Police?" Mr. Hiroshita almost screamed. "Mexican police would demand map for own use. Appealing to American police, what answer would be received to such a story? Baron von Kaz sees very misjudged man. Because wear face that is Japanese no one trusts poor Mr. Hiroshita." His voice was breaking with self-pity. "Once, twice, procuring opium for very sick friend, find character permanently blackened. No, Baron, cannot go to police. Here in Honolulu in Police Department also many bad men. For personal gain willingly steal map," Mr. Hiroshita nodded violently.

"Most deplorably bad fix, Baron. When Mr. Braunbach introduces the brave Baron von Kaz, showing great wisdom Mr. Hiroshita accepts proffered services. Studies character to find Baron very honest, most honest man—"

The Baron bowed.

"—but reputation not good," said Mr. Hiroshita with the candid air of one who tells all. "No, reputation not good. Forever quarrelsome. However, very honest dealing with client. When cabled to Europe, that is what learned."

"Cabled? My dear sir, did *you* cable to Europe—"

Mr. Hiroshita poured himself a third drink. "Taking no chances, please. In Mexico City, while awaiting news concerning brave Baron von Kaz, cautiously remain in club where most safe. But very long voyage from Mexico to Honolulu, Baron. Mr. Kohler most determined man. On voyage greatly fearing attempted theft of map. While anticipating pleasing responses to cables, brave Baron suggests to poor Mr. Hiroshita very clever idea. Brave Baron recounts ingenuous exploits in Carmel where met beautiful Miss Miquet. Displaying love for Miss—"

The table rattled as the Baron's fist dropped upon it. He roared like a stuck bull, "Mr. Hiroshita, *never* have I said—"

"Please," Mr. Hiroshita hissed, and the Baron sank back in his chair, ashamed at his outburst.

"Please, brave Baron never admits love. But most obvious so much talking of charming Miss Miquet. Reading in San Francisco paper Miss Miquet sailing to Honolulu, brave Baron respectfully requests changing ships. Then Mr. Hiroshita conceives very simple plan. Knowing jeweler in Mexico City who cuts very cunning soapstone plaques, order two. In one insert map. Folded, map requires very little space. Second Green Lion plaque with map safely deposited in club vault. In San Francisco, write Mr. Herdazo, honorable manager of club, instructing withdrawal of Green Lion to mail to Miss Miquet."

"So?" said the Baron. Slowly he lit a cigarette, then asked abruptly, "Did the unfortunate Mr. Kohler know Mr. Sargent in Mexico?"

"Mr. Sargent? Very possible. In Mexico all white men friendly."

"How did Miss McKay meet Mr. Sargent?"

Mr. Hiroshita pondered over this question. "Have heard last year Mr. Sargent has business in San Francisco. Same time, Miss McKay visits Carmel staying with cousin,

Miss Miquet. Not inconceivable mutual friends introduce. Cannot say."

"Mr. Kohler worked both for Miss McKay and for Mr. Preacher on their ranches. You knew that?"

Mr. Hiroshita blinked. "Yes."

"You cannot say why Mr. Kohler departed from Miss McKay's ranch?"

"Have heard Mr. Kohler buy three thousand acres from Preacher Ranch without permission. Miss McKay most angry. Mr. Kohler loses position."

"Did Mr. Kohler ever see Mr. Preacher?"

"Mr. Preacher resided always in Paris. Think unlikely Mr. Kohler traveled to Paris. Preacher Ranch managed by very clever Scotchman who engaged poor Mr. Kohler before hired by Miss McKay."

"Why did Mr. Kohler purchase three thousand acres from the Preacher Ranch?"

"So sorry. Have not heard."

"Mr. Hiroshita, you do not appear to be— A moment, if you please!" Hearing voices in the hall, the Baron silently went to the doors, unlocked and pushed the wooden one ajar.

The five were back again, gathering around Caryl's door. "I don't call two dances much of an evening," Mary McKay was saying petulantly while Caryl opened the door.

"Well, I'm tired," came a man's voice. It wasn't Bolton's. It was either Mr. Sargent's or Mr. Preacher's, decided the Baron.

"I'm certainly not going to bed at this hour."

"We'll have drinks sent up here, Mary, and rest awhile and go down later. The floor's so crowded now you can't move, and when people start leaving . . ." The door closed.

When the Baron turned, Mr. Hiroshita was at his shoulder. Mr. Hiroshita was nodding and smiling, pointing to the next door. "Very great trouble, Baron, arranging room beside beautiful Miss Miquet." He sat on the bed, pleased with himself.

The Baron wasn't pleased with Mr. Hiroshita, himself or anyone else. "And this second soapstone plaque with the—ach!—the map? Where is it now?"

Mr. Hiroshita tittered. "Directions for sending to Miss Miquet written at San Francisco. Mails more private than wireless. Very clever, please? Miss Miquet boasts many friends on Islands. No matter where staying, post-office here will know where to deliver package. Should be arriving in ten days." And as the Baron remained silent Mr. Hiroshita again tittered. "See how simple? When package reaches destination, Miss Miquet reads note: 'From Admirer.' Who is admirer, please? The brave Baron von Kaz! One day brave Baron inquires concerning plaque. Miss Miquet graciously shows present. Baron substitutes for plaque received by mail plaque given by Mr. Hiroshita. And then poor Mr. Hiroshita safe. Duty to friends completed. Mr. George Tuung comes to hotel. Baron presents plaque with map. Mr. Tuung gratefully presents one thousand dollars. When lost city found by expedition headed by Mr. Tuung, unworthy Mr. Hiroshita has one eighth share. Is not simple?" All of Mr. Hiroshita's teeth shone. Then he asked, unable to conceal his anxiety, "Now understanding why brave Baron stops here ten days, two weeks, please?"

From the other room came the sound of the radio and laughter and voices. The plaster walls were too thick to permit distinguishable sentences to pass through. The Baron realized that not one of the five in room seven thirty-two could hear what either Mr. Hiroshita or he had to say. But he had an uncomfortable feeling. He was too worried by what he had been told even to become angry with the little Japanese for so callously, so thoughtlessly, doing this to Miss Miquet. The little man apparently was unconscious of the danger in which he had placed her. As far as he was concerned, his plan was ideal. It was simple, practical. Mr. Hiroshita stood smiling, his hat in his hand.

The Baron lit another cigarette, blew out the tiny flame of his lighter. "Mr. Hiroshita, what would you say if I informed you that this afternoon I discovered Miss Miquet's mail had been opened before she received it?"

Mr. Hiroshita's hat dropped to the floor. Mr. Hiroshita picked it up, looked at the Baron, the shock of this announcement sticking out on his face, his lips stretching against his teeth. His hat again slipped from his hands. This time he didn't reach for it. "Mail is opened?" he squeaked.

Although the Baron didn't believe that a map of a fabulous city had been inserted in the second Green Lion, he willingly accepted the fact that something of utmost value *had* been placed in it. And that it was being sent to Miss Miquet. And someone, someone perhaps among the four who were with her, knew it!

He felt as though a sharp piece of ice were being drawn along his spine. Accordingly he said very gently to the frightened little man, "If Mr. Kohler had friends assisting him in Mexico City, could they not learn that you ordered a second plaque constructed?"

"No." Mr. Hiroshita shook his head, and his voice shook also. "Not possible. No."

"Suppose, my dear Mr. Hiroshita, that someone *had* asked about the package and the hotel manager—" The Baron halted with a stupefied expression. "Not the manager," he said slowly, "the *assistant* manager. Du lieber Himmel! Mr. Hiroshita, if you please, was not the assistant manager of the Cosmopolitan Club in Mexico City a friend of Mr. Kohler?"

Mr. Hiroshita said he believed so, but why. Why Baron ask?

Like an underexposed negative forming its picture by the action of strong chemicals, that faint recollection of words whipped to the Baron by the wind on the *Kohala* returned, became more distinct, as his trained memory forced itself to recapture that message; the words the murdered man had spoken: "I'm not double-crossing you. I'll prove it. The assistant manager of the club's a friend of mine. . . ."

"Ach!" exclaimed the Baron, his eyes lighting. The one who murdered Mr. Kohler had learned that the map—if it was a map—had been mailed to Miss Miquet. But evidently that evil someone didn't know the exact date when it was mailed, or whether it was concealed in a package or an envelope; otherwise Miss Miquet's letter wouldn't have been tampered with so soon. The Baron's jaw shoved forward. "My dear Mr. Hiroshita, what if this unknown murderer discovered that Mr. Kohler planned to sell his information to you? Have you thought of that?" Mr. Hiroshita's breath was whistling between his teeth, and from the terrace they could hear the merry strains of "A Little Grass Shack."

When the door knob rattled, both men jumped.

After reaching in his closet for his green umbrella, the Baron opened the two doors. Jameson entered, looked around the big room. "Good evening, my dear Mr. Jameson." The Baron bowed.

"Where's Hiroshita?"

"If you please, my dear sir?"

"Where is he? The clerk downstairs said he was with you. Thought I'd drop up and ask both of you if you'd mind coming to my office for a little chat."

Mr. Hiroshita stepped out from the closet, rubbing his hands nervously. "So happy to see Mr. Jameson. Always pleased to accompany."

"Get your hat, Baron." Jameson picked up Mr. Hiroshita's hat, tossed it to the little man. "The car's waiting."

The Baron glanced once at Mr. Hiroshita, shrugged faintly, then went to the closet for his hat. Jameson kicked the doors open, put his finger on the electric light switch, paused. "You don't need an umbrella in this climate, Baron."

The Baron hooked the green umbrella over his left arm. "But, my dear sir, how can one be certain? This afternoon it rained—"

"Rains every afternoon. It's liquid sunshine." The electric switch clicked; the room was in darkness. The Baron passed into the hall as Jameson ordered impatiently, "Hurry, Hiroshita. Nothing to get scared about. I only want you both on a small matter. No dope this time."

But Mr. Hiroshita said nothing at all.

"See here, Hiroshita." Jameson clicked the light on again, and the yellow light came down upon Mr. Hiroshita standing by the bed, his left hand on the bedpost where the wood was carved in the shape of a pineapple. He was staring fixedly at Jameson, and his body wavered slightly.

"What the hell's the matter with you?" demanded Jameson irritably. He walked over to the little man, placed his hand on Mr. Hiroshita's shoulder and was going to shake him from his lethargy when Jameson saw something which caused him to lift his hand.

"Baron!" His words were just above a whisper. "Baron, get in here. Lock the door."

"Pardon?" When he thrust his head in through the door and saw Mr. Hiroshita's face he had no need to ask questions. He locked the wooden door as Mr. Hiroshita rocked forward into the detective's arms. Jameson placed the little man stomach down on the bed.

"Get the room clerk at once." He didn't look around. He didn't raise his voice. Something hard came against Jameson's shoulder and pushed him to one side, and the Baron's shoulder rubbed Jameson's arm as the Austrian bent above Mr. Hiroshita. "Don't shove," said Jameson.

Both the Baron and Jameson saw the same thing. A tiny bunch of feathers protruded from the nape of Mr. Hiroshita's neck.

The Baron pointed to the balcony. "There?"

Jameson ran silently to the balcony. "No one there now. There are balconies on either side. We'll have time for that. Here—" He took the telephone from the Baron's hand. "This the room clerk? Jameson speaking. Get this quick. There's a bad accident in room seven-thirty. I've got two men outside in my car. Send them up. Wait a minute, damn it! Get the manager. I don't want anyone to get away from this wing." He turned to the Baron. "What?"

"He is dead. He just died." The Baron sat down on the bed, put his hands on Mr. Hiroshita's shoulder and patted it as though even now he were trying to console the frightened little man for the horrible thing that had happened to him.

5

Dancing Hibiscus

The Chinese gentleman in the police laboratory removed the wicked little steel dart from under the Zeiss microscope. Placing the dart with the blood-bedraggled feathers in a small cardboard box labeled "Hiroshita, 9:45 p.m., 4/7, Ex. 1," he reached for the telephone.

In the chief of detectives' office the telephone rang. "Jameson speaking."

The man in the laboratory said, "You don't need a microscope to see the groove marks, Chief. The thing was shot out of a rifled barrel."

Jameson looked over the telephone, admitted, "You were right, Baron," and then spoke into the mouthpiece, "You checked through?"

"The gun catalogue shows a Haenel with darts like this. Says the air gun is deadly between ten and fifteen yards and as accurate within that distance as a target-shooting thirty-two."

"Mention anything about noise, Oquat?"

"Just a minute." There was a long pause, then the laboratory man picked up the telephone again. "Claims the gun is silent. Slight hiss of air. Refers us to *Mutzmann's Abhandlung über der Feuerwasse,* whatever that is. It isn't in the library."

Jameson thanked him, clicked the receiver, asked the
Baron if he'd ever heard of a feller Mussman or Mustman
who wrote in German on air guns.

"Mutzmann? *Mutzmann's Treatise on Guns.*" The Baron nodded. "But it is out of date, my dear Mr. Jameson.
Three years ago I saw one of the new Haenel air pistols. It
shot a small two-and-one-half-inch steel dart. Mutzmann's
book was published ten years ago."

Jameson walked back and forth behind the moon-
shaped desk. "Oquat says the damned dart has rifle marks
on it and that it looks like a Haenel in our catalogue. He
paid twelve dollars for that gun catalogue just six months
ago, so the catalogue should be right. By Jesus! I still can't
figure an air gun shooting that hard. And you say Kohler
was killed with the same kind of a gun?"

The Baron agreed.

"Well?" Jameson sat on the desk, holding his knee between his hands, his old leathery face bent toward the Baron. "You've said you're a smart feller. What do you think?"

"Think?" The Baron shrugged, smiled.

"Hiroshita hid when he heard me coming. That shows
the feller was scared of somebody, don't it? But how the
bloody thunder did they get the pot at him unless somebody in the next room jumped across from the other balcony? That don't make sense." The telephone whirred in the
brightly lit room, and Jameson jumped quickly, grabbed
it. "Jameson. . . Hello! It's you, Cobb. Well? All right."
Looking like an old pelican under the bluish light, he jerked his head at the Baron. "Hand me that pencil, will you?"

Jameson wrote the names of all those who were in the
wing where Hiroshita was murdered. This took five minutes. When he had finished he said, "What do I care if
Berenday is stinking sore? Tell him I said no one could
leave that wing until you're through. Hey?" Berenday was
the manager of the Imperial Hawaiian. While Jameson

listened he helped himself to a thin brown cigar. The bluish light struck the cigar, and the long shadow jerked from side to side across his weathered cheeks. "All in seven thirty-two have alibis? No, guess you'd better let 'em go. Mary McKay's got too much influence. You're sure about the feller Poling in seven thirty-one? Let 'em go then. Hey?"

As a pelican who has swallowed a fish too large for its gullet, Jameson choked when his assistant Cobb, who had taken charge at the hotel after his chief and the Baron had departed for the police station, said something.

"You do, hey? Well, let me tell you he didn't. That's final. The Baron stepped out of the room before *I* did. I and Hiroshita were the only ones in it when he was shot, and the Doc said Hiroshita couldn't 've lived with that dart in his neck more'n a minute or so. No," shouted Jameson angrily. "The Doc knows what the hell he's talking about, don't he? Besides, I was there, and I searched the Baron afterwards to make sure. He didn't have a gun. Let the others go. Search the grounds again. Beneath all the windows. See if anybody's tried to climb up from the room below. . . . Oh, you did? Locked and empty. Well, do something man. How do I know?"

He slammed the receiver hard, faced the Baron. "That feller Cobb thinks you did it." He lit his cigar, the wise old eyes shrewdly watching the Baron. "You didn't, did you, while my eyes were closed maybe, or when I was hiding my head under the bed?"

"You joke, my dear sir."

"Joke hell. Lucky for you I was there." He showed the Baron the piece of paper. "Here's the list and how they were in the rooms."

The Baron was in room seven-thirty; opposite him in seven-thirty-one was a man, James Poling; next to the Baron's room on the left side of the corridor, room seven-thirty-two were listed Miss Caryl Miquet and Miss Mary

McKay; opposite in seven-thirty-three was Mr. Harry
Bolton; at the end in seven-thirty-four, Mr. John Sargent;
and opposite him in seven-thirty-five, Mr. Jeffrey Preacher. "The hell of it is," explained Jameson dryly, "five of 'em
were in seven-thirty-two: Mary McKay, her cousin Caryl
Miquet, her fiancé Sargent, Jeff Preacher, and the fat feller Bolton. All of 'em stick by each other and are ready to
swear none left the room. No, wait a minute." He glanced
at the paper. "Caryl Miquet said that Bolton got sore—"

He looked up. "Cobb says she didn't say 'sore' but
that's what she meant. She and Jeff were discussing mixing
drinks, and Bolton decided Jeff shouldn't hear such talk or
something like that. Bolton's a nut, I guess. So when Jeff
wouldn't leave—I don't blame him not wanting to leave a
pretty girl like Caryl—Bolton walks out."

"At what time, please?"

"Jeff told Cobb around nine-thirty, but Caryl says it
was a few minutes later." Jameson wrote on the paper:
"Check Bolton's time." He shifted in his seat. "Anyway,
Bolton came back a few minutes later, and that should
alibi him. Besides, I know his kind. Those fat fellers aren't
dangerous. John Sargent and Mary McKay were mooning
on the balcony most all the time. Jeff said he and Mary
went out together to join Sargent, but Jeff realized three
wasn't company, so he went back to Caryl and the drinks.
And there you are. They alibi each other. Sargent claims
it's ridiculous that anyone from the girls' room could 've
got to your balcony, and, by Jesus, Baron, it seems like
he's right. I can't arrest one of *them*."

"But Mr. Bolton?"

"Forget him. If Jeff Preacher's as hot-tempered as his
dad was, *he* might go after Hiroshita if the two had been
arguing. Or Sargent might. Those two girls could take care
of themselves, too, but this fat feller couldn't step on his

own shadow. And the hell of it is, there ain't any motive for any of them to kill Hiroshita. Or Kohler either."

"What room, if you please, is the boy in?"

"What boy?"

"The young brother."

"Billy? Billy McKay?" And when the Baron nodded, Jameson demanded, "Billy's staying at the hotel?" He reached for the telephone, told the operator to check through to Cobb and ask how he'd missed Billy McKay's room. "How'd *you* know Billy was here?"

The Baron told him and then said blandly, "In Vienna there was a case where a small boy killed three men for his mother, and I assumed that it would be interesting to—"

"What 're you talking about? Billy's a good kid. Where were we? The feller opposite your door? Poling. He was taking a bath and drinking brandy. How the hell do I know why he was drinking brandy in his bath? Anyway, when Cobb opened the door he was in the bath, hadn't heard anything, and there were no marks on the floor his feet might 've made. He could 've wiped his feet dry, but if *he* did it how could he 've gone to the window in the elevator corridor, jumped to your balcony, shot Hiroshita, and got back without me seeing him? Hey?"

The Baron shrugged.

"What was Hiroshita afraid of?" quickly cried the old man. "Why'd he hide in the closet when I knocked? Why'd he come to see you in the first place?"

The Baron's dark face showed regret. "I do not know, my dear sir. Otherwise, assuredly I would tell you."

"Assuredly, hey? Look here, Baron, I've played fair with you and given you the facts. Now suppose you come clean. Why'd Hiroshita want to see you?"

"I had met him in Mexico. We traveled on the boat together. I invited him to my room for a drink."

"Baron," said Jameson, "I think you're lying like hell. Yes?"

A stalwart man in plain clothes who had knocked entered. "Busy, Chief?"

"This is the Baron von Kaz, David Kaniela. What d'you want?"

"Cobb sent me to see if the *Advertiser* had pictures or interviews with Poling. While I was there I got all the photographs they took this morning of the others on the floor where Hiroshita was bumped off." He handed Jameson a list of names, a newspaper, four photographs, and several sheets of yellow newspaper copy paper.

"Thanks, Dave." Jameson sorted the photographs on his desk. "You better stick at the Imperial tonight and see if anything funny turns up. I'll have you relieved at one."

Kaniela went out.

"Know this girl, Baron?" Jameson slid the glossy print along the desk.

Moving the desk lamp so that the light wouldn't shine into his eyes, the Baron took the photograph taken that morning. It showed a round-cheeked, smiling girl. He studied the caption written in long hand:

> *Miss Mary McKay, owner of the McKay Ranch in Hawaii, whose engagement to Mr. John Sargent was announced four weeks ago. Accompanied by her cousin, Miss Caryl Miquet, and her fiancé, Miss McKay arrived in Honolulu yesterday on the Kohala. She plans to take her guests to her ranch for a month before departing for New York, where the wedding is planned early this fall.*

Jameson unnecessarily observed, "The picture's for tomorrow's paper. That's why they've got the 'arrived yesterday.'"

"I saw her once on the boat, again this afternoon at Waikiki and in the lobby of the hotel tonight. I can tell you nothing else concerning her."

"Take a glance at the others."

The Baron discarded the photograph of an uncomfortable-looking gentleman staring dazedly from the picture with his hand supporting a thick clump of leis circling his neck. This was; "James Poling, New York business man on vacation trip." The Baron was not interested in tourists.

The third photograph held the Baron's attention. The tall young man was caught in the position of restraining a short fat man who was lunging toward the camera as though he were trying to stop the picture from being taken. The caption read:

> *Mr. Jeffrey Preacher, owner of the famous Preacher Ranch, returns to the Islands after twenty years abroad. Mr. Harry Bolton (right), a friend of Mr. Preacher.*

Underneath this caption in red ink was written: "Scrap this picture, Mike, and get a decent one of Preacher tomorrow without his friend."

The final photograph was one of John Sargent and Caryl Miquet, both loaded with leis, both amused, and smiling. The caption:

> *Miss Caryl Miquet and Mr. John Sargent of New York and Mexico City.*

"Well?"

The Baron dropped the photographs on the desk. "I have met all five," he replied blandly. "But except—" the hesitation was slight—"except for Miss Miquet, the others I have not known before."

Jameson adjusted the lamplight so that it would again shine in the Baron's face. He leaned on the desk. "You don't know why Hiroshita was frightened, Baron?"

"No, my dear sir, as I have said—"

"Forget what you've said. You don't know why Kohler was murdered, hey?"

"'Tedium vitae,'" suggested the Baron pontifically. "In other words, translating from the Latin—"

"Hey?" shouted Jameson.

"Perhaps he was disgusted with life. That is the English translation."

Whatever Jameson was about to say concerning the value of translations from the Latin in a murder case unfortunately was interrupted by the telephone whirring. He listened, hung up, said briefly, "Billy McKay isn't at the hotel. He's staying with one of his playmates, the Hall boy, overnight. Now see here, Baron . . ."

And then followed an hour's questioning. Jameson wasn't ugly or threatening. His questions were dry, caustic. He had the Baron repeat how he had first met Hiroshita. The old man was persistent. And he had a tenacious memory. And he sat there leaning on the desk with his head nodding pelican fashion and the little shrewd eyes boring in at the Baron, chewing on his unlit cigar, taking his time, not hurrying the Baron. But where other suspects had crumpled under the impact of the tireless question after question, had grown angry, had bluffed and then had been caught in their bluffing, or had screamed and shouted, this one followed none of these procedures. He was quiet. He was bland. Despite himself, Jameson found he was becoming exasperated. The clock had struck midnight.

The man opposite was like a damned graven rock worn too bloody smooth. The Baron was infinitely polite. As the old man's voice edged with sarcasm, the Baron's candid blue eyes seemed to show his hurt by such suspicion.

Jameson got up, stalked across the room, swung suddenly at the Baron, "By Jesus! I tell you HIROSHITA WAS
FRIGHTENED!"

"Ach, so. If you insist, my dear sir."

Jameson was prepared to go on. He would take all morning as well as night. All the next day, too, by Jesus. And
then, just as he turned, he caught a glimpse of the Baron's
face. On that impassive darkness, the lips had cut a fine,
faint smile, ironic; and it passed as quickly as it had appeared, and again the Baron was sympathetic and puzzled.

Jameson wasn't a fool. He had a queer feeling. There
was something in that instant smile as though for a moment the feller's conceit had been too much for that bland,
helpful mask and had broken through it. Jameson wagged
his head, watched the Baron dourly. "Yes?" asked the Baron pleasantly.

"You're a smart feller, hey?"

"My dear sir," said the Baron simply, "I am a great detective."

"You think I'm a fool, hey?"

"Ach, my dear Mr. Jameson." And then the full lower
lip thrust forward a little, and lines imperceptibly deepened at the corners of the guileless eyes. "Let us say you
are handicapped, no? In your North American countries
not yet have you the experience." The Baron's eyes flicked
up at the old man, dropped again as he lit a cigarette.

"I'll admit," said the old man, "that I thought you were
lying about Kohler's death being caused by an air gun. But
what did Kohler and Hiroshita have in common that got
them both killed the same way? You tell me that."

"I wish I could, my dear sir. Do you know why Mr.
Kohler went to Mexico?"

"Do I know? He had business there."

"In the paper I read that he worked for Miss McKay."

"So you read it, hey?" Jameson squinted at the Baron. "She let him go. That Scotchman who runs Preacher's ranch had three thousand acres that wasn't much good and Kohler buys the three thousand acres without telling Mary. That's why she let him go. Does that interest a smart feller like you? Does that explain why Hiroshita got shot with an air gun?"

"It could," answered the Baron politely. "Why did Mr. Kohler purchase the three thousand acres?"

"Because he was probably DRUNK!" shouted Jameson. "He was drunk most of the time, and I heard before he was fired he was claiming every time he got drunk that he was going to make hisself a million dollars." Jameson snorted. "When Kohler got drunk he'd think he was an old Hawaiian. Kohler was a damn fool."

"I do not understand," said the Baron.

"I said Kohler was a DAMN fool," declared Jameson. "See here, Baron," continued Jameson, dismissing Kohler. "These islands are a paradise. The loveliest place mortal man's ever seen. We don't have much crime here. I'm an old man, Baron, but let me tell you this: As long as I'm alive there ain't going to be crimes nor murderers on this paradise to spoil it. I'm an old man, Baron. But I can hang on." Jameson went to his chair and sat down heavily. "That's all. You can go now. You're a smart feller, and I've got nothing against you, and you've got powerful friends in Washington. And you've sat here telling me a lot of lies and thinking you're smart and clever, and maybe you are." Jameson's long New England jaws dropped wearily. He took his pen between his fingers. "When you leaving, Baron?"

"Leaving?" When was he leaving? he wondered. Tomorrow? With Hiroshita shot and Miss Miquet soon to receive a package that already had led to two deaths? He couldn't leave until he knew whether he could safely tell this old man all that Hiroshita had said and trust the old man to protect Miss Miquet or not. And first he must learn what Caryl Miquet wished him to do. He smiled. "Ach, leaving? You had suggested tomorrow, my dear sir?"

"You leave tomorrow, and I'll have you brought back and thrown into jail as a suspect," declared Jameson fiercely. "We checked on you late this afternoon by cabling Mexico City. That's why I went after you tonight. The manager of the Cosmopolitan Club's told the Mexico City police that he heard you got yourself hired by Hiroshita as a body-guard. What was Hiroshita afraid of that he had to have a bodyguard?"

"I will tell you," said the Baron amiably.

"You'll tell me. You think it over tonight and decide if you're going to tell the truth or not. Meanwhile, if you try to leave the Islands, all the Austrians in Washington, and the Democrats too, won't get you out of jail. That's all. I'll ring you tomorrow at the hotel when I want you. Good night."

"Do you wish a little advice, my dear sir?"

"Do I wish— God almighty, Baron, all I want from you are facts."

"I suggest that you cable the Mexico City police and have them ascertain whether Mr. Kohler ever met Mr. Sargent or Mr. Preacher or—"

"I've already cabled," said Jameson dryly, "Also to New York and to San Francisco. Good night." He took the telephone. "Give me the laboratory again, Sis."

"Good night to you, my dear sir," said the Baron as he closed the door.

Jameson swore, then explained into the telephone that he'd burnt his finger lighting a cigar.

The Baron started down Merchant Street, a block away from the docks. Long ago tight-lipped missionaries from Boston had walked this street, and swaggering sailors from all nations, and gaudily dressed Hawaiians in red vests with dreams of a Pacific kingdom floating crazily through their heads.

The stone buildings threw scented shadows upon the flagstone walk which had so many years ago been transported to Honolulu in the holds of sailing ships. He turned into King Street, a broad boulevard plowing ruthlessly through the older part of the city toward the modern residential section erected on the cool and perfumed heights of Moiliili, two and a half miles east.

At the corner of King and Fort streets he paused, considering if he should hail one of the taxis drawn up in front of the rococo structure of the territorial capital, formerly the home of Hawaiian kings and queens, or attempt the three-mile walk to Waikiki and the Imperial Hawaiian. In the three miles of walking he would have time to think, to decide upon a course to follow.

After Hiroshita's murder Jameson had instructed the Baron to remain in his room with the dead man. The manager and others had arrived, unwillingly complied with the Honolulu detective's incisive instructions to patrol the wing to prevent any guest in the six rooms from getting away. Jameson had telephoned for his assistant Cobb, and four plainclothes men had arrived in less than fifteen minutes with the cameraman, fingerprint man and the doctor. Jameson then, after instructing Cobb to question every guest in the wing, had departed for the police station, taking the Baron with him.

As a result, the Baron had had little time to organize his thoughts. And when Jameson had commenced firing his questions the great Baron von Kaz was too distrustful to risk giving facts to the Honolulu detective. Therefore, as he stood there at King and Fort streets, he was puzzled. What part was Caryl Miquet playing? Was she unknowingly caught in this chain of events? That was something he *must* learn. What right had he to tell Jameson Mr. Hiroshita's story? And if he did, would that, after all, protect Miss Miquet? And why should he worry about protecting her? And could a lost Aztec city be the real story of the two Green Lions? Ach! he sighed pathetically. He was sorry for himself. The poor brave Baron; he who had promised so faithfully to be in Austria by the middle of May, now delayed by the idiocies of these barbaric North Americans! And even as he commiserated with himself, he felt a warm glow at the expectation of seeing Caryl Miquet again.

Tomorrow he would converse with the obstinate young woman, and this time he would let no one interrupt them. Then he would know what to do, act quickly, and, conscience clear, depart for Austria. For Vienna! As he started down King Street he could even imagine that he heard those familiar noises of Vienna, the music from the beer halls, faint and gay and happy.

"Good evening, Baron."

The Baron spun on his toes, and as he spun, the green umbrella slid from his arm to his right hand with the point sticking outwards. "So?"

"Glad to see you, Baron." George Tuung, the Japanese, showed all his teeth. They were so big that they looked to be stuck on his face, white porcelain chips stuck in a yellow clay dental mask. "I just was passing the police station and saw you. Nice night, isn't it? In Austria, I'll bet you don't have blue clouds at night like those floating up there?"

"Good evening, my dear Mr. Tuung." The Baron permitted the tip of the umbrella to touch the pavement. "Allow me to extend my regrets. Or have you not heard the lamentable—"

"It was tough, wasn't it? Olokele, at the *Advertiser*, called me as soon as the news came in. Hiroshita was—he was okay."

"Someday," requested the Baron politely, "when you have time, perhaps you will honor me by having lunch?"

"Sure."

"Now, if you will excuse me, it is late. Good night, my dear sir."

An enclosed Lincoln came around the corner on two wheels, and when the brakes were slammed down, all four wheels ground into the macadam and made a heavy, sleezy sound like a strip of rubber being rubbed on an emery wheel. Two men were in front. Before the car lurched to a stop one of the men had the rear door open. "Get in quick," ordered George Tuung.

George Tuung saved his life by a half-second margin. He never knew that he had saved it; his left hand was resting in his pocket, and he simply withdrew his hand, disclosing the smug little automatic.

The Baron had twisted the handle of his green umbrella. The handle was already lifting from the umbrella stock, lifting with it that sure, flashing death which the umbrella could wield. Ordinarily, before Tuung's automatic could have shown above his pocket, death could have been biting into his throat, striking, hard and silent, into the soft flesh.

But the Baron had hesitated. He wasn't certain that he wished to see Mr. Tuung twisting on the pavement with his hands clasping his throat. He wasn't certain at all. This Mr. Tuung might be the one who could solve the conundrum of the soapstone plaque.

And thus he hesitated. George Tuung was not cursed with an imagination. All he had to do was pull out his gun, and he did it without any inhibitions. The Baron was a brave man. But twice before he had bravely disregarded guns aimed at him and, upon both occasions, several weeks later had recovered consciousness amid the depressing odors of ether. He bowed, surreptitiously clicked the handle back on the umbrella, philosophically accepting the fact that it was too late to recover the lost opportunity.

"Make it snappy," commanded Tuung, splendidly ignorant of those black wings which had swept close to him only to waver and turn aside. "You won't be hurt if you do what we say. Don't be afraid."

"Afraid, my dear sir?" As the Baron stepped into the rear of the car he was coldly magnanimous to this foolish little person who didn't realize how fortunate it was that his throat was still in one piece. "Never am I afraid, Mr. Tuung."

However, when he sat down he watched the automatic uncomfortably. After the Lincoln had picked up speed and had turned onto the beach road he edged away from the muzzle. He suggested to Mr. Tuung that it would be safer to close the safety lock, at least. He observed kindly that you never could tell what might happen to the weapon. Tuung was quite nasty. He said he was capable of handling an automatic, and if the Baron didn't stop shoving the umbrella at the automatic it was liable to go off. The Baron sighed. He was apprehensive that he'd made a serious error. Soapstone plaque or no soapstone plaque, it would have been more convenient if this Mr. Tuung had been killed, or at least seriously disabled.

For the first five minutes or more the Baron was too intent upon the automatic to realize what the three men had already discovered: They were being followed. Tuung was growing nervous. The three men would let loose a series of rapid-fire, staccato Japanese at each other; Tuung would glance through the rear window; the driver had the Lincoln traveling seventy miles an hour now, but those bright lights behind them continued to creep closer. They were past the Imperial Hawaiian, skirting Waikiki beach.

Honolulu goes to sleep at midnight. The long street was empty except for the two cars rushing upon Diamond

Head with the stars bright and icy above them, and the surf thundering its crash and slide and crash at the right of the road, the thudding rumble of the waves lifting and joining with the strained baying of the motors. When the Baron glanced back for the second time, Tuung viciously prodded his side with the automatic.

"I'll let you have it," he said and then gave an order in Japanese to the driver. Tires shrieked, and the sound filled the car; the car tilted and the centrifugal force lifted Tuung and flung him against the Baron. The *car* groaned. Ahead the straight road slithered. Under the harsh glare of the headlights the road twisted and curved, melted into huge black trees, into a wall which streaked past as though it were painted on a revolving panorama. The lights picked out the great hibiscus flowers on the wall, and the flowers seemed to dance madly as the Lincoln's tires spun in the soft red earth away from the macadam. In turn the dancing flowers were jerked off the panorama, the lights spun down a tunneled earth road and the road became steady. When the Lincoln had lurched heavily, George Tuung's chin had gone upward from the impact of the umbrella's weighted handle applied during the swerve into the side road.

The Lincoln started out anew. The driver, glancing briefly into the gloom of the rear of the sedan, caught a glimpse only of the Baron. He spoke in Japanese to the man sitting next to him. This man also looked to the rear. As near as he could discern Tuung had gone crazy. He was sitting on the Baron's lap.

"If you please," requested the Baron, "will you stop the car?"

The Baron had Tuung's automatic. The automatic was pointed at the driver's head. And the Baron was shielded by Tuung. The car stopped. Holding Tuung by the scruff of the neck the Baron backed out of the Lincoln. He was holding Tuung in front of him, facing the two men who had descended from the car, their hands held above their heads, when the dull monotone behind him became a roar, and the roar merged into brakes squealing.

The Buick stopped ten feet behind the Lincoln. A fat man left the Buick, approached the other car. He didn't walk with his body facing the Lincoln. He walked very carefully, as though the road were covered with eggs, and he had both hands in his pockets, and these pockets were shoved out from his body. He came to them, sidewise, looking as if he were about to lift his skirts and go into a ballet dance.

He was five or six feet away from the Baron when he stood still. The creases at his neck wrinkled and slid over his wilted collar as he nodded at the Baron, his face all filled with that cherubic expression. "I've got them covered, Baron," Bolton said. "Drop the Jap and get into my car. I've saved you."

The wind swayed the feathery boughs of a Kiawe tree across the moon, and the slim sharp leaves broke the dull light into little triangles and squares; Bolton's head and shoulders were speckled with the tiny blotches of yellow and blackness. In that soft, sticky darkness the Baron watched the moon speckles jump and quiver when Bolton's body moved.

The Baron dropped Tuung. The Japanese went down into the thick volcanic dust and put his hands into the dust, recovering from the sock the umbrella had given him on the chin. Bolton's shoe caught Tuung right above the ear. Tuung didn't stir after that. "Poor fellow." Bolton's shoe rolled Tuung onto his back. "The poor fellow. I do abhor violence." Then he waved his gun at the other Japanese and ordered in his flat voice, "Scram!" The Japanese looked at the gun. Then they fled into the night. Bolton slipped his hand through the Baron's arm. "I don't like Japs," he said.

6

The Humble Man

Instead of turning north from Kapiolani Park, Bolton took the Diamond Head Road, explaining to the Baron that it would be safer this way. They could drive around Diamond Head to the Waialae Golf Club and then take the Alohea Road into Honolulu.

"Do you not believe they are too frightened, my dear sir, to attempt to pursue us?" asked the Baron.

"You can't tell with these Jap gangs, Baron." Bolton navigated the Buick on a winding curve at full speed.

Bolton explained that he had gone to the police station with one of the detectives for further questioning. "I'm such an ordinary person that I don't receive the consideration the police gave to Mr. Preacher and Mr. Sargent and the others. Not that I'm complaining. Dear me, no. I know my place, Baron von Kaz."

The black mass of Diamond Head overhung the road. On their right the road dropped off into sheer cliff-like formations descending to the water. The sliver of moonlight marked its translucent pathway across the Pacific. "They questioned you?" asked the Baron.

"As if we could tell them anything about the murder of a Jap," said Bolton disdainfully. "My opinion, Baron, is that this Hiroshita was involved with a Jap gang. However, I know so little about Jap gangs that my opinion is worth very little." The man's head revolved toward the Baron. "You, of course, a great detective, undoubtedly have your ideas."

"Ach so. You are most astute my dear sir. I met Mr. Hiroshita in Mexico City. I also believe he was involved in a gang feud."

"Think so?" The Buick was slowing as it approached the crest of the grade. "Lucky for you that I left the police station only a few minutes after you departed. I saw you go down the street and called to you. I was going to drive you back to the hotel." Bolton applied the brakes, the Buick swerving to the left upon a rocky promontory overlooking the Pacific. Mr. Bolton sighed. "It's pretty here."

"Beautiful, my dear sir." The Baron slipped his hand along the edge of the door until he had the door handle between his fingers. He braced his feet, ready to jump.

"I think we're safe after all."

"Ach so. No one seems to be behind us, my dear Mr. Bolton."

"My car was parked a block from the police station. By the time I got it, you'd disappeared. Then when I drove up Fort Street I saw you getting into the other car. It struck me that you were being forced in. I hadn't time to call for the police. So I followed."

The Baron gravely thanked dear Mr. Bolton.

"Maybe, because Hiroshita visited you, the gang thought you were mixed up in his affairs?"

"Possibly." The Baron wondered if it would be safe to light a cigarette. He decided not to. He wanted to keep his hands free. "From what they said, I assume that they mistook me for another person."

Bolton digested this information. "It's nice here. If you're not in a hurry to get to the hotel I guess I'll have a look at the ocean. I like oceans."

"I too enjoy beauty, Mr. Bolton."

"You do? If you're not too shaken up, have a look with me. The air'll do you good, Baron."

The two men walked toward the rocks. There the Baron leaned against one of the stunted pine trees with every visible sign of casualness while Bolton ambled over the rocks.

The Baron was watching Bolton all the time. The Baron had seen men before who were dangerous and ruthless, but not one of them ever gave him the feeling that he had now, watching Bolton. There was something unreal about the man. Despite his fatness, he was nimble. He sat on one of the rocks, the moon reflecting a cold light from that round cherubic face of his, and it was as if the face were molded of butter with the nose and the eyes and the soft smile there, and the Baron could imagine that oily sluggish softness oozing out and creeping, covering him.

Bolton was saying in his toneless voice how nice it was here, but it was time to get back to the hotel, and the Baron had the sensation of waiting for something. But that something didn't come. It was like watching a man blow air in a balloon. The balloon expands, and you know it has to explode but it doesn't, and the waiting tightens all your nerves. Bolton got off the rock and came toward the Baron, his colorless lips rolled into a meaningless smile, and his eyes as bright and hard as the light from the moon. When it did happen it didn't happen suddenly. Bolton stumbled. He went down on his face, twisted, and was silent.

That was all.

The Baron had the gun he had taken from George Tuung. But Bolton's arms were splayed on each side of his body. The man groaned. He tried to rise, fell again, rubbing his legs. When he turned his head, his eyes were full of tears. "I've sprained my leg," he said. He didn't ask the Baron to help him up. He said, "You'd better drive to the hotel for a doctor, Baron." Then his head dropped, and he was silent. If he'd seen the gun in the Baron's hand he gave no indication of it. The Baron came close to Bolton.

"Mr. Bolton," said the Baron.

But Bolton didn't reply. He was stretched out on the rocky gravel a foot or so away from the cliff. The waves beating on the rocks below gave a low thunder. A white moth flew by in zigzags and paused on Bolton's head where the hair was brushed across the bald spot, and Bolton didn't move. The Baron changed his gun to his left hand, walked around the fat man spread on the rocky soil like a great fat slug, motionless.

"If you please, Mr. Bolton, are you hurt?"

When the Baron rolled him over Bolton didn't open his eyes. The Baron removed Bolton's gun from his pocket, threw it over the cliff. He searched Bolton's other pockets, made certain the man was unarmed.

If the man had stumbled and in falling had lost consciousness, the only thing to do was to return with him to the hotel. After all, he had rescued the Baron.

Nevertheless, the Baron was distrustful. He flicked his cigarette lighter. And cautiously, because in order to employ both hands it was necessary to drop the gun in his pocket, he knelt and opened Bolton's eyelid. With his right hand the Baron held open the eyelid; with his left he brought the tiny flame close to the staring eye. When the lighter was less than half an inch from the lid the eyelid spasmodically jerked. Bolton opened the other eye, smiling like an evil child, and as the Baron's hand plunged toward the gun in his pocket two huge soft arms whipped around the Baron's arms, pinning them helpless to his sides.

The Baron was more amazed that the fat man, unarmed, would dare attack him, the great Von Kaz, than disturbed. The Baron had been pinned before. He knew what to do. With lightninglike rapidity, the Baron's knees came up where they would strike into Bolton's groin, and then, as other foolish men had done before, Bolton would groan with pain and release the Baron. And the Baron would get up and bow ironically and say, "My dear sir, you should be more careful." It was most dramatic to smile at a vanquished adversary, and the Baron relished these little moments of triumph.

So, automatically, he doubled his knees. But huge soft legs had split wide apart and clamped around the Baron's waist. The Baron's knees found no groin to strike. The Baron felt himself trapped in that sickening embrace, and when the legs and arms pressed he was forced against Bolton's yielding stomach, and panic overcame him. Bolton's mass seemed to be enfolding him. The man's legs tightened. The Baron jerked, writhed, heard himself crying out as the shocking pain cracked into his ribs. With all his force the Baron tried to pull from that embrace. After the first cry the Baron had clamped his mouth shut. He would bite off his tongue before crying aloud again. Great stifling waves of pain flowed through him, and he turned his head from side to side, his face pale and strained above the placid, moonlike thing below him.

Cutting the sodden haze the Baron heard Bolton's flat voice, "How do you like it?" Bolton squeezed harder. The Baron squirmed futilely. "I used to be Middle-Western champ," said Bolton, as if that were an important piece of information. "I'm going to throw you over the cliff."

The Baron gasped, "You are . . . a dolt."

Without realizing it, Bolton relaxed the pressure. "Think so? I'm giving it to you easy. In a minute you won't feel much."

"Preacher will." The Baron went limp. "When they hang him."

Bolton shook the Baron as a monstrous snail tries to crumple a particularly tough and thorny blade of grass. "You're lying." He rolled on the Baron.

"So?"

Bolton loosened his grip.

Bolton was bewildered. He took the gun from the Baron's pocket and slowly got off his body. He pointed the gun at the Baron. "Explain," he said without emotion. "If you're trying for time you'll wish you hadn't when it starts over again."

The Baron lay on the ground without moving, "I wrote a letter."

"You're lying."

"My dear sir—"

"Cut it."

"If anything happens to me . . . the letter goes to Mr. Jameson."

"Go on."

"In the letter I state that I saw Mr. Preacher on my balcony before he shot Mr. Hiroshita . . ."

"I knew you were lying. You were in the hall. The detective said you were in the hall."

"Did that prevent me from looking through the doorway? To the balcony?"

"Jeff didn't go out of the room. I was standing—" Bolton stopped short. "You're lying. You think you've tricked me."

He jumped in the air, but his knees hit the solid rock instead of the Baron's stomach. The Baron had been waiting for Bolton to move. He was prepared. With every muscle aching he threw himself to one side and kicked the fat man's arm. The gun clattered on the rocks. When Bolton stood, rubbing his knees, he looked at the man holding the gun.

"I knew you were lying all the time."

The Baron was very pleased with himself. As a lie it hadn't been very convincing, but he had been able to make it sound convincing long enough to distract Bolton's attention. The Baron wasted no time in ironic bows. "Get into the car, please. Behind the wheel."

Bolton slowly climbed into the car.

The Baron stepped on the running board, a few feet to the rear of Bolton. "Turn to me," requested the Baron.

As Bolton's head obeyed, the blue steel of the muzzle flashed in the moonlight and struck the fat man a glancing blow on the side of his neck. Bolton shuddered, felt his neck. "What did you do that for?" he complained.

"Every time you turn your head," the Baron purred softly, "I shall do that. I am quicker than you, my dear sir. You cannot catch the gun." The Baron gripped the gun tighter, trying to forget the pain which was splintering into his sides. "Where was Miss Miquet when Mr. Hiroshita was shot?"

Bolton thrust up in the seat, at the same time twisting toward the Baron, arms outstretched, fingers grasping at the gun. But the muzzle streaked down upon Bolton's head again. Bolton's arms dropped. He slumped into the seat.

The Baron smoked a cigarette. After a time he flicked it away, then methodically began to slap Bolton's face. Bolton's body trembled, his eyes opened. "Can you hear me, my dear sir?" gently inquired the Baron.

Bolton managed to get out his handkerchief, wiped the blood from his head. "Miss Miquet was sitting on the bed." He folded the handkerchief, wiped his nose. "I'm not afraid of you. Someday, Baron von Kaz—"

"Someday, my dear Mr. Bolton, you will wish you were afraid of me. Where were the others?"

There was a long pause. When the muzzle hit Bolton for the third time, he groaned softly.

"Did you hear, my dear sir?"

"I don't know. That's the truth. The girls had rigged a screen between their beds and the balcony doors. They had their breakfast on the balcony. Miss McKay said she didn't like to eat breakfast and see messy beds."

"The screen prevented them from noticing you climb from your balcony to mine, no?"

"No," said Bolton. "Mr. Sargent joined me on the balcony. Then I returned into the room behind the screen where the girls and Jeff—Mr. Preacher were talking near the radio and drinks."

"Ach, so? Leaving Mr. Sargent on the balcony alone?"

"Not exactly. I think you cracked my skull. My head hurts." The man wasn't excited. It was a statement of fact in the same soft, flat voice. "He called Miss McKay to come and look at the moon."

"She went?"

Bolton felt his head. "She and Mr. Preacher went."

"How long was Mr. Sargent alone?"

"Not long enough to get to your balcony. Five minutes at the most." Bolton started to turn his head, remembered, gazed stolidly in front.

"What was the time?"

"Nine o'clock. Nine-fifteen."

The Baron recalled that Mr. Hiroshita had been killed a few minutes before or after nine forty-five. "That is too early," he said. "The five of you had barely entered Miss Miquet's room by then."

"How should I know when it was?"

"No?" The Baron frowned. "And you and Miss Miquet were by yourselves while the three were on the balcony?"

"For a few minutes. Then I called Mr. Preacher."

"And he complied, my dear sir?"

Bolton hesitated. "Miss McKay," he answered stolidly, "has a bad influence upon him. When I ordered him to come, he came."

"Good. And so Miss McKay and her fiancé were on the balcony. And you were with Miss Miquet and Mr. Preacher by the radio?"

"Most of the time."

The Baron's patience began to crack as the pain in his ribs increased. "That is when you became angry and left the room?"

"Mr. Preacher refused to go to bed. His mother always wanted him to be in bed by ten unless it was a special occasion. I have tried to follow her rules. But lately he has grown very rebellious, Baron von Kaz. I've tried to follow her rules, and when he refused and said he was going to dance with Miss McKay later, I walked out hoping he would come."

"You went to your own room?"

Bolton nodded and then put his hand to his head again. "For only a few minutes. When Mr. Preacher did not come, I returned and was talking to him and the others when the police pounded on the door."

The moon was floating in that deep blue sky of night, and the Baron took a breath and held his lips tight until the pain ebbed away and then asked, "Why did you attempt to run over me, Mr. Bolton?"

"It was you, wasn't it?" Bolton's voice was a flat ribbon stretching into the night. "I thought you were lying. I'm a plain man. And I know my place. Don't think you're clever just because you fool a simple man like me."

"Why did you attempt to kill me twice?" When there was no reply the Baron wondered aloud if dear Mr. Bolton would enjoy the bite of the steel muzzle again.

"It was a joke. Mr. Sargent hire'd me to frighten you. I wasn't going to kill you, Baron. That was part of the joke. I wouldn't really kill anyone. I wasn't going to throw you from the cliff. I was just going to knock you out and get you put on board a ship for Australia."

"Australia?"

This time Bolton turned, and although the Baron had the gun ready, the muzzle didn't come down. Bolton laughed shortly. "Honest, Baron. Mr. Sargent didn't want you troubling Miss Miquet. He thought if I could get you on a ship and off the Islands it 'd be better for Miss Miquet. Don't you see?"

"So? He does not wish me to 'trouble' Miss Miquet?"

"Sure," said Bolton earnestly. "I was only trying to scare you. Why, you don't imagine I'd really want to throw you off the cliff, do you?"

The Baron eyed Bolton's neck. "My dear sir," he replied evenly, "of course not."

"I'm the most tender-hearted fellow in the world, Baron."

The Baron sank into the rear seat. "If you please, Mr. Bolton, drive to the hotel. I am weary."

Halfway to the hotel the Baron leaned over and asked softly, "If you please, my dear sir. You were planning to ship me off the Islands tonight?"

"That's right," replied Bolton. "I don't know what Mr. Sargent 'll say now. I suppose you'll go and complain to the police?"

"And what boat leaves tonight at this hour?"

"Oh," said Bolton uneasily, "there's always some boat. To tell the truth, Baron, after I knocked you out, I'd probably have had to keep you till tomorrow. A boat leaves tomorrow."

"I see."

"I'm just a simple, humble man. You've been too clever for me, and I expect you'll send me to jail, won't you?"

"Jail?" protested the Baron. "My dear sir, how can I blame you if Mr. Sargent has been only doing what he considers his duty? However, if you would be so kind as to explain to him that I have no intention of troubling Miss Miquet, or Miss McKay, I would count it as a favor and think no more about tonight's occurrences. After all, how bravely you saved me from the Japanese gang! I owe that to you."

"Thanks, Baron. Those Japs might've really hurt you, too."

Upstairs in his room the Baron stripped to his waist. His body was marked with purple-colored bruises, and a welt was swelling on his forehead. He frowned blackly at the sight, and the mirror returned the frown, reminding him of the dangers of overconfidence. He drew on his shirt slowly. Every time he moved, new aches came. He thought his ribs weren't broken. If they were cracked, that was unfortunate, because he had a great deal to do before dawn.

He fortified himself with several stiff glasses of brandy, sat down, grunting, wondering what specks of truth were floating in Mr. Bolton's fantastic explanation, smiled grimly at the thought of Mr. Bolton and the appearance of this gentleman's face and throat, and slowly and with an effort reached for the telephone.

7

And the Red Diamond

Two o'clock in the morning.

The orchestra on top of the roof of the Alexander Bishop Hotel had finished playing the song concerning the tourist who's mixed up in the Hawaiian language and rubs his big opu, or something like that, which wasn't his stomach at all but the moon. The cool early morning breeze was blowing in the open windows. The majority of the dancers had departed. A few were still hanging around the bar, old-timers, mixing oke and soda water and being quiet about their drinking. The drummer was yawning, half asleep: the musicians were calling it a night; pau, through.

The Baron had a small table near the door. The aqua and silver-leaf walls and the blossoms in relief of the night-blooming cereus gave the roof garden an exotic, tropical atmosphere. Several women were looking at themselves in the mirrored panels, inserted the entire width of the oblong dance floor; and one of them in shimmering green which displayed a lot of tanned shoulders, and considerably more underneath the shoulders where they begin to swell out and mean something if you liked them that way, stopped in front of the table. When the handkerchief floated from her hand to the floor she uttered sweetly, "Oh dear," and gazed soulfully at the Baron. This gentleman recovered the square of fabric, and as he raised his body it stopped at an angle of approximately ten degrees from horizontal. "Ach Gott!" he muttered, placed his left hand tenderly over his ribs and regarded the surprised woman with concentrated malevolence, as if it were her fault.

"Are you hurt?"

"Hurt?" He thrust the handkerchief into her hand, glared at her, waved her away as though she were a stray alley cat, sitting very erect in the chair until the pain subsided. The lady flounced off indignantly. She swept angrily through the mirrored doors, narrowly escaping a collision with George Tuung. There was cork-plaster bandage stuck on his chin. He came direct to the Baron's table, sat down nervously. He took the glass of brandy-and-soda, downed it. "What do you want?"

"My dear sir, you have caused me much trouble. Do you—" The Baron made a wry face and put his hand to his side and then smiled unconcernedly.

"What's the matter with you?" asked Tuung suspiciously.

"Gout," said the Baron promptly. "Do you realize that it was necessary for me to telephone Mr. Hiroshita's establishment four times before I could persuade the gentleman there to listen to what I had to say?"

"You don't have gout in your ribs. Gout's in your feet." Tuung's hands were on the table, preparatory to getting up. "What's the matter with you? No funny stuff."

"It is German gout," cheerfully explained the Baron.

"What do you want with me?"

"Not until I assured him that I would send the police for you would the dolt promise to try to get in touch with you."

"I didn't mean any rough stuff, Baron." The man lifted the glass to his lips with both hands. "How was I to know you had a friend following you? All we wanted was to talk to you alone. My gun wasn't loaded."

"Hein?" The Baron gave a start.

"I wouldn't carry a loaded gun, Baron."

Under the table the Baron examined George Tuung's gun. It wasn't loaded. "Ach," he stated agreeably, thrusting it beneath the table onto George Tuung's lap, "I knew it all the time. I am not like your friends, I am far too clever a man, Mr. Tuung, to be frightened by an unloaded weapon."

Tuung, feeling the gun, quickly shoved it in his pocket. "You knew it wasn't loaded?" he asked admiringly. "Hiroshita said you were a pretty wise detective. Seems he was right."

"Naturally." The Baron nodded and then wiped his forehead with his handkerchief. So the gun with which he had threatened Mr. Bolton, to say nothing of George Tuung's accomplices, had not been loaded? Ach, Gott! This stupid Oriental should have been more careful. As he appreciated the horrible risk he had taken the Baron said acidly, "Next time, I inform you, when you use a gun, make positive it is loaded."

"Maybe you're right, Baron," agreed George Tuung. "But that gun's so old—"

"I assure you, I have no interest in your gun," The Baron folded his handkerchief, reinserted it in his breast coat pocket. "I have matters of more importance to discuss with you. That is why, immediately upon reaching the hotel, I telephoned for you, my dear Mr. Tuung. The desk clerk at the Imperial said the Paradise roof garden would be open until two-thirty. We can talk here comfortably. And so what is it you wished to tell me before we were— ach! disturbed?"

It took a few minutes before Tuung fully realized that this wasn't a trap, that the Baron actually had come here to see him, and then Tuung forgot the ache in his jaw and said in a businesslike fashion:

"It's this way, Baron. Hiroshita hired you—"

"Hired?" The Baron frowned. "So?"

"Engaged you, I mean," corrected the Japanese hastily. "Now he's murdered. He was scared of being murdered. That's why he cabled us from the boat to meet him. But when he went to see you at the Imperial he wouldn't let us go with him; he was afraid the police would think it funny if he was tailed. He said he was going to take you for a ride. It's funny," commented Tuung pathetically, "but since that bust on the jaw by your friend I can't seem to get a kick out of this." He held up his empty glass. "Maybe it's watered. I don't like brandy. What about some Hawaiian okolehau?"

The Baron promptly ordered a bottle of okolehau, that fiery concoction from rice and tii leaves and sugar cane. "It's this way, Baron. We had a proposition to offer you. I don't know all that Hiroshita told you, Baron. There are six of us left now. We haven't much money. Most of us own shops or are in business. I'm a lawyer. I'm not going to give the names of the other five: that isn't necessary. You saw two of them tonight before that friend of yours chased them away. God damn!" He rubbed his jaw. "I thought they'd never return after you went."

"Uhm," murmured the Baron.

"I'm telling you the truth. Hiroshita was the only one who ever busted the law, and he didn't ever do anything on a big scale. Then he came to us, and we've borrowed and mortgaged and called on our friends for all the money we could get. I'm telling you the truth. We managed to raise a total of ten thousand dollars. Hiroshita didn't put in a cent. Including your fee, he spent more than five thousand dollars, so we've got less than five thousand dollars remaining. If you'll handle this for us I'm prepared to offer you twenty-five hundred dollars now. And twenty-five hundred more when you obtain that soapstone plaque Hiroshita had mailed to Miss Miquet. That's the whole story, Baron. Short and sweet. Hiroshita told us about you. If he could trust you, we can."

George Tuung drew out his wallet, slipped a thick envelope under the table onto the Baron's lap. "Count it when you get back to the hotel. I put twenty-five one hundred dollar bills in it half an hour after I heard Hiroshita was killed."

"You wish me to determine who shot Mr. Hiroshita and—"

"No sir," declared George Tuung. "Leave that to the police. All we want is the plaque."

"If you please, what is in the plaque?"

"In the plaque?" asked Tuung suspiciously. "Hiroshita told you."

"Unfortunately Mr. Hiroshita was killed before he could divulge that point. And I can give no promises until I am told what is hidden in the second soapstone plaque."

George Tuung gulped down another glass of oke without turning a hair. Glibly he explained that concealed in the plaque was the only red diamond in the world. It was a freak. It weighed fifty-seven carats. It was absolutely perfect.

"So?" murmured the Baron, sipping his second glass of oke and wondering if it really were liquid fire.

Tuung nodded. Absolutely perfect. And during one of his trips into the interior of Mexico Hiroshita had happened upon a Japanese who had formerly lived in Hawaii. The Baron snapped, "His name?"

"Aleale," said Tuung promptly, then realized this wasn't a Japanese name, hesitated, and went on to say that the man's real name was Sako Okyo but that when he'd worked for Mr. McKay they'd called him "Aleale." The Baron didn't wink an eye. He sat in his chair, fingering that envelope with the money, smiling politely, and said, "Please continue, my dear sir."

Tuung swallowed. This Aleale—he repeated the name several times to make sure the Baron would get it properly—this Aleale had taken it from one of those old Aztec idols. Aleale didn't suspect the stone was valuable. He thought it was red glass, at the most a ruby. But Hiroshita had been a jeweler. The red stone was. a diamond and, because it was unique, was worth an incredible fortune.

Hiroshita returned by the next boat to Honolulu, formed a society among his six friends to purchase the stone. And on his next trip to Mexico had easily persuaded Aleale to part with it for five hundred dollars.

"And," concluded Tuung seriously, "that red diamond is legally ours. Already we've spent five thousand dollars for it. We can't afford to lose it now, it's too much money. It'd ruin us. I've mortgaged all my property to pay my share." His voice trembled, and it wasn't the oke that made it tremble, either. "Besides, Baron, the red diamond will bring us a fortune!"

"Ach, so?" The Baron decided that another glass of oke wouldn't burn quite so fiercely. "How do I know that Mr. Hiroshita was not shot by one of his—"

"We can prove we didn't! I was expecting that question. All six of us were waiting upstairs in his store for him to return. Besides the six as witnesses, there is his clerk and perhaps half-a-dozen people in the near-by shops who saw us enter."

"No," muttered the Baron thickly, after a long pause. He stroked the envelope. Ach, that money inside of it would be good to have. But no, he could not do it. He could not wait here. In Austria they required him. And the Baron von Kaz had promised . . .

"No, my dear sir, I cannot. You must go to the police, to that good Mr. Jameson—"

"The police?" shrilled Tuung. "And suppose the red diamond Hiroshita bought from Aleale didn't belong to Aleale? What would the police do then? If Aleale stole it, and the police are informed, our money is lost."

The Baron stood in a thickening haze composed of silver cereus blossoms, threw some money on the table and wavered out of the door, followed by Tuung. Outside, in the street, the shadows pressed toward him, and far-away bells were striking the hour of three, Tuung grasped the Baron's arm. "Baron," whispered Tuung's voice, coming softly through the haze, "You'd better not tell the police. They could lock me in jail, but there are five others. Baron, this red diamond means a lot to us. My five friends would be ruined. You wouldn't want them to hurt Miss Miquet, would you?"

The Baron stood on the sidewalk wondering if he could be drunk. He lifted his hand to his forehead, shook his head, tried to peer into the darkness at Tuung. The man came close to the Baron. "No need to get tough about it, Baron," he protested. "I'm telling you the truth. You've got the money. Keep it. All you have to do is get that other plaque from Miss Miquet when it arrives and let me know. Then you receive twenty-five hundred dollars more and . . ."

The next morning the brave Franz Maximilian Karagôz von Kaz was aroused from a series of dreadful nightmares. He had been dreaming about a giant white slug. His dreams were disconnected. He was in Carmel, California . . . in Vienna . . . but no matter where he found himself, this white slug would come crawling out of purple-green leaves and lift its head, and the head was that of a man. His dreams always ended too quickly for him to see the man's face. Someone was shaking him, and he rolled away, striking out with both hands, saying something in German, and then he opened his eyes. It wasn't a slug with a man's face.

It was a man bending over him. An old man with a missionary mouth, with tiny lines cut into leather skin. The old man was shaking him with one hand; the other held a newspaper. The Baron blinked once or twice finally sat up. "Good morning, my Mr. Jameson."

"Don't you 'good morning' me, Baron. What's the idea of putting this in the paper?" He thrust the paper at the Baron. "Scaring our tourists with all that damned nonsense."

Jameson pointed to the second page:

ATTEMPTED KIDNAPING THWARTED

Late last night, Baron Franz Maximilian Karagôz von Kaz was the victim of an attempted kidnaping by a gang of Japanese criminals. Baron von Kaz is a guest of the Imperial Hawaiian, having arrived yesterday on the *Kohala*.

Fortunately for the Baron, Mr. Harry Bolton, also a tourist, happened to be driving past King and Fort streets and saw the Baron being ordered into the kidnapers' car. Mr. Bolton bravely pursued the would-be kidnapers, catching up with them on the outskirts of Kapiolani Park . . .

Then followed a brief account of the Baron's rescue, with the comment that this kidnaping gang undoubtedly belonged to the group responsible for the death of Mr. Hiroshita. The Baron gazed innocently at the wrathful Jameson and then returned to the page. Below was a short news item saying that Hiroshita, a former dope smuggler, had been shot last night under mysterious circumstances

at one of the local hotels where he was visiting with a
tourist.

"Here I try to keep Hiroshita's death out of the papers, and then you tell them that stuff. Smart feller, hey?"
Jameson sat down in a chair, bit off the end of one of
his long cigars, "What's the idea of going to bed fully
dressed?"

The sun was streaming in the windows, marking a pattern of bright gold and shadowed stripes on the polished
floor. The Baron sat on the edge of the bed, smoothing his
feet over the cool floor. His head was surprisingly clear.
That okolehau proved a friendlier beverage than it tasted.

Jameson said he had come for the truth. He wanted the
truth.

The Baron delicately felt his ribs, saying that he too
would like to have the truth.

"I'm going to get the truth out of you, Baron, or I'll
lock you up."

"As you wish." The Baron pulled his crumpled shirt off
the wide, muscled shoulders. He stopped in front of the
bathroom door, shoved out his lower lip good-naturedly.
"I have friends, my dear sir. If you imprison me, you have
no proof to hold me."

"Wait a minute." Jameson stepped to the Baron. "How'd
you get those bruises on your ribs? I talked with Bolton
this morning before he left for Maui, and he didn't say you
were beaten."

"Bruises, my dear sir?" The Baron inspected his ribs.
"Pardon: Those are birthmarks."

With the flat of his hand, Jameson slapped the Baron's
hard flesh. The Baron winced. "Sorry," said Jameson pleasantly, "but I guess you're right. They looked like bruises,
though."

The Baron said nothing. He picked up his clothes, hung
them in the closet where, hidden from the old detective,

he felt in his coat pocket and found the envelope containing the twenty-five hundred dollars. Then he went into the shower, leaving the door open. Jameson didn't move from the seat he had resumed. While the Baron shaved, Jameson continued:

"Bolton said he left the police station right after you walked out. Bolton got into his car planning to pick you up and drive you to the hotel but he saw you being kidnaped."

"Ach, so?" The Baron dried his razor. He went to the closet, selected the white linen suit he'd bought in San Francisco, commenced to dress.

"You're pretty cool about it, aren't you?" drawled Jameson. "You know, I'm beginning to think this Bolton's a mighty shrewd feller. I checked on his time when he was away from the room last night. He says it was at least fifteen minutes before Hiroshita was killed. He wouldn't say that if it wasn't true, because, even if Jeff might lie for him, Caryl Miquet wouldn't. And then I got to talking to him, and he offered the theory that Hiroshita and Kohler might both be mixed up in some Japanese gang." Jameson chewed on the dry brown cigar. "He pretended to get the theory just one second after I told him Hiroshita was supposed to be a dope smuggler. What do you think, hey?"

The Baron inspected himself in the mirror. "Perhaps so."

"You're a lot of help, Baron. You look real nice in that suit, too. Bolton thinks maybe this same gang suspected you knew who they were and that's why they wanted to kidnap you. What do you think of that now?"

"Ah, my dear sir, it is all most mysterious. Perhaps this gang thought I was someone else. Mr. Bolton was very kind to rescue me."

"Then he did rescue you?"

"Assuredly, my dear sir."

Jameson got up. "I had a feeling maybe Bolton was lying. Seems he's a hero after all. Just wanted to check on it. Sorry I woke you. Next time you want newspaper publicity, see me before telephoning the papers, hey?"

The Baron rubbed his nose, cocked his head to one side in that infantile manner of his when amused or puzzled. "Ach, so. I will do that, Mr. Jameson."

"Smart feller, aren't you?" asked Jameson sourly. "Bolton telephoned the papers, and you knew it, and I know it because I checked the city desks." He was at the door. Instead of opening it he stood there, hitting the wooden panels lightly with his clenched fist. He turned. "Who were your friends who let you out dead drunk this morning—"

"My dear sir," the Baron protested affably but firmly, "once before I informed you that the great Von Kaz is never drunk. You will understand, please?"

Jameson regarded the Baron, and there was something so arrogant and compelling in the Austrian's attitude, despite the fine veneer of courtesy, that the Honolulu detective uneasily found himself saying, "The clerk said a couple of Japs brought you into the lobby this morning. Where'd you go after you and Bolton entered?"

Unhurriedly the Baron went into the closet again, returned with his white panama hat and the heavy green umbrella. He murmured that he had desired fresh air and had stopped in one of the little bars for a drink, and he didn't really remember who had accompanied him to the hotel for the second time. "After you, my dear sir," he said politely, holding the door for Jameson. "I go down for breakfast."

Jameson walked into the corridor, drawling, "I've not forgotten about getting the truth out of you—" and then somehow the green umbrella slid from the Baron's hand, became entangled in the other's feet, and Jameson sprawled across the corridor.

"Ach!" apologized the Baron. "One thousand pardons." He lifted Jameson to his feet, brushed off his coat with malicious little side swipes which stung through the thin linen. "I am so stupid. I shall never forgive myself. Are you hurt?"

"That's enough, Baron." Jameson eyed the dark-faced smiling man. "That makes us even. Got the handle weighted, haven't you?"

"Weighted?" The Baron shook his head, Jameson was limping slightly, and because the old man hadn't complained or lost his temper the Baron illogically regretted his action, felt ashamed of himself. "Yes," he contradicted brusquely, suddenly, while they were waiting for the elevator. "It is weighted. With lead. If I wished I could have broken your leg. But I did not wish to." He folded his arms, defiantly stared at the old man.

Jameson lifted the umbrella which the Baron was holding. "You don't say."

"I could have killed you with it." The Baron was inordinately proud of this green umbrella. "Walking ahead of you, I can throw it over my shoulder."

"You don't say," repeated Jameson dryly.

"You do not believe it?" demanded the Baron fiercely. An alabaster bowl filled with sand rested in one corner. The alabaster bowl was behind the Baron; he was facing Jameson. With one motion, the umbrella slid through his hand until he had it by the silver tip, the heavy handle came up, the green umbrella flashed over his shoulder, revolved three times in the air. The handle thudded against the bowl. The bowl smashed on the floor, white sand leaking upon the rug. Without glancing at the damage, the Baron recovered his umbrella. "Even if you had a gun and were ordering me to walk in front of you, I should have an excellent chance."

"Well, well." Jameson again pushed the elevator button. "You'd better think of something to say in case the manager asks you about that bowl. Too bad you and I can't help each other better on this damned case instead of wasting time playing with umbrellas."

The Baron didn't look at the old man. "If you please," he said in his most irritating and condescending fashion, "it may be that you can help me. I recall one of my friends at the bar. It was—ach!" He snapped his fingers. "It was a Mr. Saka Okyo."

Jameson took the Baron's arm and led him out of the elevator and from the lobby into the flowering courtyard. He glanced at the sky, "It's pretty up there, Baron. These islands are the only paradise I ever expect to see. You stay here long enough, and you'll get what I mean." He sauntered in the direction of a dusty Ford. "Saka Okyo, hey? Sure you've remembered the right feller's name?"

"Assuredly." It was hard to remain stiff and formal in that bright joyful sunlight with the birds making their foolish cheerful noises high in the coconut trees, and flowers as big as a woman's hat waving in front of your nose. The Baron nodded. When he smiled, his blue eyes smiled too, and the old man found that the impulsive smile wasn't easy to resist. "I have a phenomenal memory." The way he said it didn't exasperate Jameson this time. Jameson realized the man wasn't boasting. He probably did have a phenomenal memory.

"Was this Okyo an old feller? An old Jap?"

The Baron's momentary cordiality froze. "Ach, so." His head nodded stiffly. "Exactly."

"Well, well." Jameson continued easy and careless. "Did he talk English with a funny accent? That is, did he talk like he'd learned the language in England or from an English feller in Japan?"

"That is the man. Can you tell me where I can reach him? He was so kind—"

"Reach him?" Jameson slowly climbed into the Ford. His ankle still hurt. He glanced at the heavy umbrella hanging so innocently from the Baron's arm. "I reckon you can't exactly reach him any more. I used to know him real well. He was an archaeologist out at the University, specializing in Hawaiian things. But he went and died. Yes sir, died all of eight years ago. He had a son, a big feller, but you didn't meet his son, Baron." The old man's eyes were uncommonly bright as he leaned on the edge of the door. "No, you didn't meet young Saka. He quit working for Miss McKay over a year ago. He got into a fight with Kohler, knifed Kohler, I believe. Kohler never had him arrested, and Saka left for the mainland. That was just after Kohler was fired by Miss McKay."

The Baron reflectively touched his nose. "Miss McKay, then, has complete charge of her ranch?"

"Hey? She doesn't run it, if that's what you mean. She had to hire another manager."

"But she owns her ranch, if you please?"

"She inherited it along with Billy."

"The ranch is—uhm—valuable?"

"What 're you getting at? It's worth a couple of hundred thousand dollars. Billy's due to get the major share when he's of age. Old man McKay was French and thought the boy should carry on. But Mary's got plenty to live on."

"And," asked the Baron softly, "if Billy should die?"

Jameson took a long time to answer this question. He choked the engine, stepped on the starter. Then he replied with a peculiar quietness, "If Billy died, she'd get it all, of course."

"Thank you. I was merely curious. Good morning to you, my dear sir."

"Wait a minute!" The words cracked like a whip. The Baron returned. Jameson glared at him. "Look here, d'you know that she and Billy and all her friends have taken the airplane to Maui? On the eight o'clock this morning. That feller Bolton went along too. Damn near missed the plane, he was so busy talking to me. Well, Baron, enjoy yourself. And don't forget I expect to see you damn soon."

The Ford chugged down the gravel driveway to the first bend, where it suddenly stopped and rapidly backed. Jameson threw his long legs over the sides and called to the Baron as this gentleman was climbing the steps to the lobby.

"Say, Baron, I just happened to think. Ever hear of Haleakala?"

The Baron had never heard of it.

"It's the biggest extinct crater I guess there is in the world."

"So?" The Baron found this most interesting; or, at least, from the expression on his face you might have assumed that was in his mind.

"It's on Maui," the old man said. "As long as you've got to stick around here for a few weeks you might like to run over and see it. We've got some wonderful scenery in these islands. I don't want you to believe you have to stay cooped up in this hotel." And when the Austrian showed that he had no intention of responding to the Honolulu detective's suggestion, "Baron, you're in deeper water than either of us may realize. I've got to force the truth out of you. I don't want to put you in jail. By God, I don't. I need your help. I've tried being tough with you, and you won't tell me."

"Give me one day," requested the Baron. "In one day I may be able to discover something to tell you."

"You mean in the next twenty-four hours you'll decide whether you want to tell me or not, hey?"

The Baron shrugged.

Jameson thought a minute, started the car. He leaned over, whispered confidentially, "Did the Japs give you a bad beating, Baron?"

"Hein?" And after a second or so the Baron shook his head. "Would you permit a question?"

"Sure."

"Did Mr. Kohler meet—"

"I was wondering when you'd ask. Mexico City police said Kohler and Sargent both lived at the Cosmopolitan Club, but that doesn't mean much. And when they went North, they both stayed at the Cliff Hotel before taking the boat. But so did you, Baron."

"Ach, so?"

"However, those are coincidences. I've checked on Sargent. He's a fine, straightforward feller. Got a good name as a geologist in Mexico. Met Mary McKay last year in San Francisco when she was visiting her cousin. He's all right, Baron. What I'm thinking is that old man Preacher had a hell of a temper. Jeff Preacher might have one too, and maybe he somehow got sore at Hiroshita—"

"Mr. Hiroshita did not meet Mr. Preacher on the *Kohala*."

"Positive, hey?"

"Otherwise I would not say so," replied the Baron.

"Don't get riled. I've checked on Jeff. He and Bolton landed in New York a month ago and visited with a friend of Jeff's on Long Island and then took the airplane for San Francisco. We talked with the purser on board the Kohala. He claims that Mary introduced herself to Jeff on the boat against that fat feller's wishes. Guess Bolton was afraid Jeff might meet a pretty girl. Mary's folks were right neighborly with old man Preacher." Jameson frowned, releasing the brake. "What you said about Billy's kind of got me worried, Baron. You don't imagine anything could happen to that boy, do you?"

"What *I* said, if you please?"

"Have it your own way. Only take care of yourself, Baron, and remember, if you don't write or wire me by tomorrow, I'm going to have to lock you up. I mean it too."

On the way to the elevators the Baron was called by the desk clerk. "Here's a note for you, Baron von Kaz. Miss Miquet left it for you this morning. I was to deliver it personally, but I've been so busy with the tourists coming in off the Mariposa that I didn't have time to go to your room."

Upstairs the Baron opened the note:

> *Dear Baron von Kaz:*
> *I am leaving for Maui this morning, and so this is just a note to say good-by and wish you all kinds of luck in Vienna and to say I hope you won't think I'm always as rude as I've been to you, but I've been worried. It's silly, I suppose, but now that you are going, and I won't see you again, I wish there was someone else on the Islands with your great experience and courage to whom I could turn should the opening of my mail continue and prove to be more than someone's idea of a joke. But of course it is a joke, and I am needlessly alarmed.*
> *Sincerely,*
> *Caryl Miquet.*

The Baron read the note three times, and upon each occasion that he would come to the line containing those magical words, "great experience and courage," his face

would grow more complacent and his shoulders would
become even stiffer and his chest would rise a few notches,
and, in fact, if he had continued to read the note he would
have eventually fallen over backward, or forever strained
his facial muscles, and undoubtedly ruined all his ribs.
He folded the note, repeating those words, thinking how
frightened and helpless poor Miss Miquet must have been
feeling; and it was fortunate for Miss Miquet that one of
his friends from Vienna was not in the room to coldly
point out to the glowing Baron that only a most clever
and intelligent woman would have been able to write such
a note which, while apparently giving him up for good, in
pure reality made it absolutely impossible for him to do
otherwise than pack in great speed and rush from the hotel
like a demon to catch the next airplane for Maui.

8

Magic Island

Climbing in the still blue atmosphere to five thousand feet, the ten-passenger Sikorsky amphibian leveled off above Honolulu, passed over the Imperial Hawaiian, a pinkish dot in a cluster of green, swooped over Diamond Head at one hundred and ten miles an hour headed for Molokai, the next island forty minutes by air south of Oahu.

The noon plane was nearly empty. In the front left seat a Chinese woman was nursing a sick baby. Two seats behind her was an American with a leather sample bag stamped, "G. Murray, Paper Products, Ltd.," which was resting on his knees. The Baron had taken the rear right seat just below the trapdoor opening into the roof of the twin-motored amphibian. The Pacific spread out far below, tranquil and blue. Close to the horizon was a ring of dense white clouds extending hundreds of miles above the water and encircling the eight islands in the Hawaiian group.

As the motors were synchronized and their uneven muttering vanished into a steady pulsating muttering, the Baron eased back into his wicker seat, took out a small leather notebook and stared determinedly at the empty pages as though, from their blankness, would materialize the face of that person who already had killed Mr. Kohler and Mr. Hiroshita with the silent air pistol.

The Baron was in a quandary. Nothing marched as it should march. Two men had been murdered by the same gun. But Mr. Hiroshita had been afraid of Mr. Kohler, and it was Mr. Kohler who first was killed. The order of the deaths was not logical. And Mr. Hiroshita had certainly been shot by one of the men or women in the next room.

Until now the Baron had worked upon cases where his duties were defined, where he was given an objective. At present he was upon uncharted seas, in charge of no case whatsoever. It was as if formless phantoms were moving stealthily toward a certain point, converging, grinning, mocking at the brave Baron from Austria. There were so many apparently unrelated parts to this growing night-mare: What was the connection leading from the death of Mr. Hiroshita to Caryl Miquet's hotel room to that death on the ship? What place did Saka Okyo, the countryman of Mr. Hiroshita, have in this miasma? And was Caryl Miquet being drawn into this case in any other way than that of the involuntary, the innocent recipient of Mr. Hiroshita's second plaque? Then he thought of the note she had written him and considered if something besides the fact that her mail was being opened was not frighten-ing her.

And through this tenuous drift of evil the Baron seemed to perceive a figure looming up, still nameless, to be sure, but with a blurred distorted embodiment of elemental evil. Within himself grew a presentment of events pressing into a catastrophic pattern; and, unable to pierce to the true significance of what had taken place, his dark face grew blacker.

He was so engrossed in this tangle of fears and mount-ing doubts that not until the air felt uncomfortable in his eardrums did he raise his head to find that the Sikorsky was losing altitude, circling down to the pitted Hoolehua airport of Molokai. He swallowed, relieving the pressure.

The big wheels were lowered, and a few minutes later they bounced along the ground. He would continue to Maui, he decided irritably; he would see Caryl Miquet alone. He would tell her what little he knew, warn her of possible danger, and then he would wash his hands of the entire conundrum. Ach, certainly. That was what he would do whether Mr. Jameson liked it or not. He had his own affairs to attend to in Vienna. . . .

The Chinese woman in the front seat hugged her baby, who wailed loudly. The Sikorsky stopped with a rumbling jerk as the pilot applied air brakes. The assistant pilot jumped out, opened the door in the roof. The gentleman selling mulch paper departed with his bag. The door was closed. The Chinese woman gave the baby a stick of ginger. From the narrow windows the Baron had a glimpse of Filipino boys with slicked hair and bell-bottomed trousers waving grimy hands which reminded him of monkey paws he had seen in the Vienna Zoo. In spite of the muttered complaint of the two motors the Baron heard the tiny sound of a voice coming from the radio, and the assistant pilot's lips moved as he told the radio man in Oahu that everything was okay, visibility good.

Green cliffs trembled from the heights as the Sikorsky climbed, and the clouds still lay rounding the horizon. The wings flickered in the sunlight, wires vibrating and humming monotonously against the roar of the motors.

To his right, directly below, was the leper settlement, checkered squares dotted with white and pink houses; and far away, low in the distance, under the cotton clouds, was a brownish-green blob. That was Lanai, one of the smaller islands. The wind buffeted the amphibian as it flew between Molokai and Lanai. To the Hawaiians in the fishing boat rocking up and down in the channel, the airplane was a yellow speck in a blue and endless sky.

It was merely a larger bird with a brazen throat flying like an arrow toward Maui, half a day from Molokai by steamboat, three days by the sailing vessels the missionaries formerly employed.

Great war canoes each manned by a hundred Hawaiians had passed through these waters. Along the twenty-mile channel separating Molokai and Lanai the little brigs of Captain Vancouver must have sailed in seventeen ninety-two. He also had seen these great crest mountains, sharp and forbidding; and he had seen the dense forests, the huge brown men six and seven feet tall. And perhaps he was the first white man to appreciate the strange beauty of these islands, emerged lonely and mysteriously from the Pacific, a place of secrets and hidden legends which continued to haunt the imagination of men long after he was killed by a war spear eighteen feet in length.

Missionaries with milk cows and hens on board to provide nourishment had laboured through the oily blue swells. And merchants had come, Chinese, Portuguese, Russian, Spanish, English, and long-jawed Americans, buying sandalwood and spices; hewing down precious trees with iron axes; killing with their vices and diseases men who had grown taller and stronger than any other race time has known. . . . And far up, high in that eternal blue, a Chinese mother was comforting a frightened child. A man from Austria was bending over a column of dates he had written in his leather notebook.

Today was the eighth of April.

Unless he prevented it, Miss Miquet should receive a plaque from Mexico on April seventeenth. Nine days! Exactly nine days before April seventeenth; and every day after this date increased the danger to Miss Miquet. Because, he felt, whosoever desired the plaque would have to obtain it from her without arousing question or suspicion upon her part, providing, of course, that she was unaware of the importance of the plaque. Unless this transfer of the plaque were accomplished without accident by the murderer, the moment she refused, whether by sheer whim or contrariness, or any other reason, she placed her life in jeopardy from then on. . . . . .

And although the Baron was inclined to disregard George Tuung's threat regarding Miss Miquet, the fact remained that George Tuung was an excitable person. And the Baron had the envelope with the twenty-five hundred dollars. That was an annoyance. Twenty-five hundred dollars was an imposing sum for the Baron; the thought of returning it filled him with anguish. And should he return it—ach, du lieber Gott! He for the first time appreciated that by returning it he was not only forfeiting another twenty-five hundred dollars but was informing Mr. Tuung that he would have nothing to do with retrieving the plaque. And it was quite possible that Mr. Tuung would believe without great difficulty that the Baron, on refusing the job, had informed the police in order to protect Miss Miquet. This did not march at all well.

He closed the leather book, glancing out the window. On his left hand he could see the sheer cliffs of Maui as the Sikorsky rounded Lahaina, rocking violently in the gusts of air. The outline of Maui resembles the head and shoulders of one of those old Hawaiian warriors. The head points west and north toward the islands of Oahu and Molokai. Connecting the head with what corresponds to the shoulders is a narrow neck of land, a green and fertile valley rising toward the east to Haleakala, the majestic extinct volcano whose peak is ten thousand feet and more above the Pacific.

And through this narrow neck of land, hemmed in on both sides by mountains and the crater, rushed the wind, lifting the Sikorsky as it would a yellow-tipped feather, as small up there in that blue sky as one of those yellow feathers plucked from the Mamo bird which in ancient times had been woven into the magnificent feather cloaks worn only by the Hawaiian chieftains. Now the Mamo bird had disappeared into the grayness of past ages. The few remaining feather cloaks were priceless, and pineapple and sugar-cane fields covered old battle grounds. . . .

The Sikorsky slanted downward toward the little Hana airport, halfway between Wailuku on the north side of the neck and Maalaea on the south. Reddish earth soared upward, and the wheels struck the dusty ground, rolled a thousand feet or more and stopped. The door in the top was opened. A man in a white cap greeted the Baron as he climbed out, received the pigskin bag.

"You're Baron von Kaz?"

The Baron bowed.

"My name's Blakely." He looked at the Baron's green umbrella in mild astonishment. No one ever carried umbrellas in this Pacific paradise. He nodded at the white stucco airport building on the edge of a dusty red pineapple field. "I got a telegram saying to expect you. And about fifteen minutes ago a radio telephone call came in from Chris Jameson of the Honolulu police. He said to have you call him back as soon as the plane landed."

"So?"

In the telephone booth it was hot, stuffy. Outside, the manager of Inter-Island Airways' Maui station read an adventure story and wished to God something exciting would happen to him and break the monotony. In the receiver flowed the rush and roaring of endless waves, and these waves broke upon loose sand and then formed the dry voice of Jameson hurtling the ninety miles:

"Hello, Baron von Kaz? This is Christian Jameson."

"Christian Jameson?" thought the Baron. "Good afternoon, Mr. Christian Jameson," he said with the utmost courtesy.

"Don't be funny. Listen, this is important. We've just got word from the Maui police that Mary McKay and her party have made reservations at the Wailuku Hotel in Wailuku. If we have the Maui police question Mary, either she or her friends 'll wonder what the hell business it is of ours. I want you to see—"

"My dear Mr. Christian Jameson," shouted the Baron— it seemed necessary to shout to make his voice arc all those ninety miles of empty space—"I wish to see no one."

"If you want to leave these islands, then you've got to help. You're in this mess already."

"I informed you in twenty-four hours I would decide whether—"

"Damn it, I can't wait twenty-four hours. Listen, I've just been talking with the North Kona police on the island of Hawaii. They say the reason why Mary fired Carl Kohler was not so much because he bought that three thousand acres as because he was trying to marry her. The North Kona police say that it's old gossip on the big island that she was stuck on him for a time, but *I* didn't know. Now, look here:

"Suppose she met Kohler on the boat and maybe they started making up again and John Sargent got sore? After all, Mary's got quite a little money in her own name, and Sargent isn't wealthy. You know Caryl Miquet. And if you're smart you can manage those two girls better'n we can, Baron. You've got to see one of them and learn where John Sargent was from eleven o'clock to one o'clock on the night when Kohler was killed. While you're at it, check on Jeff too."

"And Mr. Sargent, then, killed Mr. Hiroshita too? Was Miss McKay also in love with Mr. Hiroshita?" inquired the Baron sarcastically.

"How the hell do I know? I'm working on Kohler's death now."

"Suppose," suggested the Baron, "that Miss McKay was forced to kill Mr. Kohler and Mr. Hiroshita? Both of them had dealings with this Saka Okyo, I believe. They may have learned of something concerning Miss McKay that now she is engaged to be married, she would have—"

Jameson exploded. "Don't be a Goddamn fool, Baron. Mary McKay wouldn't kill anyone, and you know it."

The Baron hung up.

When, three minutes later, an exasperated Christian Jameson again was connected with Hana, the Honolulu detective ungraciously admitted that he didn't mean the Baron was a Goddamn fool, but he should realize that Mary had nothing to do with the murders.

"Not even to gain the entire ranch?" innocently offered the Baron.

Jameson had to pause to cool off, then said sharply, "You do what I told you, Baron, and I'll get you started for Austria by the end of this week. And look: I'm chartering a plane tonight. I can't leave until eleven because of a Goddamn governor's ball. I'm flying to Lahaina. Lahaina," he repeated. "That's on the other side from Wailuku. I'll be waiting for you at the Pioneer Inn."

"You may wait," declared the Baron, "for a month, but I shall not—"

"Oh yes you will," said Jameson. "You'll be there. And you'll have the facts I want. G'-by, Baron. And take care of yourself for at least twenty-four hours, hey? I'm serious."

Jameson hung up first this time.

The Baron climbed into the airport bus for Wailuku.

The bright glare of the sun had been absent for some time. A quick shower fell, a fine soft mist of rain touched with the luminous gold of the sun. To his right, fifty miles distant, the great extinct crater of Haleakala pushed heavenward into tumbling masses of gold and purple clouds. Sugar cane succeeded the pineapple fields. Graceful, light green Kiawe trees flashed by as the road wound along the floor of the valley in long, easy curves.

Wailuku was a town of twenty or thirty thousand people: Chinese, Japanese, Portuguese, Hawaiians, mixed races and Americans. At first glance Wailuku resembled some of the little California cities in which the Baron had been during his few months in the barbaric Northern States of America, but this was only a superficial resemblance. The streets and the buildings were American, perhaps, but silvery Kukui trees draped their clustered pink flowers over old walls, giant ferns and strange violet and crimson flowers were massed in every vacant lot, and life itself took on more riotous colors and expressions, and as the autobus proceeded toward the center of the town, the Baron found himself in a country devoid of all American harshness and drabness. Near the Wailuku Hotel, a monkey pod tree formed a canopy for an old Chinese woman smoking a silver pipe, the thick leaves shielding her from the warm drizzle. She nodded at the Baron as he descended, and he bowed courteously in return before following the driver into the damp lobby.

A Japanese girl gave him the hotel register. He signed his name under that of "Harry Bolton, Paris." The other four names were above Bolton's.

After he was escorted to his room on the second floor he gave the Japanese girl fifty cents. "I see Miss McKay and her friends have already arrived."

The girl took the money dubiously. It was such a large tip. "They came this morning."

He had opened the windows and was admiring the view. Green and golden fields extended to an incredible horizon of purple spires. The girl was waiting at the door. He turned, tilting his head to the left, an inquiring expression on his dark features.

"You're really the Baron von Kaz?"

He bowed, his lower lip thrusting forward. It might be that she had never seen a baron before. At least, not an Austrian baron. She was a quaint little creature.

The quaint little creature, however, did not appear impressed. "Miss Miquet said to tell you that they'd gone to Ioa Valley for a picnic lunch. They took a blue Packard. They were going to picnic near the Ioa Needle where the river turns right."

She was out in the hall before the Baron had recovered. The Baron, who firmly believed that nothing in the world could astound him, recovered, grabbed his green umbrella, wished he had time to wash, ran down to the desk. "Now tell me again," he demanded, first being sure that no one was near enough to overhear. "What caused her—"

The girl looked at him steadily. "What caused what, sir?"

"Miss Miquet to tell you—"

She opened the cash register, removed a stick of chewing gum, inserted it in her mouth. "I really don't understand what you're talking about, sir."

A man came up and asked for the key to room sixty-four, and she gave it to him and then casually regarded the Baron, who was absently rubbing his nose in the most idiotic manner possible, as though temporarily his mind were so absorbed that his fingers were continuing mechanically a process which his brain had ordered and forgotten to halt.

Then suddenly the Baron grinned, and lights seemed to go on in the girl's eyes, but her face remained expressionless. "Ach, so," said the Baron formally. "I am a tourist here, I am a stranger. What scenery is particularly suitable in this lovely island to see between one o'clock and nightfall?"

The girl recommended the crater Haleakala. However, that would take at least six hours. If the gentleman wished a shorter trip he could go to the Ioa Valley. The valley was only thirteen miles from Wailuku. And the Ioa Needle rock and the river were very, very pretty. The Baron asked if it would be possible for him to rent a car. They had cars for hire in the hotel garage. Twelve dollars an afternoon. The Baron counted fifteen dollars and with a grandiloquent gesture refused the change. The Portuguese gentleman in the garage took twenty minutes to show the Baron on the map just how to drive into Ioa Valley and where the Needle rock was.

The drizzle had expended itself by the time the brave Baron had passed the outskirts of Wailuku, and the sun was sliding out from behind a cloud that resembled a torn, soggy gray blotter floating in a liquid blue lake.

Precipitous peaks towered on either side of the road. The vegetation was rank, tropical and humid. His four-cylinder roadster bumbled along the winding narrow road. Now and then where the heavy grass sloped to the Ioa River, the Baron would see a shambling house, roof covered with mats or grass, with little brown children playing naked in the mud. There were few automobiles on this road. For this the Baron was thankful, as his roadster had a lamentable tendency to shudder over the slightest bump, the front wheels swerving wildly.

Far ahead the green shadowed into misty grays as the cliffs on each side narrowed into a V-shaped gorge. The river tumbled down brilliantly colored rocks, and here the air had the cloying fragrance found in a hothouse filled with precious flowers and luxuriant plants. Bottle-shaped tree ferns extended along the road, their peculiar trunks mottled and half rotten, the whitish-green fronds waving softly in the sticky breeze.

"Du lieber Augustin!" swore the Baron uncomfortably, this was a strange country. It was beautiful, yes. But in those hidden clefts above him, in that wild carpet of foliage which spread over the volcanic peaks, there appeared

something unnatural to Austrian eyes accustomed to the
cooler mountains of his country. Here there was too much
of everything. The ferns he had seen in Europe were of a
size to ornament little flower pots. But these Hawaiian
ferns were as large as small trees! And the huge flowers
spread beneath that bright brassy sun as if here they belonged, and not man at all.

Ages ago, by some giant cataclysm of nature, this land
had been lifted up from the depths of the sea, shuddering
from the effort, with hot lava pouring into the water. As
centuries had slipped away, like the seconds of a clock, the
grass and the trees and the flowers had sunk their tendrils
into the crumbling lava, and strange birds had developed,
and the air turned blue, less frequently disturbed by out-
pourings of lava. Finally a race of men had come from
the North in their long canoes. These men and women
had grown taller, just as the plants increased in size. And
over these islands a veil of mystery had seemed to hang
for all the centuries; and if the Hawaiians had lived here
for a time and were sheltered, the time had come when
their race was choked off by the smaller whites. After the
whites now followed even smaller yellow people. But the
lava land remained. And when, after a few years or a few
decades, a field was permitted to lie fallow, a house deserted, the vegetation crept covering these man-made wounds,
and the green carpet, studded with strange flowers, again
spread the red earth as it had been when man was not here.
And as it would be when man was gone, wiped out. . . .

Insensibly, as the antique roadster penetrated into the
narrow valley proper, the Baron lessened the pressure on
the accelerator. It was silent here for a man all his life
accustomed to the sounds of cities. And when at last he
saw the Ioa Needle he turned to the side of the road to
stop and marvel at it. The Needle was a grotesque freak of
nature, a gigantic sliver of volcanic rock pointing upward,

hundreds of feet, as if it were a dagger planted by a once worshiped Hawaiian god as an eternal threat to the blue sky.

The green river gurgled pleasantly to his right, winding through the trees. At his left was a red volcanic cliff, twenty or thirty feet high. He sighted the river, but it had so many bends it was impossible to tell which was the right one. He did not wish to drive his car too near to the picnic place. He determined to follow the road, going past the Needle rock, hoping to recognize Miss McKay or one of her friends, then to hide the car and see how it would be possible to approach Caryl Miquet. By now his astonishment that she had expected him had evaporated, and he felt a little let down that she could be so sure of the Baron von Kaz.

He released the hand brake, and the car started to roll slowly on the slight descent. He was peering to his left, watching the river and the Needle rock, when his car struck something solid. He twisted the steering wheel. A second rock dropped and smashed on the hood. The rear wheels squeaked as he forcefully used his brakes, snatched at his green umbrella.

"Hello," called a voice.

Silhouetted above him was a boy. The boy waved, scrambled down the rocks and ran toward the car.

"Golly!" The boy's great gray eyes shone with excitement. "I was afraid I'd miss you, Baron. I'm Billy McKay."

The Baron looked at the smudge of freckles, smiled. "Ach, so it is." He shook hands with the boy. "You are building more castles, no?"

"I'm not building castles, Baron. I'm being a detective, like you are, only I haven't killed anybody yet. Did you really kill a thousand people?"

"Approximately."

"Gee!" said Billy in awe. "But I got to hurry. This is a secret, see?"

Solemnly the Baron nodded.

"Caryl was going to watch for you, but she couldn't get away from the others, and she knew she could trust me." Billy proudly folded his arms. "So she told me a secret."

"A secret? And am I to hear the secret?"

"Yes," said Billy. "She wants to see you tonight at the hotel. At ten o'clock at the end of the garden." He asked anxiously, "You can remember that?"

"Ten o'clock at the end of the garden. Very easily, my dear Billy."

"Okay." Billy dropped off the running board to the ground. "I guess she's your girl, isn't she? I'm not going to have any girls. They interfere with detective work."

The Baron swallowed. "Ah—you are engaged in detective work?"

"Somebody opened her mail this morning and swiped her candy and I'm going to find out who did it. I got to get back now. They're having the picnic around the bend. You go on." He winked knowingly. "Don't worry, Baron. I'll tell Caryl I fixed it. You can trust me."

"Billy!" called the Baron after a moment's reflection, but the boy, who was running, only turned to wave before vanishing. The Baron returned to the hotel. Tonight he would have to warn Caryl not to permit Billy to attempt to do "detective work"; it might be exceedingly dangerous for a small boy to entangle himself unknowingly in the dark pattern of evil the Baron's imagination visualized slowly forming itself among these bright magical islands.

9
Lahaina Visit

They were dancing outside on the lanai, and the Japanese girl at the counter was listening dreamily, and not until the shadow came between her and the light did she realize someone was looking down at her. She raised her head sharply. He was there, very quiet, with that wolf-like grin on his face which would come when he was inordinately pleased with his own cleverness and when there was no one of importance around to make it worth while to hide his emotions or feelings. "Miss Miquet is to accompany me on a little ride. It is such a pleasant evening we are going up toward Haleakala. If anyone asks, we will return before the dancing is finished." He lit a cigarette, glanced at the Japanese girl. "Or soon after."

The Japanese girl watched him saunter to the lanai and lean on the door. He had small feet and even in repose his body seemed to be in perpetual balance on his feet, ready to spring or leap.

The lanai was strung with paper lanterns. There were twenty or thirty couples on the floor. The Baron glanced at his watch. It was ten after ten. Then he saw her dancing with John Sargent and watched her. That Sargent was a clumsy dancer, he thought. She smiled at him. She was so very cool, so very graceful. He referred to his watch again and frowned and turned from the door. "Hello there,"

Mary McKay greeted him. Jeffrey Preacher nodded. "Caryl said you were here."

Formally the Baron bowed. "Good evening, Miss McKay. Good evening, Mr. Preacher."

Mary glanced at the tall man beside her. "Looks like it's our dance, Jeff. John's evidently taking this one with Caryl, too."

"If you permit me, dear Miss McKay?" The Baron was bowing again, and before Jeffrey quite knew what it was all about the Austrian had Mary by the arm and was saying over his shoulder, "You do not mind, my dear sir?"

"Mind? Sure, go ahead," Jeffrey said cheerfully enough as Mary smiled brightly at the Baron. "I'll get a few drinks ready. You'll need them on a night like this."

The Baron's mode of dancing was mildly old-fashioned; he did not press Mary to him, but held her very carefully and gently precisely two and a half inches from him, as he had been taught in the Viennese pre-war style. But his steps were not at all pre-war. He glided and whirled, leading her with dexterity, with the assured effrontery of a man who knows that he is an excellent dancer.

"Why didn't I meet you on the ship?" she asked, forgetting her first distrust, relaxing, enjoying the perfect rhythm of the man. "I didn't see you dancing at all."

"Ach, dear Miss McKay," he confessed in so drolly an embarrassed manner that she laughed, "I was seasick almost all the way. But the last night out I believe I did see you."

"Oh!" She missed a step, but his arm was firm about her waist. "I remember now. You were in the bar. You were the one who found Carl Kohler dead? I was terribly shocked."

He murmured that it was most tragic, swung her in quick whirls, and when she was breathless and laughing once more, he suggested that they walk into the garden. From the lehua trees the fragrance hung, a heavy perfume.

Mary broke off a blossom, placed it in her hair. "You're a grand dancer, Baron. Caryl said you were from Vienna. I was there for a winter. I loved it."

He offered her a cigarette from his heavy silver case, took one, lit both with a flourish. So Caryl had told her cousin that he was from Vienna? She had talked about HIM? Ach, perhaps, thought about him! He spun on his heel, struck his hands together, placed his head to one side, eyed the astonished Mary, laughed loudly, returned to lean against the trellis, his arms folded across his chest "The night is very pleasant," he commented. "You are charming."

She laughed softly, informing him that he was nice. Then he said that he was certain she was the beautiful girl he had seen that last night out—not in the bar but outside the bar. On A or B deck—he didn't recall. But she was so charming, leaning on the ship's railing with the faint moonlight on her, that he had never forgotten the vision.

"That's another romance blasted, Baron. I was dancing until after midnight. I didn't do any moon- or stargazing."

"Such a pity." Then he suggested it might be possible that she had at least walked on deck during intermissions.

"Don't think so. Most of my intermissions were in the bar. No, Baron. Some other gal stole your heart."

He sighed, then she had been with her happy fiancé all the time?

"Well . . ." Demurely her eyes lifted. "I danced with other men too."

"Deserting your fiancé? My dear young lady, in Vienna—"

"Dear young lady nothing. John's the one who likes to go stargazing on deck at night, and I'll take dancing anytime instead."

"How unfeeling. You remained while he wandered lonely and unhappy?"

"Don't be foolish. Just because we're engaged doesn't imply in this modern age that I have to be with John every minute he wants to walk up and down a deck. You must have seen me in the bar. I was there when you entered. Then John and Bolton left after you did while Jeff and I finished more drinks, and he told me what you said about finding Carl shot in the heart. I saw you when you came down, too. You've just forgotten." She asked for a second cigarette, having thrown the half-smoked one away, and said without emotion, "I used to know Carl. He could be nice. But he drank too much."

He lit her cigarette. "The newspapers announced that he was intoxicated."

"Intoxicated?" Mary's forehead wrinkled. "Oh. That was the best thing, instead of saying that he committed suicide. Our Honolulu papers are more decent that way than the mainland sheets."

"Suicide?"

"Naturally." She was surprised. "John said that was what the police assumed. I thought everyone knew."

"Ach, so." The Baron flicked his cigarette into the bushes.

"You see John was a good friend of Carl's."

"Hein!" Then he smiled, and slapped at a nonexistent bug, apologizing, saying that he had been bitten. "He was a good friend of Mr. Kohler, yes?"

"In Mexico. That's why he had to more or less inquire about Carl's death." She shivered. "But let's not talk of it. He's dead, and he'll be forgotten just as all of us will be in time." She slipped her arm in his. "It's too grand a night to think of morbid things, don't you agree?"

"Ach!" he declared romantically. "Still must I think of that vision on the ship who was not you."

"Why didn't you speak to it, then?" she wanted to know, very much interested.

"There was no one near to introduce her."

"And so you suffered in silence? Poor man!"

He patted her hand. "However, now have I declared myself, dear Miss McKay. And if we do not go back, will your friends not fear that you have been kidnaped?"

At the door he bowed, thanking her. "Again some other evening, dear Miss McKay?"

"I'm afraid not. We came to Maui just for a day, so Caryl could be in Ioa Valley again. She'd been there years ago with her father and wanted to see if it were as beautiful as she remembered it. You know she paints. We're taking the plane tomorrow for Hawaii. Perhaps if John and I ever get to Vienna we'll look you up."

He bent over her hand. "That, dear lady, would be delightful."

"That's quite a trick." Jeffrey was grinning at the Baron. "How about letting me try it, Mary?"

"Don't be a fool, Jeff." She snatched her hand back from the Baron.

Jeffrey's grin stretched across his face. He pointed his right thumb at the lanai. "I told John you and the Baron were probably in the bar. If he finds you here in a wicked garden with a terrible baron, undoubtedly—"

"You're a darling!" Mary blew a kiss at both of them, hurried through the lanai.

Jeffrey took his hands out of his pockets. "Swell girl, Baron."

"You think so, Mr. Preacher?" The light from the lanai rested upon the Baron's face, and it was serious.

Jeffrey's grin vanished, and he nodded, "Very much so," and added, "but John's a good guy. A good guy and lucky. How about coming in for a drink and weeping on the barman's shoulder with me? Bolton says you're a bad influence, and I feel the need of a bad influence this evening."

The Baron placed his hand on Jeffrey's shoulder, almost said something, decided not to, and shook his head.

"Okay." Jeffrey hastily glanced around, then stepped down to the walk. "Bolton's been with me for a long time," he said quickly. "But he's a funny duck. I was talking about you to Caryl, and she said you were a conceited devil, but she didn't mean it when she was saying it." He halted, embarrassed. "That is—hell! Anyway, Caryl's got a lot of sense. What I'm trying to say is, don't rib Bolton, will you?"

"Rib Mr. Bolton? Rib?"

"You know. Get his goat. You've done something to him he doesn't like. He won't tell me, but lay off, won't you? He has a funny streak in him, and I've had to buy him out of two jams already, and as soon as we get to my ranch I've got the tough job of telling him I'm old enough to keep from being kidnaped." Jeffrey was whispering now, and his head jerked from side to side as though he were afraid someone might be near them. The Baron again had the curious sensation of a strain. "I don't need Bolton any more," Jeffrey continued, "and it 'll be hard enough to explain that to him without you rubbing his fur the wrong way. I wouldn't talk to you like this if I hadn't heard so much about you from Caryl."

The Baron's head inclined. "I will be most careful, Mr. Preacher."

Jeffrey went into the hotel. The Baron sniffed the air, took the dark garden pathway. A small, angry person asked with cold restraint, "Are you aware that you have kept me waiting?"

"My dear Miss Miquet," he stated, undisturbed, "are you aware that you kept the Baron von Kaz waiting once for over an hour?"

She was above replying to this question and wanted to know where he was going now when she wished to talk with him. "My car is in the garage," he explained. "It is better to drive a little distance out of town, where we will be assured of privacy."

"I mustn't be gone long."

"Only a few minutes." He assisted her into the car and backed it out of the garage. In silence they drove down the scented street, overshadowed by the great leafy monkey pod trees which rustled in the night breeze like fine sandpaper being ground together.

When they reached the outskirts Caryl informed him haughtily, "I told Mary that I was going upstairs. That I had a headache. We'll have to return by eleven-thirty."

"Assuredly."

"This is purely a business proposition, Baron von Kaz."

"Exactly."

"I thought you might be idiotic enough to come here." Her voice appeared to break for an instant. "That is why I bribed the girl at the desk to let you know where I was."

"So I assumed."

He glanced at her slyly; he saw her face in profile with the pointed chin lifted haughtily, the mouth firm, the dark eyes steadfastly gazing ahead. As if from a great distance she remarked, "We can stop here now, Baron. I had hoped to meet you this afternoon, but I couldn't get away. I had to persuade Billy to act as my messenger."

"That was most unwise."

"I wanted to see you because— What do you mean? You don't know Billy. I can trust him implicitly."

"Exactly, my dear Miss Miquet. But do you know whether you can trust those others who know Billy?"

"Really, Baron von Kaz—"

"Permit me. It is possible that Billy could come to grievous danger; he is young, true; but intelligent, and those bright eyes of his might see too much. Did you know," he asked, "that magicians fear the eyes of children because the children are not deluded by sleight of hand movements which trick adults and therefore more easily discover what happens to the canary bird when the cage is made to vanish?"

"Baron!" she exclaimed furiously, "I don't understand you. It was perfectly safe for me to send Billy to intercept you. However—" her voice broke a little—"I won't do it again. I wouldn't have anything hurt Billy for the world. Are you going to stop?"

"Ah, is it not more pleasant to drive? What is this concerning your candy and the opened mail, if you please?" he reminded her, changing the subject.

What she had to say was brief: The hotel in Honolulu had given her her mail, a few letters from friends on the Islands and a package of candy, just before taking the airplane. She hadn't had time to read her mail before reaching Wailuku Hotel. She shared a room with Mary; John Sargent and Jeffrey Preacher had the adjoining room; and Bolton a room on the floor below. Mary had been in their bedroom with her, unpacking, for ten or fifteen minutes until John and Jeffrey had entered. Then all three had gone out so that she could take a bath. While she was in the tub John had returned, knocking on the door, saying that he had come to get Mary's leather jacket and that he had Mary's key. It was when she had come into the room to dress that she noticed the package of candy had been unwrapped.

This hadn't disturbed her. She joined her party downstairs and jokingly accused one of them of wanting to eat her candy, but all had insisted they hadn't touched the box. Oddly frightened, Caryl found an excuse to go to the desk and gave the girl a tip to deliver a message to the Baron von Kaz.

"How did you suspect I would arrive in Maui today?" asked the Baron as disinterestedly as possible. Caryl had forgotten that she was angry with the wretch. She glanced at him now, quickly, with the lips turning upwards a little. He caught this ironic and knowing glance and was so astonished and delighted by it that he practically permitted the car to conduct its own course for the next few seconds.

Ach! du lieber Gott! Then she did realize that he was in love with her. That Caryl was thoroughly cognizant of a fact the Baron firmly believed was hidden deep within his heart appeared to him as a miracle.

"Oh!" exclaimed Caryl, letting escape a tiny yelp which was entirely feminine and therefore delicious to the Baron's ears.

The Baron turned the steering wheel, and the car reluctantly thumped back on all four wheels. "Have no fear, my dear Caryl," he said with such austerity that he was unaware of the grievous laxity in his manner of address toward her, "I have driven hundreds of automobiles. In Vienna I had a racing car, a Mercedes-Benz, which would go nearly one hundred and eighty kilometers an hour. And I never had an accident. Never a serious one," he amended, wishing to be entirely truthful to this one person. "Although the man's leg was broken."

With one of those incalculable changes of a woman's mind, Caryl was again speaking to him in that infuriatingly remote voice. "I am quite willing to pay you anything reasonable for your services, Baron von Kaz. I want you to learn why my mail is being opened. It worries me." Here she hesitated, and only the rushing breeze and the steady drone of the motor came to the Baron, "It might be someone's idea of humor," she added at last. "But I shall pay you. Have no fear."

The Baron gave no response.

"What's the matter?"

His voice was incredibly polite. "You will pay the Baron von Kaz?"

"Certainly. I have utmost confidence in your—your—shall we say professional capacities?"

"You shall pay, then. One thousand dollars."

"That is rather high," she replied, "but you shall have it, Baron von Kaz. You may consider yourself . . . hired."

"Hired?" The car leaped forward. "So? I am hired, then. And now that I am hired, I should like to be told where you were on the *Kohala* while I had the honor of waiting for you on A deck?"

"What has that to do—"

"Although I have the privilege to be hired, permit me the right to discover why your mail is of interest in my own way without interference."

"Very well. I danced until nearly twelve. Then, taking John Sargent's advice, I went to my cabin. Finally, about twelve-thirty, maybe a little after, I returned to B deck to see when Mary was coming to bed."

"And you spoke to Miss McKay?"

"No. I met Mr. Preacher on B deck and there listened to his tale of unrequited affection for my cousin and almost wished that I had gone to A deck where, at least, I could see the stars."

"But you did not go to A deck?"

"No, Baron von Kaz. I did not go to A deck. I saw that my cousin was too occupied dancing to tell anyone good night. So, escorted by the woeful Mr. Preacher, I again sought my cabin."

"She was dancing, if you please, with her fiancé?"

"I don't know, I don't think so. I didn't pay much attention."

"So? And what time, if you please, was it when you reached your cabin with Mr. Preacher?"

"After one o'clock," she said impatiently. "A minute or so past one. I remember glancing at my watch."

"Thank you. And where on B deck did you first encounter Mr. Preacher?"

"Outside the bar."

"When you walked on B deck, did you go toward the bar from amidships?"

"Yes. My room was near the center of the ship."

"And you walked toward the bar?"

"Yes."

"Mr. Preacher was there? He did not perhaps pass you, also walking toward the bar?

"Hardly. I would have seen him. Is this a game? Do you imagine Jeff opened my undelivered mail on the boat while you were waiting for me on A deck?" she asked scornfully.

He ignored her questions. "And, if you please, you did not locate Miss McKay?"

"I said I saw her dancing."

"And Mr. Sargent?"

"No. But I wasn't looking for him. He was probably stargazing—"

"Did you see Mr. Bolton?"

"Why in the world should I want to see Mr. Bolton?"

"One more question. How is it that Mr. Preacher, who was brought up in Europe, speaks idiomatic—that is American idiomatic English?"

"You mean slang. He went to an American boys' school in Paris, and simply because his mother wouldn't allow him to go home, to his own country, he made a fetish of using American slang. He told me so. Just as he made a fetish of going in for athletics. Now will you explain—"

"My explanations are not included in the one thousand dollars," he coldly informed her. "You hired me merely to learn why your mail is being opened."

She said nothing thereafter.

Nor did the Baron.

Now during this stretch of silence the car was hustling along at the speed of fifty miles an hour; not very fast, perhaps, for mainland driving, but on the small island of Maui fifty miles an hour quickly covers considerable territory. As a result, very shortly the car attained the settlement of Haalaea, a few small houses at the edge of a great cane field. The Baron peered over the windshield at the sign: LAHAINA 15 miles. And turned right on Amalfi Drive to Lahaina.

Caryl, completely aware of this maneuvering, straightened up and broke the silence, saying determinedly, "I would appreciate being taken to the Wailuku Hotel. It is time I returned."

"Pardon," corrected the Baron, "not yet is it time."

Those dark eyes flicked toward him, and the wide mouth set very firmly. "Would you tell me where we are going?"

"Lahaina, if you please."

"If I please," she mimicked. "The brave Baron is going to Lahaina? And would he be kind enough to tell me why?"

"Why?" he shouted, his pent-up anger at the intolerable insult she had given him breaking. "Why? To collect my thousand dollars. To inform you the reason why your mail is being opened."

The fact that Caryl entered the Pioneer Hotel with the Baron without the slightest hesitation is an indication that she too had a temper of her own of such dimensions that, when aroused, it blinded her to all prudence, or that she had more faith in the Baron's curious morals and sense of honor than almost all of his friends who assumed that they knew him intimately.

The Baron barely gave her a glance as he assisted her from the car. That she should offer to hire him as a common mercenary when he was willing to devote all his services to her even to the extent that he would risk deserting his companions in Vienna was more than a man who considered his honor could endure. And the Baron was a man who considered his honor. Every time he thought of her insulting offer, which was continuously, a hot iron twisted into the seething pride of the brave Baron von Kaz. If she were in Vienna he would have her whipped, he assured himself; whipped without the slightest mercy . . .

The Chinese individual dozing in the rattan chair, startled out of a dream of a joss house in Canton, waggled his head and put both paws on the register. The Baron pushed the register aside. The register slid off the desk from the force of a gesture which the Baron had not intended to be anything but mildly disdainful. The register landed with a loud crash. The Chinese person blinked at the Baron. "Why hell you do that for?"

The Baron succeeded in ignoring this matter completely. "I am the Baron von Kaz. Where is Mr. Jameson?"

The Chinese person picked up the register, muttering unholy curses. A door swung open, and Jameson stepped into the hall. "What the devil's that gun going off— It's you, Baron?"

"The book slipped off the desk," said the Baron with inflated dignity, while the Chinese person sputtered loudly. Jameson pushed the Chinese clerk into the chair, then stared as he saw Caryl Miquet standing slim and straight in the shadows.

"Miss Miquet," introduced the Baron with icy courtesy. "Mr. Christian Jameson. Miss Miquet is my client. She wishes—"

But Jameson had both of Caryl's hands in his, wanting to know what in sin she was doing here. "This ain't any place for you, Caryl," he said. Then he faced the Baron, "Look here, Baron. By—" he swallowed, then, managed a feeble—"by jumping Jesus, what're you up to?"

The Baron asked, "Have you a room, my dear Mr. Christian Jameson?"

Caryl squeezed the old man's hand. "You have to humor him like a child. Have you a room for the man?"

Like a child? The Baron's hands tightened on the edge of the desk, and his head dropped as though he would spring at them. Then he immediately changed. He drew

himself erect. His feet clicked. He was the great Baron von
Kaz. These were foolish American barbarians. They were
to be treated as children, not he as a child. He smiled at
them. "If you please," he said cajolingly, "a room is more
convenient. I will not detain you long."

"Come on," ordered Jameson irritably, offering Caryl
his arm, and leaving the Baron to stalk alone behind them.
At the door the Baron bowed, insisted that Mr. Jameson
precede him. Jameson gave Caryl a chair in a large, par-
lorlike room with several framed engravings of old Hawaiian chieftains on the cracked walls, faded curtains drawn
across the windows. Pale moths fluttered close to the two
light bulbs.

Jameson watched the Baron suspiciously. "You know, I
was beginning to trust you."

The Baron's head inclined.

"All right." Jameson bit into one of his dry cigars.
"I told you why I wanted you here. And you bring Miss
Miquet with you."

Caryl apologized to Jameson for intruding on a meeting that he had planned.

The Baron waved his hand. "I brought her here, my
dear Mr. Christian Jameson. She has no need to apologize."

With that he walked to the window in a long dramatic
pause. When he glanced to see how his superb calm was
affecting them, and they were whispering and not paying
any attention to him, he affirmed that all Americans, male
and female, were dolts. He left the window for a chair,
offered a cigarette to Caryl, and she shook her head.

"So you engaged him?" Jameson was asking in bewilderment "See here, Caryl, what in the tarnation would you
need him for?"

Now she sought the Baron's eyes for some sign, but
this gentleman regarded the ceiling. She bit her lips. She

looked helplessly at the old detective. The Baron finally purred, fatherly, "You may tell him, dear Miss Miquet."

So she told Jameson that her mail had been opened twice, feeling that the Baron had tricked her, had forced her to bare her worries to the police when, because it involved her friends, she had desired to keep the matter private.

When she had finished, Jameson was even more puzzled. "Well, well," he grumbled. "That beats it. Now, why in tarnation would anyone want to read your mail?"

She pointed to the Baron. "I am paying that gentleman one thousand dollars to find out."

The brave Baron jumped as if stung. Next he smiled balefully. "You comprehend, my dear sir, she is paying me. Now, dear Miss Miquet, have you ever heard of a Saka Okyo?" He repeated the name. "Saka Okyo?"

"Of course not." She appealed to Jameson, "Will you tell me what this has to do with my mail?"

Jameson teetered on his toes. "I'll be glad to," he said, "but maybe you wouldn't mind telling me something first. Where were you on the ship between—well—between midnight and around one o'clock?"

Caryl glanced sharply at the two men. Then, without another question, very quietly and coolly she told Jameson what she had told the Baron.

When she had finished, Jameson looked at the Baron, who was now prowling back and forth as though he had forgotten their presence. Jameson asked, "Where'd Jeff go after he left you at your stateroom?"

"He said he was going back to the bar to try to find Mary."

"Well, well," muttered Jameson.

The Baron abruptly spun on his toes and pointed a finger at the old man, who had just seated himself. Jameson leaned forward to get up from his chair, sat down again

almost sheepishly, wishing the foreigner wasn't so damn
unexpected in his movements. "My dear Mr. Christian
Jameson, what was Saka Okyo's profession, the elder Saka
Okyo?"

"Profession? He was an archaeologist. See here, Baron—"

"If you please," said the Baron impatiently, "do not interrupt. Miss Miquet, let me tell you a story. . . ."

And in precise, staccato words, he told her how a Japanese gentleman by the name of Hiroshita had discovered
the plan to a lost fortune in Mexico from a compatriot. This compatriot's name was Saka Okyo. And after Mr.
Hiroshita had obtained the plan, he had placed it in a
soapstone plaque. A soapstone plaque which was one of
a pair. Then the Baron explained that Mr. Hiroshita was
afraid of Mr. Kohler; and, later, he had learned that someone else in addition to Mr. Kohler desired the content of
the soapstone plaque. When the Baron completed his tale
by saying, very stiffly, of course, that by an unfortunate
misunderstanding Mr. Hiroshita had gained the idea that
if the plaque with the plan were sent to Miss Miquet, then
he—the Baron—could be persuaded to obtain that plaque
by substituting its duplicate, Jameson snorted. Furthermore, concluded the Baron evenly with a glance at Caryl,
while he was strolling on A deck of the *Kohala,* the last
night out, he had overheard that the plan was to be sent
to Miss Miquet. "Naturally, my dear Mr. Jameson, I heard
only snatches of words, and not until later did I fully realize the terrible significance of—"

"That's the damnedest story anybody could tell," Jameson declared. "Baron, I guess you and me better go back to
Honolulu. You're under arrest."

"So?"

Caryl stood, said, "Wait a minute, Mr. Jameson. If the
Baron has this soapstone plaque that Mr. Hiroshita gave

him to substitute, wouldn't that prove his story true no matter how bizarre it sounds?" She stretched out one hand.

The Baron looked at her hand, rubbed his nose, glanced at Jameson, then smiled. He reached into his inside coat pocket, handed her the soapstone plaque, bowed most ironically. Jameson was muttering, "Well, well," and when the Baron showed Caryl how it opened, the old man said that he reckoned he didn't have the pride some folks he knew had, and he could admit he was wrong.

"My plaque, please," requested the Baron after Caryl had handed it to Jameson and he had finished opening and closing it. Caryl sat down.

Jameson dropped the plaque in his coat pocket. "I guess I'll keep it."

Caryl raised her head, looked up at the Baron interrogatingly. He avoided her eyes. Jameson was thinking. He came out with it bluntly: "Why, God almighty, Baron!" Then he saw Caryl's face and stopped.

"Say it," she said.

The Baron shrugged. "It is obvious, no? Your mail is watched in Honolulu. Now in Maui. The coincidence would be too great that one other than those with you could have intercepted it twice on two different islands."

"That's not true," she countered.

"You can't get around it, Caryl," said Jameson. "By Jesus—sorry. But you can't get around it. That's why you brought her here tonight?" Jameson gazed sourly at the Baron. "You're a smart feller, Baron, but here on the Islands we don't bluntly tell a girl one of her friends is a murderer."

The Baron finished lighting his cigarette first "No?" he queried politely, in that icy way Caryl was rapidly detesting. He could have added that only by bringing them together and dramatically presenting them with his slender shreds of fact could he shock them into believing him, could he present both to Caryl and the Honolulu police official the danger that was closing in upon the receiver of the plaque. He sat down, repeating to Jameson Mr. Tuung's threat regarding Miss Miquet should the story concerning the red diamond—and here he had to tell this version of the plaque's content—be given to the police.

"Don't worry," Jameson told Caryl. "We'll keep you out of trouble. I know the crowd Tuung's with. I can take care of them."

Caryl was busy with her mesh bag. "Have you a fountain pen, Mr. Jameson?" She laid the check book on her knee as she received Jameson's pen.

"Pardon," said the Baron steadily, "although I told you why your mail is of such interest, I have not told you the content of the plaque. That is important, no, Mr. Christian Jameson?"

"Don't call me 'Christian Jameson,'" shouted the detective. "You've told us enough. You can leave the Islands on the next boat. I'll handle the details."

The Baron looked at his cigarette. "Then you have determined who killed Mr. Kohler? Who killed Mr. Hiroshita? Who may kill more people when the mail brings that plaque from Mexico to Miss Miquet? You know when the plaque will arrive in order to be on your guard? And you feel assured as to the content of the plaque; the content which is neither a map of a buried city nor a red diamond?"

"You're such a smart feller, I suppose you've figured out all this?"

"Many thanks," said Caryl, handing the Baron a check for a thousand dollars. "I hope that is quite satisfactory."

"Quite, my dear Miss Miquet." The Baron bowed, folded the check, placed it in his pocket and started for the door.

"Just a minute," Jameson followed him. "You know so much, hey?"

The Baron stared up and down the length of James-on as though he were a strange species never before seen. Then he replied with the most insulting arrogance, "For the time being I have ascertained approximately when the plaque should arrive in Hawaii. Unfortunately, not yet do I know what is the content of the plaque." He walked out of the door, while Jameson stood there, his jaw unhinged, his eyes incredulous. The Baron turned, "But I think I may guess," he murmured.

The door slammed.

Jameson carefully bit off the end of a new cigar, said mildly to Caryl, "I guess maybe I'd better see where he's going. For a smart feller he has the damnedest temper I ever came across."

"Have you a car, Mr. Jameson?" asked Caryl, as though what the Baron did, where he went, whether or not he had the damnedest temper Jameson ever came across, were not of the slightest consequence to her. "I'd like to borrow it to return to the hotel. They'll be anxious about me."

"You sit tight, Caryl," said the old man, going to the door. "I'll get you back if he don't."

Jameson found the Baron sitting gloomily on the sea wall beneath a drooping banyan. Jameson sat down beside him. "Cigar?"

"I never smoke cigars."

"You don't realize what you're missing." Jameson folded his hands over one angular knee. "Now, look here, Baron, a real smart feller like you ain't going to let hisself get riled because an old feller like me—"

"My dear sir—"

"Lord," said Jameson philosophically, "sometimes I forget what ornery manners I have."

"If you please," said the Baron more kindly, "you have gracious manners—for an American."

"You're not sore, then?"

"The Baron von Kaz never loses his temper. I wished to—uhm—to have you follow me." The Baron nodded his head. "Exactly. It was a stratagem."

"Well, well," admired Jameson. "You mean you pretended to get—"

"Obviously." The Baron glanced at the detective; the detective was wagging his old pelican head, agreeing with every word the Baron had uttered. Enchanted by his own voice, the Baron convinced himself of the probity of his actions. "I questioned Miss Mary McKay. I wished to tell you that."

"And that's why you had me come out?"

"I did not desire Miss Miquet to hear what I discovered about her cousin."

"What 'd you find?"

"She was dancing."

"That's all?"

"Dancing. And she went into the bar during intermissions."

"Well, well." Jameson digested this momentous discovery. "If Caryl heard that she'd be pretty upset, I guess. It's lucky you were smart enough to think of a way to drag me out here."

The Baron smiled, suddenly looked sharply at Jameson. "If you please—"

"All right, Baron. Mary McKay's placed. Now you were on A deck. Whoever killed Mr. Kohler didn't leave the body and run toward you, or you'd have noticed."

"Exactly, my dear sir."

"Thank you. I'm fairly bright myself. And you didn't see Jeff running by you on A deck. And he couldn't've run forward, gone down to B deck and then passed by Caryl without her being aware of him. And she couldn't 've killed Kohler on A deck because her time is accounted for. And Mary was dancing and—"

"Permit me to observe," interrupted the Baron, "not all the time. She told me she went into the bar during intermissions. She could have gone elsewhere."

"You can trust Mary all right," said Jameson. "She didn't kill Kohler. She's too sweet a girl. The thing to do is to find out about Sargent and Bolton."

"You believe so?" asked the Baron politely.

10

Black Sand

"There are eight islands altogether," said the gentleman with the round nose who was eating mango fruit for the first time. "Eight, in the territory of Hawaii. And the largest of these eight islands is the island of Hawaii. What?" He leaned forward, keeping his finger in the guidebook.

His wife pointed across the dining room of the Kona Inn, and the gentleman turned around slightly, said he didn't see anything at all, took his second taste of mango fruit, remarked that he'd never tasted fruit like that in Iowa, and continued the lecture to his daughter and wife:

"The northern tip of the island of Hawaii, divided into north and south Kohala, is high and temperate being on the slopes of the great volcano of Mauna Kea. These outlandish names are terrible," he said, and then noticed that both his wife and daughter were staring to their left with peculiar absorption. "Are you listening?"

"He's drinking champagne," his wife whispered.

"Since when, Cora, have you interested yourself in the alcoholic beverages sots wish to pour down their throats?" He frowned severely, decided not to try any more mango, concentrated on the book again. "Cattle graze on these slopes. Here are many ranches, including the famous Preacher Ranch, the great Parker Ranch, and many others. Mauna Kea dominates the northern part of the Island. Generally, even in summer, it is snow-capped, while immense volcanic cones protrude from its lower slopes. Please pay attention!" he admonished sharply. "Just below south Kohala is north Kona, the only section in which the old native life may still be found. In the Kohala and Kona regions there are mysterious lava caverns to explore, the age-old temples, and savage lava flows which speak eloquently of Mauna Kea, the world's mightiest volcano which looms fourteen feet above—what?"

"But for breakfast?" his daughter whispered. "Champagne for breakfast?"

This time the gentleman from Iowa turned completely around, sternly regarded the dark-faced man who was calmly pouring himself his third glass of champagne. This individual's table faced one of the wide windows opening upon an immense lanai, or porch, with cool overhanging eaves. A stretch of bright green lawn ran down to a beach fronted with jagged black volcanic rocks from which grew clusters of palms. Three Hawaiians were wading in the blue Pacific, casting their nets. The dark-faced gentleman lifted his glass, as if to toast an incomparable view, emptied it, returned to his rolls, his marmalade, and books scattered over his table.

The gentleman from Iowa, appalled by such immorality, gathered his wife and daughter and departed from the dining room of the Kona Inn.

Half an hour later the brave Baron von Kaz sauntered out of the dining room with two books under his arm. A Japanese boy followed him with the rest of the books. Mr. Berry, manager of the Kona Inn, was at the desk. "Breakfast all right, Baron von Kaz?" asked Mr. Berry cordially. He was a chubby, friendly man with red veins showing on his forehead and on his cheeks.

The Baron nodded absently, glanced at the calendar. Today was April twelfth. Five days before the seventeenth; five days before the plaque should arrive from Mexico.

The Japanese boy piled the books on the counter, hissed politely, silently melted away. The Baron laid his two books on the counter. "If you keep on reading the history of Hawaii," said Mr. Berry conversationally, "you'll know more about it than those professors at the university on Oahu." He took the books. "Finished with them?" The Baron nodded. "I don't think there are any more that'd interest you. I telephoned Hilo yesterday, but they claimed they'd already sent me all the books they have on the history of Kohala and Kona. Like some on the other islands?"

"No thank you, my dear sir." The Baron asked anxiously, "Then they can give me nothing more on the old legends and customs?"

"You've had them all, Baron."

"But Kailua, here, was at one time the capital. King Kamehameha was born in north Kohala. I can find nothing on the burial rites."

"Well," said Mr. Berry tolerantly, "the natives always were secretive about their habits, and I guess the white men weren't very interested in any of their pagan doings. When the missionaries came here in eighteen hundred-and-two, or thereabouts, they were more interested in converting them; and then, after the traders came, no one gave a damn about the Hawaiians. About their habits, I mean. Aunt Ella," his head nodded backwards in indication of the ancient Royal Palace of Kailua, which was a quarter of a mile from the hotel, "over at the Palace, knows more old-time legends than anyone around here." He laughed again. He had a cheerful, pleasant laugh. "You've been talking with her steadily the past three days, Baron. If she can't tell you what you want, no one can. What're you planning to do? Write an article for one of the foreign magazines?"

"Exactly," agreed the Baron.

"Say." Mr. Berry called to him as he started for the stairs. "I forgot." He came from behind the counter and gave the Baron an envelope. "Cable arrived for you early this morning."

The hotel was built for coolness and comfort. The corridors, running the length of the hotel, serving to connect the airy rooms, were more like long porches with the one side open. The Baron walked down the second-floor corridor to his room, constantly watching the winding road and the foliage across the road. Upon several occasions when men had walked through the underbrush the Baron had dismissed his dignity to such an extent that he had ducked behind the shelter of the corridor railing. But the men had been either Hawaiians or mixtures of Hawaiian and Oriental blood. For the moment the Baron was convinced that Caryl Miquet was safe, that no harm would threaten her until the plaque was delivered. And he and Jameson had made their plans to protect her as soon as the plaque entered the post-office in Honolulu.

But the Baron, as he remained at Kona Inn, fifty miles or so from those ranches in north Kohala where Caryl and her friends were staying, was very careful in taking all the precautions for his own safety. He knew that not more than fifty miles away, perhaps nearer, was a deadly air pistol. In his solitude at Kona, his imagination frequently imaged a silent winged dart striking into his flesh. If the killer were as shrewd as the Baron thought the killer to be, that person would realize, as the time for the arrival of the plaque which had already cost two lives drew closer, that having Austria's, Europe's, greatest detective near by might prove an obstacle to the desired end. And it would be so easy to remove that obstacle. And so, while the Baron was a brave man appreciating his own worth, he could be as cautious and wary as a hunted wolf.

Not until he was in his room did he slit the envelope and read the cable which had been sent to Honolulu from Vienna, and then on to Kailua. The cable was quickly decoded:

BARON FRANZ MAXIMILIAN KARAGÔZ
VON KAZ
  HONOLULU
AUSTRIAN CONSUL INFORMS US YOU
HAVE NOT YET LEFT ISLANDS STOP SE-
RIOUSLY CONCERNED STOP IMPERA-
TIVE YOU DEPART IMMEDIATELY STOP
CABLE US WHEN WE MAY EXPECT YOU
IN VIENNA
  CHWEIK

For almost ten minutes the Baron sat at his table staring at the cable, with the blue sea outside, and the palm
trees waving, and the clouds floating lazily in a sky that
looked forever calm and then he tore into small pieces the
cablegram and the sheet of paper upon which he had written the translation, yawned, stood up. He was tired. He
had read last night until five o'clock in the morning, as,
indeed, he had done the previous three nights, as though
searching in the books for a secret which he had been unable to discover during the afternoons while exploring the
coast of Hawaii in a rented car.

Time had gone so quickly. Only a few days more before
the seventeenth. . . .

He put a clean handkerchief in his pocket, picked up
his panama hat and green umbrella and left the hotel,
stopping for a moment to buy ginger leis from one of the
Hawaiian flower girls squatting at the edge of the dusty
road.

Kona Inn is situated on the outskirts of the historic little town of Kailua. Over a hundred years ago Prince Kuakini, brother of the great King Kamehameha's queen, had
erected a royal palace under an ancient and huge banyan
tree. All this the Baron knew. Kailua itself was a strag-
gling village of some fifty ramshackle buildings, several

Japanese hotels, by the side of a peaceful bay. Across from
the Palace—a square, three-storied building resembling a
great New England house of the eighteenth century upon
which had been grafted a long porch and second-story balcony with ornate railings, as a concession, perhaps, to the
tropical influence—was the large stone church, the first in
all the Islands, built in eighteen thirty-seven by the same
missionaries who had assisted Prince Kuakini design his
own royal abode.

The lawn in front of the Kailua Palace was riotous with
flowers. Coconut palms curved gracefully, shading the
porch. Inside it was cool and musty, with that smell of
old plaster and old woodwork. A small, weazened woman
with enormous eyes was knitting behind a desk. Surrounding her were glass cases containing faded tapestries and
Hawaiian relics. On the wall hung old oil portraits of the
kings and princes of that Hawaiian kingdom, already almost forgotten. The Baron approached her, bowed to her
with all the courtesy of a gallant approaching a lady of the
Imperial Court in Vienna. He offered her the leis. "Good
morning, dear Aunt Ella," he said.

Everyone, he had been warned the first morning by Mr.
Berry, called her Aunt Ella. No one knew how old she was.
Some thought she was more than a hundred. Some eighty;
some ninety. She had missionary blood in her; and on her
mother's side she was Hawaiian. Once she had been very
beautiful and the best equestrienne on the islands. During
the eighties she had lived in Honolulu, an intimate of
Queen Kapiolani and Princess Liliuokalani, who later was
the last queen, and King Kalakaua, who died in San Francisco in eighteen ninety-one. When Queen Liliuokalani
was deposed, Aunt Ella returned to Kohala; and stayed
in Kohala during those years after the brief republic of
Hawaii. A few years ago the Daughters of Hawaii Society
had restored the Kailua Palace and placed Aunt Ella in

charge, and here she remained, living among her memories.

Only a few tourists came during the day. When the Baron had arrived, at first he had seemed very strange to her. But he was so respectful, so charming, so attentive, so interested, that gradually she had warmed to him. Yesterday morning she had closed the Palace before noon and had taken him to her little house built on the Palace grounds where they had had tea together, and she had told him of those old days which never again would return.

And she had invited him to repeat the ceremony today.

When the Baron had finished his fourth cup of tea he asked politely, "Why is it, if it was the custom of the old kings and all those of royal blood to have themselves buried in the lava caverns, that so few graves have been found?"

Aunt Ella regarded him, lifted her cup of tea. Her chinaware had been bought in Shanghai fifty years ago by her uncle. He was in the tea trade then. The Baron listened while she told him about her uncle who captured a great three-masted clipper ship, infinitely better than one of these snorting modern steamboats. Aunt Ella didn't like steamboats. She had heard of airplanes, but they never flew over Kailua; besides, she didn't believe in them. When she had completed all that she had to say concerning her uncle and modern progress, she stood up, shook out the black, crinkling skirts, looked at the Baron with that little secretive air. "They didn't want to be disturbed," she answered. "When they died a tabu was placed on the burial caverns. Only the old people knew where they were located. Now the old people are gone."

The Baron walked with her to the door. "Such a pity." He sighed, glanced at her from the corners of his eyes, sighed again.

"It isn't a pity," she countered sharply. She pointed north, toward the coast of Kohala, where the tip of the island lay. "When Mauna Kea erupted, the hot lava tunneled down from the heights, forming great tubes underground to the sea. Many of the tubes are miles in length. When I was a girl—"

She stopped, looked at him again with that secretive air. "It's time for my nap," she declared. "Why aren't you fishing or lolling around the beach with the other tourists?"

He could fish in Austria, he explained. There was something about this place that captivated him. It was a great pity that all the old customs should vanish. Now if these islands belonged to Austria—

"When I was a girl," she half whispered, "I used to go into the caves. You can't find the important ones. Only a few have been opened by the bungling tourists."

"But why," he insisted very naïvely, with the lines deepening in his dark cheeks, and his blue eyes bright and engaging, "Why should they be hidden? I do not understand."

"You are stupid," she said, tossing her head. "Do you suppose the old kings want all their finery to be found?"

"Pardon. Finery?"

"Their clothes. Their possessions. What they had was buried with them."

"Ach, so." He nodded solemnly. "But surely, dear Aunt Ella, no one would disturb a few valueless relics?"

"Valueless?" She screeched like a muted parrot. "Have you seen the feather cloak of King Kamehameha at the Honolulu museum?" She began to laugh softly, like an old phonograph record with the grooves worn jagged. "Isn't that worth half a million dollars? Where are the little Oo and Mamo birds—the Iiwi birds—from which they plucked one by one the colored feathers to make the cloaks? All gone now. And the women who had the patience to work fifty years to make a feather cloak? You don't find such women any more, with steamboats and airplanes, do you?"

"And they buried these—ach!—these feather cloaks with the old chieftains, dear Aunt Ella?"

"That they did." She nodded. "And there weren't many such cloaks made, even when the chieftains were alive. One or two only every hundred years. They found King Kamehameha's because he was vain and didn't hide his. But where's Puakini's? Aye? Where's his? He was almost as great a man as the Great King himself. But Puakini was loyal to the old beliefs, and when he died they hid him in South Kohala, and nobody 'll ever find his cavern. Now go away," she ordered crossly. "I'm old and I'm tired."

He took her hand, and the faded old eyes softened. In her youth, when the foreign princes and dukes had come to Honolulu on the warships, on the sailing boats, and she had danced with them in the Great Palace, they too had taken her hand and kissed it.

Slyly he glanced along the parched yellow arm to her face. And as he lifted his lips, he murmured very softly, "But you know where is Puakini's cavern, no, dear Aunt Ella?"

She met his smile. Her lips cracked in her face. She nodded. "And when I go, nobody 'll ever know. Nobody 'll ever know."

He looked out over the Palace grounds and then felt for a folded slip of paper and handed it to her. "Dear Aunt Ella, once you stated that the tourists do not leave money sufficient for the upkeep of the Palace. Permit me, as a token of my affection—ach!" He was going to compose an extravagant and meaningless sentence, but when he saw her expression change as she read the check he said simply, "For you."

"One thousand dollars?" She looked at him. "You're joking?"

He shook his head.

"The check isn't good. It can't be."

"Pardon." He bowed. "You can cash it at any bank. Try it, dear Aunt Ella."

"But it's not signed by you." She adjusted her glasses. "It's a woman's name. It's a familiar name, too."

"It is made out to me. For a minor service." He shrugged. "Turn the check over. You will see I have endorsed it to 'Aunt Ella.'"

She watched him walk under the palm trees, under the banyan trees, and at the stone gate he paused and blew her a kiss, and she waved at him and then went into her house, the check clutched tightly in her hand.

It was hot, and he was dusty, and in his room he took a cold shower. Little green lizards scurried on the ceiling. He changed his clothes and felt refreshed. Far down the hall a door clattered suddenly as he stretched, and with arms extended he became rigid. He moved silently, when a minute had passed, to the door, peered into the hall. He did not like this long wait. His nerves were jumpy. The strain was growing. At night it was particularly bad. Even the trees seemed to rustle warnings. He picked up his green umbrella, patted it fondly, hooked it on his left arm.

As usual, when he left his room, he glanced cautiously in both directions, then sighted over the railing to the dusty road below, to the green tangle of vegetation growing on the slope which ascended imperceptibly, not ten or twenty miles, but nearly fifty breath-taking miles, to fourteen thousand feet above sea level. One of the Kona "nightingales," a mouse-colored mule, was drawing a dilapidated cart into which were crowded a fat Hawaiian and his fatter wife. There was no other movement. The air was still. Kailua had settled into its afternoon nap. Two Japanese children had curled up by the stone wall in front of the church and were fast asleep.

Downstairs he found the manager playing one of his endless games of dominoes. The Baron wished to learn if it would be possible to drive to South Kona. The manager lazily pushed aside a row of dominoes. He didn't think so. From the tip of the island—North Kona—clear down along the west coast to Kailua, there weren't any roads. South Kona, according to Mr. Berry, was pretty much a wilderness of volcanic rock which had overflowed Mauna Kea. "There's an old pathway," he said, "the Hawaiian kings built from here to North Kona for the runners, but most of that's gone. No, you'll have to drive eastward up the side of Mauna Kea, past the Parker Ranch, till you get on the road that goes through the Preacher and the McKay ranches. That road connects with the airport at Upolu Point, and Honoipu, and all the little towns around the tip below the ranch lands."

"But I came here that way," protested the Baron. "I do not desire to view the same country."

"Well, you'll have to." Mr. Berry rearranged his dominoes. "There's a little port at Puukohola for the McKay Ranch at the edge of South Kohala. You might get a boat there to take you down the coast. But all the boats at Puukohola belong to the McKay or Preacher people. Did you ever try dominoes?" he asked. "It's a very entertaining game."

"No doubt," agreed the Baron. "How far is South Kona from here by boat?"

"About two hours. We could have a game now, Baron, if you wanted to?"

"Ah—later, my dear Mr. Berry. You could rent me a boat, no?"

"For this afternoon?" Wearily Mr. Berry moved. "It's so hot. Oh well. It'll cost you fifteen dollars for the trip. Kau Nuapo has a fishing boat with a motor he sometimes rents. I'll phone him."

By three-thirty the little Japanese fishing boat chugged around the Kiholo Point. "There," said Kau Nuapo, pointing to the jagged black coast line, a fantastic mass of black rocks as far as the Baron could see. "South Kohala. We go back now?"

"Go in, please."

On this shore, from time immemorial, Mauna Kea had poured forth its steaming flows of lava. A few gnarled ohia trees and feathery silvery shrubbery grew between the twisted rocks, coiled where the molten stream had cooled, cindery and sharp edged. In the books the Baron had read of the lava flows; of that one in eighteen hundred and one which had carried away entire villages, hissing its way to the sea; of the flow in eighteen fifty-nine, and the greater one of eighteen forty-three, which had lit the night sky so that the natives in Maui and Oahu had thought the gods were returning to the Islands. These were the most recent flows, but many others had preceded them. The hot gush of lava had melted through the rocks, forming huge cavernous tunnels extending miles beneath the surface. Here, in these caverns, in times past, the chieftains had found refuge from their enemies and a resting place after death. The Baron climbed forward to the prow of the boat as it pushed in toward the coast.

Forty feet or so from the shore line Kau Nuapo refused to continue in. "Too dangerous," he said. "Rocks very sharp." A second time he pointed. In the translucent depths huge rocks lifted to the surface. For many minutes the Baron gazed at the coast. Where the sea had washed upon the land, the volcanic rocks had gradually disintegrated, forming a loose gravel, a black sand beach. It was the first black sand the Baron had ever seen. Finally he gave Kau Nuapo the signal to return, then lay on the canvas-covered cabin deck and felt the sun rays warm him. Now and then he smeared his body with coconut oil. The sloshing of the waves, the murmuring breeze, put him to sleep. He was aroused once by Nuapo's excited cries of,

"Shark! See shark!" and sleepily rolled to his side and saw the black fins slitting through the water and then went to sleep again. He didn't awaken until the fishing boat landed.

Downstairs in the inn, during dinner, Mr. Berry came to the Baron's table. "Have a nice trip?"

The Baron nodded.

"Catch any fish?"

The Baron shook his head.

"Lots of good fish around here, Baron. Best black marlin fishing in the world." With that Mr. Berry wandered to another table and joined an old friend who had driven in from Hilo and was planning to take the airplane tomorrow from Upolu Point to Honolulu. This friend also stood up when the Baron pushed his chair back from the table. More or less by chance, the three men met in the doorway of the lobby, and Mr. Berry, who was a sociable soul, said, "Baron, I want you to meet Mr. Jameson. This is the Baron von Kaz. Jameson lives in Honolulu, but he's been in Hilo to visit his sister. The Baron's here to absorb some of our atmosphere, Chris."

Jameson said how do you do, and the Baron bowed, and a little later, after Jameson had played a game of dominoes with his host, the Baron came downstairs and walked out upon the lawn.

Jameson told Mr. Berry that he'd have a look around before turning in.

"Well, young feller."

The Baron whirled.

"Jumpy, aren't you?"

The Baron said that he was never jumpy, that once in Vienna he had been on the trail of a madman for three months, living in the same house with this madman, but his nerves were always comparable to steel.

"That's fine," said Jameson, sitting on a rock and looking toward the water. "Because as soon as I got in the place

I got jumpy. I know it isn't reasonable, but I keep wondering if we're as smart as we think we are. If that one—" here he gestured with his head toward that long ascent behind him and the Baron understood that the detective was thinking of those people on the ranches—"if that one happened to guess what we're planning, it wouldn't be very far to come down here." There was a period of silence while Jameson chewed on his cigar. "No sir. I don't mind guns. They make a noise. But air pistols aren't natural."

"Ach," said the Baron in a superior fashion. "You must be as I am. I am without nerves. I am a brave man."

"Well, well." Jameson hunched forward. "That's nice. I've given you three days. Learn anything?"

"Do you know what a feather coat is?"

"Feather coat? You mean cloak? Like the ones they've got in the Honolulu museum?"

"Exactly."

"Sure. What about it?"

"Are there many in the Islands?"

Jameson threw his cigar over the rocks. "Three or four, maybe. All in museums. Old Saka Okyo used to think there were more, but I never listened to him. Why?"

"What would you do, my dear Mr. Christian Jameson, if I informed you that in all probability the feather cloak belonging to Prince Puakini—" In the darkness he smiled modestly. "I have an excellent memory. Prince Puakini. What would you do if I told you his feather cloak was hidden in one of the caverns of South Kohala?"

Jameson whistled. His head bent toward the man in the shadows like a curious old crane spying out a bit of food. "South Kohala, hey?" Then he asked, "Know anything about those ranches up on the slopes of Mauna Kea, Baron? Most of them, like the McKay, and Preacher, and Parker, and Von Stoltz lands, go all the way down to the coast. Wonder if Berry's got a map? We might take a look, hey?"

11

Disturbed Charade

"See here." Jameson pointed at the map of Hawaii spread out on the Baron's writing table. He squinted through his glasses. "These are the division lines, Baron. The Parker and Von Stoltz ranches come in along the north coast. Then right here is the McKay Ranch south of Kawaiahae, and next to that the Preacher Ranch. Both in South Kohala."

He sat down in the chair, next stood, pulled the bamboo blinds at the windows. "I don't like an open window behind my head," he explained, again sitting down. "Now, what about this feather cloak, hey?"

The Baron was walking around the room, his toes touching the floor first, noiselessly, and then his heels, the movements melting effortlessly into one. "There can be no doubt," he declared. Jameson merely grunted, and if he knew he was being observed he made no gesture, gave no indication that he was supposed to applaud the remarkable deductive powers of the brave Baron von Kaz.

"No doubt at all," repeated the Baron, frowning at Christian Jameson. "Do you understand, my dear sir? The plaque contains a map or a diagram locating the lava cavern where this Prince Puakini is buried."

Jameson crossed his legs. "That's what I guessed from what you said, Baron. What I want to know is, what makes you think so?"

"A number of reasons, if you please. All developed the final conclusion which should now be obvious to one of even average perception."

"Why not cut the fancy talk?"

Instead of becoming angry, the Baron grinned, sat down on the bed. "If you wish, my dear—"

"Make it 'Chris,' Baron. Forget this 'my dear Mister,' and you know damn well you only tack on that Christian because it riles me."

"So?" The Baron walked over to the astonished detective, formally shook hands with him. "And you may have the privilege of calling me 'Franz.'" He reseated himself on the bed. "Except, of course, when we are with other people."

"Well, that's nice," observed Jameson, conscious that in some funny foreign way the Baron thought he was being especially kind. "All right, Franz, go ahead."

"Very well, ah—Chriz." The Baron nodded his head. "First, let us consider the plaque. You have it." Jameson unwrapped the oiled paper covering the soapstone plaque. "You notice the cavity is small. Now I have asked myself, what can be hidden in such a small space that is of such value? Mr. Hiroshita told me it was a map, and a map would fit into the space very nicely. Mr. Tuung did not trust me. His lie was not at all plausible. Have you ever studied lies?"

"I don't get you."

"Lies," digressed the Baron with the air of a connoisseur, "are most successful when they are based on a groundwork of truth. Then, because the liar is telling that which is merely an exaggeration, not a complete fabrication, he does not have to depend entirely upon his imagination. His lie has the semblance of truth. You comprehend?" he inquired politely.

"I'm listening."

"Furthermore, my dear sir, what else besides a map or a diagram could fit into this small space and still represent untold value? That is a second point which, fitted to Mr. Hiroshita's partial lie, convinced me that the content of the plaque was a map."

There was a soft sighing sound outside, and both men looked startled. Then the Baron sprang quietly to the door, unlocked it, pushed it open a fraction of an inch and returned to the bed after locking it. "One of the maids vacuum cleaning. It is nothing. You should not be so nervous."

"Nervous hell," stated Jameson, lighting his cigar. "*I* didn't go to the door, did I?"

"The maids do much of their work after dinner when it is cool." The Baron gave this observation casually, as if to explain that there was nothing unusual in a maid being outside. "You agree concerning the plaque, no?"

"From the first," announced Jameson, "I always said you were a smart feller, Franz." Eying the door uncomfortably, he shifted his chair so that he was partially protected by the chiffonier.

"Thank you." The Baron appreciated praise. He thrived upon praise and when flattered he would stretch and arch his back and cock his head and go through all the tricks that he had. "The third point is then, of what is the map? In Lahaina, I had come to the conclusion that the map was in some way connected with the Islands, or why was it brought here at such risk? The focal center was the Islands, but what island? Mr. Kohler was from the island of Hawaii. Mr. Hiroshita had obtained the map from Okyo who had worked with Mr. Kohler in Hawaii. Okyo's father was an archaeologist, and as an archaeologist he certainly would be interested in this island of Hawaii, which, from what I have learned, still contains more relics and legends of the old days than any other island."

Jameson flicked his cigar. "You are a smart feller, Franz."

"Naturally." The Baron nodded, returned to the subject. "And, my dear sir, is not Mr. Sargent engaged to a girl whose ranch is on Hawaii? Does not Mr. Preacher return to his own ranch on Hawaii? Mr. Bolton, because of his connections with Mr. Preacher, could also be said to be attached to Hawaii, at least as far as our arguments are concerned." He paused. "And the plaque is now being sent to Hawaii, since Miss Miquet is here. It would be a coincidence, perhaps, if only there were one or two connections with the island of Hawaii; but six, my dear sir, cannot be entirely coincidences. And if they all come to Hawaii, and the map follows them to Hawaii, does that not narrow the limits of what the map might represent?"

"Might at that," agreed Jameson.

"In other words, my dear sir, it is hardly conceivable that it is the map of—let us say—the lost city of the Tarb. No, because we here are not concerned with something on the other side of the world. Is that correct?"

"Well, you're using a kind of far-fetched example—"

"Agreed. But the reasoning, if you please?"

"All right."

"Good!" The Baron impatiently snapped his fingers. "Then I wished to know what in Hawaii could be hidden of great value. If we were in the West Indies, the answer might be Spanish gold. Or lost treasure. But we are not hunting for a thing uncommon. Not at all, my dear sir. Who had the map first? Saka Okyo. What information could he obtain which would necessitate a map? He worked on the McKay Ranch. He would be familiar with the adjoining ranches, such as the Preacher Ranch. From his father he would have heard of the legends about the Hawaiian kings. Old Saka Okyo, better than anyone else, might well have obtained definite information concerning the location of the burial caverns. Let us make a supposition: let us extend this supposition and then see if the facts we have support the supposition."

"Go ahead, Franz."

"Old Mr. Okyo tells his son the location of the burial cavern of Prince Puakini. This cavern is on the Preacher Ranch. That means that young Okyo cannot get to it without trespassing and being discovered. He tells Mr. Kohler but refuses to give to Mr. Kohler the exact position. Mr. Kohler is aware that he has the chance to gain an enormous fortune. You yourself, my dear Chriz, told me how he boasted of the fortune he was about to possess. So we must assume that young Okyo was able to offer Mr. Kohler proof of the existence of the burial cavern and proof that he knew the location."

Jameson waved his cigar. "You don't have to explain so damn much. Of course, or the rest wouldn't 've happened."

"So. Mr. Kohler is clever. He is the manager of the McKay Ranch. That may be why Okyo approached him. I have not yet had the opportunity to question Miss McKay as to how Mr. Kohler maneuvered her into buying—"

"Hell, she was in love with him once. That's easy. Go on."

"Ach, so. As manager, then, he buys three thousand acres. Why?" Here the Baron jumped up. "Because somewhere in those three thousand acres is the burial cave. But Mr. Kohler has overreached himself, either in buying the land or in making love. Saka Okyo, angry at the man, becomes involved in a fight with him, then leaves for Mexico. Mr. Kohler takes several trips to Mexico, undoubtedly in an effort to find Saka Okyo, and finally learns, perhaps from Okyo himself, that the map has been sold to Okyo's compatriot, Mr. Hiroshita." The Baron lit a cigarette. "What do you think, my dear Chriz?"

"I think you have hit it smack on the nail." Jameson put his tobacco-stained thumb on the map of South Kohala.

"Somewhere there is a burial place containing Prince Puakini's feather cloak. I remember hearing about the Prince
when I was a young man. He was a regular hellbender,
according to all stories. Why, by Jesus!" The old man was
excited. "Whoever gets that cloak has a fortune in his
hands. There can't be five of them in existence. Any European collector could sell it over there for damn near a
million in American money." The detective's lantern jaws
waggled at the thought. Then the dancing cigar quieted. "Here's what we've got, then. Saka Okyo tells Kohler
about the feather cloak, Kohler makes love to Mary McKay
and gets fired. Saka scrams to Mexico, disgusted with the
whole plan or maybe afraid to take any more risks. All
right." He sucked on his cigar. "Kohler tries to find Saka
and get the plan. At the same time, Hiroshita butts into
the mess and does find Saka Okyo and get the plan. And
. . . Kohler realizes that Hiroshita now has the button—"

"Pardon?" inquired the Baron.

"Button, button, who's got— I forget, you're a foreigner. Kohler learns that your former client has the plan. So
far so good. Hiroshita hires you to get him safe to the
Islands. Now comes the tough part. Did John Sargent get
wind of the map showing where the feather cloak is hidden
on Mary's ranch, deliberately go North in order to meet
her and get himself engaged to her? Or did Jeff somehow
hear about the feather cloak and come back to try to find
that cave that had been on his property? Or—your third
alternative, Baron: Did Bolton somehow get wise to the
whole affair while he was staying at the same hotel in San
Francisco where Kohler stayed; or while he was on the
boat? And—if he did, is he working for himself or with
Jeff?"

The Baron gave the detective a long, level glance. "One
more possibility, if you please. A dreadful, unnatural possibility. Mr. Kohler was in love with Miss McKay, no?

Could he have been imprudent? Could he have let her suspect what he was seeking? Could he have given her, not all the facts, but enough to persuade her to purchase the three thousand acres so the cave with the feather cloak would be on her property? Miss McKay does discharge Mr. Kohler! And she does go to the mainland, where she becomes engaged to a gentleman who lives in Mexico who already knows—"

"See here!" Jameson stood up, his spectacles quivering indignantly on his old beaklike nose. "I can't allow you—"

"Please be seated," said the Baron coldly, and Jameson did sit down. "She becomes engaged to this gentlemen who is a friend of Mr. Kohler."

"You're all wrong," shouted Jameson, "and I'll tell you why. We people on the Islands ain't murderers. Besides," he exclaimed triumphantly, "if Mary did know that feather cloak was on the McKay Ranch, she didn't have to do any killing to get it. If she finds the cloak, the half million dollars are hers." Like a crane nodding, Jameson exhibited his satisfaction.

"So?" asked the Baron mildly.

"Yes sir. That shows you're—"

"But does she own all the ranch, if you please?"

"Hey?"

"Does not Billy share the greater part?"

"Billy—"

"And would not the greater share of the feather cloak money thus come to him?" demanded the Baron. "What portion of the ranch does Billy own?"

"I looked that up. He gets more'n I thought. He gets the whole damn ranch when he's twenty-one, and Mary gets an income of ten thousand dollars a year for life."

The two men stared at each other.

Finally the Baron asked, "And if anything should happen to—"

"Mary inherits it."

"And she would also receive full rights to whatever was found upon her land." The Baron smiled. "There, my dear sir, is your fourth possibility."

"By Jesus," muttered Jameson several times. Then, "If we could figure out who killed Kohler we might get somewhere without wasting time on a lot of damn fool possibilities. Everybody's alibying everybody on the Hiroshita shooting, and we haven't a chance on that. But with Kohler there must be some loophole. Start with—"

"If you please, facts. We know when Mr. Kohler was killed. We know that Miss Caryl Miquet was on B deck, if not at the moment he was shot, at least only a few minutes afterward. And we know that it would take at least five minutes for her to run from A deck to the amidship's stairway and out on B deck and down to the bar. We know that she was with Mr. Preacher. We know that: one, Mr. Preacher did not pass me on A deck, nor pass Miss Miquet on B deck—"

"Which fixes him," declared Jameson unhappily. "All right—"

"Pardon," said the Baron. "We know that Mr. Sargent had been dancing. However, I did not see him come to A deck. He might have killed Mr. Kohler, but if he escaped by running toward the front of the ship, would not Miss Miquet have seen him?" The Baron hadn't forgotten that it was Sargent who had advised Caryl Miquet not to meet him on A deck at midnight.

"Hey? Maybe he stayed on A deck."

"Very well. We will say that he had the opportunity—a slight opportunity—to do the killing. Mr. Bolton is next. We do not know what he was doing. We have learned that he was acquainted with Mr. Kohler. But Mr. Kohler was laughing. I heard Mr. Kohler laughing. Of all the people connected with the case, the two least inclined to make anyone laugh would be Mr. Hiroshita, who is killed, and Mr. Bolton. Neither is gifted with humor. Neither is joyous. Ah no; it is difficult for me to believe that Mr. Bolton ever could persuade anyone to laugh. However, I am willing to admit that it is a flimsy reason for saying he did not kill Mr. Kohler."

"That's all?"

"Miss McKay, if you please. She was dancing, yes. But there were periods when she was not dancing."

"By Jesus! She wouldn't hurt a fly. It's one of the men. Who did it?"

"Not so loudly, please." The Baron gripped Jameson's arm. "I have but one faint indication. It is like a twig which your North American redskins employed to point the way toward the right path."

Jameson practically swallowed his cigar before he finally observed that people had been hung on twigs before and what the hell did the Baron mean by a twig?

"Ach, so." The Baron glanced at the green lizard which had crawled in through the three-inch ventilation slit above the door. "However, if you please, my twig is different. I cannot employ my twig as proof; the first indication that I have a twig, and then I would find that twig destroyed, just as Mr. Kohler and Mr. Hiroshita were destroyed. Do you understand?"

"I'll be damned if I do."

The Baron shrugged, went to the door and closed the ventilator. "I am profoundly sorry."

"I want to know what you mean by a twig."

"Ach, but I have told you."

Jameson removed his glasses, polished them. "You're bluffing."

"So?"

"You don't know any more'n I do, Franz."

"No?"

"You won't tell me?"

"'Quid timeam ignoro; timeo tamen omnia demens.' That," said the Baron showing his sharp teeth in a grimace that resembled a modest little smile as much as a counterfeit kronen piece the genuine silver, "is Latin. It translates from Ovid, 'Why I fear I know not, but yet as one deprived—'"

"To hell with your Latin. If you won't tell, suit yourself. I don't think you have a twig or anything else." Jameson made as if to leave, got to the door, paused. "Look here, about that plaque. I've got everything arranged in Honolulu. The minute a parcel from Mexico addressed to Caryl Miquet reaches the post-office they notify me. We'll hold the parcel a day to get our ten men fixed in Kohala. Now that you've told me it's a map . . ." He thought for a moment. "What we can do is get the directions, have men planted right at the cavern. Then, if we don't see who lifts it from Caryl, we can spot whoever comes to the cavern for the cloak and other things. I wish to God the seventeenth would come. I don't like this waiting."

"Permit me to repeat," said the Baron, "that I dislike your plan, You and Miss Miquet overruled me in Lahaina. It places her in too great danger."

"Danger hell! When she gets the parcel, she's to leave it lying in plain sight. Gives whoever's done the murders every chance to swipe it. Not until it's gone will she say anything. Then, when we corner the lot, we'll have her out of the way. It's perfectly safe. However . . ." He paused, regarded the Baron. "Unless you want to tell me?"

The Baron shook his head. "I would if it would do any good. You do not understand. What steps have you taken regarding the air pistol?"

"Haven't been able to do any searching, Franz. You know that."

"In Vienna . . ." said the Baron, and while Jameson impatiently shifted from one foot to the other, the Baron took a good ten minutes to relate how he had discovered the secreted Marchetti documents when everyone else had failed to find them. "However," he declared, "even if I had a chance to visit the McKay Ranch, I should refuse. If I am Miss Miquet's mercenary to be hired for one thousand dollars, it is not suitable that I should mingle with her friends." When Jameson said nothing, the Baron glided to the writing table, whirled, shouted, "Do you comprehend? It is not suitable for the Baron Franz Maximilian Karagôz von Kaz, decorated by the hand of the great Emperor Francis Joseph for—"

"I never saw such, a feller," Jameson interrupted. "By Jesus! Stomping away from Lahaina. Making me drive Miss Miquet back to her hotel and ducking out with your baggage before her friends saw me. What's the matter with you anyway?"

"You, my dear sir," sullenly observed the Baron, "are a dolt."

"You're a smart feller, but with women I'd say you're a damn fool. Besides, you act plenty jumpy here, fifty miles off from that air pistol."

"I jumpy? My dear sir, do you question the bravery of a Von Kaz? Why, if it would not demolish our plans, I would this very night stealthily enter both ranch houses and search for the pistol. Of course the risk in being caught is considerable. Yes, it would be most unwise to jeopardize our procedure for, my dear sir, in so doing—"

"Good night. You need some sleep," said Jameson. "I'm leaving at seven tomorrow morning. I'll telephone you when"—he realized that he was in the corridor—"when our friend arrives. Take care of yourself."

The Baron slammed his door shut.

Should he this very night prove to the Honolulu detective that he was not afraid of an air pistol? Should he leave now for the ranches? In his imagination he pictured himself, disregardful of all personal danger, entering the rooms of three sleeping men, searching their clothes, the drawers in the furniture, the closets, even slipping his hand under the pillows their heads rested upon! Then only if the pistol were not in these three rooms would he search among Miss McKay's belongings. And he was sure the pistol would not be far from one of the four. If he were only certain which one! True, he had a twig pointing to the right one, but he wished it were more substantial than a twig: a limb or a tree. And from Mary McKay his thoughts logically centered on Caryl Miquet. And then he knew that no matter how much he might wish to impress Jameson, no matter if his honor were insulted, he would not enter the house where Miss Miquet was unless he were invited as an equal.

Thus relieved of the terrible possibility of seeking that pistol, having satisfied his belief in his bravery, he undressed. And as he undressed he thought of something else. He covered his shoulders with the shabby dressing gown and wrote a note:

> *Dear Chris Jameson:*
> *I am enclosing the money Mr. George Tuung gave to me as a retainer to obtain the plaque. Inasmuch as I was informed that this money came from very poor people in Honolulu, I suggest that, after the plaque has arrived and I have departed for Vienna, you see the money is returned.*
> *Franz Maximilian*

Instead of ringing for a boy, the Baron, because he felt that his bravery had been impugned once that night, cautiously passed down the dark corridor, entered the lobby, where he gave the Chinese night clerk the letter to be delivered to Mr. Jameson tomorrow morning. And if the Chinese night clerk thought it strange that a guest should come down to the lobby in night clothes and carrying a green umbrella, it was, after all, no stranger than why he should come to the lobby in the first place when all he had to do was ring a bell for a boy. It was midnight. Leaving instructions that he wasn't to be awakened until noon, the Baron went back to his room, looked into the adjoining bathroom to make certain no one had slipped in, locked and bolted the door and finally, as an added precaution, closed the two windows and locked them, preferring a stuffy room to the fear of a winged dart shot from a silent air gun. The Baron had intended to sleep late. Unfortunately for this intention, next morning at nine-thirty a blue-jacketed Japanese knocked timidly on the Baron's door, saying that Miss Mary McKay was on the telephone and would he come downstairs, please? At the Kona Inn there were no telephones in the bedrooms. . . .

"That's a shame," sympathized Mary McKay next afternoon. "First we didn't know you were on Hawaii until John read in our weekly paper that you were among the guests at Kona Inn. And as soon as you come you sprain your leg."

The others were on horseback, waiting for Mary. The McKay Ranch was situated on the west slope of Mauna Kea, about eight thousand feet high. From the lanai of the main ranch house the Baron could look down twenty miles until the highlands changed from a brownish-green to black where the eighteen fifty-nine lava flow had raged north across the lowlands into the sea. Now he limped to the steps. Mary could see how brave and noble he was despite the pain. The poor man had slipped on one of the rugs just after lunch, but he hadn't complained at all. Her heart was quite touched. He was such a modest, unassuming person, not at all the conceited braggart her cousin had cast him to be.

He bowed and gracefully bent over her hand, and Mary was so affected that she failed to notice that he was sighting past her, to that slim figure on horseback talking to two men. "Do not trouble yourself," he murmured. "I was a complete dolt. Ach, so clumsy. I offer you ten thousand apologies."

"Perhaps tomorrow we could plan on going for another ride if your leg doesn't pain you? You must stay over Sunday."

"I should enjoy that." He lifted his left leg, remembered quickly and lifted his right and rubbed it. "With so charming a hostess it soon will be recovered." His lower jaw was held well back now, and when he smiled and the lights went on in his blue eyes, she considered that he was really almost handsome.

Jackson, the McKay manager who had taken Carl Kohler's place, came in sight, leading two horses. "All ready, Mary," he called.

"All right, Jackson." She sprang lightly on her horse and noticed Billy, who was standing near the house. "Billy," she ordered severely, "you're not to bother the Baron. He has hurt his leg." She smiled at the Baron. "Don't let him trouble you. And, Baron, Mr. Bolton said he might drive here later in the afternoon, so maybe you'll have company."

Billy fidgeted impatiently until the horses cantered down the road, and then he grinned shyly at the Baron. "I suppose with that sprained leg you won't want to see my castle, will you?"

"Billy," the Baron assured him, "I would be sad if I thought you were going to hide it from me."

"Well, it's a secret. I'm going to s'prise them after it's finished."

"You have the word of a Von Kaz that it shall be held as a deep and dark secret."

"Let's hurry, then," exclaimed Billy eagerly.

Remembering to produce a convincing limp, leaning heavily on his green umbrella, the Baron followed the boy to the rear of the ranch house, through one of the pasture gates and up the incline. Finally Billy halted near a clump of kiawe trees, put his finger to his lips, said, "Sh-h-h," glanced around and then ran behind the trees.

Here was a little hollow. In this hollow Billy proudly showed the Baron his great work of constructing a castle. With the aid of a small tin shovel he had dug two trenches. "These are going to be the walls," he explained loftily. The Baron examined this mighty excavation seriously.

"Ach, so. Excellent."

"I'm going to have a porkullis here."

"Pardon, a—"

"What you said. A porkullis. With fifty men."

"So. Very good. A porkullis."

"These here"—he pointed to a few twigs—"they're the cannons. I haven't mounted them yet. Hanako promised me his old revolver, but he lent it to one of the boys at Puuo, so I have to use the sticks until Hanako gets off Sunday."

"Sticks are far better," the Baron advised him firmly.

"I thought maybe you'd have a real revolver or gun or something," Billy wistfully suggested.

"A gun? But I never have need of a gun."

Billy leaned on the shovel. "You said you killed a thousand men—"

"So I did. It was in the war. The regiment was chasing us through a pass, and we blew up the pass, and I received a medal. The noise was magnificent."

"Well, I could get a real gun without waiting for Hanako." Billy began to dig, continuing mysteriously, "But
that's a secret. It's a joke. I'm not supposed to know. Do
you like jokes?"

"Not with guns." The Baron again objected to a real
gun, insisting that sticks were much better, and then asked
if the boy planned to work all afternoon.

"Gee, I've got to, Baron. I want to finish by tomorrow.
I've told Aunt Caryl and Mr. Preacher and Mr. Sargent
about coming up here when I finish so we can celebrate.
Mary's going to make a flag for me." He added, "You can
come too, if you wish. But don't tell Bolton. I don't like
him very well."

The Baron declared that he was honored, and after he
was convinced that Billy would be occupied for the afternoon he returned toward the ranch house. The Hawaiian
cowboys were in the fields. The Baron saw that the majority of the servants were gathered in the two servants' houses, in the rear of the ranch house proper, where they usually slept during the afternoon or played Chinese gambling
games. He hobbled along the gravel lane to the white guest
house built on a knoll fifty yards or so from the ranch
house. Here he paused to pat two great police dogs, tossed
his cigarette away and went inside. In thirty minutes he
had completed his examination of the baggage Jeffrey
Preacher had brought with him for over the weekend; and
the two grips and trunk belonging to John Sargent. After
carefully glancing outside in all directions, privately be-
stowing his thanks on the person who had placed the guest
house on a small knoll, he took twenty minutes more to go
through the two rooms, but he failed to find the air gun.

Not forgetting to use his green umbrella as a cane, he
limped to the main ranch house. He knew that Mary and
Caryl had their rooms in the right wing. He went into the
kitchen first. An old Chinese woman was busy with her

baking. "You want dlink?" She reached for the rope which connected with a bell in the servants' quarters.

The Baron said that all he desired was a bottle of brandy.

"No have blandy." She opened a great cupboard, gave him a large, darkish bottle. "Maybe like okolehau?"

Recalling the night with George Tuung, the Baron visibly shuddered; however, he took the bottle and the proffered glass, found his way by many doors to the long, sunny living room which extended the full length of the ranch house.

He decided that no servant except the old cook could be in the house at this hour, nor would be likely to come in much before four-thirty. He felt the need of a drink, poured half a glass of okolehau, choked on it, placed the bottle and glass on the table and, peering toward the dining room and kitchen, suddenly vanished into that part of the house which contained Mary's rooms and that of her cousin. Because he frequently stopped and returned to the living room to make sure no one had entered, not until a few minutes before four had he satisfied himself that no Haenel air pistol was concealed in Mary McKay's rooms.

He had examined, then, the rooms and baggage appertaining to the two men and their hostess. Now the Baron, because of his Viennese training, and because of a strong feeling for self-preservation, was exceedingly thorough in his investigations. Therefore, partly by habit and partly owing to the fact that he was extremely desirous of having the weapon that had killed twice in his own keeping, he proceeded to enter into Caryl's room. If he had stopped to consider, he wouldn't have entered. But he wasn't thinking, at that moment, of Caryl as a person. His mind was totally absorbed in this search and in anticipating the possible entrance of one of the servants or, though he refused to dwell on this, the rightful owner of that gun.

Twelve minutes later, when he was standing in her closet, feeling her clothes brush him, sensing the faint perfume, clean and fragrant of hidden wood flowers, did he first appreciate the enormity of his conduct. He was standing on top toe. He had finished with her hat boxes. Now he was exploring with his finger tips the shelf itself. Automatically, in order to extend his finger tips to the wall, he had jumped upwards, caught his elbows on the shelf and in this uncomfortable position was completing what had been a routine matter of business.

And as his fingers touched something cold he knew that this was Caryl's closet, that she of all five was the one who could not be concealing the Haenel air pistol. But while his mind grasped this, his active fingers had grasped a round, tubelike piece of metal.

When the Baron silently dropped to the floor his right hand was holding the curiously exaggerated form of a revolver. It had a long barrel. Twice as long as the barrel of an ordinary revolver. The front half of the barrel was slender. The latter half was swollen, bulbous in outline. Incredulously he looked at it. He was so intent that he, the great Von Kaz who claimed the ability not only to hear but to smell a man, failed to heed the footsteps in the hallway. Not until the knob of the door turned did he jump, hastily shove the Haenel air gun up on the shelf, take one of the hats and back out of the closet, trying on the hat.

He didn't dare to look around. He could hear someone breathing. He shut the closet door. The outer part of the door was a mirror. He stood in front of the mirror, and behind him he saw a large, fat man with a head like a bloated cherub. "Oh, it is you?" He snatched off the hat. "I was practicing to surprise them with a charade when they came back from their ride, my dear Mr. Bolton. Perhaps you have seen it?" He adjusted the fragile hat on his head. "I am representing what bridge in Austria?"

"I've never been in Austria." Bolton removed his cigar. His voice was absolutely flat, neither amazed nor disturbed. "I'm a plain, simple man. I stayed in Paris most of the time." He inserted the black cigar, his colorless lips curling up around the cigar. "When I came in the cook said you were in Miss McKay's rooms, and I wondered what you were doing. Personally, I don't approve of charades. Some of them, I have been told, are highly immoral."

With that he blew out a cloud of smoke, turned his back on the Baron and walked off, his feet going down on the mats and coming up again like two padded plungers in a machine.

The Baron, grasping the hat in his hand, received his second shock when he heard a faint tapping on the window. Billy was grinning at him through the pane. Dropping the hat, the Baron stepped to the window to open it. Billy whispered, "Golly! I didn't know you were in on the joke too. I told you I was going to work on the castle so I could play being a detective and shadow you. You didn't know I was watching, did you? Wouldn't I make a keen detective?"

The Baron gathered enough of his wits to exclaim, "Lieber Augustin! what do you mean?"

"The joke on Caryl. Are you in it too? Don't worry, I won't tell. I guess I wasn't supposed to see, but this morning I was chasing my dog, and he ran by these windows and I saw— Psst! Duck!" The boy disappeared.

The Baron faced Bolton as he re-entered. He regarded the Baron unemotionally and finally asked, "Is part of the charade climbing out of the window?"

The Baron closed the window and smiled blandly. "Ach, you are very clever, Mr. Bolton. You have seen the charade, after all?"

Bolton said he hadn't. The two men went together to the lanai. And Bolton talked in his flat, hard voice about how nice it was in Paris and how maybe he'd like it over here, and how a fine, upstanding young boy like Billy required a tutor, someone to look after him; and, when the Baron casually said that he thought he'd take a little walk, Bolton replied that walks were very healthful and accompanied the Baron. The Baron gave up his idea of locating Billy until later, until he could rid himself of Bolton.

12

The Castle Gun

By the time the Baron had walked to the end of the lane with Bolton, recalled that he was lame and began to limp, leaning heavily on his green umbrella, and then sadly told the man that it was difficult to go much farther, half an hour had been wasted. The Baron suggested that Bolton continue on alone, but Bolton said no, he'd had enough of a walk, and the two retraced their steps together.

They returned to find the rest of the house party drinking cocktails after their ride. There were sympathetic questions concerning the Baron's leg, and he replied that the leg was better; and Bolton asked the Baron in a loud, flat voice when he would give the charade.

The Baron, glass in hand, was edging away from the living room, hoping to escape gracefully. But Bolton's announcement that the Baron had been in Miss Miquet's bedroom getting ready for a charade was like a thunderclap smacking into a warm, still, sultry night, bringing the occupants of the room up out of their chairs, their faces expressing a gamut of emotions running all the way from polite incredulity that the Baron would have the impertinence and ill breeding to enter a lady's bedroom, to bewilderment, as reflected by Caryl's lifted eyebrows and half-amused, half-embarrassed laugh, to outright anger.

The Baron was in for a bad forty minutes. He was forced to forego his plan to find Billy. He explained, gesticulated, smiled, laid himself out to be charming and confused, hinted that he'd had nearly a bottle of okolehau, assured Caryl loudly that the idea had entered his stupid head and he had gone for her hat without thinking, and so on and so forth, and all the time these people in the room held only a surface interest for him while he considered the chances of seeing Billy, unobserved, directly after dinner.

When John Sargent, Jeffrey Preacher, and Bolton finished their drinks and started for the guest house to dress for dinner, the Baron lagged behind, pouring himself another drink in the hope that Billy might enter. But Mary said, smiling, "You've had your share, Baron. You run along and get dressed." And Caryl agreed that that was an excellent idea. Dinner would be served promptly at seven, and the Baron had best hurry.

So the Baron locked his room door, preferred to go without a shower than to leave his room to take one, shaved rapidly, dressed and, armed with his umbrella, which owing to his lameness he could not be without, came with the other men to the ranch house for dinner. Here, with great casualness, he asked if Billy were not going to eat. Mary said Billy had a light meal at night in his room. Red poi and breadfruit were served among other dishes, and Caryl wanted to know what the Baron thought of these native delicacies. The poi was a sourish thin paste. He gagged, observed blandly that it was delicious and thereafter left his dish of poi untouched. The breadfruit, however, was satisfactory. The Baron thought to himself that if he were placed alone on a desert island, after starving for four or five days he might eat breadfruit providing there was ample champagne to wash it down.

He did accomplish one thing during the five-course meal: by spacing his questions, by advancing with what he complimented himself on being the utmost dexterity, he learned three facts which he believed might prove of value.

The two cousins, Mary and Caryl, had played tennis for what remained of the morning after their late breakfast, ordering the men to leave them alone. The tennis court was near the swimming pool, several hundred yards from the ranch house, shielded from the house by high, blooming shrubs and vines.

John Sargent claimed that he had slept the greater part of the morning on the hikiee, a huge square couchlike affair composed of layer on layer of incredibly soft woven mats.

And, as they were leaving the table, Caryl mentioned to the Baron that he should have been here in the morning; if he didn't play tennis he could have gone for a ride with Jeffrey, before he hurt his leg, of course. And a few minutes after coffee was served in the living room the Baron overheard Jeffrey telling Mary what he thought of the horse he had tried that morning, going on to say that he'd left at eight and had ridden toward the Summit, a volcanic cone five thousand feet or so high, which was below the ranch house, the McKay ranch house being nearly eight thousand feet above sea level

These facts, then, more or less placed the four suspects during the morning, when the air gun had been hidden in Caryl's room. Bolton, not having been on the party of the preceding night, had presumably stayed on the Preacher Ranch until after lunch.

The Baron was through with his coffee first, and when Mary asked him what he was looking for, the Baron said that he missed her charming little brother.

Mary laughed. "Billy has instructions not to bother the guests. He's supposed to read in his own rooms, although he's probably out playing with the cowboys in their bunkhouse. I'll be glad when it's time to send him to school."

"Ach, so? He has his own suite of rooms?" asked the Baron politely.

"Hardly a suite, Baron. We're not that luxurious. He has Dad's old den and bedroom in the back of the house."

John Sargent placed his cup and saucer on the floor, stretched comfortably in his chair. "He's of an age, Mary, that he should have an older, more responsible person looking after him."

"Yes, darling," said Mary, without other comment.

"I don't think these Hawaiians and half-breeds are the kind to trust a growing boy with." John glanced across the room at the fat, solid man standing patiently in the half darkness at the side of the fireplace. "Do you, Bolton?"

"I couldn't say," replied Bolton. "I'm just a humble, plain man. And Mr. Preacher was so thoughtful and considerate—when he was a boy—that even an uneducated person like myself could raise him."

"Rats!" said Jeffrey softly to Caryl, grinned at Bolton and told him with a rough sort of kindness for God's sake to sit down and relax.

The Baron yawned, said he thought he might step outside for a little air. He picked up his green umbrella, limped through the door and waited on the lanai for a few minutes, then quietly went down the steps, intending to go to the back of the house and find Billy. But he halted when he heard the door open, and his feeling of irritation disappeared when he saw who it was.

For that second or so, while Caryl was framed in the doorway, she was as a slender night flower in the pale green evening dress, her bare and bronzed shoulders rising out of the shimmering green to a face that had too much character and determination of its own ever to be called pretty. But the raven hair, parted in the middle, exposing a serene expanse of cool forehead, had hidden glints in it;

and, as the Baron stared at her, he knew, for him at least, that she was the most beautiful woman he had ever seen.

She called to Jeffrey, "Coming? The Baron's here, and it's a perfectly grand night."

She sat down on the first step, tucking in her billowing skirts. "When are you going to produce this famous charade, Baron?"

He didn't know whether she was laughing at him or not. He replied with great seriousness that he was not in the mood for charades this evening. Somewhere below them Hawaiian cowboys were passing, thrumming gently on guitars; the stars twinkled low in that purple expanse; the breeze brought soft scents to the ranch house, and far away a dog yelped uneasily and was still. The Baron looked down those twenty miles toward a sea that glimmered darkly and faded into the horizon of night. Caryl commented that the stars seemed so near that she could reach and pluck one for her hair. The brave and gallant Baron pretended to do so, hooking one with his umbrella, and when his fingers touched the thick, silky hair she turned her face to him, shadowed, laughing a little, but softly; and then her cool fingers momentarily rested on his cheek as he drew her head to him and felt for the mouth with all the clumsiness of a cadet doing such a thing for the first time.

"Sorry!" exclaimed Jeffrey awkwardly, standing above them, both hands holding a tray with glasses. "I'm clumsy as hell." He started into the house.

"Don't be an absolute idiot." Caryl stood. "I thought you were acquainted with all the Hawaiian customs by now. What have you for me?"

"Your favorite. Rum and pineapple juice with lots of ice." He handed her a glass, gave another to the Baron. Then he took his, setting the tray on the step. He lifted his glass. "How about me too, Caryl, on this old Hawaiian custom business?"

As he approached her she raised her arm to taste her drink, and her elbow came against Jeffrey's chest. "You're a Kamaaina. That lets you out."

The Baron peered at his watch. It was a little after eight-thirty. He wondered at what time young American boys went to bed. He replaced his watch and sat beside Caryl and glumly listened to Caryl and Jeffrey bicker and tried vainly to think of a plausible excuse to leave these two and steal to the boy's rooms. Mary came to the door and asked, "Caryl, have you seen Billy?"

Caryl said she hadn't.

"Oh dear." Mary sighed. A younger brother was a great tribulation to a sister who was engaged. "I went in to tell him to go to bed, and he wasn't there."

Without realizing it, the Baron was standing.

Caryl got up. "Sit down, Baron. I'll bring you another glass as soon as I help Mary find that little devil. He hates to go to bed, and he's always running off at bedtime. Another drink for you, Jeff?"

Jeffrey said, "Please." The Baron offered to accompany Caryl, but she reminded him of his disability.

Jeffrey was telling the Baron about his new life on the ranch, and the Baron listened with one ear, adding monosyllabic comments. Then, "You will operate your ranch, my dear Mr. Preacher?"

"Me? Lord, no. I've got a wise old Scotchman to do that. McCabb. He's losing enough money without my help. Not that he isn't smart." Jeffrey laughed. "The old rascal managed to sell Mary three thousand acres of no good coast land."

"To Miss McKay?"

"No, not exactly," admitted Jeffrey. "To a chap named Kohler; he was running her ranch then. She doesn't interfere with the business end any more than I plan to do with my ranch. And I'm afraid McCabb was too good for Kohler—"

"Kohler? But not the Carl Kohler—"

"On board ship. That was the one. You knew him?" The Baron shook his head. "I first met him at the Mark Hopkins' in San Francisco, just before we sailed. I thought he was pretty much of a pig, myself. Doesn't compare with Jackson, the fellow Mary has now. But Bolton liked Kohler. Damned if I know," complained Jeffrey, "where Bolton picked him up."

Bolton, the Baron vividly recalled, had definitely stated that neither he nor young Jeffrey had ever met Mr. Kohler. Jeffrey meanwhile rambled on unheedingly, giving an anecdote about his man McCabb who had gone pig hunting and had shot a prize cow instead. John Sargent and Bolton came onto the lanai. Bolton saw the Baron. "When are you going to give us your charade, Baron von Kaz?"

The Baron didn't have to reply, because the two girls appeared. Mary was worried. "He's not with the cowboys," she explained. "Haumanau says she saw him leaving Caryl's room about half an hour ago with a gun, but there was no gun in Caryl's room. Haumanau's always thinking she's seeing things she isn't, but I wish Billy'd return. It's too late for him to be up."

"He's most likely playing cowboy in the corral," suggested Caryl. "That's where he was last night. I'll go and see.

Jeffrey said he'd go with Caryl. Bolton grunted that a boy Billy's age should be trained to be in bed half an hour before this and went into the house.

The Baron lit a cigarette. Then, picking up his umbrella, he vanished around the house. The old Hawaiian woman was in Billy's bedroom. She was surprised when she saw the Baron. He wasted a good fifteen minutes on her. She couldn't understand what he wanted, at first. She took him to the hallway, showed him Miss Miquet's room.

She'd seen Billy there. Then one of the Chinese boys entered and proceeded to help the Baron by interrogating the old Hawaiian in a loud, authoritative voice, wanting to be told why not are Master Billy to bed yet, showing all of his English and manners and knowledge for the guest's helpless benefit. When finally the Baron had managed to quiet the Chinese servant and again began to question the woman, he at last learned that Billy had run out with a gun. And when he asked several hundred times what kind of a gun, she at last comprehended and measured with her hands. "Long gun. Funny gun. Billy bad boy, too late not to be in bed."

A long gun! Very clearly now the Baron realized what Billy had meant by "the joke." By accident Billy must have seen the Haenel gun, or enough of it to surmise that it was a gun, when it was brought into Caryl's room to be hidden. And Billy had seen who had carried the gun. And he had assumed that it was a joke, an incomprehensible adult joke. But he needed a gun. So Billy had taken it. Billy had taken it.

The Baron cried out aloud, to the manifest astonishment of the old Hawaiian and the Chinese house boy. He leaped through the door. In the darkness, far away, he could hear Caryl calling, "Billy! Billy!" and, from greater distances, other voices. The cowboys were seeking the runaway youngster now, too. Their soft calls and whistles came to the Baron's ears as he pushed through the clinging vines and bushes, and after he left the ranch grounds proper and reached the incline above the ranch he ran faster than he ever could remember running uphill before.

When he topped the long rise, he panted, pausing to get his bearings. On the opposite knoll, he made out an obscure feathery mass which he knew was the kiawe trees. He raced down the hill, stumbling once and sprawling his full length. When he finally reached the kiawe trees he

called, "Billy! Where are you, Billy? It is the Baron." Then
he stood very still. He heard something. It came to him
faintly, as though someone down there behind the trees
might be caught or hurt and was trying to move, trying to
crawl back toward home and safety and shelter and a bed
where a sister was to draw up the covers and say, "Good
night," and turn off the light.

The boy was moving in the hollow behind the trees
when the Baron came to him. There was enough moonlight
in the sky to see the boy. He was pulling himself forward
with his hands, and his feet were trailing behind him,
limp, like those of a puppy who has been run over; and
when the boy lifted his face at the Baron's cry, the Baron
saw that the face was covered with blood. Near by was a
dented, bloody tin shovel. It was apparent that the shovel
had struck Billy, struck him above the nose, across the
forehead; struck through the skin with murderous ferocity,
even splintering the bone. The blood streamed into those
great eyes, blinding him; the blood covered the smudge
of freckles, and the boy was choking, crying in a faint,
high-pitched, terrified voice, digging into the dirt with
his hands, attempting to pull himself forward and each
time the hands moved so futilely, they moved more slowly.

Now the Baron had behind him years of experience. He
saw the shovel lying there. He saw the boy. And he should
have promptly called for help and remained there, touching nothing, bending closer to that small writhing object,
ordering the boy to use what breath he had to talk. By doing this the Baron would have most efficiently preserved
any possible clues; by forcing the boy to speak despite the
agony and fear closing in around him it is conceivable that
the Baron would have heard the name of the person who
had tried to kill Billy.

But the Baron, to his everlasting disgrace, did none of
this.

The Baron ruined a new flannel suit.

When he picked Billy up in his arms the suit gradually soaked red. Billy whimpered, clinging to the Baron, quivering; and the Baron, in a strange voice, a queer jovial voice, laughed, and instead of urging Billy to talk told him to keep quiet, that he wasn't hurt, that he was a great, brave lad and that there was nothing to fear. And the Baron, carrying Billy carefully in his arms, the green umbrella hooked awkwardly in the crook of his elbow, slowly walked past the kiawe trees, down the grade and up again, and although the ground was rough and pitted, Billy was carried in those arms as gently as though he were in his bed, and through that sickening pain, all through that greater horror of blackness which had filled him with such terror, he heard, ever more vaguely, the loud, cheerful voice of the Baron; a voice that made Billy realize nothing was wrong, that all boys have accidents. Ach lieber Gott! the voice was saying, are you to cry, my dear Billy? You who will build castles? Why, tomorrow, Billy, we shall build a castle a hundred times as big as the biggest castle a boy has ever built. What is a little hurt? Myself, I have fallen. I have cut myself. It is nothing, Billy. Lie still. Do not move. What would your sister say if she knew her brother had been crying? It is nothing. In a minute you will be in bed, and tomorrow—ach, tomorrow, Billy, we shall build great castles. Castles mounting to the sky, Billy. Sh-h-h, boy! To the sky with knights and barons and kings, even kings. . . . "Porkullis?" whispered Billy, then coughed, and the Baron held him close, swearing that in this castle there would be a hundred porkullises, ach, two hundred. . . .

Mary McKay left the guest house—Billy wasn't hiding in it and she was going to the bunk house to rout out all of the ranch help—when she heard a man coming down the mountain road behind the ranch. She knew it was the Baron because in that heavy, sweetish night she heard him saying words in German, and she knew what he was saying because long ago every night her old German nurse would repeat those words for her, and hearing them, Mary was frightened, and she ran.

Now this gentleman, the Baron von Kaz, a man of the most cynical sentiments as he would have you understand, a person without disgusting sentimentalities, was, perhaps without fully realizing how shamefully he was betraying all the modern philosophies with which he was inculcated, repeating a foolish and silly prayer, as if such a prayer could be of help. In truth, this can be said for the Baron, the prayer he was reciting was the only one he remembered, and as a prayer it was entirely out of place and unfitted for the occasion. And later, when he thought of this action, he steadfastly refused to admit that he had even recalled it.

"Is he hurt?" cried Mary.

"Ach, he feels it no longer," said the Baron.

During those forty-eight leaden minutes of waiting for the doctor's car to hurl him the thirty-two miles of mountain road, the Baron stood at the foot of the bed, leaning on his green umbrella, a graven wooden image. If he moved, no one saw him move. Only the blue eyes shone and showed signs of life.

The white sheet of the bed stained scarlet. The boy lay there. The Baron was watching the boy. He was watching Billy, and Mary and Caryl who were bending over Billy, ineffectually dabbing at his forehead, listening for his feeble breathing. Once or twice John had whispered to the Baron to leave the room; but the Baron didn't hear him. The den, next to the bedroom, had become crowded with hushed servants, ranch hands and cowboys. Jeffrey and Jackson, the ranch manager, had imposed absolute silence. They had supervised the heating of water, brought antiseptics and all the gauze and tape, and then stood helpless, looking into the bedroom at the two women, at the Baron, and at John who was watching the women and the Baron, and a feeling of desolation pervaded; the boy was so seriously injured that it was folly to touch him, to offer their poor help, lest what they should do would only hurt him all the more.

Once the boy stirred, cried shrilly, and then lay exhausted. Mary leaned over him and would have fallen upon him had not Caryl caught her, signaled to the Baron and John.

John carried her out of the room.

The Baron closed the door after John, again took up his post by the bed. His lips moved, "Dead?"

As if in a dream Caryl shook her head. "No." For the hundredth time she glanced at her watch. "If Dr. Saier would only come. Why can't he hurry?"

The sound of a car increased and expanded into a roar, and brakes screamed, and a small, efficient man, accompanied by a woman in a nurse's uniform, entered the room, sat beside the bed and opened his bag.

Half an hour later Dr. Saier stood up, washed his hands in the warm water Caryl had brought him, gave the nurse her directions, said that he couldn't promise anything: the boy might live through the night. If he did, he'd have a chance. It was a fracture. Billy couldn't be moved to a hospital. Without an X-ray it was impossible to discern whether the bones had splintered into the brain or not.

Aware for some time of that dark, inscrutable face staring at him across from the bed, the doctor drew Caryl into the den, now cleared of the servants, and asked who the man was. Billy must have absolute quiet. The man should be requested to leave the bedchamber at once. The nurse would do what little could be done; and later Caryl could go in, and perhaps Mary, if she could control herself.

John declared that he would go and bring the Baron out, but it was Caryl who went in, who motioned to the

Baron that he must leave now. And the Baron placed his lips to Caryl's ear, "It was not an accident. Billy knows who tried to kill him. If you love Billy, no one except the nurse must come near him. No one, until I can telephone for police protection. . . ."

The Baron closed the door softly behind him. For the moment the den was empty. The doctor and the men had gone into the living room where Mary was lying down. There was a telephone in the den.

In six minutes the Baron was put through to Honolulu. Cobb, Jameson's assistant, answered. Jameson wasn't in Honolulu. He had gone to the island of Kaui. He wouldn't return until sometime tomorrow. Concisely, the Baron related what had occurred. Cobb said he'd telephone Hilo; they'd have to take over from Hilo. . . .

Jackson, coming from the servants' quarters to the den, heard the Baron's voice at the telephone, stopped at the door long enough to understand what the Baron was implying, and rushed into the living room.

The Baron was completing his call when the door of the den again opened.

". . . and no one is to be allowed in the bedroom. No one. Tell the police that. I will stand guard until they arrive. Good."

He hung up, and John Sargent advanced into the den.

"Just what's the idea?"

The Baron absently patted his green umbrella. "The police should be here in two hours or sooner, my dear Mr. Sargent."

"The police!"

Those in the living room had followed John. With superb composure the Baron pulled a chair near Billy's door, sat on it, and then arrogantly demanded where each one, individually, had gone during the search.

Caryl heard the confused murmur of voices, slipped out of the bedroom, finger to lips. "Mary," she whispered, "go back and lie down."

John said that the Baron had called the police.

Caryl eyed John for a long minute, then said that it might be a very good idea. The Baron again repeated his question.

Caryl replied first, speaking in a voice just above a whisper, while the others, seemingly stupefied by the rapid shifting of events, held their silence.

Caryl had gone to the lane past the orchard after parting from Jeffrey in the corral. She had searched the lane as far as the old windmill and was there when the cowboys called, saying that Billy had been found.

Jeffrey spoke from the couch. In order to cover more territory he and Caryl had parted in the coral; he had taken the lower road, then retraced his path toward the tennis courts, where he encountered two of the cowboys, and they were heading for the corral to get horses to extend the search when Jackson joined them and they heard Mary call.

Jackson's face gradually grew redder and redder as he sensed that this foreigner was insulting Miss McKay and her guests. He stepped forward and informed the Baron that he had met Jeffrey, and furthermore, that he had also gone with Miss McKay and Mr. Sargent toward the south gate. And then he had returned with Miss McKay to the guest, house, where she went in and he headed for the corral, and on his way he had caught up with Mr. Preacher and two of the cowboys. A minute later they had heard Miss McKay call.

"So?" asked the Baron thoughtfully. "And you, my dear Mr. Sargent?"

John corroborated Jackson's story of meeting Mary and himself, said that he had continued on to the south gate.

He was the last one back to the house. The south gate was more than a mile from the ranch house.

Bolton was standing in the doorway. "I was here all the time," he said. "Where were you, Baron?"

The telephone call from the Hilo police interrupted the Baron's reply. John reached the telephone first. He had stated that there was no need for the police, explaining that the accident had overexcited one of the guests, when the Baron elbowed him to one side.

John lifted his fist, dropped it with a startled exclamation as a long sharp sword flashed from the green umbrella. Bolton saw the play of the sword, moved to Jackson and whispered, "Why, the man must be drunk or crazy, Mr. Jackson. The idea of threatening Mr. Sargent and getting so upset over an accident."

"He should get out of here," replied Jackson, troubled.

"I'm just a plain man, Mr. Jackson, but I do think he has no right to tell all those lies to the police at this time when everyone's so worried by young Master Billy's condition. And," continued Bolton, "look how he went into Miss Miquet's room. The man's really not safe, but it's hardly my place to do anything. I do hope you'll forgive me, Mr. Jackson—"

"Well, I'll do something," said Jackson grimly, and ran out toward the servants' quarters for help.

The Hilo police had been fully acquainted by Detective Jameson with the facts concerning the two murders, as the Honolulu police official required their assistance in preparing for the arrival of the plaque. The Hilo man, on the other end of the wire, assured the Baron that three plainclothes men were already on the way.

"Good!" The Baron replaced the receiver, very calmly inserted his sword into the green umbrella, stepped to Caryl and said loudly enough for all to hear, "No one, if you please, except the nurse, the doctor and yourself, must be permitted to enter Billy's room." Jackson reappeared with a husky Hawaiian cowboy. The doctor, fidgeting nervously, wondering if everyone was going crazy, urged Jackson to wait for God's sake and he, the doctor, would persuade the Baron to leave the room. "I'll get him away. I'm accustomed to crazy people in this country."

The doctor put his hand on the Baron's shoulder. "There's a friend of yours outside who wants to speak to you."

The Baron patted the doctor's arm. "Doctor, can the boy live? You will concern yourself with him, please. Not with me. I have no friends outside."

Jackson and the large Hawaiian took this opportunity to lunge at the Baron. Caryl jumped to interfere, but Bolton held her. The Hawaiian clamped his hand around the Baron's mouth. Sargent stepped close to the Baron, struck him very hard on the temple, and the Baron crumpled to his knees. Bolton released Caryl, apologizing for his actions. She faced John. "And you call yourself a gentleman?" Mary began to weep, not knowing what to do or to think, and in the bedroom the nurse listened to a small boy's irregular breathing grow slower.

13

Kona "Nightingale"

The next morning, about ten, the Baron was awakened in his hotel room at the Kona Inn by a boy hammering on the door saying that Mr. Jameson was telephoning from Honolulu.

The Baron got up, staggered downstairs, where he ordered an appalled Mr. Berry out of the office.

"Hello," said Jameson, "what the hell's happened?"

The Baron told him.

"I got in touch with the Hilo police," said Jameson testily. "They've placed the men at the ranch, but they say that the doctor claims it was an accident and want to know what they should do."

"It was not an accident."

"I hope to God it wasn't. You can get in more damn trouble."

"How is the boy?"

"The Hilo police say he's got a chance. They may try to fly him to the hospital. He—"

Jameson heard the sound of a crash. After a number of long minutes, while he impatiently swore, Mr. Berry's voice came into the phone, explaining that he had heard a crash and entered his office to find that the Baron had passed out. "The Baron was brought back early this morning very

463

drunk," said Mr. Berry. "I gathered he consumed too much okolehau while he was on the McKay Ranch."

"Oh, God Almighty," cried Jameson furiously, and hung up. The Baron was impossible. Jameson was sunk in work in Honolulu. The Hilo police could take care of the boy and search for the Haenel air pistol. If the Baron was drunk, the chances were that the kid had had an accident after all.

Along about four o'clock in the afternoon the Baron recovered consciousness. He undressed, sourly examined his bruised temple in the mirror and took a cold shower. Then he dressed, ordered a bottle of ice-cold champagne, and after four glasses began to feel as though he could last another few hours before the world would entirely collapse.

Jameson's assurance that the police were guarding Billy made him believe that the boy was safe from attack for the time being. The real danger of the murderer again attempting to kill the boy would come when and if the doctor definitely stated that he would live, and, if he lived, when Billy came out of his deathlike coma. The Baron knew that, with a seriously fractured skull, the boy might lie insensible for days, for even a week. For the boy's sake the Baron hoped that he would remain unconscious for many days, until the plaque arrived and the murderer was uncovered.

He closed his eyes, his hands under his chin. Billy had seen who had placed the gun in Caryl's closet. But—ach lieber Augustin! Why had the gun been placed in her closet? He knew that it wasn't Caryl's gun; he knew that she wasn't guilty. And then, as his mind began to stray around this question, his imagination visualized himself as this criminal.

He had the air gun. He had carried it with him to the McKay Ranch. On the boat, and in Honolulu, and now at the ranch, he could not be conspicuous by always carrying gloves with which to handle the gun. True, thought the

Baron von Kaz as he helped himself to more champagne in this effort to identify himself with the criminal, whenever he withdrew the gun from its hiding place, or returned it, he would wipe it to remove possible fingerprints; and also, when carrying it, he would have to be extremely careful, because it was long, bulky and awkward to conceal on his person.

And now, thought the Baron, suppose I learn that the greatest and bravest detective in all Europe is coming to this ranch? I do not fear this detective, ach, no. But I must be doubly cautious. Never can one tell. And if this great detective thinks I might have the air gun, must I not temporarily place the gun where he will not think of seeking for it? The Baron thumped the table, and above him, on the ceiling, a little green lizard was so frightened by the noise that he nearly dropped his tail.

My dear Franz, he told himself, now no longer playing the murderer, you are a dolt. A triple dolt. You have not concealed your feeling for Caryl Miquet. Have not Mary McKay, John Sargent, Jeffrey Preacher—have not they all remarked about it, or commented on it, or have heard others refer to it? Even this Bolton has knowledge of that feeling. And so you are to hunt for the air gun. And whom do you suspect? Everyone, in all probability, expect Caryl Miquet. And even if you draw blank at all the other rooms, is it likely that you will enter hers? No. However, if the Baron is as great a detective as his fame undoubtedly already has proclaimed him, in spite of this sentiment for Caryl Miquet, he may search her room. And if he does find it hidden in the closet?

And then the brave Baron finished his bottle of champagne, all at once realizing the diabolical ingenuity of the plan.

If he should violate Caryl's room and find the gun, it was presumed that he would not report his discovery.

Caryl's alibis were no more secure than those of her four friends. There would be no fingerprints on the Haenel gun. Of that the Baron was positive. When it had been inserted in Caryl's closet the prints would be wiped off. The presence of the gun alone would be sufficient to confuse Caryl's possible guilt with the evidence the Baron or anyone else might bring against one of her friends! Billy's spying and running off with the gun had been entirely unforeseen by the murderer.

This was an airtight example of the Baron's singular if involved ability to drive through to a solution of a puzzle even though many pieces in the puzzle were missing. As though he were building a bridge, blindly extending his cantilever arches into the mist, feeling for an opposite shore, having his structures break again and again, sending them forth in different directions until at last they struck ground, the Baron could take what few facts he had and construct a superstructure of theory and hypothesis to bridge between the facts which were missing. And because the Baron's one real ability did lie in what amounted to a minor genius in theorizing, an unpredictable quantity at best, he was not infallible as those worthy gentlemen who advance only when they are given established facts. He failed often enough for him to distrust this queer talent of his, and for him to try to hide it and claim additional talents in order to make up for what he believed to be a weakness.

With this reasoning completed, and the champagne bottle empty, the Baron wearily lay upon the bed and went to sleep. The following morning the Japanese boy again knocked on the Baron von Kaz's door. He knocked five times. And at the fifth knock the Baron ordered, in the voice of one who has suffered irreparable injustice, "If you please, my dear sir, go away."

The Japanese boy pattered downstairs, told Mr. Berry that the guest in room twelve-five refused to open the door. Mr. Berry asked if the bottle of iced champagne the boy had left at the door half an hour previously was there. "He take champagne, Mr. Berry. No is there."

Mr. Berry was examining the bill of one Baron Franz Maximilian Karagôz von Kaz. He added: "One qt. Veuve Clicquot '18 $6.00." Then he asked the boy for the cable-gram, saying that he would give it to the Baron. The Hawaiian girl came out from Mr. Berry's office. "Mr. Jameson's on the phone again, Mr. Berry. He wants to speak to Baron von Kaz."

Holding the cablegram for the Baron von Kaz in a moist hand, Mr. Berry mounted the stairs. Ten minutes later the Baron entered Mr. Berry's office.

The first question Jameson asked was if the Baron were still drunk.

Inasmuch as the Baron had had nothing to eat for twenty-four hours, and only champagne to drink, if he had been an honest and upright man, he would have candidly replied, "Yes."

The Baron was neither honest, upright nor candid. His reply made Jameson decide, whatever the cause or occasion, never again to inquire of the Baron if he were drunk. When the Baron's peroration was completed, Jameson said that he called to give the information that his men had learned that George Tuung had booked passage for Hawaii on this morning's plane. "What I wanted to ask you yesterday, before you passed out, was, do you know where the Haenel air gun is now?"

"No," declared the Baron.

"All right, don't yell. The doctor took a chance and had Billy taken to the Hilo hospital by airplane. The police are leaving the ranch today. They have searched the house, the guest house, and where the boy was found, and they haven't discovered the gun. I've talked with the doctor and Mary McKay this morning. The doctor says it was an accident. And Mary says you were insulting and tried to keep her from being with Billy and that there wasn't any gun in Caryl's room, and if there was a gun where is it?"

The Baron informed Jameson that he was a dolt, a quadruple dolt.

"The doctor says the boy stood the trip all right."

"He will not die, then?"

"How do I know?" asked Jameson. "He might. He can't have any visitors, so I've ordered everyone to stay on the McKay Ranch. And you're not to make a damned nuisance of yourself. Tomorrow's the seventeenth. You wait in the hotel until I get in touch with you when the plaque arrives in Honolulu." The Baron slammed the receiver, stalked from the office, saying, as he departed, "If you please, my dear Mr. Berry, send another bottle of champagne. I was compelled to pour most of the last one out of the window. It was badly iced."

"Yes sir." As Mr. Berry watched the man's legs waver, he wondered just how much had been poured out. "Here's a cablegram that came in for you two hours ago." It was a little after ten now.

In his room the Baron opened and decoded the cablegram from Vienna.

BARON FRANZ MAXIMILIAN KARAGÔZ VON KAZ
   HONOLULU
AUSTRIAN CONSUL REPORTS YOU ARE RESTING ON BEACH IN KONA WHILE IN VIENNA LOYAL COMRADES ARE WORKING TO ADVANCE GLORY OF AUSTRIA STOP WHY HAVE YOU NOT REPLIED TO FIRST CABLEGRAM STOP IMPERATIVE THAT YOU LEAVE AT ONCE STOP CABLE DATE OF EXPECTED ARRIVAL
   VON CHWEIK UND MELANESIA

"Ach, so was?" murmured the Baron, "No longer is it 'Chweik.' My good friend 'Chweik.' But the great Von Chweik und Melanesia?" He tore the cablegram, gently blew the scraps from the palms of his hands into the wastebasket. It was as if he had shredded his future, all his hopes and his plans, and thrown them, now meaningless scraps of futile wishes, into that great wastebasket which contains so many dreams and desires. . . .

At ten twenty-two the Japanese boy appeared with an iced bottle of champagne. The Baron, dressed, half shaved, came to the door to take it.

At ten twenty-four Mr. Berry ran breathlessly upstairs to tell his guest that a Hawaiian boy was outside the hotel with a message of importance for the Baron.

"Message of importance?" The Baron was lugubrious with self-pity. "Ach, my dear sir, no longer have I one friend of sufficient importance to send me a message of importance." This sounded to him such a brilliant epigram that he repeated it for Mr. Berry's benefit. But Mr. Berry assumed that the Baron was drunk. The Baron waited for a smile. Mr. Berry did not smile. Mr. Berry asked, "Are you coming down?" Even this slender reed failing him, the Baron sighed. The world was all wrong. There was nothing to do but go to bed and waste away. His tragic thoughts were reflected upon his face; inasmuch as, in its present condition, when unmoved his face would have frightened small children, when it lengthened, grew more doleful, Mr. Berry stared fascinated at it and felt a desire to do a little shrieking himself. He began to wish to God that he'd never permitted this foreign rowdy to enter the hitherto placid Kona Inn.

However, Mr. Berry was constructed of stern material. At last, after much pleading and urging, the Baron condescended, as a personal favor to Mr. Berry, to see the Hawaiian gentleman. The Hawaiian gentleman was sitting in a small, shabby Ford of the vintage of 1911 or thereabouts.

"You Baron von Kaz?" he asked, jumping out of the Ford as soon as Mr. Berry assisted his unsteady guest upon the lanai. The Baron was still clutching the champagne in his hand as though this bottle were his last contact with all that was civilized and joyous.

The Baron pushed Mr. Berry's guiding hand away, drew himself erect, gazed down at the person dressed in a flowered red shirt, scanty pants, and nothing else.

"Here." The Hawaiian thrust a stained envelope into the Baron's free hand. "Miss Miquet say come quick."

Mr. Berry smiled. All now was clear to him. The Baron had become involved in a gentleman's brawl. That was not unusual after several bottles of okolehau. Miss Miquet wished him to return, signifying thereby that he was to think nothing of what had occurred at the ranch. Evidently whatever had happened was quite forgiven.

Mr. Berry felt a flood of warmth rise in his heart toward these friendly Kamaainas up on the ranch slopes. They maintained the old traditions of true Hawaiian hospitality. Mr. Berry said as much to the Baron, hoping to influence him toward a more charitable and kindly outlook on life.

The Baron read the letter. It had been hastily written in pencil and wasn't easy for him to decipher:

> Dear Baron:
> Please come at once with Kilopeka. The plaque arrived from Mexico in this morning's mail. After what you said about Billy's accident, having the plaque has frightened me. Mary and I flew to Hilo with Billy and then right back, as the police requested that we all remain on the ranch. I have disobeyed and am at our nearest neighbors', the Von Stoltzes, and Kilopeka will bring you here. The doctor

thinks Billy has a good chance to recover, and
I'm glad he is in the hospital, as things are
rather strained at the ranch house. I don't
know what to do about the plaque. Please
hurry.

Caryl.

"You coming?" inquired the Hawaiian. The Baron nodded, swung his bottle of champagne at Mr. Berry, who dodged; the Baron had meant merely to point his finger at the man to emphasize his next remark, forgetting that his fingers were grasping the heavy bottle. "Call Mr. Jameson immediately," he ordered, lurching to the car. "I am all right." Impatiently he shoved Mr. Berry aside. He sat down in the front seat. "Do you hear, please? Call Mr. Jameson at once." The Hawaiian cranked the Ford, and the Baron wondered it at all times, an earthquake had chosen this hour, this minute, to visit the island of Hawaii. Above the clattering of the Ford he called, "Tell him the plaque is delivered. . . ."

And Mr. Berry nodded cheerfully and waved, and the Ford drove from the driveway in a cloud of dust, and Mr. Berry returned to his game of dominoes and speculated on what whack the fellow was talking about. He found a combination of 0–0, and 0–1, and 0–2, and grew so interested in completing it that the matter of the whack eventually faded from his memory. . . .

The Ford passed through a mile of green-hued coffee trees, struck the grade at Huehue and started to pant. The Baron placed the bottle of champagne between his knees, holding it with both hands. "How far is it?"

Kilopeka replied in his soft English, "Not far. Forty miles. Maybe forty-five miles."

"Excellent." The Baron looked around him. Forty-five miles. Half an hour, perhaps. "Hurry," he ordered a few minutes later.

Kilopeka pointed at the brass hand throttle. It was drawn down as far as it would go. The Ford, wheezing, panting up the long grade, might have been going as fast as fifteen miles an hour, maybe twenty, when the grade would slacken. They were in the lowlands. Cane fields succeeded the coffee trees. It was hot, humid. Far above them the road straggled, gradually changing from deep black to reddish black.

"Ach Gott!" cried the Baron at last. "Can you not compel it to proceed faster?"

"No can go faster," advised Kilopeka calmly. "Steaming already."

The Baron felt himself sweat. The plaque had been delivered. It was impossible. It could not arrive by now. Not until tomorrow, the seventeenth, should it enter the Honolulu post-office. But the plaque had arrived. . . .

He couldn't sit quietly. He wiggled. He twisted in his seat. His fingers tapped on the champagne bottle, and then he glanced at it, expecting to see his green umbrella, and discerned instead the bottle. He had forgotten his green umbrella! His first thought was to turn back. The Baron was a brave man, but not all the champagne in Hawaii could dim his remembrance of what a Haenel air pistol had done to Carl Kohler and Mr. Hiroshita. Thinking of Mr. Hiroshita, he thought of the plaque and Caryl Miquet. Caryl Miquet had the plaque and had written asking, begging, magnified the Baron, begging him to come— to hurry. And she was so near to that Haenel air pistol! Could he risk the time it would take to get his green umbrella? And besides, what would Caryl say, what would Jameson say if Kilopeka told that the brave Baron von Kaz had had him turn around, drive back to the hotel because he was afraid to continue without a weapon? As usual his caution was smothered by vanity. For six long minutes he gloried in the bravery of a Von Kaz who would, unarmed, rescue a very lovely and dark woman in direst peril, in imminent danger! With a grandiloquent gesture he started to throw the champagne bottle into the road, then thought better of this and replaced it between his knees, gripping it tighter. Ach du lieber, du Gott und Himmel!

"It must proceed faster," he cried. "It must."

"Go faster, go pau," stated Kilopeka.

"Pau?"

"Go finish."

The green low country edged into grayish, volcanic-ash covered hills. The road descended into a small valley, and here the ancient lava flow had coiled down the heights from Mauna Kea, searing all life in its path. Humped, blackened, twisted rocks reared, ugly and sinister. A stunted red kukui tree emerged from two tortured rocks. To his left, the Baron saw the black smear of rock cutting downward to the ocean, trees and grass growing on either side of the lava path. Then the Ford again hit a grade. The engine began to knock, steam spurting from the radiator with every revolution.

"Must go slower," Kilopeka announced after half an hour of this. The wind was fresher, cooler now. No more palm trees lined the road. The soil was reddish gray, and the grass growing on it had turned brown. The sun was a brassy smear in the blue sky. Miles away, obscured by shifting clouds, the Baron could now and then glimpse the snowclad peak of Mauna Kea. Far over there, on one of its sheltered flanks, were the ranches. Miles away. . . .

By noon the Ford had covered thirty of the forty-five miles. At increasingly frequent intervals Kilopeka was forced to stop it to permit it to cool off. The Baron, during these intervals would leap out and walk, circling the car, forgetting his aches, forgetting his disheveled and dust-stained appearance, forgetting everything not connected with Caryl Miquet.

Would that one at the ranch know that mail from Mexico had been delivered? Would the murderer by now have possession of the plaque? What would Caryl do? Had she left the plaque in her room or had she taken it with her? She had found refuge at a neighboring ranch. Would she wait there? Would that one, that murderer, killer, follow her to this ranch? "Ready to go!" called Kilopeka, cranking the Ford. The Baron jumped onto the creaking seat, shaking the bottle of champagne at Mauna Kea, and at the hot sun.

But the Ford this time would not go.

Kilopeka cranked it until he was exhausted.

The Baron took the crank. He threatened the Ford in Austrian and in English; and in those barbarous North American words which he had picked up. The Ford was resolute. It would not go. The Baron danced around the machine, kicking it. Kilopeka undertook another siege at the crank.

The Ford would not go.

"No can start," panted Kilopeka at last, eying the raving white man in wonderment, "Must get help."

"Where?"

"Nearest town there." Kilopeka pulled off his red-flowered shirt and wrung it dry. "Anola. Eight miles back. You stay. I run. Telephone ranch for new car. This no damn good."

Kilopeka trotted down the hill, and the Baron sat on the sagging running board, and the sun flamed above him in the sky. And the little birds paused in their flight, astonished that such speech could issue from one insignificant mortal man.

After fifteen minutes of waiting the Baron could sit no longer.

If a car would have to be sent from the Von Stoltz Ranch, then the nearer the Baron could get to that car the more time he could save.

Tucking the bottle of champagne under his arm, the Baron commenced to run up the long, endless grade. The heat was unbearable. The sharp, powdery dust collected in his nostrils. The road was composed almost entirely of crushed volcanic stone. His run slowed to a steady jogging. Now and then, from utter exhaustion, he would stumble, pick himself up, swearing incoherently, and stubbornly start off again. Upward. Always upward. When the sweat stung his eyes, he rubbed it away. . . .

He had advanced five or six miles when from around a curve a young Japanese plant inspector coasted on a bicycle. The young Japanese plant inspector applied the brake as he saw a man stumbling up the grade, and when the man rocked to a stop by the bicycle, the young Japanese, wishing to show that he was acquainted with all the vagaries and whims of the Caucasian race, lifted his lips to reveal large almond-shaped teeth and pleasantly inquired, "You running fast on bet, sir?" He laughed. "Very jolly, and how far running, please?"

Then the young Japanese plant inspector suddenly felt uneasy. The dark-faced person had approached him, heavily grasped the handlebar of the bicycle, and after taking a great breath, said feebly, "I wish to . . . purchase . . . your bicycle." With that effort he lurched drunkenly, and the young Japanese regained his balance with difficulty.

The young plant inspector did not think this was jolly. Preserving his natural dignity he elbowed the vulgar, sweaty, dirty, panting, wobbling white man to one side so that he could climb upon his bicycle to descend to Anola, where, cognizant of his duties as a citizen of the United States of America, he would have telephoned the nearest police, in Kaawaiiakae, forty miles on the coast north of Kailua, informing them that a dangerous madman had molested an official of the South Kona Department of Agriculture, Hawaii, T.H.

Shuddering with the effort, the Baron lifted the large bottle of champagne and tapped the young Japanese plant inspector upon the head. Then he inserted the bottle in his coat pocket, paying no attention at all to the splitting of fabric, mounted the bicycle and proceeded toward his destination at a rate of speed one and a quarter miles an hour faster than before.

Now a new set of leg muscles were brought into play. Steadily the bicycle ascended that unending grade. No longer did the Baron waste breath on multivoweled curses. His teeth were white in a gray, sweat-streaked mask of dust. He bent low over the handlebars. The pace he had set in the first rush of confidence gradually diminished. The grade grew steeper. Below him the whole great vista of the Kona coast stretched from north to south, black angry paths of lava cutting into the greens and browns. If he had looked, he could have seen the half circle of Kealakekua Bay, where stood the little grass shack in the song, where in times past many grass shacks had been erected, where at present was only the mournful blackened city of refuge and the white monument to Captain Cook. Northward was Keauhou in shimmering palm trees, near the picture rocks; and then Kailua, and farther north the green coast line changed into the drab blackness of South Kohala. . . .

The Baron was able to get up when the bicycle fell. He landed on his right side. The champagne bottle was not broken. Slowly, painfully, he clambered upon the bicycle, pushed downward on the pedals and wobbled forward. Minutes and hours and days seemed to filter by him, and only the slow, tortured grind upon the sprocket wheel was of consequence to him. Vaguely he realized that an automobile eventually should be driving this way, down this deserted road, traversed ordinarily by two buses, one in the morning and one in the night, and a few cars of ranchers and tourists.

He coasted down a little incline, felt for the pedals, was unable to find them. His feet had lost their feeling. The hot needle pains in his calves and ankles had been replaced by numbness. The bicycle coasted a few yards uphill and then fell again, and this time the Baron lay for several minutes panting in the dust before he could crawl to his knees and examine the damage.

The champagne bottle, apparently, was the only object that had resisted the fall.

The front wheel of the bicycle had collapsed, the chain was broken.

A fat Hawaiian who was sitting on a small mouselike mule on a shelving projection above the road was a witness to this catastrophe. The Hawaiian thumped his Kona "nightingale" with his bare legs, leisurely descended into the road. The mule halted wonderingly a few feet from the man trying to drag himself to a standing position in the middle of the road.

"Pilikia?" asked the Hawaiian helpfully. "Trouble?"

The Baron got to his feet, saw before him a means of conveyance, fell upon the soft startled side of the mule. The mule, who was a sensible creature, reared, protesting at such treatment, and the Hawaiian, who had no conception of the possibility of violence, tumbled off backward, landing upon the rear wheel of the bicycle, complaining mightily.

The Baron disregarded all complaints. Grunting, he pulled himself upon the sleek back of the mule. The mule also complained in a voice which had brought upon his kind the appellation of Kona "nightingale."

When the mule would not move after being kicked, the Baron fell upon the mule's neck, embraced the neck, viciously chewed at the leather skin.

Completely appalled, the mule reared. Unable to unseat the terrifying object on his back, the mule thereupon

lost his head and galloped, then trotted madly on up the
grade. . . .

The Chinese cook came in and told Mary McKay that
the steak would be ruined if dinner wasn't served without
further delay. Jeffrey, dressed in dinner clothes, was tick-
ling the ears of one of the dogs in front of the fire. Mary
asked anxiously, "Jeff, you haven't seen Caryl, have you?"

"I saw her drive up in someone's car a couple of hours
ago when I was taking my bath. Thought it was funny.
Isn't she here?"

"No. And she isn't in her room. I've had Jackson looking for her for the past half hour. She's always late dressing, but she doesn't usually wander around the ranch at
dinner time. You didn't see her, John?"

John and Bolton were playing cards. "I've got you, Bolton."
John's big shoulders moved as his body turned. "Sure she
isn't in her room? She ran in here about five as if the devil
were after her and went into her room. Maybe she went out
to the pool afterwards. You see her, Bolton?" John stood.

"No." Bolton's cherubic face raised toward the geologist, the colorless lips rolling up and down, exposing the
small, jagged teeth. "I have you, sir. Not that a simple man
like myself wishes to argue, but three aces and a king do
win, don't they?"

"She's been acting funny ever since Billy's accident,"
John said, ignoring the fat man. "You don't suppose she
disregarded what the police said and went to the Von
Stoltzes'?"

Jeffrey left the dog and pulled the curtains of the window aside. "The car's in front," he informed them quietly.
"She wouldn't walk six miles."

Bolton's head whipped back and forth between the two
men, his lips twitching. He, said softly, "But where can
Miss Caryl be?"

Outside, feet dragged across the lanai floor. Mary said, "There she is. John, please go to the door."

John flung open the door, started back in surprise. "You!" he exclaimed. "I tell you Baron whatsyouraame, that if you—"

John Sargent failed to complete his sentence.

The Baron didn't appear to appreciate that his way was blocked. When the door opened, as an automaton beginning to function, his feet moved forward, and as he encountered the big bulk in front of him he swung the champagne bottle down onto the man's head.

John fell, the glass and champagne exploding into a shattering white froth. A piece of glass cut the Baron's cheek. None of this he noticed. He walked over the stunned man, still holding the neck of the bottle in his hand. "Where is Miss Miquet?" he croaked hoarsely. The others all looked at him. "Where is Miss Miquet?"

14

The Shiny Water Rock

It was two minutes of two o'clock on the morning of April seventeenth.

"You're at Kona Inn now?" Jameson's voice came from Honolulu over the telephone; he was excited, impatient. "Talk louder!" he shouted. "This damned storm's making the static bad. I can hardly hear you, Baron. What the hell happened at the McKay Ranch?"

"My dear sir, I had no time to telephone you from the ranch—"

"I got that much. I've telephoned Williams at Hilo to put an extra guard around the boy's bed in the hospital. Damned lucky they were able to get Billy to the hospital before all the ruckus at the ranch. What about Miss Miquet—"

"I requested Miss Mary McKay to telephone you after we found her." The Baron spoke rapidly. He had much to say. The time was growing short. His words shot out, hard, fast, precise. The map, the plaque had been taken. But the Baron still had a chance to find the feather cloak before the murderer came for it. The storm sweeping northern Hawaii, lashing north as far as Oahu, would probably keep the murderer indoors until daylight.

"Sargent called instead of Mary," said Jameson. "Told me you'd finally found Caryl trussed up under the bushes

481

by the swimming pool." The old man's voice crackled. "What the hell's it all about, hey? Sargent took half an hour to demand your arrest for attacking him. For attempted manslaughter. For abduction. You didn't take Caryl to the inn with—!"

"She kindly drove me here." The Baron sounded grim. He had been in no condition to drive down a slippery, rain-washed road to Kona, and he didn't like to be reminded of the fact.

"Drove you to Kona!"

"She was not hurt. She wished to come."

"Wait a minute. I can't hear you. . . . Operator, I can't hear with this damned static. . . ."

Caryl, coat around her shoulders, poured the Baron another drink from Mr. Berry's bottle of Armagnac, asking the Baron if he were feeling any better. He returned the empty glass, absently patted her on the shoulder, listening intently all the while for Jameson's voice.

"Nice Rover," murmured Caryl, delicately removing the Baron's hand from her shoulder, and he was so absorbed in the attempt to distinguish Jameson's voice through the pounding surge of static that he didn't even glance at her. Mr. Berry, collapsed in a chair, was staring at both of them, the girl and the man.

Jackson's voice came through again. "Hear me all right?" The Baron said he could. "I didn't get it straight from Sargent why Caryl was tied up. What the hell's it—"

The Baron said that when the plaque arrived Miss Miquet had risked disobeying police orders and had gone to a neighboring ranch to send for him.

"What plaque?" Jameson was shouting.

"The plaque from Mexico," replied the Baron, wondering if Jameson had lost his head.

"What plaque? WHAT PLAQUE?"

"The Mexican plaque."

"I can't understand you. All I can hear is Mexican plaque. Operator, for God's sake—"

"It is the Mexican plaque. It arrived yesterday."

"ARRIVED yesterday?"

"Exactly, and—"

"The Mexican plaque, ARRIVED YESTERDAY?"

"My dear sir, I had Mr. Berry telephone to you and— One moment, please." The Baron's lips swung two inches from the phone, and when he said, "Mr. Berry!" the hotel manager jumped as if he'd been shot and admitted that he hadn't telephoned anyone about the whack because he didn't know what a whack was. "Quadruple dolt!" This piece of gratuitous information on the Baron's part struck Mr. Berry like a cartridge wadding, and he fell back into his chair, helplessly protesting to Caryl, who merely took another drink. "Pardon," said the Baron, "Mr. Berry did not telephone."

Hearing Jameson's voice surging out of the receiver, Caryl asked pleasantly, "Is Mr. Jameson having a stroke, or is it just the static from the storm?"

The Baron frowned at her to remain quiet. Now Jameson was insisting that the Baron was ab-so-lutely crazy. The Mexican plaque couldn't be in Hawaii. He'd checked at the Honolulu post-office last night. It wouldn't arrive until ten this morning.

"I examined the paper it was wrapped in," declared the Baron, his voice taut. "It had a Hilo postmark. Hilo, Island of Hawaii. Why, my dear sir, did you not inform me that mail boats also landed at Hilo?"

"Hilo? By Jesus. That can't— Wait a minute." Again came that twisting mixture of voices, questioning, answering. . . . "Please," said the Baron to Caryl. He swallowed the Armagnac. He was feeling better. When Caryl had driven him down from the ranch he had slept during the ride.

Jameson was apoplectic. "Ashiti just checked with the postmaster. God damn!" In his excitement, for a moment Jameson grew incoherent. "Woke him out of bed. Once a month there's a Japanese boat leaves Manzanillo, touches Hilo on the way to Japan. But it hardly ever leaves mail. How was I to guess the Mexicans would send the plaque to Manzanillo? How was I to guess, hey?"

The Baron said, "Hiroshita addressed the plaque to Miss Miquet, care of Mary McKay, Hawaii. Perhaps the Mexicans assumed it was the island of Hawaii."

"What d'you want me to do? Telephone Puueo to arrest everyone at the McKay Ranch?"

"Ach!" The Baron had to make up his mind. If the four at the ranch were arrested, would his evidence be strong enough to hang one of them?

"Who does Caryl say slugged her?"

"She does not know. She was standing by her table, taking the plaque to bring it to me." The brave Baron did not feel it necessary to say that by his haste in attempting to reach Miss Miquet he had somehow missed her on the road when she had borrowed the Von Stoltz Packard to meet him after receiving a message from Kilopeka saying the Ford had broken down. When she did not find the Baron on the road—and who would have recognized Franz Maximilian Karagôz von Kaz astride a Kona "nightingale"?—she had lost her head and returned to the McKay house to see if the plaque were still in her room. "The next thing she remembers, she regained consciousness under the bushes. She was hit from behind, on the left temple. I wasted an hour, my dear sir. An hour attempting to pick up clues. Either Mr. Preacher or Mr. Sargent had the opportunity to follow her to her room. Bolton claims he was in the corral talking to the cowboys."

"Was he?"

"For half an hour. The time is indefinite. Whether he was in the corral before Miss Miquet entered her room or during the short time she was in her room I could not determine."

"Then it's one of the three men?"

"One moment, please. I cannot understand—"

"I'll telephone Williams in Hilo to drive north at once with a couple of men. Puueo's alone at Upolu. Despite the storm, Williams should be there by six."

"Too late," said the Baron. "No, my dear sir. It will not march."

"What're you talking about? I can hardly hear you with this static. Puueo can handle it with you until Williams comes."

"When can you arrive at Kailua?"

"Did you say Kailua?"

"Kailua. Du Gott!" Was he to lose more precious time talking to Honolulu?

Jameson said he'd have to call the airport, for the Baron to hang on to the phone. In forty-eight seconds Jameson reported back: Upolu had no landing lights, and the Inter-Island people wouldn't risk their amphibians in the Kailua harbor during the storm. They'd take off for Upolu at dawn. Jameson could reach Upolu by six. The McKay Ranch was half an hour from Upolu.

"Not the McKay Ranch!" shouted the Baron curtly. "You will come to Kailua. Here." And as he listened to Jameson's question as to why he should come to Kailua the Baron snapped at Mr. Berry, "Raincoat!"

"Get him a raincoat," said Caryl, urging Mr. Berry on. "A raincoat. How do I know what he wants one for?"

Mr. Berry feebly tottered to his bedroom, and Caryl accompanied Mr. Berry to make sure he would return.

"Listen to me," commanded the Baron over the telephone. "I know who did it. Our only chance to prove

who the murderer is, is to be at the cave before the murderer arrives. The one who killed Mr. Hiroshita did so by
climbing through the bathroom window and jumping to
my balcony. The vines protected him from being seen by
those of Miss McKay's party on the balcony, and he probably had the water running to cover any noise he might
make. But we cannot prove who climbed out of the bathroom window because, during the course of the evening,
more than one may have gone into the bathroom, and if
we asked, then we would arouse the murderer's suspicions
and might frighten him into flight . . . do you hear? And
whoever killed Mr. Hiroshita and Mr. Kohler was opening
Miss Miquet's mail because he heard from Mr. Kohler that
Mr. Hiroshita had sent the plaque to Miss Miquet. But he
did not know when the plaque would come—"

"Hey?" shouted Jameson. "I can't hear . . . louder . . ."

"And," continued the Baron, "he knew that Billy was
building a castle. He knew that, and when the old woman
was said to have seen Billy run from Miss Miquet's room
with a gun, he knew that Billy had found the Haenel air
pistol he had hidden, and he went to the castle behind the
kiawe trees because Billy must have told the others as well
as myself that he wanted a real gun . . ."

"I can't hear you at all." Jameson's voice was barely
distinguishable in a welter of static. "Maybe you can hear
me. Look! I'll be in Kailua as soon as possible. We'll have
men to block all the roads leading to North Kona . . . wait
for . . . be there soon . . ." And Jameson's voice faded, and
the operator told the Baron she was sorry but the Honolulu connection was temporarily drowned out by the static
caused by the storm.

The Baron turned from the telephone as Caryl and Mr.
Berry entered. Without a word she handed the Baron the
manager's raincoat and followed him to the door. "Shall I
put a candle in the window for you?"

He buttoned the coat. "Hein?"

"Never mind."

"Please request Mr. Berry to have a motorboat ready in half an hour."

"He's so scared now, he won't—"

"Inform him I shall slit his throat." The Baron's face swung close to hers, grinning quickly. "That will cause the little man to march, no?"

Caryl peered through the window. She saw the Baron stagger as the full shock of the driving rain and wind struck him. The tropical rain fell in slanting sheets of solid water. He disappeared into the blackness. No sign of early morning could penetrate that cloudburst. Caryl shivered, returned to Mr. Berry.

Aunt Ella had the blood of kings, of princes. She was an old woman. She was old and tired. But she was an aristocrat. She knew what it was to have the responsibility of traditions. And she sat straight in the rocking chair, the heavy silk gown around her where the Baron Franz Maximilian Karagôz von Kaz had so gently tucked it in after hammering on the door and awakening her.

She listened to him. The little house shook and trembled as the rain smashed upon it. The wind howled. It was a wonder she had ever heard the Baron's poundings. She was used to the rain and the wind. From her windows she had seen the tall palms bend to touch the ground, and in the morning they would be upright again, and the land would be fair and sweet and the flowers brighter. The waves rolled heavily upon the black rocks at the edge of the Palace grounds. The waves gave a heavy, thundering roll like carriages, enormous and fantastic carriages, riding through the night.

She said nothing. He sat opposite her. He bent toward her, hands resting on knees. He was racing with time. She could see that, the way he talked. He made no attempt to impress her. He was almost motionless. Only his mouth moved, wide, flexible. He was unshaven. His eyes were haggard. The bruises on his face were mottled, blue and purple. But he was clean. On reaching the hotel he had taken five precious minutes for a cold bath, for clean clothes. This wasn't vanity. The cold bath stung him into wakefulness, helped lift the fatigue. That and the Armagnac. And the clothes were fresh. Not sticky. They had helped to erase from his mind the grotesque figure he had appeared at the Von Stoltz Ranch. It was a wonder they had ever believed that the disreputable, seemingly half-drunken tramp brandishing a champagne bottle could conceivably be a friend of Caryl Miquet! As he had talked to Jameson, as he had run in the rain to the Palace, as he sat now in the chair and spoke to the old woman with the wrinkled yellow face and the great old eyes, he could feel his body responding to the spur of this final drive to trap that murderer. He could move his legs. His arms. The ache, the pain, had been forgotten. Or camouflaged.

He was through now.

He stood up. "Will you tell me where it is, Aunt Ella?"

The old eyes went into him, and he withstood their gaze, and her hand, yellow and aged, lifted from the silk and dropped to her lap.

In one corner was a clock. It was a tall clock. It had been made in England two hundred and forty-five years ago. It went tick-tock, tick-tock, tick-tock, and the old woman's eyes went into the Baron, and the clock continued tick-tock, tick-tock. It had seen death. Tick-tock. Many deaths. Tick-tock. Kings had gone. Queens had gone. Tick-tock. It had crossed oceans. Fat, smiling Hawaiian princes with elaborate costumes had offered love to women who were not fat, who had hair which reached to the floor, and the women had looked at the clock and had said that it was time to go to bed. Tick-tock. What was time? An hour or a year? Tick-tock. Tick-tock . . .

The old woman said nothing.

The Baron slowly placed his hand to his forehead, shut his eyes. The windows rattled as the rain came against them, and the thunder of the waves mounted, and the wind struck in quick surging rushes, but the clock's tick-tock, tick-tock never wavered. Each second it marked slipped away. Lost.

"They will take it?" came that whisper.

"He will," corrected the man. "Unless you tell me. And he will go unpunished. Remember it was he who attempted to kill little Billy McKay."

"It could not have been an accident?"

"No."

And then she asked, "If you are there first?"

"What do you wish?"

"Not to defile the grave. Take the cloak if you must. Place it in a museum. Let people stare at it. But don't disturb the dead."

"You care so much?"

"Do you promise? You are a Von Kaz. That is something in your country?"

When the lightning streaked out of the sky and sent its pale greenish light into the room, the Baron jerked nervously, but the old woman did not stir.

"Your family was something in your country?"

"My grandfather . . . he was very great."

"As a Von Kaz you give me your word?"

He bowed.

"You will protect the grave?"

"I will protect it."

"In the parlor there is an old book. You cannot miss it. It is big, with lead corners. I am too tired. Bring it."

It weighed nearly thirty pounds. Here were letters, memories, documents, her diary. Her whole life. She found what she was seeking. Her voice was thin and strained and weary. "My great-uncle was a great Kahunapule, a priest." She tried to smile a little. "As great perhaps . . . as your grandfather. I was young. Fifteen. Foolish, I suppose. He wished to have written on paper what . . . what his father and his father's father had handed down." She asked for her glasses. The Baron's hand trembled as he gave them to her. Time was so fleet. "There is a little inlet near Kiholo. In daylight you cannot miss it. And old Heiau—an old temple was once built there. The Heiau of Anuinui. The temple of Rainbow Hill. The lava came down hundreds of years ago and shoved the hill into the sea like water melting a sand pile, and they built a Heiau over the lava. The lava formed a great cavern . . . My great-uncle said it went upward nearly to Mauna Kea . . . I do not know. One of the rocks in the Heiau is called the Waiohinu. Shiny water. When it rains this rock has the resemblance of water. Why I do not know. I have never been there when it rains. It is tabu."

15

The Dark Cavern

The Baron shouted to the Portuguese fisherman in the stern of the little boat, "How long will it take to attain the Anuinui inlet?"

The lightning ripped across the sky, a jagged strip of flame. Two miles behind them the shore line stood out distinct in the greenish flare, vanished.

The fisherman bent against the rain. "One hour. Two, maybe."

"You can find it?"

The fisherman nodded. "Goddamn, for hundred dollars I find way to hell for you. I seen badder storms. Boat all right. Better you go below. When we cross point, bad waves maybe come over."

"What about you?"

Bracing himself with the tiller, the fisherman nodded confidentially. "Tied here. Can't wash away. You go below. Much better."

The Baron ducked his head, climbed into the oily hold lit by a single lamp which was gyrating from the cabin beam. He sat down on the bunk, took off his rain hat and wiped his eyes.

When he opened his eyes, Caryl was sitting on his lap. "Damn this rocking," she said, pulled herself up again. "I brought hot coffee in a thermos bottle. Better have a cup."

He finished the coffee before speaking. "Mr. Berry said you were in the hotel."

"I thought he would."

She sat on the other bunk, holding to the woodwork. The lamp flung its shadows on them. "In fact," she explained dispassionately, "if he said anything else, I told him I would slit his throat." The crimson lips smiled at him. He didn't smile.

He got up.

"Do you want more coffee? It's about half Armagnac."

He spoke heavily. "We shall have to retrace our course, my dear Miss Miquet. Your imprudence may make me too late."

"Don't be an idiot!" She barred the way angrily. And when she was angry her eyes sparkled, her olive face lost its cool repose and he thought her very beautiful. "When I was a girl my father and I spent a summer exploring caves. I know more about them than you do. You may need help. And Joe can't help you. He'll have to watch the boat."

They climbed the crumbly hill. Their flashlights gave blurred puddles of light in the rain. When the lightning leaped across the black sky, above them they could see nothing but a tormented, running waste of desolation. Below, in the inlet, Joe's *Maribelle* rocked violently, its motor going, resisting the waves, helping to hold the anchor.

The Baron pulled Caryl up the battered rocks, the remnants of the old walls. Another screeching tear of lightning momentarily showed them a square expanse, a hundred feet wide by a hundred and fifty feet long. The floor was composed of huge irregular rocks, uneven, sharp, dangerous if fallen upon.

Caryl cried in his ear, "No one's here. We're the first!"

The rain whipped her face, and she exulted in the sting. "We're the first!" she cried, not to the Baron this time, but to the elements, and the rushing wind took her words and flung them away.

"Stay here, please." She did not understand what he was saying. He pushed her down under the shelter of a towering volcanic slab. The rain slashed onto the rock, but it stood firm as it had for so many years.

Flashlight in one hand, he held his green umbrella in the other, using it as a cane to prevent himself from slipping. Crouched, half shielded, she watched his flashlight as he circled the Heiau. She wondered why he didn't open his umbrella. She thought it was odd. He was a queer person himself. As violent and changeable in moods as Hawaii; cheerful, amusing, he had a genius for appearing in the worst possible light; then, without warning, being dignity itself or lashing out in black anger. Vain too. And proud. As were the Hawaiians. But they weren't as vain as he was. And she wondered if he'd ask her to marry him. And what she would say if he did. All this she thought as the rain poured down and lightning cracked overhead. . . .

He was searching the stones. He didn't know what he was looking for. Shiny water rock. What was a shiny water rock? The Waiohinu, old Aunt Ella had called it. Slipping, jumping from one rock to the next, he had the fantastic feeling that this was a nightmare. It couldn't be real. A Waiohinu rock. Ach du lieber Augustin! That was but a fragrant of a dream, and Caryl was another fragment of the dream; she wasn't over there, smiling at him with the rain streaming down her face. He was in Vienna, and tomorrow he would awaken and tell his good friend Chweik how he had dreamed that he was deserting old friends and remaining in Hawaii.

This time he raised his arm, instinctively. Protecting his face. The lightning had struck very close. The night was saturated with that electric discharge. This was sheer insane madness. Lieber Gott! A Waiohinu rock? He was

completing the circuit. He was nearing Caryl. She snapped
her flashlight. He was pointing at her. He looked so
peculiar, so strange, in the dripping beam of light that
she laughed nervously, came to him, asked if he had hurt
himself. He placed his hand on her shoulder. She felt his
hand. She thought he wanted her to put her ear to his
mouth and her damp cheek pressed against his. He shook
his head, turning her toward the huge rock, pointing.

Both their flashlights hit the shiny black surface.

A foot or so from where Caryl had been huddled the
rock seemed to be alive. It writhed as the water poured
down in tiny rivulets, following natural grooves. Or perhaps the grooves weren't natural. Perhaps in the old days
one of the great Kahunapules had found this gigantic slab,
set it up in the temple and slowly ground the grooves in it.

Caryl gasped, "It's moving. Don't touch it."

The Baron poked the rock with his umbrella. The
water was gliding down its surface. The rock was solid.
"The Waiohinu rock," he muttered solemnly, for no one to
hear. Then he darted to the foot of the rock. He examined
it. He ran his hand over it, oblivious of the rain and the
streaming water. She stood to one side, holding the flashlight beam on the surface. He climbed the broken wall of
the Heiau, waited for the next streak of lightning. The
rock was at least ten feet high, four feet thick. He jumped
from the wall, slipped, went to his knees.

He got on his feet quickly, then went down on his
knees again in the water. The water ran from the rock
along a narrow groove chiseled into the floor of the temple. In other days, other centuries, blood had flowed along
this same groove. Caryl was positive he had hurt himself
this time. He motioned her back impatiently. Along the
base of the rock were a series of stones. He began to dig
them out from under the base, tearing his fingers, cutting
his skin. The base, on the side facing him, was curved

upward. It was apparent that the Waiohinu rock did not have a square base. Time and weather had worn away many of the smaller rocks; the Baron removed more which were not wedged too tightly. He gazed up at the shiny rock. "Stand over there," he shouted, coming close to Caryl. Then, getting in front of her, he reached for the automatic he had brought with him, which he had borrowed from Mr. Berry, placed the muzzle some ten feet from the base, turned his head, pulled the trigger.

The gun spurted. The sharp cracks smashed into the night.

When the magazine was exhausted he again peered at the base. The steel-nosed bullets had cracked one of the rocks, bracing the left end of the tall rock. By pushing at the pieces with his umbrella, and with one of his feet, he got them out. He loaded the automatic, again pulled the trigger. He repeated this process four times, using all his bullets. He asked Caryl for the automatic she also had borrowed from Mr. Berry. There was one larger, oval rock held firm in the center. He believed, if he could only crack this, the Waiohinu would totter.

Caryl tried to warn him. The great gusts of wind striking the Waiohinu were making it shudder and tremble. When he had finished, when there were no more bullets, the center wedge was cracked. The volcanic stone was brittle, more like clinkers than real rocks, easily shattered by the steel-nosed bullets. He beat the Waiohinu with his hands. It will still upright.

"We've done all we can," she shouted.

They started toward the opening of the Heiau, toward the rough path which led down to the boat.

As Caryl was stepping onto one of the fallen rocks in the entranceway a mass of wind and rain flowing from the heights of Mauna Kea drove against her. She would have fallen if the Baron hadn't caught her. Then both pressed hard, holding each other, as the roar spread into the storm, and their flashlights showed them where the Waiohinu had been. The wind had completed the Baron's work.

Breathlessly they scrambled over the rocks. Great broken chunks. The remnants of the Waiohinu. Never would blood again twist its way on the shimmering cobalt surface. Never would blood lick into the grooves. The wind shrieked, its impalpable fingers tearing at the man and the woman who had started this havoc.

"There!" The Baron lifted Caryl over what remained of the base.

His flashlight dripped light upon a square opening. The opening had been covered by the base. The opening was about two feet long, less than two feet wide.

"Be careful!" she warned him. "The rocks here may be loosened by the fall of the big one."

The wind roared too loudly for him to hear.

He put his hand down into the opening. A foot below he felt a smooth rock, and then another below the first one.

His flashlight smeared dull light along rough steplike stones. These stones seemed to be arranged one above the other upon a slanting floor of a shaft penetrating downward.

He lowered his feet into the hole, both hands supporting his body on the flat stone where had rested the Waiohinu rock. Deprived of the massive weight of the Waiohinu, these flat stones tipped as though the fall had ground them enough off their own base to make them unstable.

Standing on the slanting floor of the shaft, the Baron reached for his flashlight and umbrella which he had placed on the stones by his shoulders.

Caryl was inspecting the rock base where the Waiohinu had been placed.

She came to him, cried in his ear, "You must be careful. These smaller rocks are loose. Without the Waiohinu to hold them, they may slip into the entrance."

He smiled encouragingly at her.

She was angry with him for his placidly superior confidence. "Do you hear? The rain is washing between the cracks!"

He nodded. He lowered his body until only head and shoulders protruded. "There is no danger," he shouted. And he ordered her to return to the boat. He explained cunningly, "Joseph will be worried. You must tell him I will join you in a few minutes. Half an hour at the most."

The Baron's conception of a cave was a large opening underground.

He believed that as soon as he descended these steps he would reach the cave, there find the feather cloak. But the Hawaiian lava caverns were not caves; they were long natural tubes, lined with cold lava formed ages ago, and after each eruption more molten lava would pour through these tubes, widening them, just as water pours down natural earth conduits.

Caryl, surprisingly, didn't protest.

She nodded, this time restraining her impulse to tell him to be careful.

As he slowly felt his way downward, he decided that all women were alike: Be firm with them and they would obey. Henceforth he would be as firm as steel with Caryl.

Centuries ago some great priest, a Kahuna Moi, had found this lava tube, had ordered his people to dig down to it from Rainbow Hill. The shaft slanted. The rain leaked in from the opening, ran in little streams. The Baron descended steadily. Once he lifted his head. He could see a faint luminosity above him where Caryl's flashlight was held at the entrance. Then the flashlight winked out.

Unreasonably, he wished she had not decided to follow his orders to depart at once. She could have waited a little longer. Ach! Thus it was with women.

His umbrella hampered him. When he lowered his head, trying to peer below, his head struck sharp volcanic rock, and he swore, nearly dropping both umbrella and flashlight.

The hole dug down to the lava tube slanted. The slant was an angle of approximately forty-five degrees. If it had been steeper by as much as five degrees the Baron would have slipped. Centuries had passed; the water had seeped into the opening, wearing the stones smooth. Dankish moss grew on them. The moss was sticky. When the Baron's fingers gripped into the moss it broke away. It was like touching a furry animal. A furry animal which was rotten, which disintegrated into sticky particles.

After twelve minutes of this the Baron reached the bottom of the tube. He stood up, hit his head again, crouched. His flashlight swung back and forth across the space. As the molten lava of recent eruptions had neared the sea, it had choked the ancient tube. It was ten or fifteen feet wide, hardly five feet high, sloping downward past the opening.

With a curious feeling of elation he turned, penetrating farther. He was able to advance only a few yards. The tube narrowed, was blocked by gigantic rocks. He retreated, then proceeded slowly, crawling on his stomach. Gradually the tube widened, and soon he could walk upright. He was glad Caryl was not with him. Never would she have been able to come this far.

Fifty yards past the opening, going towards Mauna Kea, which was so many miles distant, the floor of the tube flattened. Smaller flows of lava had rushed down the tube, had cooled. The ripples had solidified. His flashlight showed the swirls and patterns where the streams had hardened.

In here it was dry. And there was no sound. The earth and metals of the soil, melting, mixing with the streaming lava, had changed the blackness in places, streaking it with grays, with dull reds and greens.

Becoming absorbed in the patterns formed by the lava currents on the floor, he failed to notice a twisted, knobby stalactite hanging from the ceiling.

It gashed his forehead.

He stopped, grunted, ducked under it. Small crevices cracked the surface of the floor. Again, at times, the floor was glass smooth. Then there would be stalagmites. His breath came sharper. Along the sides, where the lava had dug a kind of embankment, his exploring flashlight showed indications of primitive habitations.

Stones had been piled in regular mounds. His fingers touched a mat. The mat crumbled, turned to dust. The tube was not straight. It curved, twisted like the burrow of a gigantic ancient mole or snake. After some twenty minutes he paused. The air he breathed was fresh. He licked his forefinger, raising it. He shivered, as though something cold had been rubbed down his back. From somewhere in front of him a current of air, steady, chill, rushed in.

He turned. The silence was broken by the slide of a rock.

He snapped out his flashlight, waiting. Absolute darkness closed around him, total darkness. The darkness smothered him. He wanted to fight it off. Only by the greatest effort of his will could he resist the temptation to use his flashlight.

Around the sharp corner of the cavernous tube spread a faint glow. The Baron knelt. He pointed his gun. Then he remembered that he had no more bullets. He had been a dolt! But he had not expected anyone to come. Not at night, during the storm. That had been in the back of his mind: by venturing here during the storm, he would

be first. He could get the feather cloak. Then, when the
police arrived, they could hide in the vicinity of Rainbow
Hill. And when in daylight that one from the ranch would
come . . . it would be ended.

A dazzling glare shot at the Baron.

He stood, the sword in his umbrella streaking out of
the umbrella scabbard. "Don't be an idiot!" Caryl snapped
off her light.

"Lieber Augustin!"

She was smiling in the light of his flashlight. Her clothing was torn. Her shoes were muddy, scratched. There was
a streak of mud on her forehead, grimy dust on her nose.
The dark eyes were brilliant. Excitement flared in them.

The Baron was furious.

She waited until he had completed all that he had to say.
In the rock cavern their voices vibrated, echoed sullenly.

"You think I'd miss this?" she asked when he had finished with an imperative demand that she immediately turn
back and go to the boat. She dismissed his words concerning the value of a woman's word, and other high-minded
and thoroughly indignant remarks, as if they were not of
the slightest concern to her, which, as a matter of fact,
they weren't.

"From what I remember," she declared with a thoughtful frown, "we'll have to walk on quite a way. Probably two
or three miles. When these tubes neared the coast and the
sea they always choked. And the old-time Hawaiians left
the tubes as they were at the openings. They thought that
if any of their enemies managed to enter and saw no signs
of habitation they'd be safer."

The Baron said stiffly, "But I have already detected
signs of former habitation."

"Those?" She was scornful. "I saw the mat, too, and the
stone fire bed. That was recent. Not more than fifty years
or so ago."

"If you please, and how do—"

Her black eyebrows lifted as his flashlight outlined her face. "My dear man," she said, "because the stone fire bed was on a black bank of lava. The old lava had started to crumble. Look." Her flashlight explored ahead of them. "The floor and most of the walls are grayish black, or streaked with colors. Only along the sides can you see the deep, glistening black from recent lava flows."

"Ach!" he stated, listening to his voice rebound. "Must we lose time?"

They plunged on.

The lava walls widened, narrowed. From the roof, stalactites hung low. Now and then the tube would spread as though, from above, greater forces had squashed it. At times the incrustations were of such startling beauty, etched and coiled into the rocks, traced with colors, that the Baron would pause in amazement.

When Caryl first saw the round, polished stones on the floor she cried out. They were ancient rolling stones used in a Hawaiian game. And the Baron was next to find two rotted kahilis, ancient feather standards.

Then, without realizing it, they spoke in whispers. Once, in the past, an entire village had been located here. They found skeletons along the walls. Perhaps a group of Hawaiians had been trapped here, killed by their enemies. Or, perhaps, as the race had slowly begun to die, here they had crawled to meet the greatest adventure among the bones of their own people. . . .

When the tube again widened, before them they saw what resembled a dais. They had to climb to reach this dais. A semicircle of polished stones, each as large as a man's head, guarded a center stone. This center stone was nearly seven feet long. It was crudely chipped into the form of a man! Both Caryl and the Baron looked down at this stone. It was hollowed out. In it were bones, white under the flashlight. At the head of the stone was the skull of a man.

Caryl felt a strangling sensation.

She turned away. The Baron saw a faint yellow sheen underneath the bones. It was a fuzzy yellow. Not the yellow of metal. But an old yellow. Of cloth or feathers. The Baron whispered, "It is the cloak. It is—"

"You found it, didn't you?"

At first the Baron thought Caryl had asked the question and without moving his head said, "Yes, I found it," and afterwards in the ensuing stillness was aware that something was wrong; that Caryl's voice had never been so terribly flat, so devoid of all shade and inflection.

When his flashlight danced away from the stone image, rested upon her, he saw that her face was white.

There was a little hiss.

In the quietness of the cavern the hiss was magnified. Then followed a metallic click. Caryl jumped. A small object struck the stone image, dropped to the lava. It glittered. At one end, when the Baron's flashlight shifted and the light made a pool, a round pool circling it, they saw the blue feathers of the dart.

The flat voice echoed vacuously, "I heard you coming."

Caryl's lips formed the single word, "Bolton?"

"I didn't have time to find it myself." They couldn't tell from what direction the voice originated. It was flat, emotionless. "How does half a million dollars look? Thought you'd get it for yourselves?"

"Bolton!" cried Caryl. "Where are you? Are the others—!"

"The others, ma'am?" The Baron had never heard Bolton laugh before. The laugh was high, womanish. "The others? With all their wealth? All their high and pretty ways looking down at me, a poor simple man? Do you think I'd let any of them know?"

The Baron had stepped in front of Caryl. He remained there, listening. His head cocked to the left. He leaned forward, holding his umbrella as a man resting upon a cane. His body was tense.

"You can't see me," said the voice. "If you use your flashlights, I'll shoot. That first dart was a warning. Keep your flashlights till I tell you to throw them away. Shine the lights on your guns."

"My dear sir," the Baron spoke, "I assure you, we are unarmed."

"You're lying." The flat voice broke and went up higher again. "You can't fool me. You can't trick me any more. You wouldn't come here without guns."

The Baron shrugged. He threw his down. "There is nothing to do but comply," he told Caryl. He heard the clatter as her gun hit a rock, bounced and hit another. "Now your flashlights," ordered that echoing voice. "Don't turn them off. Throw them while they're lit. Hurry!"

Caryl's flashlight spiraled across the vaulted cavern, crashed, extinguished. The Baron dropped his gently, and it rolled from the dais and fell, dim and obscure, in the center of the solidified lava, a tiny patch of light.

"All right." Behind them a light was turned on. Above and to their right they saw the round glow. "Climb up here," said Bolton. "You first, Miss Miquet. And if there're any tricks, I'll shoot to kill, Baron von Kaz."

Caryl crossed the dais. The Baron watched her ascend. Bolton was standing, faintly revealed behind the round blob of light. "Now you, Baron," said Bolton.

The climb was steep but not particularly dangerous.

In the far distant past, one of the lava flows had melted through the original lava tube, forcing a smaller tube at right angles. Bolton was standing in this second tube, looking down into the central chamber. This tube was wet.

Water dripped from the roof. It was nearer to the surface of the ground.

"You weren't so bright after all, were you?" The flashlight blinded the Baron. "I heard you coming. How did you get in?"

The Baron didn't grasp the significance of this at first. Bolton was panting.

Then the Baron understood. There was another entrance to the lava tube below. The map Bolton had taken from the plaque had indicated the other entrance. Bolton didn't know about the Waiohinu rock.

The Baron told him. He didn't want to irritate Bolton. He told him the truth. The Baron was a brave man. But he was afraid now. Terribly afraid. No time now to regret that he hadn't forced Caryl to remain on the boat. No time now to regret her presence. He had believed that no one could come while the storm lasted. He had not considered the possibility of two entrances.

Bolton had remained silent.

He broke his silence. "Miss Miquet, you walk ahead. Walk ahead without looking back."

The Baron interrupted, "Mr. Bolton, please—"

"Stop!" said Bolton to Caryl, who did. Then the flashlight rested upon the Baron. Bolton said in an even tone— it was matter of fact—"Listen to me, Baron von Kaz. I'm only a plain, humble man. I haven't your tricks."

"I assure you, my dear sir—" The Baron was feinting for time. If he could keep Bolton satisfied for a few hours, then Jameson and the men from Hilo would be at Kailua. They'd learn the Baron hadn't returned. They'd discover Bolton's absence.

"You'll assure me nothing, Baron. You two will walk up the tube about twenty feet until I tell you to stop."

The Baron's head inclined.

"When I say stop, you will step to the left of Miss Miquet. Then," said this voice, completely without excitement, "I shall shoot Miss Miquet. You next. It will be quite painless. In the back of the neck. However—" and the voice seemed to waver, to become a thin thread—"if you try any of your famous tricks, Baron von Kaz, I promise you this: I'll shoot you first. You can imagine the reason why."

The stillness was broken only by Caryl's quick intake of breath.

Then the Baron bowed, turned his back to the flashlight. He turned his back to the flashlight and stepped to the left, very casually. By this he was directly in front of Mr. Bolton. Caryl was a pace or so in front of him.

"And drop your umbrella," ordered Bolton. "I haven't forgotten the sword in it. You won't threaten me like you did Mr. Sargent."

"As you wish, my dear sir."

The umbrella moved.

Then with all his force the Baron lifted it by the silver tip. His fingers caught it. It circled over his shoulders. As it left his fingers, he dived at Caryl. He gripped her below the knees. They fell. Not until he was on the ground did the pain fill his shoulder. Not until then did he know that Bolton had shot. Bolton had seen the green thing coming. It had taken him by surprise. In the air it looked awkward, wobbling. He shot, pulling the trigger convulsively as he dodged.

The weighted handle struck him under the eye as he was jerking away.

The man staggered, lost his balance. He dropped the flashlight. It went out.

He fell backward.

Caryl struggled. The Baron held her, shielding her with his body. They heard the shrill cry from Bolton, drawn long and dying, and then far off a faint thud, something like a bag filled with sand dropping upon a hard surface, then heavy shocks of rocks falling, then smaller stones. . . .

After that there was nothing.

He could feel her body under his. He whispered, when all was still, "Are you hurt?"

"Bolton?"

"Lie as you are."

He crawled from her. When his hand reached and encountered empty space he knew that he was at the edge of the opening above the cavern. Far below he saw a faint speck of light. It was his flashlight.

"Franz!" It was Caryl's voice.

"Bolton has fallen," he whispered.

She crawled to him. They climbed down the rocks, groping in that abysmal darkness. The Baron found his flashlight, played the light over Caryl. Her leather jacket was ripped in two. She said she was only bruised.

He asked her to look at his shoulder.

She saw the bedraggled bloody feathers sticking into the raincoat, just below the shoulder bone.

"Pull it out," he requested. "Pull it out."

The dart had penetrated as far as the feathers.

The Baron's shoulder didn't hurt very much, but he could feel his shirt sticking to his skin. He whirled his flashlight to the semicircle of stones. They saw the white mass there. Bolton was lying in a lump. The upper part of his head was against a rock. The rock was red. His eyes were open. He was watching them. "I can't feel anything," he said, when they stood above him. "But I can't move."

The Baron bent down. When the light shone on Bolton's back the Baron didn't speak to Bolton. Bolton watched the two draw aside, heard them whispering. His eyes didn't close.

The Baron said softly, "I think his back is broken." Then he gave Caryl the flashlight, told her to go to the

boat and get Joe. He would remain with Bolton. He wanted to talk with Bolton.

The Baron sat on one of the polished stones. The flashlight flickered along the wall and disappeared, and the two
men were in darkness. Bolton refused to talk. The Baron
waited.

An hour passed. Or more than an hour.

When the flashlight was seen, it was duller. Caryl
climbed to the dais, met the Baron. "Where is Joe?" he
asked.

She said in a small, strained voice that the rocks had
slipped into the opening, blocking it. She showed him
her fingers. The flesh was torn off. She had tried to move
the rocks. The rain had washed down, and the rocks had
slipped.

"There is the other entrance."

He returned to Bolton. The flashlight was growing feeble. Bolton glanced up at them with that face of an evil
child. "A plain, humble man like me," he said, "hadn't a
chance with a clever fellow like you. My back is broken,
isn't it?"

"You are not seriously hurt," the Baron assured him.
"How did you get in? How far is your entrance? We will
get help for you."

"You'll never find it," said Bolton, his colorless lips
rolling, showing his teeth. "And you can't trick me. And
if my back wasn't broken, I'd feel pain, wouldn't I? You
can't fool me any longer. You've been after me all the time,
haven't you, Baron von Kaz? You didn't want me to get
the cloak. You hoped to have it for yourself. But I tricked
all those other fine gentlemen. And I nearly tricked you.
Only you're not really a gentleman, are you?"

"Let's go," said Caryl. "Let's get out."

They left him there. But fifteen minutes later they
reached a place where the tube branched into three tunnels.

When they again came to the dais, half an hour later, Bolton was waiting for them, his white smile on his face. The Baron methodically went through his pockets. When he had finished, Bolton said, and his voice was slower, like heavy glue which was turning cold and poured with difficulty, "You won't find the map, Baron. You'll never find it."

The Baron snapped off the flashlight. He told Caryl that it was best to conserve the battery. "Let me think," he said to Caryl, with a flash of his old confidence, and she gave him her hand, and Bolton's voice poured slowly into the congealing darkness.

"How did you decide I killed Kohler?" he asked.

16

The Feather Cloak

The Baron squeezed Caryl's hand, warning her to remain quiet.

Then Bolton cried, "Where are you?" his voice lifting in panic for the first time.

"We can help you if—"

"If I'll tell you how to get out?" Bolton sighed. "No! You'll stay here. You'll stay here and rot. And it 'll be harder for you because I don't feel anything." Again came that tortured sigh. "If I'd had money and an education I could have killed you first."

"How did you know about the feather cloak?" asked the Baron. "How did you get Mr. Kohler's letter?"

"You heard about the letter Kohler wrote from Mexico City?" Bolton chuckled softly. "It was addressed to Mr. Preacher. But I open all of Mr. Preacher's mail. Mr. Preacher . . . trusts me . . ."

"I can't stand it much longer," Caryl murmured. "Do we have to stay with him?"

The Baron held her hand tightly.

". . . and when Kohler wrote that Saka Okyo had the map and told what the map was and . . . and said he could buy it from Saka Okyo if he could get ten thousand dollars . . . I tore up Kohler's letter. I told Mr. Preacher that I'd learned he was threatened with kidnaping and the Islands would be the safest place." The voice died away, and the Baron left Caryl, kneeled over the man.

"And?"

"Oh . . . you want to know? I'm cleverer than you think, Baron. . . . I realized that Mr. Preacher wouldn't give me the money. He didn't have that much to give. He was even trying to get rid of me," complained Bolton, "because he'd lost most of his money during the depression. So I—" the evil chuckle came again, weaker—"so on the boat I met Kohler, and that last night we got into an argument. And I . . . I killed him because he was going to double-cross me. . . . And then . . . in the hotel, I saw Hiroshita in your room and was afraid Kohler'd got to Hiroshita before being killed . . . so I shot him, and then Billy mixed in . . . getting the gun and . . . and I had to . . . to . . ."

Bolton's voice stopped.

A little later, after Bolton had died, the Baron and Caryl walked up the main lava tube until they were in front of three smaller openings.

They took the center one first.

But a hundred yards into it they were forced to stop, their way abruptly blocked by rocks.

They worked back to the main tube. "Ach!" said the Baron loudly, "if Mr. Bolton could enter, my dear Miss Miquet, have no fear. The great Von Kaz will find how he did so."

"Franz," she replied in an odd little voice, "if you are ever to call me 'Caryl' and I mean 'Caryl,' not 'my dear Caryl,' I think you had better start now before it is too late."

Nervously the Baron mumbled that only intimate friends called each other by their first names.

"Suit yourself," she said. "I have a funny feeling that we may be with each other a number of years."

"Hein?"

She laughed, then stopped as the laugh jeered at her from the echoing cavern. "It may be a long time before they find us. Too long to do any good . . ." The opening to the left ascended, then narrowed, and finally split into small hose-like formations.

They tried the last opening.

They walked along this for a quarter of a mile or so, entered a great cave with high walls and a ribbed vaulted ceiling, black, from which hung hundreds of stalactites. They could feel the air rushing to them, but they could find no exit, no continuation of the tube.

The flashlight flickered and went out. This was the end of the battery the Baron had removed from the flashlight Caryl had thrown away at Bolton's command. Long ago his had burnt out.

Caryl sank to the lava. "Let's stay here," she said quietly. "I don't want to go back where—where Bolton is."

He put his arms around her, stroking the soft hair.

"I'm dead tired," she said, leaning on his shoulder.

When Joe Manuela, becoming alarmed, left his little sloop to go up to the Heiau, he saw where the rocks had fallen. By two in the afternoon he reached Kailua.

Jameson, disregarding the Baron's instructions, had driven to the ranch. He had arrested Sargent and Preacher, had his men searching for Bolton.

Neither of Mary's guests, nor Mary, knew when Bolton had disappeared. He had been playing cards with John Sargent before the Baron knocked and slugged John with the champagne bottle. Then, during the search for Caryl, Bolton had vanished. One of the Hawaiian cowboys explained that he had let Bolton take Mary's car as Bolton said that he had received permission to fetch clothing from the Preacher Ranch.

Mr. Berry telephoned Jameson from the Kona Inn.

Jameson drove to the Kona Inn, arrived at four. He found George Tuung there and sent him back to Honolulu. By six, ten police headed by Jameson climbed upon the Heiau. With crowbars they broke into the opening. Not until eight o'clock did they reach the dais and find Bolton and the Haenel air pistol well covered with fingerprints.

At eight-thirty they came upon Caryl. She said the Baron had told her to remain where she was until he returned.

At nine-ten, two of the Hawaiian policemen, climbing up along the walls, found the Baron. His empty cigarette lighter was beside him. He was lying where he had fallen, on a kind of shelf, with the blood soaking through his shirt and coat, forming a puddle at his shoulder.

One of the Hawaiians, seeing the lighter, and from previous experience in similar tubes, realized what the Baron had been doing.

This Hawaiian lit a candle, raised it above his head. A draught of air sucked at the flame. The Hawaiian called down to Jameson, "There's an opening near here, Chief."

They found the opening a little later.

The Baron would have found it if he had had fuel for his lighter, and if he had not slipped, hit his head on the sharp volcanic rock and lost consciousness. . . .

After they had rushed the Baron to the hospital, Caryl told Jameson what she had heard Bolton say. Jameson told the reporters. The Hawaiian newspapers came out the following morning with the amazing story; the news services cabled the story to the mainland.

As a result, three days later, when the Baron was permitted to see visitors for the first time, he learned that he was a hero. However, he was less and less a hero in direct ratio to the number of miles separating him from the Northern States of America and Europe.

By the second day the news had spread to Vienna, and two of the Vienna newspapers carried a few lines on the rear pages announcing that the Baron Franz Maximilian Karagôz von Kaz, formerly of this city, had assisted in locating the murderer of two men in Hawaii, T.H. One of the Baron's former friends happened to read this item and immediately wrote out a cable.

And so, on the third day after Bolton's death, the Baron was sitting up in bed with Caryl Miquet and Christian Jameson sitting beside the bed, telling him that he was a hero. Jameson handed the Honolulu and Hilo newspapers to the brave Baron from Austria. Caryl said that Mary, John and Jeffrey were waiting outside and sent their love to him but were afraid to come in, that too many in his room might disturb him.

Jameson bit a cigar, started to light it, guiltily extinguished his match. "You're quite a hero, Baron, hey?" He grinned. "By Jesus, there's half a dozen reporters camping around the hospital just begging to be let in to see you."

The Baron finished reading the headlines in the newspapers, dropped the papers to the floor. Caryl said that a cablegram had arrived this morning from Vienna for the Baron. Mr. Berry at the Kona Inn had sent it to the McKay Ranch. "A cablegram?" murmured the Baron.

"I read it," she admitted. "I'm sorry, I shouldn't have done so, but I wondered if it were important. It didn't make sense. I understand enough German to know that."

"Pardon?"

"It was about the weather and shipping hides."

"If you please, may I have it?"

She handed him the cablegram. He read in German:

WEATHER HERE FINE STOP THANK YOU FOR ORDER STOP TWO DOZEN HIDES SENT RETURNED REFUSED WHICH ENDS THE MATTER ENTIRELY STOP SUGGEST NO MORE BE SENT

It was signed with a long, formal name beginning with Prince.

The message was easy to decode. Because of his disloyalty, because he had deserted the cause in time of need, now that the coup again had failed, he was invited to keep out of Austria for all time to come.

The nurse came in as the cablegram slipped from his fingers. "I think he's had enough visiting for today."

Caryl and Jameson started for the door. Caryl anxiously regarded the cablegram. "I hope it wasn't bad news. I didn't know whether to show it to you or not."

"Ach, it is nothing." He snapped his fingers. "A little joke from a friend. From a former friend. 'Trahit . . . trahit sua quemque voluptas.'" The prognathous lower jaw shoved forward in a wry smile. "That is Latin. It translates, 'His own desires . . .' Someday I shall translate it for you. I am very tired now."

"Well, we can't have a tired hero," said Jameson cheerfully as he opened the door. "I'll see you tomorrow before I fly to Honolulu."

Mary McKay and the two men were standing in the corridor, and they glanced in and smiled at the Baron. Caryl said, "See you tomorrow."

Jeffrey called, "How do you like being a hero?"

"Ah, but my dear sir," said the Baron, "not yet am I the hero."

Jameson turned. "Don't tell me that crack on the head's made you modest, Baron?"

The Baron didn't reply; instead, he asked a question.

"How is Billy? Is he—"

Caryl answered, "The doctor says Billy's fine."

"Wait, please! Billy is yet unconscious?"

The nurse reprovingly interrupted, stating that the Baron shouldn't be excited, but the Baron half lifted himself out of the bed and shouted his question, and Caryl soothingly explained that Billy was much better and was coming out of the coma nicely and that they were stopping in to see him now.

"Now . . ." The Baron swung to the floor. Both Jameson and the nurse caught him. The nurse rang for the doctor. The Baron cried to the old detective, "We have no time, my dear sir, if I am to be a hero. Your gun, please."

"My gun?" Jameson's jaw dropped in astonishment.

"I wish to show you a little trick."

Sargent, watching from the doorway, whispered to Mary, "We'd better leave. The man's out of his head."

Jameson gasped. The Baron's right hand had whipped the detective's coat aside, grasped the revolver from the holster. The Baron swung the revolver toward those at the door. "Come in. Come in or I shall shoot."

The nurse said, "He's delirious. Humor him." The nurse feverishly kept on pressing the bell for the doctor, while slowly the three in the corridor entered the room.

Caryl approached the Baron, "Franz, you mustn't—"

The Baron's eyes passed over her, rested on the man in the center of the three.

"My dear sir," he said, "you killed Mr. Kohler; and because the murderer of Mr. Kohler killed Mr. Hiroshita, it is you who climbed through the bathroom window to my balcony, and if you move even so much as a hair wavers in the wind, I shall shoot you between the eyes, in the same place that you struck when you tried to kill Billy. On board the *Kohala*, then again in Wailuku, I heard Miss McKay say that Mr. Kohler was shot in the heart. Only I and the murderer knew that he was shot in the heart. You were the only one who told her about the murder; and you, forgetting that no one else except myself had seen the body, accidentally, by a damaging slip of the tongue which will hang you, said to Miss McKay that Mr. Kohler was— not merely shot, ach no; but shot in the heart."

Boldly Jeffrey Preacher looked around at the others, said easily, "Why, Baron, you are delirious. You know I was on B deck with Caryl when Kohler was killed." Unwaveringly the gun pointed at Jeffrey as the Baron, by way of explanation, said more to the others than to the tall, smiling man with the yellow hair:

"At first this clue dropped by Miss McKay was too weak to employ. She herself might have killed Mr. Kohler. Or it might have been Mr. Sargent, and she could be protecting her fiancé by throwing the guilt on Mr. Preacher. But, if you please, after Billy was attacked, I knew. Miss McKay had not the opportunity to hide the pistol in her cousin's closet, as she spent the morning with her cousin. And it was not Mr. Bolton, no! He knew that Mr. Kohler had written to you about the map and that you were after it because you needed money; he knew that you owned an air gun. He knew you were the murderer. And he admitted as much to me the night he tried to kill me in Honolulu after practically kidnapping me from Mr. Hiroshita's friend, George Tuung." Forgetting that he had named Jeffrey as the murderer in a desperate expedient to free himself, the brave Baron mentally congratulated that great instinct of his which, although he had had no factual evidence to support it, had so astounded Mr. Bolton into releasing him. "Mr. Bolton tried to kill me to save you. He was the only man who could not have hidden the gun in the closet, for he was not on the ranch that morning. And, also, Billy had not told him of or showed him the castle he was building, so even if Mr. Bolton had left the house to seek Billy that night, which he didn't, he would not have known where Billy had gone. And if Miss McKay had been shielding her fiancé, the murderous attack on her brother would have caused her to reveal what she knew. But she knew nothing; what Mr. Preacher had told her had not aroused her suspicions. And, my dear Mr. Preacher, how was it that you were on B deck, not when Mr. Kohler was killed, but one or two minutes later? Ach, that is simple. Mr. Kohler was shot on the platform. You are agile, athletic. Mr. John Sargent is also athletic. But it was not he, my dear sir, who met Miss Miquet on B deck. It was easy for you to swing down from the platform, climb down the stanchions, and be near the bar without passing me on A deck or Miss Miquet on—"

Jeffrey leaped for the door.

When the Baron pulled the trigger, the noise of the gun exploding caused the woman upstairs to jump in such surprise that her husband was informed three hours before he expected to be relieved from the strain that he was the father of a new baby boy, weight nine pounds, and doing nicely, thank you.

"You're a complete and total idiot," Caryl Miquet told the brave Baron Franz Maximilian Karagôz von Kaz, one evening two weeks later, "Why aren't you going to Vienna? You don't like our country. You think we're all barbarians. Admit it. Don't you?"

They were sitting on the steps of the lanai, and Jameson was standing, looking down that long twenty-mile stretch to the sea.

The Baron glumly thought of that cablegram forever barring him from his beloved Vienna. "Ach!" he stated lightly, "in your Northern States of America there are some very nice people. As a matter of fact," he glanced at her, took a breath, said loudly, "As a matter of fact, Vienna no longer has the attraction for me that it had in the past."

"You're joking."

"I tell the truth. What do I care for Vienna? Ach!" He snapped his fingers. "'Veritatis simplex oratio est.' That is Latin. It translates, 'Simple is the language of truth.'"

"Well, don't think I'm simple enough to believe you. What's happened? Don't they want you in Vienna?"

Shadows flickered across his face, and all at once Caryl wished she'd held her tongue, and she reached out to touch the man, to comfort him, and then her hand dropped to her side instead, and she laughed very cheerfully and said of course she believed him; was he so inflated with conceit over his great exploit that he couldn't even be teased? "Never," she concluded, "have I seen so conceited a man."

The Baron began to smile a little. Lieber Gott! after all, he was a great detective. "You may say to me all you wish, my dear Caryl," he conceded. "I do not mind in the slightest. Although I do not like Vienna any more."

Jameson bit into his cigar and spat disgustedly. "See here, Baron, I can't figure why Jeff went to pieces as soon as we stuck him in jail when he was able to hold up calm and cool all during the murders. I never saw the like. Jeff told us, himself, about Bolton; he gave Bolton to understand that he'd been forced to kill Kohler and Hiroshita in self-defence, after failing to get the map from them. Bolton either believed him or pretended to, and Jeff promised that he wouldn't take any more risks to get the map, even said that he didn't know where the map was and didn't care. It come out that Bolton hadn't known of the plaque at all, not until the rumpus over Billy getting hurt, and then Caryl disappearing, made him suspicious. Jeff admitted that he'd swiped the plaque containing the map from Caryl. So Bolton, realizing the danger Jeff'd got himself into, grabbed the map and the Haenel pistol from him and then beat it through all that rain and storm to the lava tube."

The Baron held his cigarette lighter to the detective's cigar. "Mr. Preacher was an actor. And when the show was finished, my dear sir, Mr. Preacher collapsed. Mr. Preacher was not remarkable nor exceptional. He was merely a glib, cheerful, and likable—"

"Likable!" exclaimed Caryl. "After what—"

"If you please," said the Baron, "did you not like him? A man can be likable and still be without morals or scruples, without the sense of doing wrong. There are thousands in this world. Mr. Preacher was one. But Mr. Bolton—although never did I care for him, greatly must I respect that man's loyalty. It was he, my dear Mr. Jameson, who was exceptional."

"Oh, *I'm* 'Mister' Jameson, hey?"

"One thousand pardons, my dear Chriz," apologized the Baron, "but for the moment I forgot. This Mr. Bolton . . . you do not often meet men of his kind, who are as bulldogs in their tenacious, unyielding devotion even to death."

"Jeff didn't deserve a feller like Bolton," commented Jameson thoughtfully. "By Jesus, I damn near could 've hit Jeff when he sat there in his cell complaining how Bolton had taken the map and had gone to destroy the feather cloak."

"Mr. Bolton realized that if Mr. Preacher went for the cloak, we would have him trapped. I believe that Mr. Bolton went to the lava tube expecting to find us, and, even after he thought our way was blocked and we would die with him, he carried out his plan to save his master just as a bulldog hangs on to something that is dangerous long after that dangerous thing seemingly is killed."

"Well, well." Jameson flicked his cigar, gazed at the stars. "Somehow I wish you'd killed Jeff instead of plunking him in the leg. Jeff said he killed Hiroshita because he thought the Jap might 've known that Kohler had gotten in touch with him. Kohler had threatened to tell Hiroshita if Jeff didn't pay what Kohler wanted, and Jeff was nearly broke. Jeff was afraid Hiroshita'd suspect him of killing Kohler. You know, Jeff tried to get Hiroshita on the boat but didn't have time. Jesus!" exclaimed Jameson suddenly remembering. "Didn't I hear about Hiroshita having an accident and coming off the boat with his head bandaged?"

The Baron smiled grimly.

"That's how Hiroshita got the bump on his head, hey? Well, Jeff said, when he heard from Kohler that night on A deck that the map was being mailed to Caryl here, he didn't have no more use for Kohler."

"Uhm," murmured the Baron thoughtfully. "Did Mr. Preacher realize that I overheard—"

"Say, that's right. You did overhear Kohler. I forgot to ask Jeff, but he must of guessed you'd heard something. He claims he never wanted to kill you but was afraid of what the Jap might've told you. Says he ordered Bolton that last night on the ship to scare you off the Islands, giving Bolton the excuse that John said you were in love with Caryl, and Jeff liked . . ." Jameson stopped, embarrassed.

There was a long silence which endured until Mary McKay came to the door. "Chris, San Francisco is on the telephone. I think it's a newspaper again."

Jameson went up the steps, growling that somebody was a smart feller but sometimes he acted like a damn fool.

Caryl said after another dragging interval of silence, "Now that Billy's all right, I'm leaving next week for San Francisco. I don't know whether I'll go to New York for Mary's wedding or not. I suppose you'll go on to the Orient?"

The Orient? No, the Baron thought he might go to San Francisco too. Jameson had asked him to stay until after Jeffrey was hung, but the Baron wanted to take an early boat to the Northern States of America.

"Talking about San Francisco," said Caryl lightly, "the San Francisco papers arrived today. You remember Marge

Courtwell, don't you? She lives in Carmel. The papers said she'd married an Englishman. A 'Sir' somebody or other."

"Englishmen," stated the Baron moodily, "are all barbarians."

"Marge is wealthy," continued Caryl as though she hadn't heard the Baron. "She can afford a title. It seems quite the thing, doesn't it? I mean for wealthy women to marry titles. However, I'm not at all wealthy." She sighed very tragically and watched him, and her wide scarlet mouth flicked up at the corners. "I doubt if my income's much over eight thousand a year. I suppose it would cost a lot more for me ever to have a title. Still," she added reflectively, "I do know a German Baron in Hollywood. If I gave him encouragement . . . But he's fat. Oh dear. And it would be nice to have a title."

Jameson came out again, planting himself on the steps. "You should've heard that feller on the telephone," he said, "when I told him how all the fuss was caused by a feather cloak and how the feather cloak had rotted to pieces and wasn't worth a damn when I found it."

"When I found it," corrected the Baron mechanically; mechanically, because he was thinking of something else which had no connection with the feather cloak at all.

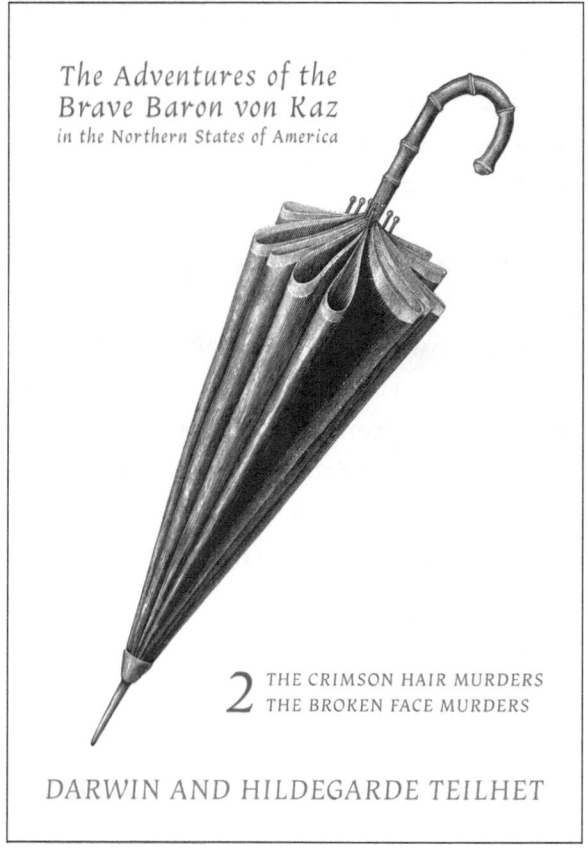

The Adventures of the
Brave Baron von Kaz
in the Northern States of America

2 THE CRIMSON HAIR MURDERS
THE BROKEN FACE MURDERS

DARWIN AND HILDEGARDE TEILHET

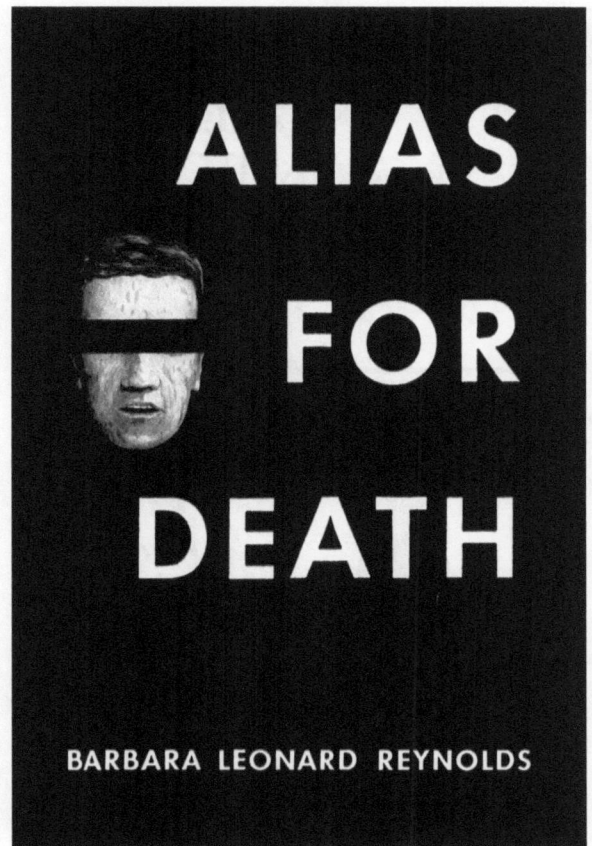

Also Available

CoachwhipBooks.com (print)
Coachwhip.com (epub)

THERE IS
NO RETURN
THE ADELAIDE ADAMS MYSTERIES
ANITA BLACKMON

ALSO AVAILABLE

CoachwhipBooks.com (print)
Coachwhip.com (epub)

A MYSTERY OMNIBUS

Ready for
Death

This
Murderous
Shaft

Murder
Rings Twice

HELEN JOAN HULTMAN

www.ingramcontent.com/pod-product-compliance
Lightning Source LLC
Chambersburg PA
CBHW032258020726
47495CB00001B/157